The Spark Drowned in the Night

Olivia Ocran

THE SPARK DROWNED IN THE NIGHT

To anyone who was told they couldn't do it. Don't let them win by listening.

PREFACE

This book contain instances of violence, death, blood, discrimination, suicide, murder, and mass murder

Edited by Karena Akhavein

Cover by Murphy Rae

Map Design © 2023 by Catherine Bloomfield

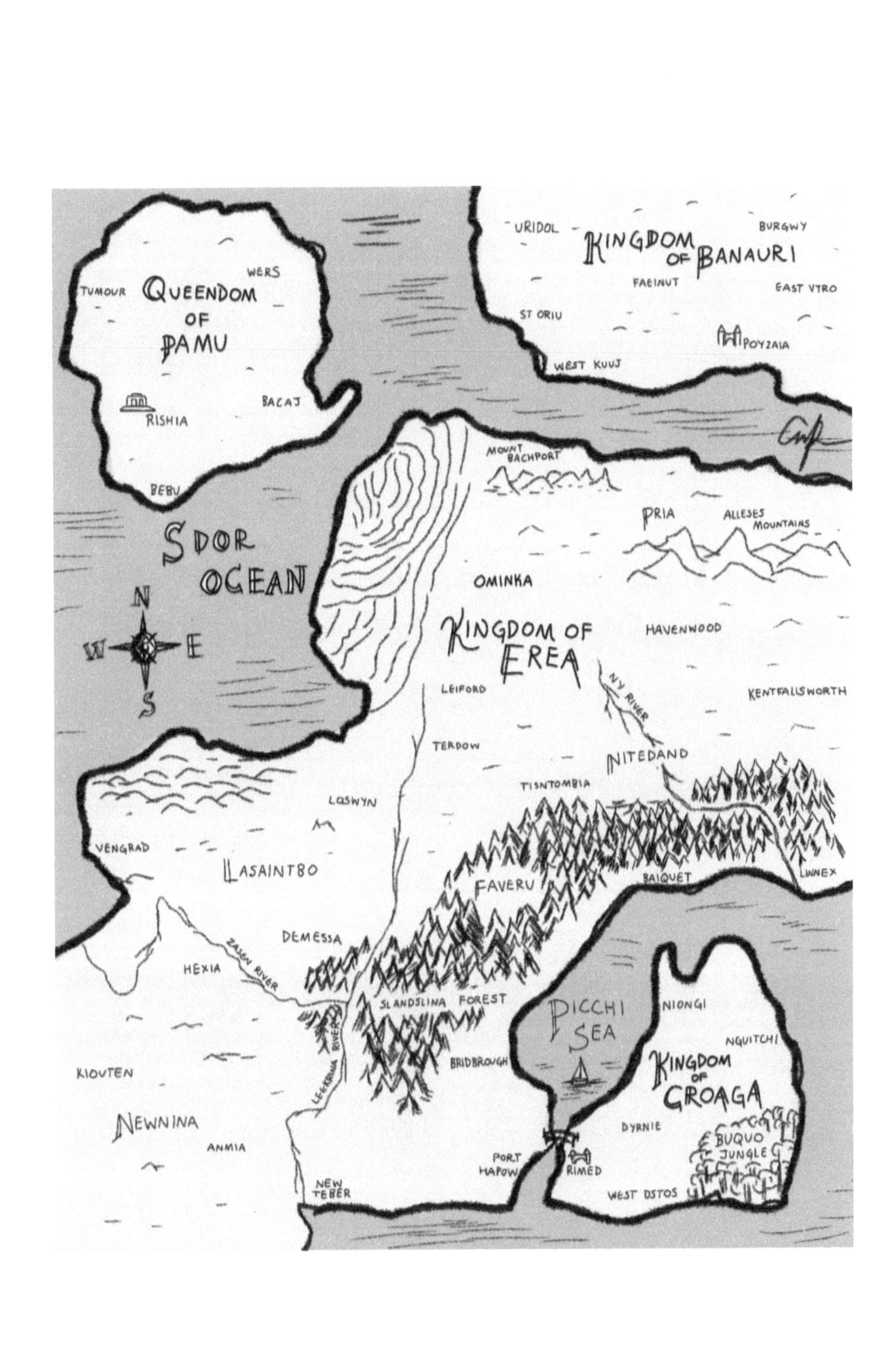

QUEENDOM OF PAMU
TUMOUR
WERS
RISHIA
BACAJ
BEBU
KINGDOM OF BANAURI
URIDOL
BURGWY
FAEINUT
EAST VIRO
ST ORIU
POYZAIA
WEST KUUJ
SDOR OCEAN
N
W E
S
MOUNT BACHPORT
PRIA
ALLESES MOUNTAINS
OMINKA
KINGDOM OF EREA
HAVENWOOD
LEIFORD
NY RIVER
KENTFALLSWORTH
TERDOW
NITEDAND
TISNTOMBIA
LOSWYN
VENGRAD
LLASAINTBO
FAVERU
BAIQUET
LINNEX
DEMESSA
ZASEN RIVER
HEXIA
SLANDSLINA FOREST
PICCHI SEA
NIONGI
NGUITCHI
LEEERNIA RIVER
BRIDBROUGH
KINGDOM OF GROAGA
KIOUTEN
DYRNIE
BUQUO JUNGLE
NEWNINA
ANMIA
PORT HAPOW
RIMED
NEW TEBER
WEST OSTOS

CHAPTER 1

YORENA

I WAS A FAKE—NOTHING more than a pawn to be used and discarded. I was no more important than the dirt underneath my feet. I held back tears as we trekked away from the palace, away from the only role I'd believed I was meant to fill. Looking back to my old home one last time, I noticed that it looked particularly majestic with the sun beginning to dip below the highest towers of the palace. We were far away enough to where it appeared no bigger than a child's toy in the distance. Much too small for me to possibly have spent every waking moment of my life within its walls. Preparing, waiting, wishing for the day I would become Queen. And now, that dream had been reduced to something no more real than a child's toy.

The remaining two members of my former team of servants, Mathias and Chafik, trailed behind me, looking no less defeated than I felt. I tried to keep my head held high as we followed the Leekrina River away from New Teber. I wanted nothing more than to stop and kneel in the dirt, to cry until there was nothing left inside me. But we had to keep moving. I had to keep the boys alive.

A cool breeze blew through my blood-matted hair, the sun stealing away the muggy heat as it dipped its toes below the horizon. We had to get as far from the palace as possible before nightfall. It would only be a matter of time before Ilise sent the guards after us. Or as I should now call her, Queen Ilise. Queen. That was what I was supposed to be by the end of Heircestrial. And yet here I was, without a family, chased from my home, and without a clue of what to do next.

The air was heavy around the three of us as we walked in silence, as if the sky above had decided to rest itself upon our shoulders. Even Mathias had stopped his sarcastic commentary for the time being. We walked until the moon replaced the sun and chirping crickets replaced singing birds. My feet ached after hours without a break and my skin itched from the tall grass that was intent on slapping my face every few seconds. But I wasn't taking any chances with our lives, and that meant moving as quickly as possible. A heavy thump sounded behind me and I whipped around, my exhausted muscles tensed for danger. But it was only Mathias, who had slumped on the ground, with yellow grass protruding out from the brown curls of his hair. His face had a reddish tint, and the brown freckles dotting his face were darker than ever. My heart ached for him. He wasn't used to being outside like this—none of us were.

"We're tired, Yorena," he whined. "Exhaustion will kill us before any palace guard can even try." I looked past him in the direction of the palace. If no one had been sent by now, it should be safe enough for us to rest. At least I hoped so. Luckily, he'd waited until we stopped in an empty field. Nothing but tall grass surrounded us for miles. It was the perfect place to conceal us while we slept.

"Okay. We can sleep here for tonight and continue once the sun rises," I said.

Chafik groaned, peeling a black curl from his sweaty brown skin. "Sunrise? Are you sure we can't rest for longer than that?"

I cut him an apologetic look and shook my head. The two of them used their bags as pillows and fell asleep within minutes. I tried to do the same, but while my body begged for rest, my mind was more awake than ever.

I sat up and started taking inventory of what Nikos had given me, just to give myself something to do. Nikos had been my competitor during Heircestrial—a competition to determine who deserves the title of Heir through a series of trials. Maybe the mindless task would quiet my head. He'd packed two orange fire crystals, a compass, a filled canteen, some strips of dried meat, a bottle of alcohol, a small roll of bandages, a pouch of coin, and two silver daggers about half the size of my forearm. *How did he manage to get all of this?* He must have been preparing for a few days before we left, but how could he have known Imogen would take control of Ilise? Had Imogen told him? Or had he come to his own conclusions?

Imogen was the eldest sorceress on the council and had decided *she* was what the kingdom needed. Sorcerers could control people's souls as well as all four elements. It was terrifying. We'd been on the verge of defeating her after Ilise had discovered her dual-elemental power, but Imogen had taken over Ilise's soul and turned her into a mini-me. Now Imogen had the most powerful Imperium in the kingdom that wasn't a sorceress at her disposal.

I strapped the daggers to the empty sheaths on my trousers and repacked all my supplies. The only thing we didn't have in abundance was food. We would have to stop in a village eventually, but stopping anywhere in Newnina would be too dangerous; too close to the palace.

Ilise had offered me the role of princess-consort, but I'd declined. So, Ilise had locked me, Chafik, and Mathias in the dungeons until I "reconsidered" and she'd likely already started the man-hunt for us. Guards would be swarming this province, and I was already out of my element. I had *some* combat training, but not enough to fend off an entire squad of guards on my own.

I stood to pace, keeping my eyes and ears scanning the space around us for the heavy crunch of guard boots, the unnatural shake of grass. I should sleep, but I might as well do something productive until then. Stars winked above my head and under better circumstances, I would have lay down in the grass to watch them.

It was what I used to do on the rare days I'd been able to just be a child, not the Princess, not the Heir; a normal girl. Sometimes, my mother would come with me into the palace gardens once the moon rose and we would find shapes in the stars together. I would pretend there were horses galloping through the dotted black, even though I was sure they looked like random blobs to my mother. But she'd never corrected me, she had succumbed to the silliness with me.

Tears stung the back of my eyes at the memory, begging to fall. I didn't stop them. If I pushed her away now, she would only come back to haunt me later. Even if she hadn't been my real mother, it had felt real. She'd still held me when

I'd been upset, she'd still helped make me into the person I was today. She'd been my friend when I was younger and most of the other noble children weren't able to play with me. She and Father were still my parents, even if it had all been a cruel lie. Silent tears streamed down my face. Though she and Father had let themselves be influenced by Imogen and the nominees, I still missed them. I wanted nothing more than for them to appear in front of me and take me home.

The last time I'd spoken to them, the last time I would ever speak to them, was when they'd been sitting on their golden thrones and ordering the deaths of the Primis Defense Union. They were the antithesis group to The Progression, also the only ones who had the guts to go up against them. I'd never gotten to make things right with us, all because of Imogen.

I imagined Ilise sitting on one of those thrones, with my mother's crown of golden vines atop her head. I imagined she wore the dress she'd been wearing at the ball when I'd first met her, with maroon silk pooling at her feet and two new crystals hanging around her neck. She was regal, powerful, dangerous. As long as she was under Imogen's control, she wouldn't do this kingdom any good.

"I thought we were supposed to be resting, not moping," Mathias said, startling me. I turned around to see the two of them sitting up. I must have accidentally woken them.

I wiped the remaining tears off my face. "You guys can go back to sleep. I will rest eventually," I said, my voice wavering.

Chafik stood and brushed the dirt off his uniform before sitting next to me. "We'll keep you company. Right, Mathias?"

Mathias stayed sprawled out on the ground. "I am perfectly content with going to sleep. You two can stay up as long as you want."

Chafik sighed. "I said, *we'll* keep you company, Right, *Mathias*?" he said with more bite.

I smiled a little. The world could be crumbling around us and these two would still find a way to argue. At least something in my life hadn't changed. Leaving them at the palace without me there to hold off a changed Ilise would've been ten times more dangerous than anything we would encounter out here.

Mathias groaned but moved to join us. "I don't understand why I listen to you," he said.

Chafik ignored his comment and turned back to me. "Have you been crying?"

"Of course not," I said.

Chafik looked unconvinced.

"Haven't we all cried at this point? It's not a new theme to the night," Mathias said.

"That's not what I had in mind when I said we should keep her company," Chafik deadpanned.

"What could be better than the company of someone in the same boat as you?" Mathias said.

"Personally, rather than wallowing in our self-pity, I'm a bit invested in being part of the decision about where we should go. Not to put too fine a point on it, but it is kind of a life or death situation," Chafik said.

"I've been thinking about that since we left," I said. In between fearing for our lives and feeling like a complete failure, I've managed to find all the places we *shouldn't* go. Erea was Ilise's now, and anywhere within its borders would have some level of danger. However, I've yet to determine which place would have the *least* danger.

"We could go to Ominka, it's mostly peaceful there," he said.

A good idea in theory, but not in practice. Ominka was one of the most densely populated provinces in the kingdom. More people meant more anonymity, but it also meant more chances we could be spotted. Plus, it was much too far of a journey from here, and a cold one at that. Ominka was the northernmost province, and we didn't have the supplies to not die from frostbite when fall hit.

"We need to go somewhere without people. And preferably somewhere not so cold," I said.

"Well where would that be? Unless you suggest we go live in the forest with the wolves, there's nowhere we can go that we can completely avoid being spotted," Mathias said.

I opened my mouth and then promptly shut it. All the places that came to mind wouldn't have enough supplies for us to survive on our own. We could hide out where the Leekrina River met the Slandslina Forest and camp out there while we planned next steps, but we could easily be spotted on the edge of the forest, and finding food beyond a few rapidly spoiling fruits would be difficult. Or we could hide out in the plains of Lasaintbo, but they were too open and the only supplies would be in the villages and towns. And not to mention, I needed to take us where the boys would be safe. I had to get Ilise and my kingdom back, but I couldn't put the boys in danger. They'd hardly lived their lives yet at eighteen and twenty years old, and it wasn't fair of me to be the reason it was cut much too short.

"Why don't we go to the people Nikos named before he left?" Chafik suggested.

"Do you mean the Primis Defense Union?" I asked. They would be the most equipped to combat Imogen and The Progression, but I was sure they'd rather fight the Council of Sorcerers with nothing but their fists than work with me. The Union's entire mission was to defeat The Progression, and they *would* know the most about the weakness the organization had, maybe even that Imogen had. But they saw me as no better than my parents who'd tried to execute them all while The Progression ran wild through the kingdom.

Chafik nodded. "They're who we need to find. Ilise said they were supposed to be coming to the palace, so they might be close by." She had told us that, but she hadn't specified when. And based on what Ilise had thought of me when we'd first met, they were unlikely to be friends of mine. I couldn't blame them. I'd been completely blind to how my kingdom, Erea, was dangerously close to breaking apart, until Ilise had opened my eyes. How had I been blind to the fact that an extremist group was destroying villages and killing large masses of people, and that our monarchs were intent on going on like it wasn't happening by killing anyone who protested their disagreement? The murder of an innocent had been "justified" by a basic level of suspicion.

"Where would we even find these Primis Defense Union people? I highly doubt they are intent on being found," Mathias said. That was true. I didn't know the first thing about the Union, especially where their bases were. Well, besides the one near Hexia my parents had ordered destroyed. My parents had put their energy into ridding the kingdom of the Primis Defense Union and had had guards follow two Primis Defense Union members so they could destroy the base and smoke the rest out. Chafik was right: if foot soldiers from the Primis Defense Union were coming to the palace, most of them would be outside their bases, maybe even close to where we were.

"Do either of you have a map?" I asked. The boys rummaged through their bags, Chafik opting to pour out all the contents to search. He had the same supplies I did except for the crystals. I doubted he knew how to use the small knife Nikos had packed for him, but it eased my mind to know he wasn't unarmed.

"I found one," Mathias said. He handed me a rolled bit of yellowing paper. I placed rocks on the corners to keep the map from flying away in the breeze as the boys huddled around me. The map was an older version, but most of the information was still correct.

"How is the map supposed to help us? It'll be difficult to determine our location before we have the sun as a reference," Chafik said, nodding to the dark sky. The lack of light also made it a challenge to even read the map. I could barely read the tiny town names scrawled on the parchment,

"We need to look for potential hiding spots not too far from the palace like caves, tunnels, or thick forests that are also somewhat close to villages, for supplies, but still far enough to remain secret. " I said. If we headed in the direction of a possible base near the palace, we might run into Union members, maybe ones Ilise had known. And if these camps were set up similarly to the Hexia base, we might be able to find the entrance. Having a base closer to the palace would be a strategic advantage for the Union. There was no chance there wasn't at least one. We'd only have to find some type of door in the ground. Hopefully it wasn't a door created by Earth Imperium, then we'd have no chance of getting it open.

"Even if we're lucky enough to find a base, the soldiers will likely be long gone before we get there," Mathias said. Chafik elbowed him and Mathias winced. "What in four hells was that for?" he asked, rubbing his side.

"Could you be optimistic for one second? We're already stressed out, and your negativity isn't helping," he said. Mathias grumbled and fell quiet.

I wasn't angry at Mathias' negative comments. He was only echoing the thoughts already swimming in my head. How was Ilise able to come up with plans so easily? My overworked brain cells were on the verge of collapsing. My eyes landed on a specific area of the map. Just outside the Slandslina Forest was a small village by the river, where I knew there was plenty of dense forest that could hide any man-made structures around it—the perfect place for a base.

I pointed the area out to the boys. "Here," I said.

Chafik moved my finger from the map to look closer. "Depending on where we are, this doesn't look too far," he said.

I nodded. The Leekrina River ran into Lasaintbo and Ominka, so we were north of the palace. "If we leave in the morning we could get there in a day and a half. But we have to get some rest before we start moving again."

The boys nodded and rested their heads on their bags once more. I carefully folded the map and tucked it into my bag. This map, which seemed like it had been packed as an afterthought, was in fact our lifeline, the only thing keeping us on track to save Ilise and the kingdom until we found the Union. I placed my head atop the bag and closed my eyes.

We finally had a plan. I just hoped we would be able to catch the Union before they arrived at the palace. If Ilise thought the same way as Imogen now, she would kill them the moment they set foot on palace grounds. Once she became her true self again, if she was able to shake the spell Imogen had cast, which was currently keeping her spirit captive, Ilise would never forgive herself if she hurt them.

The Union would have no way of knowing Ilise had been turned—they wouldn't see her for the monster she'd been turned into—until it was too late. Imogen had likely pumped a bunch of anti-Union propaganda into Ilise's head by now, and the group had already been the kingdom's public enemy number one in our parents' eyes. The Primis Union soldiers' arrival at the palace would almost guarantee their likely extremely painful deaths.

We needed to find the Union, *fast.* For their sakes, for the kingdom's, and for Ilise.

Chapter 2

Ilise

ALL THIS IMBECILE HAD to do was take Yorena back to the dungeon. I'd given him one simple task. And yet, he'd failed miserably. I stared the man down from my throne. I finally realized why monarchs loved these chairs so much. People were so much smaller, so much weaker when they were below you. This skinny gnat of a man who had once dared to call himself my superior kneeled before the dais, begging for forgiveness. I'd already blown out every candle in the room in frustration, leaving only dim light filtering through the few open windows. Nikos kept his gaze trained on the floor. He was afraid of me.

Good.

I'd sent him away with Yorena hours ago, expecting him to inform me that he had completed the task I had ordered. Yet, only now was he coming back to me. He'd walked in the door, head down, shoes squeaking as he dragged them across the marble, looking defeated, a pitiful little thing. Like a child who had lost an argument with their parents.

The dungeon guards had already told me that Yorena and the boys had escaped. And after ordering them to scour the areas surrounding the palace, we'd found nothing. She thought she could run from me. The one thing I knew she wanted more than anything was to be Queen. I'd offered her the next best thing, and by running away she had basically spit in my face. But I wasn't worried—there was nowhere she could run that I wouldn't find her.

She always liked to put herself into a box, thinking being Queen was all she could do. She was made for more than that, but as long as she refused to see her potential, she would be back. With her trusting heart, she may think she'd be able to revert me to what I'd been before Imogen had shown me the truth.

And in hindsight, I shouldn't have pushed her away so much when I'd first returned to the palace. Maybe then she would've known I would never allow any harm to come to her, that I would sooner let the world go up in flames. All I wanted was to be able to run my fingers through her cloud-like hair, to be able to hold her close. I wanted to find out what it would feel like to kiss her heart-shaped mouth. But I would solve that issue later, now I had to see if Nikos knew anything.

"All you had to do was take Yorena back to her cell," I said after a long period of silence. From when he had walked in, I knew there had been a fight from the cuts marring his face and skin around his eyes. But surely, he couldn't have been overpowered by those three. Yorena was weakened without a crystal, and those pitiful boys couldn't fight. I rose from my golden throne and stepped down to where I was only mere inches from his face. I grasped his chin and forced him to meet my eyes.

"What did you do?" I demanded. He held my gaze with a new level of ferocity. A challenge? Pride? Cockiness? Did he still think he was in a superior position to me? I was the Queen now, and I didn't tolerate people disappointing me. He was in no position to have any sense of pride.

"They overpowered me, Your Majesty," he said plainly. I released his chin and crossed my arms.

"Overpowered you? Yorena didn't have her crystal, and the boys have about as much combined strength as an anemic mackerel. What in the five Spirits makes you think I would ever believe that?"

He shrugged as if I couldn't reduce him to a pile of ash the second if I wanted to.

"It's what happened, Your Majesty. I don't know what else to tell you." I had a sudden desire to watch this room burn, but my fire wouldn't do much with all the gold and marble. It wouldn't bring her back.

"Fine. Then tell me, do you at least know where they went?"

His eyes darted around the room. *Is he forming a lie?*

"I don't know. I walked down the tunnel they used and it let out on the northeast side of the palace. They might have fled for Ominka." Ominka? Yorena was smart and determined; she wouldn't flee after being chased from her home. Nikos could be telling the truth, or maybe he was trying to lead me astray. I would have to send search parties in both directions.

"Simply because the tunnel let out that way doesn't mean they went that direction. I thought you were better than this, Nikos." His face remained impassive, an unreadable stone. What was he hiding?

He rose out of his kneel. "If you'll excuse me, I think I've told you everything."

Before he could walk away, I trapped him in a ring of air. The whistling sound echoed in the room, mimicking a hurricane. I tightened the ring to where he had just enough room to breathe, barely. He grunted with the effort of trying to break free. I would never get used to the rush of strength I received from using crystals to control the elements. It was intoxicating. Air was surprisingly easy to control—to weaponize. And especially helpful for when someone was stupid enough to walk away from me.

"I didn't dismiss you. I don't think you've learned your lesson yet." I squeezed the ring tighter and his skin turned a pale pink.

"Please," he choked out. "Need... air." So *now* he was begging for my mercy. Just a few days ago he had been one of the many who would have loved to see my head on a stake. I understood their desire, but it still wasn't a nice memory.

"Release him, little one." Imogen strolled up beside me. I hadn't even realized she was in the room. It was unnerving how quiet she could be, the way it felt like she was always watching me.

"They're gone because of this incapable buffoon. And he doesn't seem very apologetic," I seethed. She placed a hand on my shoulder. It was cold enough to feel through the leather of my suit.

"I think he has learned his lesson, we still need him alive." The pink flush in Nikos' skin turned bright red. I guess we did need him alive—so I would let him go. *This time.* I deactivated my crystal and he fell to the floor, coughing. "I hope you have learned a valuable lesson, Nikos," Imogen said. He wobbled as he picked himself up.

"You are dismissed," I said. He bowed, albeit shakily, and left the room. The wooden doors slammed behind him.

"I know you're here for a reason beyond saving the life of that rat. What do you want?" Imogen did not respond. Her plum colored robes fluttered behind her as she waved for me to follow her out the door. "Where are we going?" I asked.

"I see you already have quite a firm grasp on how to use air, but fire is a bit more tricky," she said.

She spoke to me as one would to a toddler, like I couldn't understand basic concepts. Part of me wanted to tell her *exactly* how I felt about that comment. I was the Queen now. I didn't have to stand for others speaking to me in this manner. Though the strategic part of me knew I needed to control this element, and Imogen would throw me into a wall if I responded in an unsavory manner. I kept my mouth clamped shut.

We strolled through the golden hallways to the staircase. Guards straightened their backs when they saw us coming. It felt nice to be the one with power for once in my life. And unlike the past monarchs, I would use it to set this kingdom on the right path. Even if it took some collateral damage to get there.

"Controlling fire is similar to the way you control water, so Mx. Li is going to help you learn to wield it properly." Ugh. Oliver. A lifetime ago, they were the third competitor, along with Nikos and Yorena. Too bad for them, I now had the crown, not them.

Imogen lit a torch hanging on the wall and we walked down the dark stone stairs. I kept my hand on the wall to balance myself. *This isn't you.* What was that? A voice echoed faintly inside my head, but it wasn't my voice. *Break free.* The words sounded feeble, they had no more strength than an ant. I was shaken for a moment, but decided to ignore them. I'd been exhausted. It was probably my imagination.

We arrived at the underground level of the palace and walked toward the training room. The dark stone dripped with leaks from Spirits knew what, and torches sparsely lit the long hallway. The last time I'd been there, I was enlisting Yorena to help me prepare for the arrival of the Union—that traitorous organization. They were another thing on my list of what I would fix in Erea. Servants bowed and curtsied when we passed them. Imogen halted in front of the training room door.

"Before you go in there, I need to remind you of something." Remind me? I wanted the same thing she wanted. Reminding me felt insulting and condescending. "You are about to be crowned Queen, which means you also need to control yourself when people upset you."

I crossed my arms. "I'm in control," I said.

"You only let Nikos go when I told you to. I admire how ruthless you are, but you need to rein it in." She spoke to me as if I were nothing more than a child. The past King and Queen hadn't held back when they'd had my friend Aerilyn killed, and they hadn't held back when they'd basically stripped Yorena of her power. I didn't see why I had to hold back. But Imogen and I *were* working toward the same goal. Listening to her wouldn't be the worst idea.

I let out a loud breath. "Fine. I'll rein it in."

Her wrinkled face turned up in a smile as we walked into the training room.

"Good. Have fun training."

Oliver stood in front of multiple stacks of hay they'd piled in the middle of the room. They wore a white tunic that washed out their pale skin in the dimly lit room. Oliver was "One with the Spirits," as we called them. The five Spirits were more than just a "he" or "she", they encompassed all aspects of life. Hence, why we referred to them as "they".

"What's with the hay?" I said.

Oliver strode up to me and bowed. "You need flammable material for fire practice, Your Majesty."

A smile tugged at my lips. Now we were speaking my language.

"Then let's get started."

Lessons with Oliver hadn't turned out to be as unbearable as I'd thought...at least in the beginning. They guided me through the basic motions—how to move a tiny flame, and how to will it to not burn anything I didn't want burned. All but one of the hay bales had been reduced to no more than a few charred bits of straw. And all the smoke permeating the air mixed with the sweat on my skin created a gritty layer over my face.

But things went south when Oliver had me practice controlling multiple fires at once. It was much harder to split my focus on more than one flame. I would manage to snake one stream of flames around the hay without burning it. But then the other one would gain a mind of its own as my focus shifted to the one I was bending around the hay.

Oliver came dangerously close to incurring my wrath due to the many ex- pletives they leveled at me. Then again, I couldn't blame them. I'd accidentally burned some of their shirt and pants in the three hours we were training. But it was entertaining to watch them struggle to douse the flames with water.

They stormed out after I'd almost burned off some of their hair, and I was hav- ing so much fun that I decided not to punish them for their insolence. Wielding fire was more fun than I could've imagined. And as long as I wore my leather gloves when I used it, I didn't feel like it was touching me, like it was adding to the scars on my arms.

Those scars were a reminder of when a Progression Fire Imperium had burnt me during an attack on a village years ago. For years my scars had only brought back traumatizing memories of that day, but now they were something I could look upon with pride. Whoever had burned me was justified. I'd been a deluded child to think I would do this kingdom any good working with that spiritsdamned Union. These scars were a testament to the strength of The Progression and the future of the kingdom.

Exhausted but exhilarated, I left the training room and went to find Imogen. We needed to plan what our next steps would be. One of the crucial steps, for me at least, was finding Yorena. I had to get her back. She just needed to open her mind to see all the good we would do for the kingdom if we were united.

Imperium were the superior peoples. We were the ones with power over the elements, and we were the ones who'd been in power for centuries. Yorena's big-headed ancestor may have thought she'd changed that, but even after her rebellion, Imperium were in power. Primis were powerless, small-minded. If the Spirits had meant for Primis to take up as much space as they believed they deserved, they would have been given power too. Primis were lucky to even be allowed to live alongside us.

I ran up the stairs to the third floor. I assumed Imogen would be in the King's old study. After the sorceress had shown me the way the kingdom should run, I almost had a sixth sense when it came to finding her. Guards bowed to me as I ran past them. I had almost passed an open doorway when I saw the flash of familiar plum robes. I didn't know what this room was. Multiple shelves stood in the middle, the few lit candles casting a yellow glow over the space. I stepped inside and was hit with the smell of old books.

"I figured you would find me," said Imogen, her cracked lips turning up into something that was doubtless meant to be a smile but looked predatory. She sat in one of the armchairs in the corner of the room. She closed the leather-bound book she'd been perusing and set it on the arm of her chair.

"We need to discuss my next steps," I said. She motioned to the chair next to her and I sat down. I propped my feet up on the little table in between the chairs.

"What did you have in mind?"

"I need to get the Imperium population on my side before we can make any more changes. They're the only ones I need to worry about pushing back against me considering my...unorthodox rise to power."

"As long as your little Union friends don't cause a fuss, I wouldn't worry your head over the possibility of much pushback," Imogen said with a wave of her hand. I bit the inside of my cheek at her use of the word "friend". The Ilise that considered that band of traitors friends was gone for good, and I hardly appreciated the reminder.

"We don't have to worry much about the Union. They should be here in a few days, and we can deal with them then. But we need to get around my kingdom-wide reputation of being a traitor to the crown," I said. After Aerilyn's murder, I'd incriminated myself as a Union spy by running away from the palace. Posters with my name and face had been plastered on every wall of the kingdom, and it would take more than a crown to erase that image of me from people's minds.

Imogen tilted her head.

"Are you going to give any suggestions, or are you just going to stare at me?" I asked, my patience beginning to wane.

"Who is the next most powerful group of people in the kingdom?"

Of course. How could I have been so blind? The most powerful people below me were the Dukes and Duchesses—they were like the monarchs of their provinces. Having the reigning monarch in charge of every little issue would be impossible, so tasks that could be settled at the province level were handled by the Dukes and Duchesses.

"The Dukes and Duchesses will have to come for the coronation. As long as they pledge their allegiance to me, then none of the provinces will have a choice," I said.

Imogen smiled. "You're learning. That horrible Union always focused on the little people," she said as she stood up. "You have to go bigger to get what you want." She was in a good mood. Now would be the perfect time to ask her about what I truly wanted to do.

"I also need to find Yorena."

The smile vanished from Imogen's face as she stared me down. It didn't matter how much new power I had, she could always make me nervous.

"You need to let her go for now. We will find her eventually, and I am not risking my future Queen by letting her go on a mission the guards can do for her."

My nails dug into my palm. I needed Yorena. And I was the only one who could bring her home.

"Imogen, please," I pleaded. I did not like the whiny tone of my voice when I said this. It sounded weak. But if I had to have one weakness, it would be Yorena.

She rubbed her temples, as if I was giving her a headache.

"Order a squad of guards to look for her. Or better yet, send a kingdom-wide alert to bring her back here on sight, and get rid of the other two she ran off with." That wouldn't bring Yorena back fast enough. But it was a start. Imogen might be saying no now, but that didn't mean she would say no later. She had won, for now. But I would gain the favor of the Dukes and Duchesses, I would rebuild this kingdom into the force it had been before Anora Schaefer's sorry excuse for a revolution, and I would prove myself to Imogen until my final breath. I would do everything in my newly expanded power to justify bringing Yorena back to me. It was what I was meant to do.

"Fine," I bit out.

"Good. Now we can focus on planning your coronation."

I wanted to be Queen, but at the same time, thinking about planning a coronation quickly made my head throb.

"Or, you plan the coronation. I'll focus on how to persuade the Dukes and Duchesses to see things my way when they arrive for it," I said.

Imogen looked unamused. "Okay. I'll handle it. But you had better be ready when the day arrives," she said. She started to leave the library, but I stopped her.

"And what should I do if they refuse to be convinced?"

Imogen paused at the door. "Then show them what you can do. You'll only have to do a little 'convincing'."

Chapter 3

Nikos

Imogen, I could deal with. Oliver, I could deal with. What I could *not* deal with was Ilise: the equivalent of two Imogens, with only half the sanity. I rubbed my chest from where Ilise's ring of air had almost killed me. I was sure it had left a bright red souvenir of the debacle, but I didn't want to see.

I pushed open the door to my room and ordered two servants out of the room. I needed to be alone right now; I needed to rein myself in. Just a few days ago I'd been at the top of the palace food chain. The King and Queen had been doing anything they could to keep me happy lest they aggravate my province, and I'd been on the same level as Yorena. Actually, I'd been above her. The past monarchs had lost all hope for her, and I'd become their top choice for Heir.

A glass bottle filled with amber liquid glinted at the edge of my vision, a clean cup set beside it. Dying light from the almost set sun gave the cup a weak glow. Maybe a drink would take the edge off, calm my nerves, which were on the verge of exploding. I poured a heavy serving of the liquor and drained the cup.

The drink seeped through my veins, the warmth spreading to every part of me. But I felt the same as before. How could I have stooped so low? Drinking to drown out the world around me? Needing a deranged sorceress to save me from getting killed over a good deed? That wasn't who I was supposed to be.

My father had told me all I would have to do was act like a normal Heircestrial nominee until we could plan out The Progression's infiltration. I was supposed to pretend I wanted that dumb crown, and then he would get off my back. I wasn't supposed to still be here. I should've been far away from here at this point, not walking on eggshells to keep myself alive. Ilise was reaching for *any* justification to get rid of me. It was a miracle she hadn't killed me yet, but it wouldn't be safe for me forever.

I'd been awful to her. And now, she had two elements at her disposal and a general dislike of everything and everyone around her. Well, everyone except for Yorena. That sorry excuse for a Princess owed me her life at this point. Why did I have to suffer because I'd decided to be a decent person for once? I needed to get out of here.

I needed to get Daeva out of here. She was the only reason I'd even agreed to be a fake Heircestrial competitor for The Progression in the first place. She was the one good thing in my life, the one person who had ever truly loved me. Ilise was already on the verge of murdering me, she was sure to target Daeva next.

But I couldn't simply retrieve Daeva and leave. Guards swarmed just about every area of the palace, and they were on the lookout for both Yorena and members of the Union. Waltzing out like I owned the place wouldn't work this time. I needed to plan a time when the palace would be at its weakest, when Ilise would be too distracted to give me a second thought.

I poured another glass and sipped it—more slowly this time. I needed my head intact. Ilise's coronation would be in the coming days, but security would likely double. Erratic Primis citizens might decide to protest her rule then, and I didn't want to get caught up in the bloodbath that would ensue if that happened.

The room was almost black at this point, faint moonlight filtering through the large windows. I stared at my dark reflection in the glass. Trapped. I chucked the half-empty glass against the window and delighted in the sound of the shattering cup.

"What am I supposed to do, Daeva?" I asked the empty room, burying my head in my hands. If it were only my life on the line, I would risk it. I would escape via the tunnels I'd shown Yorena and her servants, and never look back. But Daeva... My father had banned her from having any crystals on her, and a Progression footsoldier was to be with her at all times. I had to pull it together. For her.

The Progression. That was it.

My father had said The Progression was coming to the palace, but he hadn't specified when. He'd planned a coup by The Progression to put Ilise on the throne. Imogen had done the grunt work for them so The Progression wasn't really needed, but they were still coming. If I snuck the two of us out while they were here, Ilise would be too busy discussing her various nefarious plans with my father and Imogen, and the guards would be preoccupied keeping anti-Progression citizens *out* of the palace. No one would be focused on keeping people *in* the palace. I just needed to find out when this was all to happen.

My father was never one for verbal communication—never fulfilling a deal unless it was in writing. That man hadn't changed for as long as I'd been alive, and I highly doubted he'd changed in the short time I'd been here. My mind went to the hidden tunnels that seemed to be in every room of this palace, but I only knew how to get to other bedrooms on this side of the palace from here. If there was one thing Yorena had been good for, it was navigating those convoluted tunnels.

I would have to get to Ilise's room the normal way. These guards likely had about as many collective brain cells as a rock, so I could make up a reason why I needed to enter her room. I hadn't survived living with my father for as long as I had without quick thinking.

I left the room with my head held high. The guards pacing the halls watched me suspiciously until I walked past them. I gathered that they didn't like me very much, but one didn't survive the palace by being *likable*. A soft pattering sounded behind me. I could swear there was another set of footsteps but I refused to turn. By turning my head, I would incriminate myself, as if there was something I was running from. The sound could simply be from a servant.

Ilise had likely moved into the previous monarchs' room, so I quickened my pace until I reached the gilded door. Two burly guards stood watch, tall as the trees in the Slandslina Forest. Each rested a nervous hand on the sword sheathed at their hip, and I'd bet there were crystals under their shirts.

"State your business, Mr. Vikander," the taller one said. His eyes were dark, almost black. He stared down at me, challenging me.

"Her Majesty sent me to retrieve documents," I said, my voice steady.

The guard looked at his partner, then back at me. I knew they didn't believe me. I wouldn't believe me. But who were they to question the orders of the Queen? Ilise would burn them just for asking. I raised an eyebrow as they continued to stare at me, deciding whether they should risk Ilise's wrath.

The taller of the two guards spoke again. "You may enter, but make haste," he said. The pair pushed open the doors and stood at the entrance. I paid them no mind. Ilise wouldn't keep correspondence in the sitting room anyway. This bedroom was unlike the apartments. There wasn't a kitchen as soon as you entered, but an assortment of gilded seating for any guests the monarchs had. Golden columns stood in the middle of the space. Moonlight flowed in from the large wall of windows, reflecting off the marble tile. This room was grand. It was impressive. It reminded me of Vikander Manor.

I hated it.

I made a beeline for the bedroom, where I was sure I would find her desk. And I was correct: an oak desk sat tucked in a dark corner, its surface bare. Peering over my shoulder to make sure the guards hadn't followed me in, I attempted to open the drawer. Locked. No matter. I had noticed a potted plant on the windowsill. I hastened to retrieve it and the guards took a step into the room.

"What exactly are you doing with that plant?" the shorter guard asked.

"I don't expect a pair of guards to understand the needs of the Queen. And I doubt she'll appreciate guards entering her room without permission."

The pair of them released a low growl in their throats but stepped back into the hall.

I returned to her bedroom and placed the pot in front of the desk. Green light filled the edges of my vision as I grew another vine, easing it into the lock. I twisted it around until it opened with a soft click. I opened the drawer and flipped through a haphazard pile of letters. I searched for my father's nearly illegible, loopy handwriting.

There.

In the back corner was a letter that had been sent about three weeks ago, addressed to Imogen. At that point, they hadn't known if Imogen would be able to make Ilise her puppet, so it made sense for this to be addressed to the old witch. Just as I peeled open the letter, a weak hand clamped down on my shoulder. I whipped around, elbow out. It connected with a nose and there was a recognizable yelp.

Oliver.

I groaned and turned around to Oliver holding their now bleeding nose closed.

"You didn't have to elbow me, you barbarian," they said, their voice congested.

I slowly tucked the letter into my waistband as I said, "And you didn't have to sneak up on me." I paused. "What *are* you doing here?" Ilise hated me, but she was utterly annoyed by Oliver. If she was a tiger, I was the wolf she hunted, and Oliver was like the bothersome field mouse.

"You're not supposed to be here either," they said, still holding their nose. I slowly ambled toward the doorway, hoping that the letters I had tucked into my waistband could not be seen. Something cold rolled down my back and I was sure it was the sweat collecting under my shirt. Oliver was a snitch. They would do anything to gain Ilise and Imogen's favor, and reporting me was the best way to make them the deranged pair's right hand.

Oliver cleared their throat and I turned around, only to see that, between their fingers was my spiritsdamned letter. I patted my back for the paper and my fingers only met with smooth, slightly damp, silk.

"Did you know that soil harbors enough moisture for Water Imperium to use? And that it can be used almost like another hand if wielded correctly? Makes for a very useful device to find what a certain Vikander is hiding." They surveyed the letter like it was a priceless treasure.

"I was sent by Her Majesty to retrieve that," I said, my hand outstretched.

They giggled. *Giggled.*

"As if the Queen would trust the likes of you tainting her space," they said. Okay, tainting was pushing it. Oliver paced and I rushed them for the letter. They swerved out of the way at the last minute, the grin on their face spreading wide.

"Ratting me out to the Queen will hardly put you in her favor," I said, remembering the potted plant on the desk, which was still within my control. A thin runner of ivy shot out at Oliver, but they managed to form a wall of water to contain it. This water, and the now-dead plant, were then returned to the pot.

"But me telling on you *would* lessen her tolerance for you."

I scoffed. Calling what she had for me a tolerance was a joke. The only thing keeping me alive at this point was my family name. I stormed up to Oliver and swiped at the letter.

"Oops," they said. I noticed their crystal glowing and then, a dark stain began to spread across the paper. *No.*

I started for the letter and the stain only spread faster.

"Attempt to take it, and I allow the water to ruin the ink," they said.

My eyes locked with theirs. They wouldn't be able to ruin it if I broke their concentration. I tackled them to the ground, pinning their body down with my legs.

"Ruin that letter and I'll break more than just your nose," I seethed, my face inches from theirs. The blood had dried up at this point, and I was sure the use of their crystal had at least partially healed the break. I wasn't above breaking it again. I wasn't above anything until I could escape.

"I have a proposition," they drawled. My eyes flew to the letter, to the ink beginning to seep across the parchment. Why couldn't they break the damn hold they had on their crystal's power.

"Talk faster then," I said, yanking at the collar of their tunic.

They chuckled lightly. "I won't tell Ilise or Imogen you were snooping as long as you agree to obey three requests from me. And if you refuse, I will report you. Got it?"

I look back at the letter. Half of it was soaked with water, but I could work with half a letter. Daeva and I needed anything we could get, though the idea of having to be ordered around by this mouse made my skin crawl.

"Fine," I said through gritted teeth. "Now stop soaking the letter." The light of Oliver's crystal died and I scrambled off them to the ruined letter. I peeled it open and my heart dropped.

All the ink was smeared. It was useless. And I'd just signed my soul away to a mouse.

Great going, Nikos.

Chapter 4

Yorena

"**C**AN WE TAKE A break?" Mathias groaned. Clouds covered the sky in a thick blanket, blocking the moonlight we'd once had to navigate by. My feet cried with every step, begging me to stop. Humidity weighed on my shoulders, and sweat glued stray hairs to my forehead. But we couldn't stop yet. The longer we spent in the open, the more likely we were to get caught. And if we were caught without finding the Union, our chance of escape would be almost nonexistent.

But we should have found *some* sign of a base by now. My legs trembled at the thought of walking any further, but I was trembling on the inside, too—terrified that I had made a devastating miscalculation.

"We'll stop once we find the Union," I said.

"How much longer, Yorena?" Chafik asked. I clamped my mouth shut. No answer I could give would be much of a motivator. Our pace slowed to a crawl. Our feet couldn't handle much else. Wilderness was wildly different from the palace gardens, or even the small forests surrounding the palace. Every other plant sprouting from the ground could kill us in one way or another, dirt managed to get stuck on every part of my body, and the grasslands offered no reprieve from the unrelenting sun during the day.

"Can we stop for the night, please?" Chafik begged. I let out a long breath, staring into the sky. Thunder rumbled as lightning lit up the blackness.

"We'll stop when we find cover. It looks like a storm is about to come through." A flash of lightning illuminated a stout acacia tree standing erect in the distance.

The thick leaves should be enough to keep most of the rain off of us. We trekked for another few minutes, arriving at our destination just as the first droplets of rain were beginning to fall.

"Finally," Mathias said. He dropped to the ground, settling underneath the short tree. Chafik and I joined him around the trunk and pulled out some of our food. I devoured a strip of dried lamb, licking the saltiness off my fingers to make it last longer. My stomach roared, begging for more, the feeling not unlike a storm drain trying to guzzle any water it could. But there was no telling how much longer we would be out here. A hungry belly was better than a starving belly. I'd taken my unlimited access to food for granted.

Our journey had avoided any and all villages nearby. We'd managed to arrive where I thought the base would be in a single day, but an uneasy feeling turned the meat in my stomach sour. I'd thought we would have found at least one person from the Union by now. They were supposed to be marching on the palace, yet we'd seen nothing but the occasional rabbit. Finding these soldiers was my entire plan—they couldn't be gone.

"Yorena," Mathias said with an annoyed twinge.

"What?"

He ran a hand through the unruly curls on his head.

"We asked you how much longer it would be."

Oh right. But I couldn't give them an answer they would like.

In fact, I didn't even think I had an answer.

"Not much longer," I said. Thunder boomed, as if it was enraged at my lie.

"Then let's get some rest and find the Union tomorrow," Chafik said as he rested his head on his bag.

"I've been wanting to do that for hours," Mathias said. Within minutes, their breathing slowed. They had fallen asleep in record time. I was working them into the ground. I had no business being out here, and these two didn't even have the added strength I'd gained from combat training. But all of this was necessary, because getting caught would be a hell of its own.

I should sleep. My body begged me to rest, to take a few hours to prepare for the next leg of our journey. Yet, I stayed awake. I needed a backup plan in case we couldn't find the Union. If the kind of training Ilise had demonstrated as a spy had been any indication, the Union soldiers had probably detected our approach and had eluded us. I was a fool to think we could find them.

Goosebumps rose on my arms. I scanned the landscape, now asleep for the night. Nothing seemed to be around, but I had the distinct feeling of being watched. A branch snapped. My hand flew to one of the sheathed daggers. Keeping one hand on the weapon, I shook the boys awake.

"I thought we had a few hours," Mathias grumbled.

"I think we're being watched. Get Chafik up and get ready to run." Mathias silently shook Chafik awake. He brought a finger to his freckled face as Chafik peeled open his dual-colored eyes. A moment later, they both nodded to me. They were ready.

"Is someone there?" I called.

Crickets.

"Maybe you're just tired. You need sleep as much as we do," Chafik said with a yawn.

"I'm not going crazy."

I stalked through the grass, in the direction of the branch snap. My heart raced, braced for an attack. Mathias and Chafik shuffled after me.

"There's nothing there, let's just go back to sleep," Mathias said. I held a finger to his mouth, listening.

Silence. Too much silence. Crickets ceased their constant symphony, the frogs had stopped croaking. Someone was definitely here. Then I saw it. I almost thought it to be a figment of my imagination. A shadowy figure moved, crouching low in the grass.

"Stay here," I whispered to the boys.

I sprinted in the figure's direction, fueled by pure adrenaline. Luckily, the rain wasn't too strong, so I didn't have to slip through mud. The dagger shook in my hands as I neared it. Where I'd last seen the figure. Scanning the grass, I saw nothing amiss. Not even a footprint, or another snapped branch.

"Where are you?" I said.

A large hand covered my mouth. I flailed the dagger around, hoping to meet a body. Panic set in. Another arm went around my waist, squeezing the air out of my lungs. I clawed at the hand, begging for air. Black spots dotted my vision. I would not pass out here. I kicked my foot back, aiming for the groin of whoever held me. The figure released me with a grunt and I fell to the ground, gasping in lungfuls of air.

"Identify yourself," a familiar voice said. The figure yanked me up by my braid. My energy spent, I twisted around to see the figure, and the panic eased out of my veins.

"Yorena?"

It was Kieron. Palace guard, and my childhood friend. He let go of my braid and pulled me into a hug.

"How'd you get all the way out here?" he asked, releasing me. I eyed him warily. He may have been my best friend, but the royal guard was completely loyal to Ilise now, and who was to say Kieron wasn't as well? Maybe Imogen had sent him to spy on me or to foil my plans. I tightened my grip on my dagger and pressed the sharp tip to his neck. He inhaled sharply, raising his hands.

"Who sent you?" I said, my voice low. He looked at me as if I were speaking another language, mouth agape.

"I would greatly appreciate it if you took your very sharp weapon away from my neck." His voice was pinched. Maybe he hadn't been sent by Imogen. Kieron was as tall as me, but he was at least twice as big. If he'd truly been compromised, he would easily have been able to get out of this. I sheathed my dagger, and he let out a breath of relief.

"Sorry about that. I had to flee the palace after Imogen gained control over Ilise, and one can never be too careful when it comes to that sorceress."

His jaw dropped in surprise.

"Wait. Do you not know about what happened?" I asked.

"I haven't spoken with anyone from the palace in over a week," Kieron said. "Hells. I'll need to hear the rest of that story."

We walked back to where I'd abandoned my bag. Oh right, I realized. Kieron's squad had already been dispatched to Ominka to search for more Union bases by the time Imogen took over Ilise.

Visible relief crossed the boys' faces. "I thought you'd died for a second there," Mathias said.

"Always the vote of confidence, aren't you," Chafik said. He paused, eyeing Kieron's attire. "Isn't he a palace guard?" He scooted away from Kieron, warily.

"Not anymore. I'm with the Union now," he said. I sat next to Chafk.

My jaw dropped. "Since when?" I said.

Kieron had tried so hard to get me to believe Ilise was a spy, how could he have joined them so easily?

"My brother is the one of the leaders and I wanted a way out of the palace."

He has a brother? A brother in the Union?

"I thought you said the rest of your family was still in Pamu?" I asked. That was what I thought he'd said when I'd been getting to know him. And a brother? One of the first things we'd bonded over was the fact that both of us were only-children.

"I may have told a *little* white lie," Kieron admitted.

"Little? How could you have blatantly lied to my face all these years?" I said, standing up and staring him down. He gulped, a hint of fear flashing in his gray eyes. "Well?"

"Ilise lied to you too, and you're not nearly as mad at *her*."

The world seemed to go quiet. The wind ceased, the bugs stopped skittering about, and the few birds had terminated their chirping.

"I think that was the wrong thing to say," Chafik whispered.

I stepped up, so that my face was only inches from Kieron's. Close enough that I could see dark stubble dotting his skin.

"Ilise would have been killed if she told me the truth. You could have at least told me you had a brother, that you had family in the kingdom," I said. If he'd lied about this small thing for so long, there could be other things he'd been lying about. Maybe he wasn't my best friend at all, and was just another spy the Union had planted in the palace.

Kieron put two hands on my shoulders, his gaze soft. "Yorena, my brother would have *killed* me if I told anyone we were related. Being in the Union isn't just dangerous for its members, it's dangerous for those related to the members as well. I didn't want to lie to you, but I also wasn't keen on being burnt to a crisp or tortured for information."

I took a deep breath. He was right, and I hated that he was right. I hated that so many people had to lie about themselves to survive—to be seen as a person instead of nothing more than a bug to be exterminated.

"Do you forgive me?" he asked.

"I suppose. But if you're lying about anything else I will actually murder you."

His face cracked into a crooked smile and he brought me in for a hug. The rain stopped and our little group expanded out from the cover of the tree.

"Does this mean we can finally stop walking?" Mathias said.

Kieron's brow furrowed. "What's freckles talking about?" I settled into the grass and threw myself into the story of how we escaped the palace, and the makeshift plan we'd made to find the Union. Mathias managed to doze off halfway through, and Chafik's eyelids fluttered, barely open slits. His head somehow landed on my shoulder.

"Yorena, that is the dumbest plan I've ever heard," Kieron said.

I rolled my eyes. "But it still worked, didn't it?"

Kieron shrugged. "We'll still have to convince the others to let you come along. They aren't your biggest fans."

I snorted. "No kidding." I looked around. If Kieron was here, then where were the others he spoke of?

"What are you looking for?" he asked.

"You said there were others. Where are they?" Kieron joined me on the ground, leaning back on his arms.

"I've been gone for a while. Val will come find us eventually."

"Is that your fancy way of saying you're lost?" I asked, an eyebrow raised.

He averted his gaze to the grass. "No," he said an octave higher.

"You're a palace guard, how are you lost?"

"I lost my compass about an hour ago, and the clouds are preventing me from using the moon or stars." Losing your compass in the grasslands was like a death sentence. Unless you found a village, it was like walking in circles.

My head whipped to the sound of rustling grass. The wind was a slow breeze, like a light caress on my cheek. But the grass moved as if in a tornado.

"Uh, Kieron. I think your brother is coming."

He glanced over his shoulder with disinterest. "Took him long enough," he said, standing to brush the dirt off his uniform.

I shook Chafik and Mathias awake, ignoring their mumbled protests.

"Look who finally found me," Kieron said. A man stepped out from the grass. He towered over Kieron with his lanky form, but I could see their resemblance easily. Both had bronze skin, glowing in the cloud-covered moonlight. And they both had the same silver-gray eyes. Though his brother had had the smart idea to cut his brown waves so they just brushed his ears, unlike Kieron, whose hair fell below his shoulders and was almost always in a messy ponytail.

"Val, meet Princess Yorena and friends." Val raked his gaze over the three of us.

"Val, can you help us?" I said, without preamble. His gaze narrowed, but I continued on. "Imogen has taken over Ilise and made her Queen. I need help from the Union to get her back and defeat Imogen." Val blinked at me, as if trying to understand what I said.

"Aren't you the same person who was ready to get rid of us a few days ago?" he asked.

"That was what the King and Queen wanted. I tried to stop them," I said. Val crossed his arms, his face set, unbelieving.

It's true. She failed horribly and embarrassed herself in front of the entire royal guard, but she tried," Kieron said.

I pressed my mouth into a thin line. "You could have phrased that in so many different ways."

"It's my duty as your best friend, to phrase things in the *worst* way possible."

I pushed myself up from the ground. "Will you help us?"

Val crossed his arms over his chest. He circled the three of us, like a hungry shark sizing up its next meal. He stopped. His gray eyes were piercing. They shot right through me, as if he was searching my soul for every dark deed I'd ever done, for every reason he surely had to not trust me. My blood ran cold, though that only made the sweat on my face fall faster.

"Who's side are you on?" he asked in a low voice. Val crouched in front of me, forcing me to look up at him as he leaned closer to my face. I knew that he and the rest of the Union had no evidence to prove I was on their side now, but it still hurt that they were questioning it. I was in the middle of the grasslands with barely any food, quickly depleting water, and no shelter to speak of. Nothing about this would indicate I was still with the crown, but I supposed my name was enough to tie me to the throne. A name that had meant nothing in the long run.

"I'm on your side," I said. My voice cracked and I swallowed the lump forming in my throat. "We want the same thing."

Kieron poked his brother in the side.

"Come on, I've known this girl for years. You can trust her."

Val stared at me for a few more moments before pulling away.

"Fine. We'll help you, *if* you can get the others on board. And that's not a given. I will not force my people into a fool's errand."

But I knew I could convince them all of how important this was. I was so relieved, I almost wanted to hug him.

"Thank you so much. You have no idea how bad it's gotten in the last few days."

Val did not respond. He only waved his hand for us to follow him. I pulled the boys along as we trailed after Val. Kieron walked in front of me, fraying a path through the tall grass.

"How did this Imogen character you mentioned take over Ilise? The Ilise I know would never have let her. And why her?" Val asked. He walked at a hard pace and I almost tripped multiple times. Val didn't seem to notice, or maybe he didn't care.

"I think you'll want me to wait until we get to the others. It's a long story."

Val groaned. "Everytime someone says that, things get worse."

"You're the one who decided to join the Union," Kieron said flatly. "Kind of comes with the job."

Val halted, turning his head to look at his brother. "Let's not start this today. We have bigger problems to address," he said, continuing our trek. Kieron frowned but said nothing in response.

"What was that about?" I asked him.

He shook his head, refusing to look me in the eye. "It's nothing," he said with a sad smile. "Nothing you have to worry about." I knew that was a lie, but interfering with these brothers made getting Ilise back look like an easy task.

We walked in silence for what felt like hours. Annoyance rolled off Val as the three of us dragged behind him. I wanted to drop. The need to find the Union had been the only thing keeping me going. Fear of failure was a great motivator. And I hadn't failed, I had found the Union, I had found a safe place for the boys, and I had found people who would help me. Hopefully.

But I had a sinking feeling I wouldn't be received well. I could tell Val was holding in his resentment. Since we'd started walking, tension had burrowed in between his shoulders. And it didn't go unnoticed how he kept his fisted hands close to the many sheaths on his leather outfit. We were led into a dirt clearing. There were a few people gathered around a fire. Their heads all turned toward us upon hearing our footsteps.

"Val. Why in four hells is the Princess with you?" a girl with inky black hair asked.

"She claims to be on our side now. *And* she knows what happened to Ilise."

The girl's scowling face softened when he spoke Ilise's name. "Where is she?" she asked. She jumped up from the fire, as if she could go get Ilise right now.

"Still in the palace. Imogen took control of her," I said.

The girl fell back to the ground in shock and the others stared at me for an explanation. Mathias and Chafik shuffled toward the fire. They needed to rest now—they would have snapped if I had made them stay awake any longer.

"What do you mean, Imogen took control of Ilise?" a redhead snarled.

"Imogen used her soul crystal to basically make Ilise do her bidding."

"So Imogen *was* the voice in her head," a boy with a short afro said, mostly to himself. Voice? When Ilise had returned to the palace because of Imogen's ultimatum to kill everyone she knew, she had mentioned being pulled into her soul to talk to the old witch, but had never mentioned a voice.

"Tell us everything that happened," a blonde girl said.

Chapter 5

Ilise

THREATENING THE DUKES AND Duchesses had been a brilliant idea. They had poured in from every province, ready to accept me as their Queen, with the same fake smiles I'd seen them don hundreds of times. Before, I'd always despised how easily nobles were able to plaster on a smile and pretend to be enamored by everything that came out of the monarchs' mouths. But it was at this moment that I realized it didn't matter how artificial they were. As long as they were loyal to me, I had no care for how they truly felt.

I'd managed to convince Imogen to do away with an over the top coronation. Such a waste of time. I wore one of Yorena's gowns to the brief ceremony. It was slightly too long and still permeated with her signature rose scent. It was as close as I could get to having her by my side, and that brought me a small amount of comfort. Mauve silk fell around me in waves, pooling behind me in a long train. The off-the-shoulder neckline connected with puffy tulle sleeves, and pieces of gold twinkled at the waistline, cascading down the dress like a shower of stars. I'd even switched out my leather gloves for golden ones reaching my elbow.

I was ready to receive my crown. I craved the gentle weight of it on my head. Duke Dewei of Ominka had the honor of overseeing the ceremony. Under the pink streaked sky of the setting sun, I swore an oath. To lead, to protect, to put the kingdom first until I drew my last breath, and to lead the kingdom the way the four—which really should be five—Spirits intended. The golden vine crown rested upon my head, and I was finally Queen.

I'd expected the crown to be much lighter. And it shifted with every step I took, as if it wanted to jump off my head. But I would learn to bear the weight. The crown did not come without cost.

The Dukes and Duchesses spared no time in leaving the palace shortly after my coronation. I'd expected nothing more from them. I *had* threatened their status if they didn't come. The only way to persuade people in power to do something was to show them a world where they had none. Even a small glimpse into a life like the one I'd lived as a servant and as a spy had been enough to scare them into bending to my will. Resentment had rolled off them in waves throughout the ceremony, but I didn't mind. Who cared if they hated me? I had the power, I had the crown, I had two crystals for Spirits' sakes. I had it all...except for her. Yorena.

Back in the study, Imogen and I already had my first action as Queen planned out. We'd modeled our plan after the kingdom Letita had envisioned. Letita had been one of the first Imperium to exist, and she had been the first to take power. Her perfect kingdom had been one where Imperium were in their rightful place at the top, and Primis lived off the scraps we didn't need.

Letita had envisioned a world where Imperium were in control of everything and everyone, but then, Primis had managed to claw their way to the top of the ladder in too many places. I needed to start by giving some of the power back to Imperium. It was the way the world was meant to be. There was no reason to meddle with something that had been working perfectly for thousands of years until a few people decided their way had been better.

"Are you ready, Your Majesty?" Imogen said. The parchment sat in front of me on the desk. Moonlight illuminated the spot where I was to sign and plant my royal stamp.

I'd finally made the late Queen's study my own. After I'd killed her and her husband, clearing out their rooms had been something repeatedly knocked to the bottom of my to-do list. The study was sparse to begin with, only containing a chaise, two half-full bookcases pushed against the wall, and a desk overlooking the sprawling city below. I'd burned every personal touch she had to piles of smoldering dust. Smoke permeated the space and I had to open the window to air it out, allowing a smooth breeze into the room. There was no point in keeping any of her belongings, I refused to think of that woman as my mother. I felt no connection to this room, no sense of longing for the mother I had never known.

She was a stranger to me. And any thought of her made my stomach lurch. All I saw was the sword being plunged into Aerilyn's chest while my screams had been ignored. The Queen and her husband had had Aerilyn executed simply for having a piece of mail in her room. She hadn't stopped to properly question Aerilyn, and the King hadn't stopped to approve of the Commander's decision before he'd made the order. It was their fault she was dead, and taking over the Queen's space was my last piece of my revenge, erasing the last remnants of her from this palace. I would make the changes she had been too cowardly to make.

I stared out the window in front of me, oil lamps twinkling down the road into New Teber. All these people were mine to command, and I would get a front row seat to watch my kingdom change for the better. I shifted in my seat and gripped the fountain pen in my hand.

"I'm ready," I said. I dipped the gold tip into the black ink. The pen hovered over the parchment, begging for my signature. *Don't do this,* said the voice I had heard earlier, in the palace basement. *Remember who you are.*

"What is it, little one?"

I forced the traitorous thoughts from my mind. Nagging voices would not hinder me.

"Nothing, Imogen."

My pen met with the thick parchment and I signed. Setting down the pen, I stamped the document with the black outline of roses—the royal crest. I stared at my signature. I didn't feel different. I'd expected a more excited feeling after signing. All I felt was crashing waves in my stomach, and the off-putting feeling that something was missing. It was the same feeling you got after a disappointing gift trading ceremony for each of the spirits.

The nobles had thrown elaborate balls, while people in the villages had gift trading ceremonies. One year, I had received a pair of used wooden shoes. They were the most uncomfortable things I had ever worn, and didn't come close to the doll I had been hoping for.

"How do you feel?" she asked. Imogen hovered over me, mouth curled into a rare proud grin. I drummed my fingers on the wooden desk.

"Good," I said finally. Imogen rested a wrinkled hand on my shoulder.

"You should be proud of yourself. Our people will rejoice in your name."

A ghost of a smile graced my lips. "How long do you think it will take for this to take effect in every province?" I asked.

Imogen moved her hand from my shoulder, pointing to one section of my decree. "According to what you wrote, this is effective immediately."

I scanned over the lines that had been rendered in elegant calligraphy by the Palace scribe, my cramped signature thrown into stark relief.

"All rules outlined below are to be put into effect immediately. Refusing to act will be considered treason for opposition of direct orders from the crown. A grace period of three days will be given to every Primis business owner and not one day more."

I would have allowed The Progression to continue their method of driving Primis out of their homes, but they were too messy. Burning down houses and murdering those who refused to leave their homes left nothing intact, and Imperium still needed places to live. But at least The Progression had a nearly perfect success rate. Nothing was a better motivator than mortal fear.

This decree would give Primis a more discrete reason to leave their nice villages and towns. Without a business to support themselves, they would have to move somewhere they could find work, or live completely independent of their community. It was a much classier and cleaner method to scare away the Primis. But of course, if they refused, we could always go back to the old way.

"That may be what it *says,* but that doesn't mean it's what they'll *do,*" I said.

Imogen clicked her tongue. "Have I taught you nothing? We will tackle that issue if we come across it. And based on the meek behavior of all the Dukes and Duchesses at your coronation, I doubt you will have much trouble."

A knock sounded at the door. "Enter," I said. Nikos walked in the room and bowed to me.

"You summoned me, Your Majesty?" he said. I would never get used to the sound of my new title rolling past everyone's lips. It surpassed the bewitching melodies of the most renowned orchestra.

"I summoned you. I have an assignment for you," Imogen said.

Nikos clasped his hand behind his back and stared at me. "I thought our new Queen said I was an incapable buffoon who couldn't follow simple orders," he deadpanned, glaring at me. The muscles in my jaw twitched. Quite a bit of confidence for someone who I'd recently almost suffocated.

"I suggest you fix your tone before I fix it for you," I said sweetly. I smiled at the sneer he attempted to hide.

"My apologies, *Your Majesty.*"

"You will treat Her Majesty with respect, or else," said Imogen. "You are to pass a message on to your father."

Bitterness rolled off Nikos in vigorous waves. I stared him down as his hands curled into tight fists, tight enough for me to see the whites of his knuckles.

"What could you possibly need from him?" he spat.

"The Progression is to oversee the implementation of my new decree," I said, holding up the thick parchment to Nikos. He grabbed it from my hands, sweeping his eyes over it.

"What's the point of this?"

Imogen snatched the decree from his hands, carefully rolled it up, sealed it with melted wax and my stamp, and handed it back to Nikos. "This is not for your eyes. It's for your father's."

"I'm returning some of the power Imperium had ripped away from them after Anora Schaefer was wrongly made Queen," I said.

Nikos pressed his mouth into a thin line. Comments were doubtless on the tip of his tongue, and luckily he had the smarts to bite it. He would understand soon, this was for the better. He had to have something to do with Yorena's disappearance, so I wouldn't put it past him to harbor sympathy for Primis people.

"The people won't be willing to give up their businesses," he said. I stood from my chair, leaning into his face. "Most of the Primis population in Erea makes a living through their businesses. Taking that away from them would ruin their lives. They may be powerless, but they won't stand by and have their livelihoods ruined."

"They won't have to be willing."

Nikos gulped.

"You are dismissed. Pass my message on to you father," I said. Nikos bowed again before walking out. "And remember, the only reason you are in a better position than Oliver is because you know how to bite your tongue." I maintained eye contact as I opened the drawer with my gloves, slipping on the smooth leather. He knew what this meant—he knew the threat I was making plain as day. "Don't make me change that."

His finger dug into the door frame before leaving.

"Don't worry little one. He will learn to see our way very soon," Imogen said as she massaged knots of tension out of my neck.

"It would be a lot easier if we could be rid of him," I said. And I could think of at least thirty-seven ways in which I could happily do that in the next five minutes. Imogen glided to the green upholstered chaise.

"Unfortunately, I made a promise to his father to leave him be, for now," said Imogen.

I quietly seethed. Why had she done a stupid thing like that? She doubtless had a good reason, but Nikos was another annoyance I'd rather not deal with. As long as Imogen had to adhere to her promise, Nikos would continue to be a thorn in my side. I could work around him, but his lack of respect infuriated me, and he needed to be reminded of his place. However, that was a problem for another day.

An air message flew under the door. Air messages were what Air Imperium sometimes used to send notes over short distances. Other times, they could carry their voice with the wind, making people able to hear them from impossible distances away.

I bent to pick up the scrap of paper.

Union soldiers sighted on palace grounds. Have been taken into custody and await questioning

-Commander Hynkel

"What is it, little one?"

I handed Imogen the slip of paper.

"Some of the Union soldiers have arrived. I think we should pay them a visit."

Imogen's lips curled into a smile. "Agreed." She trailed me as I left the study and bounded down the stairs. Finally, I would be able to get rid of some of these pesky Union roaches. The rest of them should be arriving overnight and tomorrow. As far as I knew, none of them were yet aware of my transformation, my new rank, my new mission. They would be expecting a Progression siege on the palace. When I'd been part of the Union, I'd told them Imogen's plan for The Progression to start a palace takeover. Having me on the throne had eliminated the need for a siege. Assuming no one had intercepted them, the Union would still believe the siege was coming. It was elating to think the Union would never cause problems again. They would never recover from what was going to befall them in the coming days.

Bright chandeliers and sconces gave way to dim torches lining the walls as we reached the deepest level of the palace. Guards broke their formation to allow me passage when I arrived at the door of the dungeons. I pushed open the old wooden door that led to where prisoners were kept, to the mass holding cell at the end of the corridor. This was one of our bigger cells—slightly larger than an average servant bedroom. Gray and brown stone made up most of the space, with the only reprieve from the darkness being two torches on either side of the cell. The guards had removed the thin bed that should've been tucked in the corner, but the bathroom bucket still remained. Though none of the prisoners would be left alive long enough to have to use it.

I was shocked at how few Union soldiers were assembled in the cell—only sixteen pathetic souls, not even two complete squads of ten. I'd been expecting at least half the Union to be coming tonight. Most of them should have left their bases at least a week ago. There was no way only two squads had managed to make it.

"Where are the rest?" I asked a young soldier who was no more than a boy. Dark bruises marred the pale skin under his eyes, and dried blood was caked in his blond hair. He couldn't have been older than fifteen. Yet, he looked up at me as if I was the one in the cell, as if I was the one whose life was in danger. *Cute.*

"Why should I answer you, traitor," he spat. "You should be in this cell with us." I raised a brow. Traitor? They were the ones who wanted to go against the crown. I had been shown a better way to run the kingdom, a better rule to believe in—my own.

"If you don't plan on answering me, I'll assume you don't need your tongue anymore. I'll gladly have a guard cut it out for you." I leaned closer to the bars, gripping them hard. No one spoke. Not the boy, not the pair of twins huddled in the cramped corner, not the woman shooting daggers at me from the center of the floor, not the guy who wrapped a strong arm around another man, his partner, I assumed, and not even the girl who trembled at the back of the cell, nervously yanking on the thin strands of her black hair. Fine, we would do it my way, then. I nodded to the closest guard, a burly Earth Imperium. He unlocked the bars and grabbed the boy, who squirmed in his grip. "You've forced my hand."

The guard shoved him to the floor and I grabbed him, pressing the boy against the rough stone wall and grinned as his eyes widened. "I'm giving you one last chance," I sneered.

"No," he said. I shrugged. If that was his choice, then so be it. I formed a ball of flames in my hand, inching it closer to the boy's face. Sweat beaded his brow as the flames grew closer.

"Who needs to cut your tongue out when I can burn it away," I mused.

I inched the small inferno mere centimeters from his face, noting with some satisfaction that his eyelashes were singeing. Curling and then turning to powder. The heat on his tender skin had to be unbearable. Tears sprung to his eyes. I would break him, just a little more.

"Ok I'll tell, just let me go," he begged. I snuffed out the fireball and let the guard hold him in place.

"Now was that so hard? Tell me where the rest of you went."

Waves of blond hair fell into his face as he trained his gaze to the floor. "They're not coming. We got the message too late."

I crossed my arms. "What message?"

"A message warning us that you betrayed us and the mission was off."

I gaped at him. *Yorena.* That girl had managed to find people from the Union and warn them about me. I would have to find them the hard way.

"Kill them all," I said, breezily. Their pleading voices echoed off the walls. "I don't care how, just get rid of them," I told the guards.

The Union wanted to hide from me. No problem. Erea was mine now. Every tree, every cave, every hideout belonged to me. There was nowhere they could run. There was nowhere I would not find them.

Chapter 6

Nikos

YORENA OWED ME, BIG time, for what I was about to do. Guards trailed behind me as I walked through the dungeons. I hated how it smelled down here—like desperation, defeat, and rotten fruit. Water dripped from every crevice in the stone, creating black puddles on the ground. Ilise had ordered all the Union members to be executed in any way the guards chose. But I'd managed to convince her to keep one alive for questioning. I hadn't asked how the guards had chosen to kill them, but my imagination could fill in the blanks between the smoldering fleshy smell and the thin layer of water that shouldn't be covering the entire corridor. And I suspected that to be the source of the faint metallic scent of blood.

Without knowing when The Progression would get here, or even if they still would, these Union members had been my only shot at getting out of here—my only shot at discovering any small morsel of information that could help me and Daeva. But no, Ilise had to have almost twenty people murdered in cold blood. A small part of me felt the pit forming in my stomach to think this was only the beginning of Ilise's reign, but I ignored it. I owed those Union soldiers nothing. I couldn't fathom why I felt this shred of remorse—of guilt.

All it had taken was a little smooth talking, a little pleading, a huge hit to my pride, and some more begging for her to let me be the one to interrogate the girl. After I'd let Yorena and her servants out, Ilise prowled over me like a hawk, hungry, and waiting to strike. If not for Imogen's interference, I might have died in the throne room. But this interrogation would make up for that blemish on the events of the past few days.

I nodded to the guard stationed in front of the solitary cells, and he opened the door for me, sliding the seamless door to the side with his green crystal, casting a ghostly glow around him. I stepped through the opening, ordering the guards to stay outside. If nothing else, this assignment from Ilise had given me a semblance of control over the guards, for once.

I walked down the short hallway, stopping in front of the last cell. A girl lay slumped against the corner, staring me down through the bars, eyes burning with the promise of violence. The look was almost comical on a girl who couldn't be older than sixteen. Though I *had* left her for the night, hopeful the time alone would lower her defenses.

"We can do this the easy way, or the hard way," I said. Her fingers pulled on a black strand of her hair, ripping it from her scalp. Of course the one they had let live was a dramatic one. They were always the hardest to get to talk. No sense of preservation to speak of.

"You already killed my people, what do I care what happens to me?" she said as she stood.

The closer she walked to the bars, the clearer I could see paths of dried tears on her dirt-streaked skin. I fisted my hands behind my back. I couldn't feel remorse now.

"Why didn't you just kill me too? Why make me suffer alone?"

Because you can help me out of here.

"Because you have information I want," I said coolly. She wrapped a fist around the iron bars of her cell, jaw clenched.

"I won't tell you anything. Might as well kill me now and get it over with."

I activated my crystal and parted the metal bars for myself, stepping into her cell. The girl backed up to the wall, as if it would help her. This cell was the size of a closet, with barely enough space for three people to stand in comfortably. Her eyes widened as I stalked toward her.

"I warned you," I said.

Her eyes darted to the ground as it began to shake beneath her, a web of cracks forming under us. Thick vines sprouted from the cracks, snaking their way around her legs.

"This is your last chance to tell me where the rest of the Union went."

Little did this girl know, I didn't need to know to help Ilise. I needed to point Ilise in the wrong direction. The more time I provided for Yorena to find the Union, the closer I would be to getting me and Daeva out of here. And it would be entertaining to see Ilise go on a wild goose chase.

"I'll never tell you," the girl said, spitting at my feet. "I'd rather die than endanger the others. They will defeat you, and you will pay for all you've done."

Her hateful words shouldn't have bothered me. It's not like they weren't the same ones echoing in my nightmares. But still, I felt a jab of guilt stab through me, lessened after all these years, but still painful. I was only doing what I needed to survive, I told myself. Something this girl should've done rather than defy me and become a martyr.

She wouldn't tell me anything. She was a child without a family, a soldier without the rest of her army. Yet nothing I could say or do would convince her to betray the few Union members remaining, not even if it would spare her life.

I wrapped the vines fully around her torso. She looked upon me without fear of what was about to come of her, ready to die for the Union. She was young, but her face told a story full of trials, every scar another chapter of her story. I'd probably helped write the ugliest chapters of that story, and now I was about to end it.

I closed my fist, tightening the vines around her. Her pale skin quickly reddened as she squirmed against the vines, desperate for air that wouldn't come. Ilise had given me two instructions: get any information about the Union's whereabouts, and then kill her when I was done.

Her eyes fluttered closed, finally unconscious. I couldn't save her, her life was void, but I could at least offer her this small mercy. I snaked the vines around her neck, squeezing them hard to separate her head from her body with a sickening crack. The head rolled in front of me as the rest of her body slumped to the ground. She didn't feel it. She'd died without pain, I tried to tell myself.

I took one last glance at her decapitated head, feeling sick to my stomach. *She died without pain.* I returned the vines to the dirt below and closed the cracks in the stone. I'd hoped the girl would at least give me some directions, but I was no better off than when I'd started. All I'd gained was another person's blood on my hands. I reasoned with myself that this was at least better, more humane, than Ilise's idea of an execution: a more... hands-on approach.

I walked down the corridor back into the main dungeons. "Dispose of the girl's body," I told the stationed guard. He nodded grimly and walked back into the small hallway with one of my guards, a Fire Imperium.

Ilise wouldn't be happy to know I'd learned nothing. At least I had killed the girl. That would have to be enough to appease her for now. The other two guards followed me as I hurried up the stairs to the third floor. If there was anything Ilise hated more than my "incompetence," it was being kept in the dark about it.

The guards left me at the door to the Queen's old study—now Ilise's study. I knocked on the door, mentally preparing myself to speak to her. Ilise opened the door, her mouth already turned downwards. *Great.*

"Nikos," she said. I bowed deeply. "I trust you got the information I asked for after begging to keep the girl alive for so long." She opened the door further and motioned for me to sit on the chaise.

"I apologize, Your Majesty, but I was unable to gather anything from the girl." Ilise sat at her desk chair, still facing me.

Her lips curled into a deep frown. "You must not have tortured her enough." Ilise's finger grazed the dagger she kept strapped to her side. I didn't know why I had ever underestimated her. She was a nightmare. Given, most of it was probably Imogen's doing, but I was sure she would have no qualms about killing me the moment I proved to be useless.

"I tried, Your Majesty."

She sighed, playing with the silk of her peach dress. "I thought you were going to finally prove yourself to be helpful, but clearly, I was wrong." She twisted around in the chair, focusing back on the papers littering her desk. "Did you at least kill her? Were you capable of doing that?"

I dug my fingers into my knee. "Yes, Your Majesty. I decapitated her," I said, knowing she liked knowing the gruesome details.

"Excellent. You are dismissed for today, and I hope tomorrow you will not fail me."

I stood up from the chaise and hurried out of the room. Ilise was now no more than a less controlled, slightly less powerful version of Imogen. Yorena had better find the rest of the Union. I didn't know how much longer I could stand being stuck with the two of them before I snapped.

I walked down the halls to my room, or rather, the room next to mine. I wanted nothing more than to escape this place, to cut my ties with The Progression and Imogen. But I couldn't, for Daeva. Imogen had never objected to me visiting Daeva, and she had never tried to stop me. But keeping my love so close, easily within reach, was nothing more than another way to keep me on Imogen's leash. I pushed open the door to Daeva's room.

"Darling," I called.

Daeva walked out from the main bedroom, rubbing sleep from her eyes. Without servants assigned to her, the apartment was nearly empty. She had the curtains in her room drawn, letting only one candle light the room. I opened my arms and she ran to me, hugging me tightly. I pressed a soft kiss to the top of her head, brushing back a strand of her flowing black hair.

"Did I wake you from a nap?"

"No," she said quietly.

Keeping one arm around her waist, I walked with her to the velvet settee in one corner.

"You haven't visited me in a while," she said as we settled onto the couch.

I tucked her head into the crook of my neck.

"I've been busy, darling. But things should be calming down soon."

At least that's what I hoped. She sighed into my shoulder and I inhaled her lavender scent.

"I'll get you out of here soon, I promise."

"You said that two months ago."

The comment stung, but it was true. Despite all that I subjected myself to, it did nothing to help her. We were supposed to get married once upon a time, until my father and Imogen had the bright idea to use Daeva to keep me in check. She popped her head up, flashing that gap-toothed grin I loved so much.

"But as long as we're together, I guess it isn't too bad."

That was Daeva, always the optimist. She lifted her legs onto the couch so she was fully on top of me.

"Can you stay here for a little? It gets lonely."

I pressed a long kiss to her forehead as I held her closer to me.

"Anything for you, darling."

Chapter 7

Yorena

I AWOKE AS DAWN broke over the grasslands, accompanied by the soft chirping of birds. Blades of grass dug into my cheek and dirt coated my tongue. I really needed to stop sleeping with my mouth open. I stretched my stiff muscles, finally having gotten a few hours of sleep. I rummaged through my bag for my canteen and drained the remaining dregs of water, only a few sips, really. The cool liquid barely quenched my desert-dry throat.

"I see someone's greedy for water," the short Air Imperium I had met the night before said. "But I suppose I shouldn't expect anything else from a palace rat." They paced around the dying embers of the fire, keeping their eyes trained on me. I'd learned their name last night—Rori. I had also learned they had a personal vendetta against me.

"Why are you watching me so intently?"

They walked up to me, arms crossed.

"Don't think that just because you claim you decided to switch sides, I'll automatically trust you. Thousands of lives have already been uprooted because of your cowardly family, and I'll be damned if I let you betray us the way your parents did."

"None of you would have known about Ilise without me, and you would still be marching to your doom, " I responded.

Rori stared down at me not unlike the way a snake did their prey before they attacked. They leaned in close. "Great. I've still got my eye on you," they hissed.

The freckled girl, Orla, yawned. "Back off Rori," she mumbled. They could try as hard as they wanted, but I wasn't going anywhere until we took back the kingdom and saved Ilise.

"Don't kill each other yet. We still need to hear the rest of what happened at the palace," Val said. He brushed stray grass from his hair, rubbing the sleep from his eyes. He shook awake his brother's sleeping form beside him as I woke Chafik and Mathias, both of them trying to slap me away.

"Just need a few more hours. Or days," Mathias mumbled.

Chafik rolled over, his unique, heterochromatic eyes draped over by his heavy lids. "I second that."

"For the love of the Spirits, get up. You guys got way more sleep than us," Cain said, nibbling on a dried piece of lamb. Ignoring their protest, I dragged my sleepy boys toward the rest of the group. Rori shot daggers from their hazel eyes. *And I thought Nikos' stares were cold.*

"Okay Princess. You told us how Ilise got taken over, but you didn't tell us why she went there in the first place," Val said. After I'd told them all about Ilise, Rori had sent air messages out to every group who was about to storm the palace. I hoped they'd all received them in time. Otherwise, they would be walking straight into a trap. These Union soldiers may have been the closest thing Ilise had to family, but Imogen had managed to demonize every person Ilise had ever cared about. Well, except for me.

"I told the kid not to do something stupid. And yet she turned around and did the stupidest thing possible," Kass grumbled.

"It wasn't stupid," I said.

Maybe questionable, but she was brave and honorable to sacrifice herself for her friends. Imogen had given her an ultimatum: return to the palace and turn herself in, or all allow all her friends to be killed. Granted, sneaking into a palace of enemies may not have been the best course of action, but it had kept the people in front of me alive. Though they didn't seem very grateful. Unless, she'd never told them about the dream. Did she let them believe she'd abandoned them for some unknown reason?

Rori stormed up to me, leaving mere inches between our faces. Every muscle in their jaw clenched, and I could almost see steam pumping out of their ears.

"Not stupid? We lost Ilise because she decided to abandon the plan and leave us for your over-pampered ass."

I gaped at them. "Do you think I don't wish the roles were reversed? Do you not think I wouldn't trade places with her in an instant if I could?"

Kass stepped up to Rori, pulling them back from me. "They're just upset, they didn't mean it. Right, Rori?"

Rori huffed, backing down from me. I dropped the cold mask I had cultivated as Princess over my face. These people were not my friends, and I needed to stop trying to convince myself that they were.

For a brief moment, I was no longer in the woods, I was in the throne room again, standing before my parents as I attempted to lay claim to the power I'd been raised to wield. They'd raised me to be Queen, to lead the people of Erea into greatness. And the moment my vision of greatness had differed from theirs, I'd been belittled and knocked down.

And now I was back, in the middle of a field, chased from the only home I had ever known, after finding out my whole life was a lie.

"Did Ilise tell you about the voice she'd been hearing?" I asked.

"She mentioned it in passing to me when she first came back to base," Cain said.

"Did she tell you whose voice it was, though? It was Imogen."

Cain shuddered. The very name of the sorceress was enough to make one's blood run cold.

"I assume you know of her?" I asked him.

"Who doesn't? She's the oldest and most powerful sorceress in the kingdom, possibly the world. Ilise told us about the voice, but we didn't think it could be Imogen."

I tilted my head. "Why not?"

Cain shifted uncomfortably. "Because she was hearing the voice before she ever met the sorceress. And there's no record of a sorcerer being able to talk in a person's head, *and* without ever being close to them."

"Just because there's no record doesn't mean it's not true. The only reason Ilise came back was because Imogen gave her an ultimatum."

Rori leaned in. "What kind of ultimatum?" they asked.

"Imogen threatened to hurt all of you if Ilise did not come back and hand herself over," I said. Shadows seemed to grow on the faces of the people grouped around me. I could have heard a pin drop with the silence that fell over them as they contemplated this idea.

Val fisted the grass in his hands, staring straight ahead. "She screamed in her sleep the day before she left and told us it was just a dream. We should have seen it."

I could see the guilt in his and the others' expressions. But it wasn't their fault. Ilise always put her friends first. Even if they'd known, they wouldn't have been able to stop her. I hadn't been able to stop her either.

It's what I admired most about Ilise—her willingness to do whatever it took to protect the people she loved, even if her own fate was unknown. If the world had more people like her, then maybe we wouldn't be in this predicament.

"Don't blame yourselves for not noticing," I said. An empty laugh bubbled to the surface. "If Ilise doesn't want you to know something, you won't find out."

"But we still should've known she had a reason for abandoning the mission," Rori said. "She's the most resilient out of all of us. She wouldn't just quit."

Val clapped his hands together, snagging everyone's attention. "Now that we know the situation, it is even more urgent that we plan our next steps," he said.

I dragged my finger through the dirt. Yes, we needed a plan. But what could we do? There was no telling where the rest of the Union had fled to. And there was a very real risk that Ilise might guess anything we came up with—she knew how her people thought. She had trained with them, bonded with them, gone on missions with them...We needed to do something outside the box, enough so it would take Ilise by surprise.

"What if we gathered the Union to march on the palace together like we originally planned? We would have strength in numbers," Cain said.

I shook my head. "She's expecting the Union to show up, it would be a suicide mission," I said.

Orla blew out an exasperated sigh. "Ilise knows us. She knows our strategies. We can't expect to devise a plan she won't be able to guess," she said.

She was right. Nothing *they* could think of would be outside Ilise's realm of thinking. But she hadn't spent years of her life with *me*, so she wouldn't be able to guess what plan I could come up with. I was the one who needed to come up with an idea. How could we undermine a sorceress with thousands of years of knowledge, and the powerful two-element Imperium queen she controlled? We couldn't defeat them with brute force, and we didn't want to hurt Ilise. Based on how many guards were already at the palace when we'd left, it would be impossible to go back now. But the nine of us couldn't go against her alone. We needed outside help, a lot of it.

"What if we asked another kingdom for help?" I offered. Val's cold mask broke briefly as bewilderment painted his features, and Rori simply scoffed at me. The rest stared as if I'd grown two heads, even Kieron and the boys.

"What? Did I say something wrong?"

"As if we knew anyone from either of the neighboring kingdoms," Val scoffed. "And it's very unlikely they would help us even if we did."

My lips turned up in a smile. I could finally make myself useful.

"Oh Spirits, she's doing the idea smile," Kieron said.

Orla turned to him, a questioning look in her eyes. "The *what* smile?"

"It's the face she makes when she gets an idea that most of the time sends us on a wild goose chase."

I cut him a look.

Rori glared at me, already impatient. "What's your idea?" they asked.

"Why don't we ask the King and Prince Consort of Croaga to help us? Their borders are still open, and it's not too terribly far from here, is it?"

"As if you know them," Rori said, skepticism bleeding through their tone.

"I was the Princess of Erea for my whole life. I met them multiple times. I used to write to the Prince Consort, Alyx, for advice. If anyone will help us, it'll be the Croaga monarchs."

Kieron rolled his eyes.

"Did you have a better idea, Kieron?" I asked.

He opened his mouth and then promptly shut it. My idea was perfect. King Titus and Prince Consort Alyx were big advocates for equality between Primis and Imperium. All we had to do was make it to their castle, and my face should be enough to earn us an audience with them. Rimed—the capital—was just on the other side of Faveru. The trek wouldn't be as painful as trying to go to Banauri or Pamu up north.

"I think it's a good idea," Orla said, cautiously. "We can't get Ilise back with just the nine of us. And maybe the monarchs would have more suggestions."

Val weighed the idea, scratching the brown stubble on his chin. "Is everyone in agreement?" he asked.

"Always wanted to see Croaga. I hear the beaches are beautiful," Cain said.

I turned to Kass and Rori. "Are you guys in?"

A muscle in Rori's jaw twitched. "I don't like it. But we don't have any other ideas, so I guess I'm in," they said.

"Kass?"

She nodded. I clapped my hands together.

"Great. I have a map in my bag and we can plan our route."

I dug through my bag and handed Val the map.

"Can we make one stop on our way there?" Chafik asked.

Val blinked at him. "What kind of stop?"

Chafik walked to Val, taking the map in his hands. He dragged his finger along the creases until he found Bridbrough.

"I've been thinking, and to fight a sorcerer, we need to know the extent of their powers. The Faveru Archives are more extensive than even the palace archives. If a book exists about them, it's in there."

Cain leaned over the map. "I thought there weren't any books on sorcerers."

Chafik grinned. "There are not many. My adoptive father is in charge of the Archives. I've seen him stock books about them multiple times. And it wouldn't be too far out of the way to get to Rimed."

He made a compelling case. The detour would only take half a day at most, and if he was right, we wouldn't be as clueless anymore.

"But wouldn't the building be armed to the teeth?" Rori asked. "We know you might be able to convince the guards to let us in, but it would be dangerous to let anyone know we were there."

"I know a few different ways in."

Compared to the danger of the rest of the journey, this paled in comparison. And if there was a way to break Ilise from Imogen's control, it would be a heavy blow to the sorceress. Too much about Imogen was unknown. She was too unpredictable. Even a small amount of knowledge about sorcerers' powers would be helpful. Just something to knock Imogen down a few rungs.

"I think we should go. Even with help from Croaga, we wouldn't get far if Imogen surprised us again," I said, turning to Val.

He sighed. "We'll plan to go there. But if you can't find a discreet way in, we won't go inside. Deal?"

"Deal," Chafik said.

"Ok. Everyone gather your belongings, we'll move in an hour," Val ordered. He handed me the map and I carefully rolled it, packing it away. Someone tapped my shoulder. I whipped around to find Rori crouching behind me.

"Do you truly think you can get the Croaga monarchs to help us?"

I placed a hand on their shoulder. They swatted it away.

"I do. And I will stop at nothing to get Ilise back. You can count on that."

"I hope so."

Chapter 8

Yorena

MY FEET THROBBED AFTER the third hour of arduous travel over rougher and rougher terrain. I wanted nothing more than to drop where I stood. To nap for a few hours, or a few days. Mathias was chatting with Cain at the front of our line, cracking jokes, as I walked with Kieron in the back. The sun beat down on us and sweat dripped nonstop down my skin, gluing my ruined dress to my back. Wearing a riding dress to fight Imogen may have been smart when I was inside the palace, but out here, the short trains still caught on every branch, the cotton kept in the heat even when wet, and the blue fabric stood out in the green and brown grassland.

"In case you haven't noticed, Val, there are some of us who are dying back here and would appreciate a break," Kieron said to his brother. Val sighed, annoyed. This was the third time in a single hour Kieron had asked this. The bite in his tone I'd heard when Val had first found us was back, and it was foreign to me. Kieron had never been the type to lash out at someone, especially not someone he was close to. What in the four Spirits was going on between him and his brother? I would have to ask him in private the next time I had a chance.

"We need to get to the Slandslina Forest before we take a break. We're too exposed out here," Val said. Mathias groaned from up front. "It's only another hour away, stop whining." I kept my mouth shut.

Rori already saw me as a pampered princess, and I couldn't let the others think that I was too. But I was out of my element. Two months of training with Ilise paled in comparison to this. Until the past few days, I'd never walked farther than a couple miles from the palace, and that had been along a road. Out here, the high grass scratched against my skin, managing to get through the seams of my dress. Oh, what I would do for a bath and a change of clothes right now.

Orla slowed her pace to walk in line with me and Kieron. "I think the others are warming up to you," she offered.

I snorted. "I wouldn't exactly say that."

She turned to me, her freckles standing out against her slightly sunburned face.

"Well, Rori hasn't threatened you in hours. And Kass has moved her hand from her dagger." I hadn't even noticed Kass had a dagger. I peered up the line and saw the glint of her silver blade, strapped to the outside of her thigh. I had a sudden realization: these people could easily get rid of me if they wanted. What was I doing, teaming up with people who had every right to turn me away? At least when I'd first started training with Ilise, she couldn't have hurt me without dooming herself. And she'd hated my guts then. The few times I'd sparred with her, there was always a certain ferocity in my eyes. Like she thought that the fight was real. But she always pulled back to avoid risking herself. These people had no such limitations.

"Is there anything else you know about Imogen?" Kass asked.

I kicked aside a stray rock in my path, trying to distract myself from a painful seeping wetness on my heel. Another blister. What *did* I know about her? I hadn't even known she could communicate with Ilise without being near her until Ilise had told me. I knew she was the oldest sorceress in Erea, possibly in the world, but that was where my knowledge ended.

"All I know is she's thousands of years old, hates the way the kingdom is being run, and she wants to return the kingdom to the way it used to be," I said, recalling the conversation I'd had with Ahn—a sorcerer on the Council who had warned me about Heircestrial being a diversion. "Also, she's controlling the entire Council."

It'd been the night I passed my first test of the competition and I'd needed some time outside the palace. Ahn had approached me in the garden, erratic, talking in riddles that had taken me much too long to understand. By the end of our conversation, he'd acted as if we had never spoken before. As if someone had erased any memory he had of warning me.

"Define control," Rori said.

"A few days before Ilise came, one of the sorcerers came to warn me about Imogen. And seconds after he warned me, his crystal glowed and he completely forgot he was even talking to me." The memory of his blank stare, the shell of a person he'd become, still haunted me.

"Cain? Got any explanation?" Val asked.

Cain looked to Chafik, seeing if the scholar-in-training knew anything else. Chafik shrugged.

"No clue. Imogen is another level of powerful, and I can't even guess what rules she's bending to maintain that level of control," Cain said. It would be nice if we actually knew the rules she was supposed to be held back by. There didn't seem to be any when it came to her.

"Maybe we'll find out when we get to the Faveru Archives," Orla said, her voice filled with hope. I prayed we would. If we didn't, it would mean going in blindly, again. And I would hate to see how much more Imogen would manage to steal from me, and from the citizens of the kingdom, this time.

We traveled in silence for the next hour. My legs trembled with every step, unused to the landscape.

"We should reach the forest once we crest this hill, and then we can take a break," Val said.

Thank the Spirits. If this went on for much longer I would drop. Our pace slowed to a crawl as we trekked up the grassy hill, roses poking their red and pink petals through the grass. My heartbeat was in my ears from the exertion. How was I going to make it all the way to the Faveru Archives, let alone Croaga, if I was already exhausted on the first day?

We reached the top of the hill and I nearly cried from relief as the Slandslina Forest filled my vision, thick with lush pines. The towering timber blocked out the sky, only allowing the smallest amount of sunlight to peek through. Vines caressed my cheek from where they swung on low-hanging branches. Instead of yellow grass and dry soil, my boots sank into the soft dirt, which retained moisture from the expansive shade above.

"Finally," Mathias said as he sat down under the drooping branch of a willow.

"We'll rest here for an hour and then we'll keep walking until nightfall," Val said. I walked into the thick brush, stopping at the closest pond. The lofty trees blissfully blocked the sun, the relief falling over me immediately. I splashed some of the cool water on my face and sighed as it washed away much of the heat and grime. What I really wanted was a long bath, but disrobing in the middle of the forest wasn't a good idea. Instead, I needed to make this dress better suited for the journey ahead.

Digging in my bag, I retrieved one of my daggers and began cutting. I first cut off the sleeves and sliced them into thin strips to use as hair ties. Then I sawed off the long back of the dress, the navy blue now stained brown with dirt. I could cut the pants into something shorter, but then I wouldn't be able to use any of the sheaths or holsters. With the extra fabric gone, I stretched out on the shore of the pond.

I didn't want to think about how much animal dung and bugs I was lying in, but I would accept them if it meant being off my feet. A branch snapped behind me and my body tensed. It could be an animal, maybe even a panther. They weren't common but apparently this forest was their last habitat. Long canines and predatory yellow eyes flashed in my mind, making my blood run cold.

My dagger was too far away for me to reach it, and I didn't want to use my crystal so soon in our journey, on an endangered animal of all things. Nikos had only given me two crystals, and I wanted to save power for later. I forced my hands to remain still as I slowly turned. Orla smiled at me and came to rinse her hands in the pond water.

"You can calm down, I'm not here to capture you," she joked.

I let out a breath of relief. "Sorry, I'm a bit paranoid. I thought you were a wild animal."

Orla pulled off her leather boots and kicked her feet in the water.

"We're all a little paranoid. It's what keeps us alive," she said. She eyed my newly cut dress. "Good thinking, getting rid of that extra fabric. I wish I could do the same but..." She trailed off, tugging at the leather neckline of her suit.

The soldiers in our group all wore similar suits to what Ilise had worn when she'd returned to the palace. They were practical uniforms, full of places to stash weapons, but they must not have been comfortable or breathable. I rose from the ground and sheathed my daggers on my pants. Orla picked at her fingernails, looking down at the water before her. *She came here for something else.*

"Why are you really here? There are other ponds to choose from. Anything you want to say?"

Orla opened her mouth to protest, but I cut her off.

"I was raised to be a Queen, I can read faces."

The corner of her lip turned up in a smile.

"I can see why Ilise likes you," she said. "I came here to see how you were doing. I know this isn't what you're used to."

That was an understatement. I relaxed a bit.

"I'm alive, we finally have some direction of what to do. So, I'm doing as well as I can," I said.

Although, I still wasn't sure if my best was going to be enough, especially if we ran into any guards. I doubted the rest of my group would have any quarrels with fighting, or even killing anyone who came after us.

"Orla, Yorena!" Kieron shouted.

A panicked expression spread across Orla's face and I sprang up, grabbing my bag and running after her to the tree line. I saw Kieron gesturing wildly. Orla seemed to understand, and cut back into the tree line, just as I started to say Kieron's name.

Kieron reached me in a few lightning fast strides and clamped a hand over my mouth, pulling me into the trees before I could leave the forest.

"Ouch!" I protested, panicking. What was going on?

"There's a guard squad coming up the hill," he whispered. "We're going to have to fight them off. Are you ready?"

No, of course I wasn't ready. The only people I'd ever fought were Imogen and the other Heircestrial nominees, and we all knew how that had turned out. Compared to everyone else, I was pathetically weak. I could barely climb this spiritsdamned hill.

"Ready?" Kieron asked again.

"Yes," I said, my voice surprisingly steady.

The other Union members, who had been hiding behind the trees until this very moment, unsheathed their weapons. The faint sounds of hooves crunching the dirt reached my ears, and I quickly looked through my bag. My fingers met with the smooth texture of the crystal at the bottom of the bag, and I clasped it around my neck. Now was as good a time as ever.

Val directed the others into position and ordered Mathias and Chafik—whom he obviously considered to be incapable of being any help to us—further into the forest before coming up to me.

"Have you ever fought before?" he asked.

I nodded, too nervous to speak. "Good. Just be prepared, we might have to kill them."

My empty stomach lurched. *Kill them?* They were just following orders, they didn't deserve to die for it. But I nodded anyway.

"Remember to not let them get you on the ground," he said before moving closer to the tree line.

As far as I could tell, there was just a single squad of soldiers coming, so the odds weren't completely against us. And the only non-Imperium fighting were Kieron, Val, and Cain, so we had the elements on our side. But there was no telling if this was a Primis squad or an Imperium squad. Maybe if it was a Primis squad, we could scare them away instead of having to hurt them.

The soldiers crested the hill on white steeds. Even from a distance, I had the uncomfortable feeling that their eyes were all drilling directly into me. The golden rose of the royal crest gleamed on the breastplates of their uniforms.

"Yorena Scheafer, we are here to return you to the palace on order of Queen Ilise. Surrender now."

I jumped as Rori clasped their hand on my shoulder.

"Why didn't you say there was a warrant out for your capture?" they seethed.

I wiggled from their grip.

"I didn't know," I pleaded.

"Anyone aiding Yorena is to be executed. Step forward now and we shall be merciful." Based on their predatory grins, I highly doubted that. The first guard hopped down from his horse and the others followed. The guard's gray eyes held the promise of violence in them, the jagged scars on his face a testament to what he could endure. He was the tallest among them—a full head taller than Val. *Spirits help me now.*

"This is your last chance, Yorena," the man warned.

I stepped past the tree line, ignoring Kass' hushed curses.

"I will never surrender," I said, my chin held high. A pinprick of white light shone from under the guard's jacket.

"So be it," he said.

With a forceful gust of wind, he knocked me back, kicking the air from my lungs. *Don't let him get you on the ground.* I planted my foot behind me to keep from falling backward as the remaining guards rushed the others behind me. But I couldn't worry about them now, I had to try and disable this guard. Preferably without killing him.

I ducked to avoid another wind attack and charged the guard, elbow out. My elbow collided with his nose, causing crimson blood to flow down his face.

Anger burned in the guard's gaze. I was sure that Ilise had told the guards to capture me alive, but chances were, they would relish hurting me if they could. Judging by what she'd done to the last guard who'd hurt me, I highly doubted Ilise would appreciate me being hurt, but that didn't seem to matter at this point. The guard planted his boot in my stomach. Tears stung in my eyes from the pain of the brutal kick and my dagger flew down the hill. *Spirits.*

Kieron let out a string of curses behind me as two guards descended on him, a sword in each of their hands. All he had was a shortsword and any hidden weapons in his uniform, though I doubted he would have time to grab them. Clutching my stomach, I started toward Kieron and was jerked back by my braid. My scalp pulsed from the yank. The guard behind me chuckled.

"Trying to run, are we?" he taunted. His breath against my cheek was hot, stale. I kicked his groin as hard as I could and he dropped me. I tried to catch myself, and my knees buckled. Pain shot up my legs, every joint pulsing in time with my heart. A ring of air wrapped around my middle and I was thrown into the thick of the battle, colliding with Rori. Rori tumbled to the ground with me, and the guard who had been fighting Rori charged the two of us. Rori threw a knife, the flashing silver sailing through the air before landing in the guards throat. He grasped at the blade. He fell to his knees, blood gushing from the wound. *Hells.*

"What in four hells is wrong with you?" they grunted, pushing me off them. Before I could respond, I was yanked back to the guard. My head was spinning. My heart pounded in my ears and my muscles screamed at the thought of having to move. I landed a weak punch to his stomach and he tossed me on the ground.

He gripped my arm, trying to pull me down the hill. I activated my crystal, almost sighing with relief at the rush of energy and strength, and focused all my fire to where the guard's hand gripped my bare arm. He screamed in agony as his hand sizzled like oil on hot coals, and he dropped me. I scrambled to my feet and rushed back up the hill.

Kieron and the others had already defeated the other guards. My stomach lurched to see the bodies, no breath making their chests rise. Taking advantage of my attention being focused on the bodies, the guard I had been fighting smacked the back of my head with the handle of his sword. I swayed on my feet as the world spun, tasting dirt as my face was shoved into the ground. *Stupid.*

"Your little flames don't impress me," The guard hissed into my ear, his knee digging into my back.

I needed to get up, I was better than this. I forced my muscles to obey me, managed to gain purchase with my feet, and pushed myself from the ground, shoving the surprised soldier back. Black spots dotted my vision, shrouding half the world in darkness, and then the guard had me again—he roughly yanked me to his chest.

"You're coming with me," he seethed.

I fought against the arm he wrapped around my neck, but he held strong. I couldn't waste my crystal on this one guard. Val's warning echoed in my head. *We might have to kill them.*

The guard began dragging me back down the hill, barely slowing as I dug my heels into the ground. I couldn't reach any part of the skin he had exposed. My fire would do nothing except drain the crystal. I reached for the second dagger sheathed in my pants, gripping the handle. *Spirits forgive me.* I buried the blade to the hilt in the guard's side, making him release me with a pained grunt.

I stood frozen in front of the man as a river of blood flowed from the wound and he fell to the ground. Val rushed down the hill, bloodied shortsword out.

"You need to aim for the heart or else you only make them suffer," he chided. He plunged the sword into the guard's chest, finishing the job for me. The scant contents of my stomach ended up in the grass as I vomited at the sight. I'd never wanted to kill someone, never wanted to see it. I hadn't even been able to watch Aerilyn's execution. The guard was just doing his job. Who was I to decide he deserved to die for it?

"Rest. We'll be waiting for you at the tree line. We leave in half an hour," Val said.

He removed my dagger from the dead guard's stomach and handed it back to me before walking back up the hill. I kneeled before the guard, trying to offer him some honor in death. I closed his still open eyes, and whispered the words of farewell.

"May you be guided away from this world, and lead the Spirits home to you."

CHAPTER 9

ILISE

“T HE FLAMES ARE SUPPOSED to be an extension of your body, not a weapon you wave in front of you,” Oliver chided.

“I'm trying,” I said through gritted teeth. I attempted to snake the flame around another hay bale. Oliver had moved our practice sessions to the courtyard behind the palace after one too many close calls. Sweat dripped down my brow, my gloves made my hands feel like they were in the middle of the Slandslina Forest in the middle of summer, and the cloudless sky offered no reprieve. But at least now, I had stopped wearing long sleeves all the time. There was no reason to hide my scars anymore. If anything, it gave people a blatant reminder of who I was. And what I could survive.

I managed to snake the flame around the hay bale three times, and silently applauded myself as I held it in place. I'd learned the air element could help my flames stay close, but not burn. All I had to do was create a tight coating of air around my flames, acting as a barrier. Almost like the flames were wearing a flame-proof jacket.

Oliver narrowed their eyes, taking a few steps closer to me. “Are you using air?” they accused. I looked down toward where the air crystal was hidden beneath my shirt. No light was penetrating the fabric. How had they noticed?

“No,” I said, hoping my voice was convincing. They reached for the string to the necklace of my air crystal, ripping it off.

“Prove it, then,” they said, smirking. I scowled. Edges of the hay smoked, threatening to burst into flames. I imagined the fire was my own arm, and strained to keep it just shy of burning the bale. The flames wobbled as a cooling breeze blew through the courtyard. "Keep them steady," Oliver said, pacing around me.

"No, really? I thought I was supposed to let the wind snuff out the fire," I said. They pressed their mouth into a thin line in response. I held up my other hand to steady the flames until the wind ceased. The fire held around the bale, no longer burning the hay.

"Good. Now try to create a fire shield without breaking your hold."

I scowled. Shields took most of my concentration, but they were useful. I raised my free hand and started to weave a flaming shield together. Tiny sparks knitted together in a circle, just big enough to block most of my torso. The other flame began to burn the edges of the hay, releasing black smoke into the air.

"Maintain control," Oliver said.

I forced the flame to stop burning the hay, snuffing out the rest of the small fire.

"Give me a second," I said.

Focusing back on the shield, I fused the remaining holes. My crystal glowed bright orange, rivaling the sun as I solidified the shield. It was thin and shaking, but it was a shield nonetheless.

"Done," I said.

Oliver stepped back, planting their feet into the tan stone below. "Now let's see how it holds up," they said, a smile spreading across their lips.

Their crystal glowed a deep blue the color of the twilight sky, forming a sphere of water above their head. I let the flames around the hay disperse and focused all my energy on keeping the shield intact. I thickened the flames, making them hot enough to scald a person in less than a second.

Oliver released the ball of water in my direction. I dropped to avoid it, rolling on the ground to soften my fall.

"I said to test your shield, not avoid my attacks," Oliver complained.

"You never specified. Why would I make it easy for you," I said, jumping to my feet. Using my free hand, I formed a line of fire, wrapping it around my gloved hand to use it as a whip. "And I'm bored. Let's have some fun," I said.

A wicked grin spread across Oliver's face.

We circled each other, sizing each other up. I raised the fire whip, lashing the ground in front of Oliver's feet. They hopped back with every strike, until I had them backed against the palace wall.

"Come on, you can do better than that," I teased.

They shot a jet of water into my face, forcing liquid up my nose and into my eyes. I staggered back from them, wiping my eyes and blowing the water from my nose.

"That was a cheap shot," I said.

I almost didn't notice Oliver rushing toward me, their water-covered fist aiming for my shield. Using the whip, I wrapped it around their fist, the water evaporating away with a loud sizzle. Oliver's bare fist collided with my shield, dispersing the flames. *Dammit.* Oliver landed a punch to my chest, knocking me onto my back.

"Come on, you can do better than that," they said, echoing my taunt.

I frowned. I sprung up, tightening my control on the flaming whip.

"I was just getting warmed up," I said.

I lashed out with the whip, wrapping it around Oliver's sleeve. Their sleeve burned away, leaving behind a red mark on their pale skin. Oliver grimaced in pain, but didn't make a sound. I knew that hurt more than they wanted to let on. Fire didn't need to touch you for long to do its damage.

I rushed them before they could generate another water attack, punching them square in the chest. They fell onto their back, rubbing the space between their ribs. I planted my boot on their chest, keeping them pinned to the ground.

"Told you I was just getting warmed up."

They frowned.

"You were supposed to focus on keeping your shield up," they said with slight disinterest.

I removed my foot from their chest, holding out a hand to help them up.

"One of the most important defense tactics is creating a shield," they said.

I brushed off dirt from my leather leggings and blew the last of the water from my nose.

"I can create a wall with less effort. *And* they're more effective."

Oliver sighed. Who cared if they thought they were right? A wall would do me more good during battle than a measly shield. It was made of fire, for Spirits' sakes. They needed to remember that not every single aspect of controlling water applied to fire. They were opposing elements. And I would always have my air crystal to aid me. I'd only allowed Oliver to take it from me since they knew the consequences if I didn't get it back. No one else would get close enough to take it from me like that.

"Give me my air crystal," I said, holding out my expectant hand.

They removed the necklace from their pocket and dropped it into my palm. I smiled down at the little gem; I didn't know how I had lived so long without my crystals.

I gathered a small ball of flames in my hand, admiring the way the flames danced in the light breeze. For the past few years, the thought of being anywhere near fire had terrified me. Now, I was its master. I threw the ball on the remaining hay bale, reducing it to a large pile of ash. Oliver shot me an unamused look.

"Was that necessary?" they remarked.

Who were they to speak to me like that? I only got rid of a job for one of the little farmhands.

"Is your hand necessary? Because I can relieve you of it, if you so please."

They clamped their mouth shut and walked toward the palace door.

Heavy footsteps sounded behind me, followed by a familiar sensation of the air compressing around me, almost like it was running from something. *Imogen.* I turned around to see Imogen and the Commander walking toward me. The Commander always had a slight smirk on his face, as if he found everything amusing. So it sent an uneasy feeling in my stomach to see his lips turned down in scowl, lines wrinkling his spotty forehead.

"Do you have news for me, Commander?" I asked.

Imogen and the Commander dipped into a bow before speaking.

"The squad we sent after Yorena and her accomplices has not been heard from all day," the Commander said.

"Unless you have Yorena en route to this palace, I don't see the point in telling me this," I snapped.

Imogen shot me a look in silent warning.

"You should really listen to your Commander," Imogen said through my soul.

"He's giving me incomplete, unimportant, and useless information," I said back. I had always wondered how Imogen could talk to me through my soul so easily. It was probably something I should address, but I was almost afraid to think about it lest she know. The Commander cleared his throat. I gestured for him to continue.

"I dispatched a team to go after them, and all they found were the dead bodies of the squad in Faveru. Yorena and her accomplices were nowhere to be found."

I clenched my fists. Yorena's progress during combat training had been impressive, but not enough to kill a squad of guards. I doubted she would have the stomach to kill even one person. She was too kind. The only way she could have escaped was if she had teamed up with those Union traitors.

"I'll come up with a solution myself," I said. "You are dismissed." The Commander bowed before walking around the corner of the palace, toward the front gates.

"I know what you're going to ask, little one," Imogen said.

The soft breeze fluttered her plum robes, blowing through the gray coils of her hair.

"Walk with me," she said.

I followed her into the palace, feeling the immediate relief from the heat as the door shut behind us with a clang. Servants passing through the halls bowed to me as I passed.

Yorena was becoming too much of a nuisance. I needed to bring her back before she caused more damage to my rule, and I didn't want her getting hurt out there.

My heart ached at the thought of being separated from her any longer. I needed her by my side. We went into this together, and I intended to follow through.

"I wasn't going to ask anything," I said finally, wondering if Imogen knew I was lying.

We walked up the dark staircase to the third floor, into my study. Imogen perched herself on the edge of the chaise.

"Are you sure? Every time that Princess of yours is mentioned, you ask me the same question."

Okay, so maybe I was thinking along the line of that particular question, but I didn't *ask* this time. Imogen had searched for me my entire life. How was that any different than me trying to find Yorena?

"I wasn't going to ask. I already know what your answer would be."

But it would be ten times easier if I could go after her. Yorena would never hurt me, the Union wouldn't *want* to hurt me, so it would be easy for me to neutralize them and take Yorena home.

"Even though I wouldn't be in danger," I added.

I slumped down in my chair, cracking my back against the rigid wood.

"You are the Queen. You must understand that you cannot go gallivanting through the woods to find that *girl.*"

I shot up from my chair, moving inches from Imogen at a surprising speed.

"Her name is Yorena, and you will not speak of her in that tone. Like you said, I am Queen. And disrespecting my Princess is disrespecting me."

Imogen's violet eyes seared into mine, challenging me.

"Of course, Your Majesty," she said with a smile.

I backed up from her, settling into my chair. Sometimes, I wondered if Imogen thought I intended to share my power. I appreciated her occasional guidance, which, to be honest, had taught me more about ruling than any book could, but I still needed to be trusted to bear the weight of the crown. Preferably *without* her hovering over me the whole time.

"So, make a decision about what to do about her. *Without* leaving the palace," Imogen sneered.

My fingers drummed on the oak table. The remains of the squad were found in Faveru, but that didn't make any sense. Why would Yorena and the Union want to go into Faveru? All Faveru had was most of the Slandslina Forest, fishing towns, and a smattering of tiny villages. Except... of course.

"Yes, little one?" Imogen asked, as if she wasn't in my head.

I rummaged through the desk drawer, pulling out the detailed map of Erea.

"Faveru is mostly empty except for the forest. And I doubt they would waste their time in tiny lumber towns and fishing villages," I said.

I ran my finger on the thick paper until it landed on a small town on the edge of the Picchi Sea—Bridbrough. Imogen stood up from the chaise, gliding to my side.

"The only relevant thing in Faveru is the extensive Archives."

Imogen's lips spread into a grin.

"Chafik must have convinced them to go there to find out more about you and your powers," I said.

Before I'd switched sides, Cain had always complained about how he didn't know much about Imogen's powers. And Chafik always spoke about the Archives—his father was in charge of them.

"Then we should plan a little surprise for them," Imogen said.

Maybe more than a little one. I was going to get Yorena back, and I didn't care who I had to go through to get her.

Chapter 10

Yorena

VAL LED US THROUGH the thick brush of the forest, whacking away low-hanging branches. We traveled in silence for the rest of the day. Not even Mathias dared to complain.

My throat was thick. My skin tingled, as if every part of me was stained with blood. I think Kieron and Orla tried talking to me, but I couldn't say for sure. All I could think about was the guard's blood and the way it flowed over my dagger, the way I had been able to see the second the light had left his eyes. There must have been some other way to escape without killing him. I could have tried to knock him unconscious long enough for us to escape, or I could have tried to scare him away, and we could have run.

But the others didn't seem too shaken up about it. And we'd decided against telling Chafik and Mathias what had happened—they were too sensitive, and I envied them for their ignorance. They'd been too far into the forest to see, but still, I think they assumed what had happened based on the blood on our clothes and weapons.

Val led us into a clearing in the forest with a small pond in its center, in which we could clean ourselves.

"We'll stop here for the night, and keep walking at dawn," he said.

I tossed my bag into the grass, throwing off the bloodied weapons. I didn't want to hold them anymore. I didn't even want to see them anymore.

"You should probably wash those off," Orla said, causing me to jump.

I hadn't noticed her approaching.

"It'll get hard to scrub off after a while."

I stared at the blades in the grass, the metal glinting in the moonlight. The blood splatter almost looked like it could be nothing more than paint. It taunted me as it lay in the grass—judging, accusing, incriminating.

"I killed someone," I said. Ten guards. Ten people with lives and families who will miss them dearly. And they were dead, dead because Ilise had sent them after me.

Orla pressed her mouth into a thin line.

"You did what you had to," she said.

I settled in the grass beside my bag, taking the dagger in my hands, but careful to only touch the blood-free handle.

"And I didn't even kill him fully," I said, my voice beginning to crack. "I stabbed him in the stomach, just creating more pain for him."

Hot tears rolled down my face, dripping onto the dirty blade. I hadn't even been able to offer him a quick ending.

Orla placed a hand on my shoulder and I looked up into her eyes, filled with sympathy.

"You did what you had to to escape."

I wiped a tear from my eye. I was certain I could've found a different way. There was no reason for the guard to pay for doing his job with his life.

"How come you aren't fazed by it?" I asked.

Orla sat down beside me, staring at the ground. It was so dark the only part of her I could fully see were the dark freckles on the bridge of her nose.

She looked up.

"The first kill always hurts the most. What you're feeling is normal."

I scratched at the dirt.

"Does it ever get easier?"

I hoped I'd never have to kill someone again. To think that guard was supposed to go home to his family after bringing me back to the palace, but instead his body was rotting in the dirt. To the others, I did the right thing, but it did nothing to ease the guilt welling in my stomach. It churned—an ocean of acid.

"It gets easier. Sometimes there's only one option, unless you want to either get captured or killed."

Orla gave my shoulder a reassuring squeeze before standing up.

"We're going to start planning the Archives mission. You can come join us when you're ready. We need you for this."

I bit my nail as her footsteps receded behind me.

My eyes strayed back to the dagger on the ground. I'd learned to use this to defend myself, not take another's life. There was always another way, and yet I hadn't been able to find it, sentencing a man to a death with no reason, and no honor. That wasn't how a Queen behaved, it wasn't even how a Princess behaved.

"Yorena," Val called, after a while. "Are you coming?"

I nodded and stood up. I just needed to ignore these thoughts, then maybe they would leave me be. Steeling myself, I joined the others, already sitting around the map. I sat next to Kieron, who shot me a concerned look. I shook my head, as if it would shake away any of my thoughts.

"If we're going to do the Archives mission as cleanly as possible, we're going to need to plan before we get there," Val said.

Throwing myself into the mission ahead would surely ward off any unwelcome memories. I pulled the map from Val's hands, studying the faded parchment.

"Most of Bridbrough is shrouded in trees, so that could help cover our tracks," I said.

"And there's a back entrance into the Archives that's almost completely surrounded by forest," Chafik said, pointing to the town on the edge of the forest. "If we go in at night, we'll be almost untraceable."

"We can't *all* go inside," Rori countered. "A few of us need to keep watch outside."

I definitely didn't want to get stuck outside. Only the Spirits knew what I might have to do... again.

"How about me, Cain, Kieron, and Mathias stay out, and Yorena, Val, Chafik, Kass, and Orla go inside."

Thank the Spirits.

"Why do I have to stay out?" Mathias groaned.

"Because based on the small amount of time we've been together," Kass started, "You'll be more focused on complaining rather than looking for relevant information."

Mathias opened his mouth to speak, but Orla beat him to it.

"And all you would have to do is sit and relax for a few minutes. The others will focus on keeping watch," she said.

At that, he seemed to agree to his position.

"We shouldn't stay inside for longer than fifteen minutes," Val said. "To minimize our chances of running into any guards."

And to minimize my chances of having to kill someone again.

"What's our contingency plan if there's a lot of security around the Archives before we go inside?" I asked.

Val considered me for a moment.

"We'll send one person in. It's a risk, but otherwise this detour will be a waste of time."

Cain frowned. "Fifteen minutes isn't enough time for one person to find a single book in that place," he said.

Val stared at him, unblinking, his hands in tight fists. "Then you better hope there aren't a lot of guards," he said, a bite in his tone. His whole body was tense, every expression on his face pinched. Val didn't want to go to the Archives in the first place, and his frustration was beginning to show. Cain said nothing, and pressed his lips together.

The crickets filled the void our voices had left. With every second we stayed silent, it was as if the air was getting thicker, like the oxygen around us was quickly depleting.

"How many guards would usually be around the Archives?" Kass asked Chafik, dispelling the tense silence.

"I've never seen more than four at any given time," he said. "One for each side of the building. And they were usually Primis guards carrying no more than a shortsword."

If no changes had been made since Chafik was there, then we should easily be able to get inside. And we wouldn't even have to worry about other Imperium guards, who would have made this mission much more difficult.

"I think we have a decent plan," Rori said as they stood to go to the pond. "For once." Everyone else dispersed from the circle, finding a place to rest for the night. But I already knew the guilty visions that would come to me in my sleep, so I volunteered to keep the first watch.

After the first hour, I was surrounded by the sound of quiet breaths and chirping crickets. The moon shone high over my head as I started to wash the grime of my hands. I scrubbed off dried blood and caked on dirt in the grimy pond water. I would never take my bathtub at the palace for granted ever again, I started thinking, until I realized that it was not *my* bathtub any more. I didn't feel much cleaner than before, just no longer covered in blood and dirt. With more time to kill...More time to *waste*, I finally found the strength to rinse the blood off my dagger.

It wiped off the silver blade easily. But it felt like I was trying to erase what I had done with this weapon, as if I actually thought that the simple act of cleaning the blade would clean away my sins. I tucked the dagger back into the sheath on my pants and returned to where I had been sitting. I heard a rustle. My muscles tensed. Another soft sound. I took a relieved breath. It was just Kieron stirring. He sat up, rubbing the tiredness from his eyes.

"It's not your turn yet," I said. I was exhausted but I was not ready for guilty dreams.

"I know you wouldn't have woken me up anyway," he said as he sat next to me. "How're you holding up?" I took a deep breath, resting my head on his shoulder.

"I'm doing the best I can," I said, still staring at the ground. "It's not everyday that you go from being next in line to the throne to having to kill a man just to survive."

I tried to laugh it off, but the sound came out strained, forced. Kieron threw a heavy arm around my shoulder, pulling me closer for a hug.

"You don't have to pretend like it didn't happen, Yorena," he said in an uncharacteristically soft voice. "It's okay to want to move forward, but you can't just distract yourself from thinking about it."

A single tear escaped my eye. Distracting myself seemed like a much easier option. What wouldn't I give to not have to imagine the guard's blank eyes staring up at me as I knelt over his dead body. Or how it felt to drive the blade into his stomach, sealing his fate with a loud squelch.

"I'll be okay," I said, mostly to myself. "This wouldn't be the worst thing to happen to me in the last week."

Kieron let out a weak chuckle.

"That's the spirit. Now, I'm going to take over the watch, and you need to get some rest."

He patted me on the back, urging me to lay down. I was about to settle into the grass when I heard a whisper behind me. My head whipped toward the sound.

"Did you hear that?"

He opened mouth to retort but then shut it as the whispers sounded again.

"What in four hells is that?" he said, mostly to himself.

I had already started walking back toward the forest when Kieron grabbed my elbow.

"Are you crazy?" he said in a hissing whisper, trying not to wake the others. "You don't wander off into the forest when you hear weird voices."

I ripped my arm out of his grip.

"I'll be fine. I have a new fire crystal and a dagger with me."

Not like I would be able to bring myself to use it, but it was there for intimidation. Kieron grumbled but gave me a few more inches of space.

"I'm not letting you go alone. Either I come with, or I'll sit on you if you try to leave," he said.

"Fine," I gritted out. "But we're not coming back until I find out what those voices are."

I pushed aside low-hanging branches and we ventured deeper into the woods. The whispers grew louder the further we went, sounding almost like a dark chorus. The crickets and other bugs ceased their chirping as we neared another clearing. Crumbling dirt, snapping branches, and Kieron's heavy breathing were the only sounds around me the deeper we went.

"Spirits," Kieron whispered as we beheld the structure in front of us. My eyes widened. It looked like an ancient temple. Almost two stories high, made of gray bricks stacked upon each other. Vines covered the majority of the temple, winding around gold columns at the top of the stairs. Was this where the voices were coming from?

"I thought all the temples in this province were gone," I said. They hadn't been widely used in centuries, possibly millennia. Once the four Spirits had disappeared from the world to chase after the Soul Spirit, so had the need to use the temples to offer our gifts and let Them hear our requests. Temples were scattered throughout Erea, and there were very few still in use, mostly in Nitedand and Ominka. I didn't remember one being in Faveru at all, let alone near Bridbrough.

The world around me felt muffled as I stepped closer to the abandoned monument. A frieze of the four Spirits adorned the top of the building. Like many renderings, this one pictured the Spirits as ginormous crystalline beings, handing the first Imperium their power crystals. But there must have been something else next to the four Spirits. Something that had been chiseled away, leaving behind a patch of stone slightly lighter than the rest.

"Follow me," a dark voice whispered. It sounded as it came from the very wind blowing through my matted hair.

"Who are you?" I said, bracing myself for an attack. My eyes darted around the clearing, finding nothing but tipped over moss-covered statues and trees. "Show yourself."

"I will reveal myself in time," the voice said.

My heartbeat was in my ears as I spun, trying to find someone to attach the voice to.

"Claim your crystal for it will serve you well," it said.

My crystal? "What are you talking about? Show me who you are."

A chill spread through the air, raising goosebumps on my arm.

"Yorena," Kieron called, though his voice sounded distant. As if he were back with the others rather than a few feet behind me.

"Remember what I've told you."

It would help if I understood what the voice was telling me. I took one last glance at the temple and walked back to Kieron. Bewilderment painted his face.

"Why were you talking to yourself?" he asked.

"You didn't hear the voice?"

He shook his head. But the voice had been so loud, so present. It'd been like the owner of the voice was in the clearing with us. How could he not have heard it? He'd heard the original whispers. What had changed?

"We should get back to the camp before you run after more 'voices'," Kieron said. I noted the obvious sarcasm in his tone, but also, I saw his worried expression. It was like he didn't want to believe me, because the ramifications of me actually hearing real voices was even worse than the very real possibility of me just going crazy. But I was sure that I wasn't hallucinating. The temple had spoken to me; it *wanted* me to find the voice. I needed to figure out why.

"Let's go," I said, looping my arm through Kieron's

Claim your crystal for it will serve you well.

What did it mean?

Chapter 11

Nikos

"I HAVE MY FIRST request," Oliver said. Their voice sent a jolt of fear through my sleepy body. I couldn't begin to guess why the guard had let them in my apartment, let alone my bedroom. But the whole palace was either afraid of me or hated me, so I doubted the guards felt I needed much protection. It had to be close to midnight. I was hoping they'd forgotten about these so-called requests, but I suppose the chance to get me to do their dirty work was too enticing to pass up.

"How did you get in here?" I seethed. I fumbled for my matches in the dark and lit the stubby candle on my nightstand. It did little to brighten the space, but it did illuminate Oliver's outline in the doorway. They waltzed into my room with a smirk on their face, and the confidence of someone who couldn't be touched.

"It would appear the guards posted to your room left," they said, amusement coloring their tone. *Those bastards.* "Not like they would have kept me out anyway."

I glared at Oliver. They were basically still a child—freshly eighteen years old. And yet, they were the one people in the palace tolerated, the one who could walk down the corridor without glare, and the one who didn't have to fear for their life every time Ilise was in the room. What could I have done to deserve getting ordered around by this person?

"Unfortunately for you, I have retired for the night," I said. "I'll fulfill your stupid request tomorrow. Good night." I snuffed out the candle and burrowed further under the covers, though I could still feel Oliver's heavy gaze burning a hole in my head.

"I said you have to fulfill my requests or else I will report you to the Queen. Either get up, or you can say goodbye to your lady friend."

My eyes shot open and a vine was wrapped around Oliver's neck before they could even blink in surprise. I always kept a pot of soil in my room for this very use. I stormed up to them so that I was mere inches from their face. Their quickening breaths warmed my face. And the small glint of fear in their eyes brought me a bit of joy.

"Keep Daeva's name out of your filthy mouth," I said in a low voice. I wanted to cut out their tongue. Daeva was an innocent caught in crossfire, she didn't deserve to be a ploy for the weak to use against me. "Threaten me all you like, but she is not part of this."

Though their face turned a sickly pink, Oliver smiled. "Then fulfill my request," they said. Their voice was thin, reedy. They would likely pass out in a few seconds. I could let them, but then they'd awaken with a new grudge against me—and against Daeva. My pride would have to be bruised. I would have to lose my dignity, but if it meant Daeva's name stayed out of Oliver's mouth and off Ilise's list of people to torment, it would be worth it. The light in my crystal extinguished and I let Oliver drop, gasping to fill their lungs.

"What do you want?" I asked. Might as well get this over with.

They let out a string of coughs before shakily pushing themself up from the floor.

"I need you to sneak into one of the Council sorcerers' rooms and find out what they're scheming about."

"Do you ever hear how idiotic you sound?" I said.

No one in their right mind would break into a room full of the most powerful and dangerous beings in the kingdom. But I supposed Oliver wasn't in their right mind.

"One of the sorcerers had warned Yorena about Imogen using Heircestrial as a distraction and I doubt he's the only one who's trying to create pushback. I need you to tell me what they're talking about, so I can report them to the Queen."

"Is reporting people the only thing you know how to do?"

"Considering only one of us is on the verge of execution every time they're in the Queen's presence, I'd say I have the right idea."

I controlled my hands before I could punch Oliver and worsen my predicament. "How do you expect me to even get into that room?" I asked.

Oliver handed me an old crumpled map. Half of the ink had faded away, and the creases marring the parchment made the remaining ink nearly impossible to read. It was...just a bunch of lines. It was like looking at someone's drawing of the inside of a cobweb.

"How is one of your scribbles going to help me?" I asked.

They narrowed their eyes. "This is a map of all the tunnels in the palace that should lead your right to the room."

Were these tunnels even a secret at this point? Only a select few people were supposed to know about them, yet it seemed everyone in the palace was aware of their existence. That would make any escape plan via the tunnels a no-go.

"If you're not back in an hour I'll assume you've deserted, and I'll have to report you," they said.

I held the retort on the tip of my tongue. I needed to find some dirt on Oliver before this power went to their head. Well, it already had, but it could always get worse.

"If you'll excuse me," I said, pushing past them into the sitting room with my candle in hand. Being one of the rarer types of Imperium came in handy most days, except when I couldn't light a damn torch with the snap of my fingers. This dim light would have to do. Though it barely illuminated the crudely drawn map. The only orienting feature was a circle around where I assumed my room was leading to another unidentified room.

The sitting room was dark, dusty, and stale. The yellow armchairs smelled like they hadn't been cleaned in years, but at least they were comfortable. The space would be a relaxing area if not for the threat of someone entering the room from the hidden door. Behind the chairs, I felt for the thin seam in the wall and pushed it open. Dust swirled around me as I creaked open the aging door, dozens of ants and spiders quickly skittering away.

Deplorable.

The last time I'd been in these tunnels was when I'd captured Ilise so we could kill her for the last trial. And look where that had gotten me—right back in these dank corridors. I held the candle above the map and slowly followed the trail Oliver had pointed out. I could've been walking in circles though. Each new corner looked the same as the last: cobwebs, dust, insects, and so on.

After what felt like an hour but couldn't have been more than fifteen minutes, I reached what I hoped was the door the map had marked. The wood paneling was peeling and the metal lock was coated in a thick layer of rust. My skin crawled at the thought of touching it. There wasn't any dirt or dead plants I could even use to open this. *You're doing this for Daeva,* I tried to tell myself.

I was sure there was a key somewhere, but my candle was on its last dregs. I needed to get in there as quickly as possible before I ran out of light for the walk back to my room. The lock was old, and the chance of it having any strength was low. I grasped my hand around the handle, ignoring the way the corroded metal made my skin crawl, and twisted as hard as I could. The lock broke easily.

I cracked the door open, only allowing a large enough gap for my eye to see. As I had expected, the door opened right into the living room. Convenient. A huddle of dark robes and aging faces filled the gap. Their voices were quiet, but I could just barely make out what they were saying.

"We can try to sway Ilise to our side all we want, but it will be a fruitless effort as long as she's under Imogen's thumb," one sorcerer was saying. His dark brown beard was long, falling halfway down his chest. I hadn't bothered to learn which provinces all the Council sorcerers were from, but I guessed this one was from Faveru.

"Simply distracting her will only delay the inevitable," a sorceress said. Based on the nearly translucent skin and pale blonde hair, I supposed she was either from

Pria or Nitedand. Oliver wanted to report the Council for distracting Ilise? These were supposed to be the most powerful people in the kingdom, but I supposed that didn't mean they were the most intelligent.

"Then why don't we try convincing one of the two nominees to help us?" another sorcerer said. This one had black hair that fell to his shoulders and only a few strands of gray. I compressed the gap in the door before those golden eyes could spot me. He had to be one of the youngest on the council—he couldn't be older than forty. Though sorcerers' appearances were always deceiving, he could easily be hundreds of years old, despite his naivete.

Oliver would never help them. And aligning myself with a group of people that had already been banished *and* were almost always under Imogen's control was the last thing Daeva and I needed.

"Ahn," the long-bearded sorcerer said, "The last time you attempted to push a nominee to our side, she went straight to the enemy, and you also approached *the enemy*." So the golden-eyed sorcerer was who Oliver had been talking about. He didn't seem so intimidating.

"If we told the Vikander boy what his father and Imogen did, he would almost certainly work with us," Ahn responded. "It would change his life."

My father and Imogen? They'd done all sorts of unspeakable acts together, but something told me this sorcerer wasn't talking about those. What could possibly sway me to their side? Whatever it was, this must be something major. Something personal.

"Fine. Talk to the boy," another sorcerer said. I was too focused on Ahn to see who the gruff voice belonged to. Ahn had a smile on his face. He was happy. Was he this happy because he had a way to forcibly get me onto their side, or was there truly something deplorable Imogen and my father had done to me?

The blonde sorceress spoke again. "But don't give him all the information until you are certain he won't report us to Imogrn. We don't need a repeat of last time."

Ahn nodded. "I will speak with him soon," he said.

My candle flickered. The last bits of wax were starting to melt. I closed the tunnel door. I was pushing my luck.

As I walked back to my room, I pondered what the Council had been discussing about me. My father had disregarded me as a child, nearly disowned me as a teen, and exploited me now as an adult by threatening the one person who loved me. There wasn't much else he could do to me. The deed that sorcerer had been thinking of was likely something from my childhood I hadn't cared enough to feel upset about. But had my father known Imogen by then? She didn't fit into this.

My candle burned out when I was mere paces from my door. I opened the creaking wood only to find Oliver standing in the entryway, their arms crossed.

"I'm shocked. You made it back with twenty minutes to spare," they drawled.

"Move out of the way," I said.

They didn't move. "Tell me what you learned, and then I'll move."

I groaned. A child. I was being bossed around by a child. I thought of Daeva's smiling face and the short period of time we'd had together away from my father, away from The Progression. I just needed to remember that. What it felt like to be free. Or else I wouldn't survive here much longer.

"The Council only plans to slow down any decision-making processes when they meet with the Queen," I said. Oliver didn't need to know about what Ahn had said: it had nothing to do with them.

I tried to push past them but they threw up a dense wall of water, soaking me to the bone. My thin nightclothes stuck to my skin uncomfortably. I shivered. They destroyed the wall with a smirk on their face.

"That's not enough information to satisfy the Queen. I know there's more than that. What did Ahn say?"

For the love of the Spirits why were they so obsessed with Ahn?

I gritted my teeth. "Ahn wants to tell me something my father and Imogen did to me to get me onto their side."

Oliver smiled a slow, predatory smile, full of teeth. They likely didn't know how to smile properly and this was their best, stiff imitation.

"It appears I already have my next request for you."

CHAPTER 12

ILISE

S UNSHINE STREAMED IN FROM my open window, a soft breeze blowing in a
rose scent from the gardens. Lovely, but I didn't have time to dwell on that.
They should have returned with Yorena by now. I had been pacing in front of
the window of my new bedroom, so much so that I was surprised I hadn't worn
a path into the wool rug. If Yorena and the Union were planning on infiltrating
the Archives, they would have done it under the cover of night. Unless they were
trying to confuse me and were planning to go inside in broad daylight.

I cracked each of my knuckles, trying to ground myself with each soft pop. Val
would never risk a mission during the day just to surprise me, it wasn't his style.
It wasn't any of their styles. Although, I could have miscalculated the *day* they
would arrive in Bridbrough. Assuming Val was taking the lead, he would force
them to go through the forest rather than taking the quickest path, to avoid being
discovered. He was overcautious to the point of near insanity.

Unless, Yorena was taking the lead. But she'd hardly left the confines of the
palace, let alone navigating a thick forest. Though having her choose the route
would be a good way to throw me off their trail. But I doubted she would *want*
to take the lead, not to mention Val would likely fight her on it. The group would
arrive at the Archives eventually though, so it shouldn't matter which route they
took. We would be ready for them.

I crossed the room to my desk and searched my drawer of carefully rolled maps.
I pulled out a map of the kingdom, scanning the paper for Bridbrough. I traced
my finger along the route I assumed they would take. Based on where and when

they'd left the guards to rot, it would take them no more than a day. And if they were going to try and get inside after nightfall, then they should arrive there today.

And I would have my soldiers waiting for them.

This isn't you. Call off the guards and complete your mission.

I froze. What was this meek voice in my head? I had noticed it a few times now, always deciding to speak at the most inopportune times, babbling pure nonsense. It was the antithesis of everything Imogen and I were trying to accomplish. My job would be a lot easier if I didn't have a little voice fighting against me.

Break free of her.

Break free? Break free from what? I had everything I could ever want, well, except for Yorena, but she would be returning soon.

I just needed to get through today and wait for nightfall. Then I would doubtless get a message saying my soldiers were returning Yorena to the palace and that the Union was finally gone forever. I walked to my armoire, throwing open the oak doors. For today, I chose a simple dress the color of fresh moss that fell right above my knee, allowing for easy access to the new dagger I kept in a sheath on my thigh. Imogen constantly berated me for wearing the weapon, claiming it was "unqueenly", but I didn't need anyone to think I was going soft, getting a little too comfortable with my new crown of gold. If how I'd dealt with the previous monarchs was any indication, even Queens weren't safe from danger.

With my new healing power from my crystals, I didn't need to keep my upper arm wrapped anymore. It was already completely healed, but the scars would never fade, nor would I want them to. They were proof to myself that I could survive some of the worst pains this world had to offer. And to others, they were a clue to not even attempt to come for me. I would survive, and I would punish anyone who dared.

The crown glinted out of the corner of my eyes from where it rested on my jewelry shelf. Imogen kept chiding me for keeping it in such an informal place, but the crown wasn't the symbol of power. I was. A ring of metal didn't need a ceremonial place to rest. No one but me and Imogen were ever in my bedroom, anyway. I retrieved my crown from its place on the shelf and placed it on my head.

Looking in the mirror, I could see how the golden vines almost glowed in the light, as if I had the very sun perched above me, illuminating my face

A knock sounded at the door.

"Who is it?" I asked.

"Oliver. We have a situation, and Imogen told me to come get you," they said through the door.

Ugh. I crossed the room, opening the door to a slightly distressed Oliver. They bowed deeply.

"Lead the way," I said.

I followed Oliver to my study, with Imogen and Nikos already waiting. They both stood up to bow to me as I walked through the doorway.

"Now, what's the problem?"

Nikos moved from where he leaned against the wall, grabbing a crate from the floor.

"You called me in here for a crate?" I said, crossing my arms.

Nikos' placid expression broke for a second, a ghost of a smirk spreading across his lips, before disappearing as if it had never been there.

"I don't see why you're smiling, Nikos."

He stared into my eyes, as if daring me to do something. The audacity.

"I didn't mean to smile, Your Majesty," he said coolly.

I narrowed my eyes at him. I knew a smile when I saw one. Was he mocking me? Did I need to teach him another lesson?

"We have gathered countless complaints and significant backlash since you took the throne," Imogen said.

I rummaged through the crate. It was overflowing with pieces of paper. I selected a few at random. They were pamphlets and angry notes, slandering my name, calling me a murderer, and a fake. I'd honestly expected more resistance against my rule, even though I got rid of the King and Queen who'd lost the trust of their kingdom. *You're not much better than them.* Ugh. That voice was beginning to get more annoying with each passing day. I had hoped that if I ignored it, it would go away, but it was only getting stronger.

"And what do you want me to do about this?" I asked Imogen. "A few angry people can't do much against me."

The sorceress studied the nails on her wrinkled hand.

"A *few* angry people are harmless. But there are a lot more than a *few* angry people going against you. Multiple rebellious groups have started to drum up trouble throughout the kingdom."

Did they seriously think their puny rebellions would do any damage? They were more a nuisance than anything; small and inconsequential.

"Then let's send out squads of Imperium guards to squash their miserable excuses for a rebellion," I said.

Imogen nodded her head approvingly.

"Nikos, go tell the Commander what I said and tell him to get those guards on the ground immediately."

Nikos stared at me, unmoving.

"Do I need to talk more slowly? Because I'm pretty sure I gave you an order," I hissed.

I stepped closer to him, close enough that I had to look up into his eyes.

"Are you sure sending a bunch of soldiers to deal with the issue is the best course of action? Won't it exacerbate the situation?" he asked, not breaking eye contact.

I circled him, crossing my arms over my chest.

"Are you the King?"

He shook his head.

"Are you my advisor, a military specialist, or anyone of *any* importance?"

"No, Your Majesty."

I stopped pacing, keeping his gaze captive.

"Then who are you to question my decision?"

I inched closer, amusement coursing through me when I noticed his nervous gulp.

"You are only here because your father is insistent that I keep you alive. But don't think that means you can speak to me as if we were on the same level. Understand me?"

"Understood," he said.

Satisfied, I stepped back and almost laughed as his shoulders relaxed.

"Now go."

He bowed before leaving the room. That boy was getting harder to keep in my control. What he needed was a not-so-subtle reminder of what would happen if he continued to act this way. Or else I may have to break Imogen's agreement with his father.

"Oliver," I said.

They perked their head up, rushing to my side. Now this was how Nikos should've been acting.

"I need you to go after Nikos and bring him to the throne room once he's informed Commander Hynkel."

They tilted their head.

"Of course, Your Majesty. But if I may, what are you going to do?"

I patted their shoulder.

"I'm going to give him a little reminder of who's in power here," I said, a wicked grin spreading across my face.

Oliver's lips curled in a playful grin of their own.

"Right away, Your Majesty," they said with bow.

This would be fun. Well, maybe not for Nikos, but definitely for me. I was about to leave, when Imogen cleared her throat.

"Do you need something?" I said, slightly annoyed.

"How have your lessons with Oliver been going?"

I sat at my desk chair, sensing there was more to her question.

"Fine," I said. "I've gotten a lot better at controlling fire."

Imogen flashed a tight-lipped smile.

"Is something wrong?"

She waved her hands.

"No, it's just your gloves."

My gloves? I looked down at the smooth leather gloves I wore every day. They were the only things that allowed me to use fire in the first place. If I didn't wear them, it would send me into a panic, stuck in a shaking, crying ball. I never wanted to feel that weak again.

"What's wrong with them?"

"They're holding you back, little one. There may be a time when you don't have your gloves, and then you won't use fire."

I stared at her.

"Anyone close enough to try and take them off will die a painful death. There's no reason for me to remove them."

Imogen sighed, but I didn't care. She could be disappointed in me all she wanted, but it wouldn't force me into training myself to use fire without my gloves. Only one person besides Imogen knew about my small weakness. And Yorena would never use it against me, she wouldn't have the heart. Strong as she was, I knew she could never try to hurt me.

I stood up from the chair, smoothing the wrinkles on my dress.

"If you'll excuse me, I have to go teach Nikos a lesson,"

I started walking out the door then paused when Imogen spoke again.

"Remember you can't hurt him, little one," she said. "His father would not be very pleased."

I waved a hand. "I know. He'll come out mostly unscathed," I said with a smile.

"Do you know why I've called you here?" I said to Nikos as he knelt before my throne.

Sunlight streamed in through the windows, making the gold decorations of the room shine.

"No, Your Majesty," Nikos said, still staring at the floor.

I rose from my throne to join Nikos in front of the dais. He knew exactly what he had done. Despite my power, despite my crown, despite all the threats I've made to him, he has done nothing but defy me. And in front of Oliver? I didn't need them getting similar ideas to this pest.

"If I have done anything to your displeasure, you have my deepest apologies."

Pathetic.

"You can't apologize if you don't know what you've done wrong." I circled him like a vulture. "Clearly you don't value your life." I stopped in front of him and gripped his chin in my hands and forced him to look at me. Those bright green eyes shot daggers at me, but I paid him no mind. That look would have frightened me once, but I was the one in charge here. I was the one who held his life in my hands. Or in this case, someone else' life. "So, you've forced me to move onto drastic measures."

I released his chin and signaled the guards at the door to let my secret weapon in. Two Imperium guards brought inside the girl, her long black hair shrouding her face. Her long gray dress dragged so much, I was surprised she didn't trip across the floor. As she passed Nikos, his muscles tensed, already knowing who it was.

"I thought I would bring in your dear Daeva to remind you what happens when you defy me."

The guard pushed the shaking girl to me.

"Hello, Daeva," I said.

She didn't dare look me in the eye, instead lowering herself into a deep curtsy.

"Hello, Your Majesty."

I gripped the girl's pale arm to keep her from running. Though I doubted she would have the gall to run from me.

"Nikos, would you tell Daeva how you've been behaving?"

I moved the girl behind me as Nikos took a step forward. He wasn't going to get to her that easily.

"Now," I ordered.

His hands curled into fists at his sides and I could tell he was forcing his mouth to not form a sneer.

"I have defied your orders on multiple occasions and I have questioned your authority."

I nodded.

"Very good. Now, you are going to stay exactly where you are while I punish you," I said, raising my hands above my head.

Wind howled in the large room, echoing off the marble and stone. Daeva's hair whipped ferociously and she huddled to the ground to keep the wind from biting her skin. Nikos was someone who despised showing weakness, so I relished at the sight of him hunched over from my power. The few candles adorning the chandeliers extinguished, and my crystal became the brightest object in the room.

Nikos looked up at me and I smiled. Using air, I threw Daeva to the far corner of the room, not hard enough to break bones, but hard enough for her to be sore for a few days. She slumped to the ground, curling in on herself. To my surprise, Nikos stayed put, finally with a hint of fear plain on his face.

I immediately wrapped a air ring around his middle. If only I could finish what I'd started the last time he'd been in this predicament. But I had to keep him alive for now.

"Remember this the next time you think about opening your big mouth," I said.

He nodded quickly, his face a bright red. I released him and he let out a loud gasp, falling to the ground.

"You can go get her, and you are dismissed."

Nikos dragged himself up and ran to Daeva's side, gathering her into his arms before he stumbled out the door.

This isn't who you are. Do not drown your spark in her darkness, free yourself, the voice whispered. How stupid this voice was. I *was* free, more free than I could have ever been believing in the Union's mission. This voice spewed nothing but lies. It had to be the work of one of the Council sorcerers. Imogen had been able to talk to me through my soul before I'd turned, and who was to say there weren't other sorcerers capable of the same?

There was a meeting with the Council tomorrow. I would find out who was to blame for this distasteful phenomenon, and I would make them cease the whispers.

One way or another.

Chapter 13

Yorena

WE WALKED IN SILENCE for the entire day, only stopping for a few necessary short breaks. Branches stuck out from my hair, but I didn't care enough to remove them. If anything, they would help me camouflage. Once night fell, stars twinkled through the breaks in the trees, helping the moon illuminate our way through the thick foliage.

A white stone building came into view as we left the tree line just at the bottom of a hill. The structure rose three full stories, with green vines climbing up the walls. The only windows were at the very top of the building, probably to lessen the amount of sunlight that could damage any of the texts inside. I envisioned the Archives to be more... well more. From here, it looked like a blank box, with a few doors on the sides.

"We'll split up here," Val said.

We all nodded.

"Chafik, you'll lead us inside, and those staying out should spread out around the perimeter."

My eyes strained to see any guards in the darkness. I couldn't spot any from our vantage point, and I would have thought that if there were any, someone would have marched around the corner by now. Why weren't there any guards?

"Rori," Val said.

They looked up as they sheathed all their weapons.

"At the first sight of trouble, send us an air message. But we shouldn't be more than fifteen minutes."

I just had to survive fifteen minutes. Surely nothing bad would happen in that little time.

Kieron clapped me on the back. "Good luck in there," he said.

I hoped I wouldn't need luck.

I emptied my bag of everything to make room for any books we found and gave my things to Kieron for safekeeping. I double checked that my daggers were sheathed and then followed Chafik down the hill. Crickets and other bugs sang as we walked to the back of the Archives, flinching at the sound of our shoes crunching in the damp grass. We winded through the trees surrounding the building, taking extra care to make as little noise as possible.

The process was tedious—stepping over gnarled tree roots, staring at the ground to avoid snapping branches. Eventually, we stopped in a clearing, only a few minutes' walk from the Archives.

"What now?" I asked. "I thought you said there was a back entrance."

Chafik gestured to the ground.

"This *is* the back entrance," he said.

He kicked away a pile of vines to reveal a metal door in the ground.

Why does everywhere in this kingdom have an underground tunnel?

"There's another entrance, but it's probably guarded, and since we have Kass here," he said, waving her forward, "She can open this Earth Imperium-made entrance."

Kass kneeled in the ground and placed her hands on the door. Her crystal glowed bright green, and soon, a quiet rumble shook the ground beneath my feet. The door slid aside, revealing a dark tunnel.

I hated tunnels. Kass rubbed her dirt-covered hands on her leather leggings and we followed Chafik down the steps.

The tunnel was narrow, just wide enough to accommodate my shoulders. Packed dirt made up the walls, metal beams stabilizing the structure every few feet. Kass, Orla, and I activated our crystals to illuminate the way, but they hardly helped.

"How did you even know about this entrance?" Orla asked.

"I stumbled across it when I was younger. We should be arriving at the door any minute," Chafik said.

I took a few deep breaths to calm down my speeding heartbeat. There was nobody outside, so I shouldn't have reason to worry about this mission. Val had insisted that we would only be in here for fifteen minutes, and hopefully, nothing could possibly happen in that short time. I was just making myself more nervous by thinking about it.

Chafik stopped our line and turned the handle to a wooden door in the ceiling.

"Here it is," he said, pushing open the small door. "This opens up into one of the back rooms, so no one will hear us while we go over everyone's tasks."

Val came up last behind me as we all climbed through the door. There wasn't a ladder, since the ceiling was only a little over six feet, so we had to help each other up.

My breaths were coming in pants by the time I managed to hoist myself inside. I lay on the concrete floor to catch my breath, marveling at how Val had been able to climb inside on his own. Chafik lit a discarded candle he found in an alcove, casting a flickering glow over the small room. The only thing inside was a dusty table that looked as old as Imogen, and a few half-destroyed books, their yellow pages falling out of the spine.

"Chafik," Val said, "Where in the building do you think what we're looking for would be?"

Chafik drummed his fingers on the table. He drew an invisible picture in the air, as if we could see the imaginary diagram he was thinking of. Orla shot me a confused look and I shrugged.

"All information on sorcerers is on the far side of the Archives."

Val clapped his hands together. "Okay, me and Chafik will take the top, and you three will take the rest." We nodded in unison and followed Chafik out the door. My head was on a swivel as I scanned the quiet Archives. Shelves rising almost two stories high filled the space, and the smell of old books wafted into my nose.

I didn't see a single guard as we cautiously made our way to the other side of the building. The only sound was the echo of our feet shuffling across the carpet. I let out a yelp as a book fell, slamming to the ground.

"It's just a book, Yorena," Chafik said. "Some of the shelves are so overfilled, they fall over occasionally in reaction to vibrations caused by people walking."

We kept our slow pace all the way to the section Chafik had mentioned. The books were along a single wall, but the shelves were tall, and filled to the brim.

My palms were damp with sweat and I rubbed them against my pants. I could do this. After all, this wasn't a battle. We just had to look for some books. And we hadn't seen anyone else in here during the whole walk over here.

"Fifteen minutes," Val said.

We broke off into our groups and started scouring the shelves. Dim moonlight filtered through the windows at the top of the wall, barely letting in any light. I had to squint to read any of the titles along the aging spines.

"What should we be looking for exactly?" Orla asked as I removed a promising looking book from the shelf, coughing as it released a large puff of dust.

I cracked open the book, squinting to read the faded ink in the dim light.

"We need something that talks about their abilities," I said, placing the book on the floor. This one simply described how sorcerers came to be.

"Our goal is to know sorcerers' weaknesses, or if there's a way to reverse the effects of their powers."

If only we could find the Soul Spirit Themself and ask.

I flipped through more books and soon, my eyes caught on something interesting. *Thank the Spirits.*

"Kass, Orla," I whispered.

They approached and crouched to the floor on either side of me. "This has a whole chapter on powers." Kass flipped the books to read the cover.

"I can't read the title," she said.

The book was so old the title had completely faded. The only thing left visible was a barely legible *S*.

"Let's take it. We need to go."

I closed the book and stood from the floor. The fifteen minutes were up already? It didn't look like anyone else had found anything useful. I'd hoped we would find more than one chapter. But it was better than nothing.

I saw Chafik and Val's shadowy forms heading back to where we had started. Maybe we were going to get out of here without any trouble after all. Maybe we had time to make sure that what I had found would be useful.

"Chafik, you know these tomes better than anyone. Do you think this one could help?"

I handed the tome to Chafik and he ran his hand along the cover.

"This must be one of the oldest books in the Archives," he said in awe.

I would never understand how he got so excited over old books, but now, I was excited too. Maybe this was progress at last. But my elation was short-lived.

All at once, a sense of awareness washed over me. My skin prickled the way it did when I knew someone was watching me. Tiny hairs on the back of my neck rose, and my body grew rigid. Chafik continued to look through the book as I scanned the room. Nobody had been here when we came, and we would have heard if someone came in. Right?

"Did someone come inside?" I whispered, my fingers resting on the hilt of my dagger.

Val looked around the room, his brows furrowed in confusion.

"I didn't hear anyone, and Rori would have sent a message if someone had come in."

True, but something didn't feel right. Rori might not have seen someone come in through another entrance; it was a big building. I hit the ground as the sound of an arrow slicing through the air echoed in the room.

"I told you," I huffed.

The others dropped to the ground and covered their heads in preparation for another arrow. Boots pounded on the floor from the level above.

"We need to get out of here," I hissed.

"Let's all split up and get to the tunnel exit," Val hissed.

Split up? There wasn't space for that.

"Chafik, stick with me. Everyone else, run," Val continued.

I didn't waste another second on the floor and sprinted down the walkway. There was only one soldier as far as I could tell, so hopefully I could make it out without much trouble. My boots skidded as I turned a sharp corner and ran in the direction of the back room.

"No use in running," a deep voice called.

The ground shook underneath my feet, almost knocking me over. Flames streaked through the air, lighting every candle in the dozens of chandeliers hanging from the ceiling. Still, I continued to run, albeit more slowly, to avoid tripping on the unsteady ground.

"Yorena," a feminine voice called, "We are under orders to return you to the palace. Surrender now and make this easier on yourself."

Like hells I would. The sound of boots against the floor grew louder behind me. Against my better judgement, I turned my head to see two soldiers sprinting toward me.

"Stop in the name of the crown!" a female soldier screamed.

I forced my feet faster as I swerved to avoid the dozens of books tumbling from shelves. One hand still rested on my dagger, but I couldn't bring myself to use it. These soldiers were only doing their job, and it wasn't my place to sentence them to death because of it. I would just have to knock them out long enough to escape. I took another sharp turn to buy myself time.

It wasn't enough to lose them. The two soldiers were gaining on me with every step, their crystals glowing like twin stars around their necks.

So we have two Air Imperium, a Fire Imperium, and an Earth Imperium. Just peachy.

But I had a crystal of my own, and I had no problem with using it.

My eyes caught on Val and Chafik sprinting into the back room as the rumbling ceased, hopefully thanks to Kass and Orla intercepting the source. I couldn't let the guards get to them. I skidded to a stop a few bookshelves shy of the back room and turned to face two soldiers, a man and a woman. They stopped in front of me, wearing twin smirks.

"Surrender," the man said.

I curled my hands into fists, watching their eyes widen at the brilliant orange glow around my neck.

"You wish."

I gathered a ball of flame into my hands, not sparing a second before throwing it toward their heads. They ducked to the ground before it could hit them. The female soldier knocked me onto my back with a gust of air to the chest. I rolled over before the second soldier could land his punch to my face.

I sprung to my feet, and shot up a wall of flames around me. I needed to think. What would be the least painful way to knock them out? Frigid air pushed against my fire wall, diminishing some of the flames.

"You can't hide from us," the male soldier taunted.

I collapsed the fire wall and charged him, my elbow out. I landed a hit into his eye, and crimson blood streaked down his face like gory tears.

The other soldier rushed toward me with her sword out. Fueled by my crystal, I snatched the weapon from her hands with surprising speed. I then snaked a thin flame around her wrist to pull her toward me, and brought the hilt of her sword down on the back of her head. She slumped to the ground.

I was about to attack the other soldier, but my eyes widened in horror to see a gleaming sword through his chest, with Orla on the other side.

"You're welcome," she said.

There was blood streaked through her blonde hair, hopefully not hers.

"The others already got out, let's go," she said, grabbing my hand.

We hurried toward the back room but stumbled when the shaking ground returned with a jarring ferocity. We both fell, barely catching ourselves before we face-planted.

"I thought you and Kass took care of the Earth Imperium," I shouted over the rumbling.

"We did, but he must have done some pretty bad structural damage before we killed him," she said, trying to push herself off the ground.

I heard the crack of splitting stone and my heart dropped. The entryway into the back room crumbled into a heap of white rubble, kicking up decades' worth of dust and stinging my eyes. Orla hoisted me up by the hand.

"We need to find another way out."

I nodded, but we turned around to find a soldier in front of us. Blood dripped from a wound in his chest, no doubt inflicted by Kass or Orla.

"I won't go down without completing my mission," he said.

I didn't even notice Orla draw her sword until I saw the flash of silver metal in her hand, already stained with blood. The soldier's face broke out in a chilling smile. It was a miracle he was still standing. The wound on his chest looked fatal.

"If I'm to die, I'm taking you with me," he said, holding up a flaming hand.

Orla threw her sword into the soldier's neck just as he placed a flaming hand on the bookshelf closest to him. He sank to the ground in a large spray of blood.

Fire spread quickly across the old and dry books, tearing its way through other bookshelves. The whole place would be up in flames in instants. Orla tugged on my arm.

"There are windows on the upper level," she said.

I ran after her as she charged toward the nearest ladder.

"Why can't we go back the way we came?" I asked.

I narrowly avoided a flaming book as it fell where my head had been a second before.

"Too dangerous. There are probably soldiers waiting for us. Also, you might be able to protect us from burning, but the smoke could kill us before we escape," Orla said.

We took a sharp turn and started climbing up a wooden ladder. Already, flames were snaking up the aging rungs, warming the soles of my boots. I urged Orla to climb faster and we reached the upper level. The room was an inferno.

Orla started kicking the glass of the window, but it only created a few tiny cracks. I joined her, already wracked with coughs, and with a few more kicks, we were able to break the glass, letting it rain down outside. Cool night air rushed in, a welcome relief from the black smoke permeating the room.

"You first, Yorena," Orla said.

I poked one foot out the window, trying to ignore the way my stomach turned as I looked at the steep drop. I found the ledge from the frieze decorating the building and brought the rest of my body out.

"Your turn," I said.

Before Orla could even get a foot out, the floor holding her up crumbled. I rushed to grab her hand, but was only able to meet her fingertips before she plummeted into the inferno inside.

"Orla!" I screamed.

She was a Water Imperium. She wouldn't do well in fire. The ledge I was on began to shake as the rest of the building inside collapsed.

She couldn't be gone. No. She would find a way out, there had to be one. The ledge underneath me crumbled and I plunged to the ground, landing hard, my back screaming from the impact. Tears stung my eyes. I had to save Orla. My resistance to fire would keep me alive long enough to get her out. I gritted my teeth against the pain, got up from the ground, and ran to the nearest entrance. But before I could enter, the roof of the Archives crumbled to a smoky pile, forcing me to flee to avoid flying debris. *No.* I slumped to my knees, bringing my shaking hands up to wipe away tears. Nobody could survive that. If only I'd been faster...if only I had caught her hand.

"Yorena!" a voice called.

Strong hands gripped my shoulders and turned to find Kieron.

"I thought you were still in there."

He pulled me to my feet and brought me in for a hug.

"I couldn't save her," I said in a tear-choked voice.

I heard more footsteps as I sobbed into Kieron's chest.

"Who couldn't you save?" Rori asked.

I turned to them, trying to make the words come out. But I couldn't make myself say it. That would make it too real. Rori looked around until it dawned on them.

"Where's Orla?" they asked.

More tears welled up in my eyes as I watched their face fall.

"Why didn't you save her?"

Tears began to run down Rori's freckled face. The words tried to come out, but were choked by a sob I couldn't hold back.

"Answer me!"

"Leave her alone, Rori. She'll tell us when she's ready," Kieron said.

I buried my face in his chest again, unable to look at the pain in Rori's eyes anymore. Eventually, Rori's boots crunched the branches on the ground as they walked away.

"Whatever happened wasn't your fault," Kieron said as he stroked my head.

If only that were true.

Chapter 14

Ilise

I paced in front of the mahogany table, my gloved hands behind my back, trying in vain to dispel some of my restless energy. I was pretty sure that if I stopped, I would destroy the table in front of me. The sorcerers were debating how to win over the kingdom. And although I was already getting a headache, they were substantially less insufferable than the nobles of the court. The amount of idiotic disputes I'd had the displeasure of witnessing was ridiculous.

There was simply no winning over my Primis subjects. They were lucky I was even allowing *some* of them to stay where they were. It wasn't as if I was enslaving them; I was simply returning them to their rightful places. Was compliance too much to ask for?

And I wasn't any closer to figuring out who the source of the annoying voice in my head was. I'd made sure to glare at each of the sorcerers before the meeting started, just on principle. Guilty people would often confess to their crimes if they thought someone knew about them, but I'd only gathered the normal amount of fear from each of them. Tracking down the source of the ever-louder whispers in my head would have to wait.

A dissonant chorus of voices echoed off the high ceilings, clashing together as the six sorcerers threw out more ideas. Some suggested we take a royal tour so that I could talk some sense into these people, while others suggested I completely ignore the lack of support. And I was quickly reminded why none of the monarchs ever took a true council.

At this point, I was convinced the sorcerers had forgotten I was there. I halted my pacing and slumped in my gold seat at the head of the table, slinging my legs over the arm of the chair. Imogen stared at me expectantly from the opposite end of the table. I shrugged in response.

"*This is your meeting, little one. Reign them back in,*" Imogen said.

I didn't think I would ever get used to hearing her in my mind.

"*I don't know what you expect me to say,*" I retorted.

Imogen crossed her navy robed arms over her chest. I removed the golden crown from my head and threw it into the center of the table. Five heads whipped in my direction as the heavy ring of gold slammed onto the wood, the clang reverberating throughout the room.

"Is something wrong, Your Majesty?" Ahn asked.

The seven-hundred-year-old sorcerer stared at me with his golden eyes, confused. He always had a dazed look to him, as if he wasn't quite sure what he was doing at any given moment. But it didn't stop him from consistently acting in precisely the way that would get on my nerves the most.

"You people are wasting my time with this nonsense."

I pushed away from the table and rose from the chair. Six pairs of eyes followed me as I slowly paced the table, taking the time to glare at each sorcerer. My crystal glowed a brilliant white as I used a gust of wind to place the crown on my head. *You never wanted this.* The incessant voice had yet to leave me alone. I could ask Imogen about it, but I didn't want her to see me as weak. She made me the Queen because I was strong.

"How about, you only speak when you have a *good* idea," I said.

The sorcerers' rainbow of vibrant eyes stared blankly at me.

"That's what I thought. You don't have any good ideas." I walked back to my chair at the head of the table and leaned over the short back.

"If I may, Your Majesty," Imogen began, "Maybe you could think of a way to give the *impression* that we are working in the Primis citizens' favor. We need to give them something they want."

I was taken aback. What she proposed was not a bad idea. Why hadn't we been taking this angle from the beginning?

I thrummed my nails on the dark oak, trying to put myself in the people's place. This led me to thinking back to my childhood. As a child, I had never seen the monarchs, or even come close. They were such an abstract entity to me, there was no thought of being loyal to them or supporting them in any way. So possibly a royal tour could help? But parading through a kingdom full of enemies would be stupid, even for me. When I was a child, the elders around me, people I respected, told me how and why I should act in accordance to the laws of the kingdom, or not. Now that I so needed credibility, maybe I needed the people to be told to trust me from someone else, too. An endorsement perhaps, from someone they all knew, someone they all trusted. If only I had Yorena with me. She may not be the entire kingdom's favorite, but they sure as hells liked her more than me. But without Yorena, I needed to look outside of Erea. A smile broke across my face as an idea formed in my mind.

"Being crowned Queen isn't enough. I need to be recognized and endorsed by another kingdom," I said.

The sorcerers traded satisfied looks with each other. I looked at Imogen, and accomplishment flooded through me as she gave me a slight nod.

"Erea has always had a strong trade relationship with the neighboring kingdoms," Ahn said.

"But which kingdom still supports us?" a silver-eyed sorcerer asked.

I hadn't learned many of the council members' names, and it was very low on my list of priorities to do so. He took the moment of silence as an invitation to keep talking.

"Pamu has closed off their borders to us, Banauri has refused to communicate with us until you step down, and Croaga has been accepting our citizens to cross the bridge border, as refugees."

For a moment, I worried how all these kingdoms had become our enemies, but I pushed back the uncomfortable thoughts, pushed away from the chair, and stalked toward the sorcerer. Now, amusement tickled in the back of my mind as he gulped. *There. That was better.* I bent down so I could look him in the eyes.

"If I wanted someone to shoot down the only decent idea to be spoken in the last hour, I would have asked."

A single bead of sweat formed on the sorcerer's brow.

"Do you agree with me?"

"Of course, Your—Your Majesty."

I smiled. "Good."

He visibly deflated as I stepped away from him. Pamu and Banauri were off the table, but just because Croaga was accepting refugees didn't automatically mean they were protesting my reign. Our kingdoms had a long history of peace. The rulers were sensible people. They wouldn't dare deny me a meeting. The Dukes and Duchesses had bent to my will with little fanfare. I could deal with the King and Prince Consort of the only neighboring kingdom not to openly declare its hostility.

The door burst open, stealing everyone's attention. The uninvited guest strode into the room with his head held high. If the silver-streaked blond hair wasn't a clue as to his identity, the shiny black detailing on his dark gray vest certainly was. The leader of The Progression. Nikos' father. A thorn in my side.

Wayne Vikander.

"I highly doubt any of the other crowns will recognize you as the true Queen," he said coolly, without preamble.

He breezed past me, settling down into *my* chair. If he hadn't been the leader of The Progression, with control of one of the biggest military forces, second only to the royal guard, I would have killed him by now. He rested his feet on the table, as if he owned the place. A visible chill ran through the other five sorcerers as my eyes narrowed on him.

"First of all, you do *not* barge into my rooms any time you please."

I stalked toward him, the flames on the chandeliers growing to twice their size, matching the orange glow of my crystal.

"Second, you do not disrespect me in my palace, especially over the only viable option we have."

My hands curled into fists and I stood over him, keeping his gaze captive.

"Third, *that* is *my* chair. Get up," I sneered.

He pressed his mouth into a thin line and said nothing as he stood from my chair. I took my seat.

"Why are you even here, Vikander? This meeting does not concern you."

He scratched the bushy mustache above his lip.

"I would assume you want my Progression forces to help subdue any 'rebellions.' And without me, you get nothing."

He was right. I hated that he was right. But he didn't need to know that. Vikander was the type of man who, if others validated his power, he would use it.

It was hard to believe he and Nikos were related sometimes. Nikos' face was angular and drawn out, where Wayne's was circular and covered in wrinkles. Wayne flaunted the power he had, while Nikos held any he managed to scrounge up close to his chest. The only thing they had in common was the hair and the bright green eyes.

"You will lend me your forces because I am your Queen, and if you don't, it won't be hard for me to take it all away," I said with a smile.

Wayne's green eyes flicked to the sparkling crown resting on my head and the two crystals hanging from my neck.

He bowed. "Very well, Your Majesty."

I waved him away and he retreated into the corner, having lost the battle of wills. I couldn't even guess why Imogen still kept him around. She could have gotten rid of him and made Nikos the new leader. That boy was firmly under our thumb so long as Daeva was in our custody. And though he got on my nerves with his impudence, he was worlds better than this man.

The door flew open once again. *Does anyone know how to enter a room properly?* The Commander strode in, two guards at his heels. I rubbed away the beginnings of a headache.

"What is so important that you needed to barge in on my strategy meeting, Commander?"

The Commander scratched his graying head before dipping into a low bow.

"Apologies, Your Majesty, but I come with urgent news from Faveru."

Faveru? I knew Yorena would try something there eventually. I peered over the Commander's shoulder, looking for a head of long curls.

"Where is she?" I asked before he could continue.

He rubbed the back of his neck.

"Did your men fail me, *again*?"

"Yorena and her accomplices have evaded capture once again, and they burned down the Archives in the process."

I couldn't care less about a building full of books. I needed Yorena back by my side.

"But one of them did not escape."

I pushed away from the table, moving toward him. He kept his cold blue eyes trained on me, watching, waiting. He stared at me like I was a predator.

Good.

"Did you capture them?"

He cleared his throat.

"No, but my men did find their charred remains in the rubble."

I crossed my arms, waiting for him to continue.

"From what was left after we extinguished the fire, we can assume the body was a female, quite short, and she had a water crystal around her neck."

Orla, I guessed. I would have thought one of those stupid, inept boys would be the first to die. But with Orla dead, morale would be at an all time low. This would be the perfect time to capture them. Even better, they were now down one of the elements. The only element they had over me now was earth, but that could be dealt with easily.

"Have your men scour the area for them," I ordered him. "With Orla gone, they will be demotivated, sloppy, grieving."

Wayne cleared his throat from the corner.

"If I may, Your Majesty, I think your search for the girl is futile."

I whirled in his direction. The old me would have wanted to murder him because he was The Progression's leader. Now I wanted to murder him for pleasure. The number of headaches I would be saved from was immeasurable.

"When did I ask for your opinion, *Vikander*?"

I stalked toward him, my air crystal glowing a brilliant white.

"She does not concern you," I said.

"I just think if you forgo your search for her you could spend more time solidifying your rule."

I formed a line of air, snaking it around Wayne's waist. His frail body stiffened.

"She's just a girl, she is irrelevant," he said, his voice full of misplaced bravado.

That did it.

"You do not speak of her like that," I seethed.

The next person to talk about Yorena in such a disrespectful manner would become a pile of ashes. I wrapped the air into a ring, squeezing Wayne's stomach. His pale face reddened as I floated him off the ground, squeezing just tight enough for him to remain conscious.

"When I let you go, you *will* apologize. And you will take this as your *last* warning."

I released him from my hold, and he dropped to the ground, coughing. I made sure to keep the light of both my crystals glowing bright, a silent warning.

Without raising his head he said, "I apologize, Your Majesty. I meant no disrespect."

I crouched down beside him, grasping his chin.

"Don't lie to me. Your intention was to disrespect Yorena," I said.

Vikander's eyes were wide from my close proximity, fixed onto my crystals.

"I apologize for lying, Your Majesty."

I released his chin and stepped away. He slowly stood and backed away from me.

You didn't have to hurt him.

When would that voice leave me alone?

You're acting insane, this isn't who you are.

"Would you shut up!" I yelled.

My voice echoed throughout the room and everyone froze.

"Your Majesty?" the Commander said.

"What are you idiots staring at?"

The people in the room shared confused looks with each other. They must have thought me crazy, losing my mind. Like I was cracking under the weight of the crown—my emotions an overflowed dam ready to burst. But I wasn't—it was merely this annoying voice that refused to release its hold on my mind. I would get rid of it soon. I had to.

"Commander and Imogen, make preparations to leave for Croaga. I want to leave as soon as possible."

Everyone bowed and I left the room.

As I stormed through the halls, I couldn't help but think of the voice. Before I knew it, my feet had taken me to the royal gardens. Gardeners scurried out of my way, taking extra care to not look me in the eye. I stopped once I reached the roses, inhaling their refreshing scents. Back in my old life, being amongst the flowers had a way of soothing me. But somehow, now, it only angered me more.

I took the crown off my head, examining the metal sparkle in the sunlight. A gust of fresh September air blew across my face, a welcome reprieve from the stifling heat. I gripped the crown, hard, letting the sharp points of the vines dig into my hands.

"What are you doing to me?" I whispered.

Let's talk, the voice said. *My crystals glowed brighter than they ever had before, enough for me to not see the engraved symbols on them anymore. The last time I'd been pulled into my soul was when Imogen had convinced me to see the truth in what she was doing. And as far as I knew, she was the only sorceress powerful enough to do it from a distance. Who was behind this?*

Suddenly, the roses disappeared. Misty shadows of purple, orange, white surrounded me, floating lazily through the black space around me, and I found myself in emptiness. But I could feel a presence there with me. I was sure of it.

"What do you want with me?" I asked.

My voice echoed through an infinitely large space.

"Hello?"

No one responded. The only things here beside me were dancing shadows, the only splashes of color in the dark landscape. These shadows were disconcertingly familiar to me. I had seen them once before. I knew where I was, now. I was inside my own soul.

The weird voice had said it wanted to talk. There had to be a person attached to the voice. Right? I squinted my eyes, trying to see further than the few feet of space around me. The shadows formed into a ball behind me, pushing me into the blackness.

"Where are you taking me?"

The shadows didn't respond, but why would they? Even when Imogen was controlling shadows like these, she couldn't make them speak.

I walked for what felt like miles into the blackness and someone had yet to appear. It was quite peaceful—aside from the fact that I was stuck inside of my own essence until whoever pulled me in here decided to release me. Was everyone's soul so black? Blackness meant emptiness, darkness, and just nothing. If not for the shadows, there'd be nothing here except the empty blackness. Did this mean I was empty? I wouldn't think that of myself. I had an entire kingdom at my disposal, I was the most powerful person on our continent, possibly out of all the kingdoms in the Sdor Ocean and Picchi Sea.

"I don't think we're empty," a familiar voice said.

Out of thin air, the silhouette of a person began to materialize in the distance. The shadows dispersed, leaving a cold space behind.

"Who are you?" I asked.

The figure slowly walked toward me. She wore a blue peasant's dress that went halfway down her calves with mismatched patches sewn throughout. Thick, black coils sprouted from her head, going almost to her shoulder. She stepped even closer so that she was no longer shrouded in blackness. I froze.

It was like looking in a mirror. Her arms were identical to mine, covered in dark burn scars that had never had the chance to heal. She had the same deep eyes sparkling with silver and gold, the same wide nose, the same full lips. The figure was... me.

"I was you," the other me said.

We circled each other. If she was the one who had pulled me in here, then I wouldn't be able to do anything to her. There could only be one me, this girl had to be an imposter. And a powerful one. I would have to play along with her ruse.

"What do you mean you were me?"

She halted, and so did I.

"I am who you were before this all started."

All this? This all started a thousand years ago when Anora Schaefer decided to take over the kingdom and run it into the ground. I hadn't been alive then, but Imogen had. And she alone knew how much better off Erea would have been without Anora. Primis would've stayed where they belonged, in their little villages. Or working for a fair wage on the estates of Imperium who were kind enough to take them in.

"Just tell me what you want so I can be on with my day."

The imposter crossed her arms.

"I brought you here to convince you to snap out of it."

"Snap me out of what? I'm thinking more clearly than I ever have before."

"Imogen is manipulating you. This isn't who we are."

This girl was nothing more than a weak villager. Before Imogen, I didn't know who I was or what I truly needed. I'd been nothing.

"You know nothing."

I lashed out with my fist, aiming for the imposter's side. She swerved out of my reach at the last second, making me stumble forward.

"Let me out of here before I do something you'll regret," I seethed.

The eyes that used to mirror mine turned pitch black, as empty as my soul appeared to be.

"You can't hide behind your power forever," the entity said in a voice octaves deeper.

A frigid chill ran down my spine.

"You would have done anything for your friends, and now you want them dead?"

Those people were not my friends. They'd manipulated me so I would be a spy for them. Real friends would have helped me kill Wayne Vikander from the beginning. I might still need him alive for now, but the second he was useless to me, I would be the one to kill him. Not for destroying my old village, but for trying to undermine my authority.

I slowly stepped away from her...it, not taking my eyes off of the apparition.

"This is for the greater good. Those 'friends' are just collateral damage."

The imposter sighed.

"I thought I would be able to get through to you," it said.

White light filled the blackness, accompanied by a ringing and a thundering voice.

"You are drowning your spark in her, free yourself."

Chapter 15

Yorena

ORLA WAS DEAD. AND it was my fault. It was one thing to kill in battle. No matter how guilty I felt in the aftermath, there was nothing I could do to change it. When your life, and other's, were on the line, sometimes morals had to be temporarily sacrificed. But it was an entirely different thing to unintentionally be the sole blame for someone's death. She'd been *so* close. I should have let her go through the window first. I couldn't burn. I could've survived. If I hadn't hesitated, if we'd been a few seconds quicker, she would still be with us. I hadn't even known her for long but it was devastating nonetheless. The back of my throat burned, begging the flow of tears to be released.

We traveled through the plains in silence for a full day after the Archives, the setting sun a clue we'd be stopping soon. We were about half a day from reaching the bridge that would allow us to cross the Picchi Sea into Croaga. Orla had been so close to being here with us, so close to making it into Croaga. As the sun rested below the horizon, the churning, burning in my stomach grew. Almost as if the sun had found a new home inside of me.

Kieron had yet to leave my side, but I couldn't bring myself to say anything to him. He kept telling me it wasn't my fault, that I couldn't have done anything to save her. But the guards had been after *me*. Orla's life wouldn't have been in danger if it weren't for me.

Water Imperium belonged in Lasaintbo, with the cooling current of the Zasen and Leekrina Rivers. Or in the northern, mountainous reaches of Pria, where the rock harbored enough water to last them a lifetime. Allowing Orla to die in a dry and smoky inferno was the worst way I could have failed her.

After walking for an hour, all of us lost in our own thoughts, Val halted our party near a pond. My skin was still covered in soot from the fire, and pieces of debris clung to my hair. Kieron put his last piece of dried beef in my hands.

"You still need to eat," he said softly.

My stomach was in too many knots to eat, but I took a small bite to appease him and lay in the dry grass. He gave me a small smile and walked toward the pond to get clean.

"*Claim your crystal,*" a familiar dark voice whispered. I startled, and rose from the grass, peering across the empty landscape. It was that same voice I'd heard at the temple. Was the owner of the voice following me?

I looked down at the orange gem on my neck. What did it mean when the voice told me to "claim my crystal"? It wasn't like I was afraid of using it; that was probably the only reason I'd made it this far.

A sudden fear froze me in my tracks. Ilise had said she was hearing a voice before... before Imogen changed her. But she'd been able to tell it was Imogen after the first few times she'd heard it. The voice *sounded* like Imogen. This voice had a way of crawling under my skin, sending unending chills down my spine. If Imogen was dark, this voice was darker.

Grass crunched under Cain's boots as he walked over to me. He sat beside me, not looking at me, not talking to me, just sitting.

"If you've come to yell at me, take a ticket—I'm sure Rori wants to be first in line," I said.

Rori hadn't spoken a word to me since we'd left the Archives, and I couldn't blame them.

Cain sighed. "I'm not here to blame you. I'm here to see if you're ok."

I finally looked at Cain. His brown forehead was creased with worry lines, and his shoulders were sunken in, just slightly. Based on the redness of his eyes I could tell he was mourning Orla too, but from the way he clenched his fists, I knew he still blamed me, no matter how much reassurance he offered.

"How are the others doing?" I asked.

"No. First, you're going to tell me how you're doing."

I groaned. I wasn't the one who'd lost a friend. I barely knew Orla, and the only remaining emotion I had after the shock had worn off was never-ending guilt.

After a full minute of silence, Cain answered my question. "Chafik and Mathias are doing their best to comfort the others...and to keep Rori in check So everyone's doing the best they can."

That did nothing to quell my worries. I was one of the ones who had insisted we go to the Archives, and all we had come out with was a single book that might not even be useful—at the price of Orla's life. Cain waited for me to say something, but when I didn't, he sighed and stood to leave.

"Val wants us to rest here until morning before we go to Croaga," he said.

"Got it," I said in a hollow voice.

"And no offense Princess, but I suggest you try to clean up. We're going to be meeting the monarchs, after all."

I flashed him a weak smile before he walked to Val. I waited until the sun had set and everyone else had rinsed themselves before going to the pond and cupping some water with my hands, melting away the dirt and grime. I did my best to wash my face and smooth my hair. The quiet wind chilled my skin and I finished up as quickly as possible.

"Find me," the same dark voice whispered. I nearly slipped in the soft mud as I whipped around, searching for the source.

"Yorena?"

I leapt at another voice behind me, but it was only Kass perched on a tall rock for watch duty.

"Is something wrong?"

Dark circles ringed her eyes, stark against her pale complexion. The moonlight made the scars marring her face even more severe, like the jagged strokes of a paintbrush.

"Sorry, I—I just thought I heard something, but I guess it was just you."

Kass gave me a tight-lipped smile. Rori was more blatant when they blamed me for Orla's death, but with Kass, she hid her blame under a smiling mask.

"I'm sorry about what happened to Orla, I know there must have been something I could've done and—"

"I'm gonna stop you right there," she said, putting a hand up.

Kass slid off the rock, forcing me to look down at her.

"What happened to Orla was *not* your fault."

But it was. Kass hadn't been in the Archives when we were trying to escape, so she hadn't seen it. I'd heard the ledge beneath Orla crumbling, but I'd hesitated, and she'd paid for it with her life.

"You're just like Ilise, always blaming yourself for things out of your control. Ignore Rori," Kass advised. "They'll come around eventually. It's just... they were closest with Orla, and Ilise."

She patted my shoulder and told me to get some sleep for the rest of the journey.

I settled down near Kieron and shut my eyes. I couldn't imagine losing two of my closest friends in such a short time, and then being forced to stay with the person who'd had a part in losing each of them. Now I understood why Rori seemed to hate me so much. The only thing that might quell their hatred was time. A lot of time.

Val shook us all awake just as the sun was cresting over the horizon. Dew coated the grass, dampening my clothes and making me shiver for a full hour after we woke. Kieron stayed by my side as we followed Val and Chafik toward the Atheron bridge. My feet ached with every step, pain shooting up to my calf with every hill.

The closer we got to the bridge, the more signs of civilization we found. The roads began to flatten out, dirt eventually giving way to stone. Every time we heard the rattling of a traveler's cart, we had to hide behind any vegetation or shelter we could find.

The sun was high above our heads once we reached Port Hapow—the last town before the bridge. This was Erea's main trading hub. Filled with fishermen, merchants, farmers, and artists bustling around the crowded streets. Every one of my nerves was on fire as Val made us go straight through the town.

It was crowded enough that our travel-weary group could move about anonymously. Dozens of shoulders crashed into mine as we pushed our way through the thick of the crowd, trying to get to the east side of the town, toward the Picchi Sea.

Carts and stands covered with bright patterned cloths took up most of the main street. The smell of spiced meat filled my nose, barely masking the aroma of sweat. So much sweat. We reached the town center, and I quickly realized that even the market in New Teber paled in comparison to this.

Vendors advertised their handmade goods: colorful dresses with swirling black and gold patterns, wooden figurines of every animal I could think of, jewelry made from colorful shining beads, stitched murals of the four Spirits, and so much more. Kieron had to keep his hand on my elbow to keep me moving as I took in the extent of it all.

As we pushed through, I noticed something odd. There didn't seem to be visitors from our three neighboring kingdoms. This was supposed to be a trading hub for all the kingdoms. Where was everyone?

Val expertly led us into alleyways between tan brick buildings whenever he spotted black and gold guard uniforms, which happened more times than I could count. We were about to finally reach the outskirts of the town when I saw the posters, hung up for all to see.

"Kieron," I said, turning him toward the sheets of paper flapping on a wood post.

My face was plastered on every one of these signs, calling for my arrest and the execution of anyone aiding me. *You're better than this Ilise.* Val whistled for us to keep moving so we could get as far away from people as possible.

Brick buildings gave way to one lone road leading to the bridge. We were so close I could already smell the salty air from the coast. Val halted us just before we could reach the bridge. We all crouched low behind a row of bushes, peering at the two Erean guards standing guard at the bridge.

"What are we doing?" Rori asked. "Can't we just knock them out and run?"

"If you want to get captured immediately by the Croagi guards on the other side, then sure," Val said in a flat tone.

"We need to plan what we're going to say to the Croagi guards so we can gain an audience with the monarchs," Cain said.

They all looked at me expectantly, except for Rori, who looked at me like I was no more interesting than a wall of wet paint.

"I was planning on just saying my name and demanding an audience with them," I said. Not a great plan, but it was all I could think of. Alyx and Titus had always liked me. I didn't think it would take much for them to award us an audience.

"You actually think that'll work?" Rori scoffed.

"Do you have a better idea?" I countered. Rori stalked away, presumably to talk to the others, who were behind the bushes across the way.

"As long as it doesn't get me killed I don't really care whose idea we go with, but maybe we should quiet our voices before the guards hear," Mathias said.

I peeked over the bush and my heart dropped to see that one of the guards had left their post. Where did he go?

I soon had my answer as I was eclipsed into a shadow, heavy footsteps sounding behind me. My muscles tensed and my hand flew to the handle of the dagger at my thigh, I slowly turned around.

"I wouldn't do that if I were you," the guard said. "Just surrender. It'll be easier for you."

I rolled to the side just as he grabbed for me, "Princess Yorena, you are under arrest," he said, yanking me up by my arm.

I winced from the force of it and activated my crystal. Using my free hand, I slapped the guard's hand, igniting it hot enough to burn straight through his leather glove. He howled in pain and dropped my arm.

Before he could advance again, Rori, their crystal glowing a white, blew him back into a giant tree, hard enough to crack the thick trunk. I barely had time to catch my breath before a second guard tried to rush me. Kieron tackled the man to the side just before he reached me. I unsheathed my dagger and ran toward the two men as they wrestled with each other.

"Yorena Schaefer, you are under arrest," the guard said, his breaths coming in pants.

"Big talk for someone being pinned to the ground," Kieron taunted. The guard tried to push Kieron off but he was too heavy for him to move. Another man came up behind me. I elbowed him in the stomach and kicked his groin for good measure. He crumpled, next to his partner.

"I suggest you two do what we say." I said. Rori threw the first guard to the ground beside the second. I twirled the dagger in my hand. "You won't tell anyone of what happened here or I will become your worst nightmare," I threatened.

"Oh yeah, what're you gonna do to us?" The second guard teased.

I formed a ball of flames in my hand, stepping as close as I dared to the two men.

"I don't think you want to find out," I said.

Neither of the guards appeared to have a crystal, and their eyes widened as the flames lightly caressed their faces. I backed away from them, deeming them thoroughly scared.

"Stay here," I ordered.

Wasting no further time, I led our group across the stone bridge. Once we crossed the halfway point, there was no chance of the Erean guards coming after us. Erea's and Croaga's border was right in the middle of the bridge, and for any guard to try to arrest me now would be a break in international policy.

The others crowded behind me as we approached the Croagi guards at the end of the bridge. They held iron-tipped spears in their hands and stared us down as we walked.

One of the guards approached me and I halted our march. "State your business, traveler," he said in a thick, round, Croagi accent.

"I am Princess Yorena Schaefer of Erea and I demand an audience with King Titus and Prince Consort Alyx."

The guard stared at me intently, searching my face for a tell that I was lying about my identity. "I think you all are going to need to come with me," the guard said.

Kieron and Kass shot forward, swords and daggers pointed at the guard. The guard pointed his spear at us, and we stood frozen in a standstill.

My crystal grew brighter orange the longer we stood there, preparing for him to strike.

"Now, there's no need for all that," another voice said.

We all turned toward the castle balcony above. Prince Consort Alyx stood there, ordering the guards to stand down with a wave of his hand.

"Yorena, I'm sure you have quite the story for me," he shouted.

"Guards, please escort our guests to my study."

Chapter 16

Ilise

I KICKED MY CHAIR across my study, watching as it splintered into tiny pieces. It did nothing to quell my frustration. I used wind to sweep the debris into one large pile, but some of the wood dust settled onto the black leather of my gloves, annoying me.

"Did killing a chair make you feel any better, little one?" Imogen said calmly. Somehow, that irritated me even more.

"Yes," I lied.

Yorena had been reported crossing the Atheron Bridge into Croaga—the last kingdom with open borders. What I couldn't figure out was the reasoning behind her going there. Leaving the kingdom wouldn't help her get the crown back, and now that I thought of it, what had been the whole purpose of going to the Archives?

Morning light streamed in through the wide window, making Imogen's violet eyes appear more vibrant. She rose from the chaise and retrieved a scroll from the inside pocket of her royal blue robe, placing it in my hands.

"The monarchs of Croaga just responded to my letter. They will be expecting you," she said. "We will be leaving early tomorrow morning."

I unrolled the thick paper and read the letter.

To Her Royal Majesty,

It would be our greatest honor to invite you to the city of Rimed, Croaga's glorious capital. A ball shall be thrown in your honor at our seaside castle, celebrating the beginning of a hopefully long reign. Rooms will be prepared for everyone in your party.

King Titus and Prince Consort Alyx

A hopefully long reign. The golden ring on my head felt infinitely heavier. It hasn't even been a month, yet it felt like I'd been Queen for years. I had always craved power—the power to make change in the kingdom. And now, I realized it was such a fickle thing, something that could be taken by anyone. It had evaded my grasp for years, during which I'd endured the blasted Union holding me back, the previous monarchs thinking me weak, and half the kingdom thinking me weak. I wouldn't fail now because running a kingdom was stressful. This was the life of a ruler; there was no avoiding it. I would not be weak, I would not quit. I had to believe it would get better as the years went on. That was it. Ruling would stop being difficult the moment Primis people let go of the wild notion that I might ever be overthrown.

"You're doing quite well, little one," Imogen said, placing her hand on my shoulder. "When King Titus recognizes you as Queen, we will be unstoppable."

I looked down at her smiling face. I could tell she didn't smile very often. Her face was stretched so much she almost looked pained.

Stop hiding.

I pulled away from Imogen and threw the crown onto my desk. When would this voice leave me be? I'd yet to find any evidence to place the blame on the other Council sorcerers. Anyway, none of them were powerful enough to keep this little trick up for this long. This had to be the work of someone else.

I looked through the window, out over New Teber, noticing the citizens milling about in the marketplace, children running across the streets to the dismay of their parents, a horde of people storming toward the palace.

Wait.

A horde of people?

I leaned over the desk and unlatched the lock on the window. Warm air blew in from the light breeze outside, carrying with it an orchestra of voices.

"What is all that commotion?" Imogen grumbled, joining me in front of the window.

At least a hundred people marched in a blob toward the palace gates, carrying weapons, pitchforks, wood planks—really anything they could get their hands on, it seemed. *Cute.*

I slammed the window shut and stormed out of the room. Imogen trailed behind me with almost silent footsteps. The crowd looked to be made up of only Primis, so this would be quick. I needed to make another example of what happened when you tried to go against me. Maybe the last example wasn't bloody enough. Repetition was the quickest way to learn, anyway.

I bounded down the stairs, my fire crystal already growing bright enough to forgo the need for a torch. What else could the people want from me? I was only doing what was best for the kingdom, and that meant reverting back to Letita's ideals—Imperium provided all the best housing, jobs, and resources while the Primis lived off the scraps. It was nothing more than what they were. Primis were the scraps of humanity that had been unfortunately given a place in this kingdom. Imperium were the superior beings, and Primis should be lucky we had paused at merely only taking their businesses.

But I guess I gave them too much wiggle room. We shouldn't have stopped there. Servants quickly sprinted from my path as I charged toward the front gates. Primis were trying to take more than what their powerless selves deserved, and their little display would be the perfect time to enact one more change to my policies.

Warm September air blew across my face as I strode out of the palace. Guards already rushed toward the gates, awaiting my command. The nearest general spotted me and ran up to me, dipping into a low bow before speaking. I couldn't remember what his name was, but I couldn't find it in myself to care.

"Your Majesty, the rioters have started trying to break down the gates. They're calling for your head."

Screams, shouts, and wood thumping against wood almost drowned out the general's voice. *My head, they say?* I crossed my arms, thinking of the quickest way to get rid of them all. I knew I wanted this example to be a bloody one, horrible enough for the whole kingdom to know not to even attempt to overpower me. I had already given them so much. They should be thanking me. I was ushering in a new era for Erea. One where Imperium regained their rightful place. Primis were lucky to be allowed to coexist with Imperium, and serve them..

"Ready the archers to go on my call," I ordered the general.

The general broke into a sprint toward the lieutenants huddled close to the gilded gates.

I took a moment to notice the depictions of the four Spirits in all their glory that were carved into the gold. Almost everyone in this kingdom constantly tried to erase the existence of the fifth Spirit, the Soul Spirit. It was absurd. The Soul Spirit was everywhere. A piece of Them was hidden in everything and everyone. Imogen had taught me that the Soul Spirit was the mysterious piece that allowed sorcerers to manipulate a soul. Perhaps that was why people hated Them so much. But there was no soul without the Soul Spirit. If only I had Their full power at my disposal. I wouldn't have to waste my time quelling these pitiful uprisings. All it would take was one thought from me, and the whole kingdom would bend to my will.

I stormed toward the tan, stone guard tower, taking the winding steps two at a time. As I climbed higher, I could finally see over the wall. The participants in this riot had nearly doubled in number since I had last seen them. Primis dressed in all types of colored rags shouted at the guards, demanding to see me. Those who held broken planks of wood as weapons pointed the sharp edge at the guards stationed outside the palace. Pitiful.

I reached the top of the tower, scanning the walls around me. Archers were lined up, arrows already drawn and waiting for my call. The cacophony of voices from the rioters reached my ears and infuriated me.

"Quiet!" I roared, using my air crystal to carry my voice over the shouts of the crowd. Hundreds of pairs of eyes landed on me. Even from my vantage point, I could see the burning in their eyes, as if they could incinerate me purely with their glares. Others were even less afraid to make their feelings known, their lips curling into snarls, hands gripping their makeshift weapons tighter.

"I gave you everything you needed. I allowed you to keep your nice homes, I told the guards to leave you alone when they overheard your whispered threats toward me. I was willing to give you more than your weak selves deserved. And all I get in return is you spitting in my face."

I raised my hand high enough for all the archers to see.

"It's time you learn your lesson, again. From this moment forth, all Primis living in the center of towns must surrender their homes to an Imperium. This will be effective immediately. Your old homes will be searched. I had been willing to back out of enacting this policy, but you leave me no choice. I can't appoint privileges to treasonous citizens."

Cries of outrage rose as the crowd tried to push through the line of guards. My guards raised their broadswords, keeping the crowd away from the gate.

Free yourself.

If only my guards could keep away that voice as well.

"Archers at the ready," I called.

The archers aimed their bows down at the crowd, who continued to attempt to strike down the guards.

"Fire!" I ordered.

It was as if a river of arrows flowed toward the crowd. Angered screams turned to cries of terror as iron-tipped arrows met soft flesh, a horrific soft squelching sound reaching me at the tower. Despite arrows continuing to rain down, much of the crowd still pushed past those falling, using the chaos as an opportunity to get closer to the gates. These people's determination would have been admirable if it weren't idiotic and pointless.

"I have to admire their stubbornness," Imogen said through our bond.

I loved how alike we thought.

"How do I get rid of them?" I asked.

While this little rebellion was an entertaining distraction, I had to prepare for Croaga. And finally be treated like the Queen I was.

"Show them who they're dealing with, little one. I didn't reveal this power to you for nothing."

The Spirits hadn't awarded me this power to sit and let my soldiers do all the work. I had the crown; I was the crown. And this would be fun.

I cracked the knuckles of my gloved hands, stepping onto the wide ledge of the tower. I climbed to the flat roof, the open blue sky finally revealed to me. Ocean waves crashed against the jagged rocks in the distance, sunlight glinting off the white caps. A stark contrast to the carnage in front of me.

Bodies littered the ground outside of the gates, stone and grass stained crimson with blood. Most of the fallen had arrows protruding from multiple places in their body, some of them still smoldering. About half of the mob was gone, either dead or fleeing.

I climbed on top of the roof in the view of everyone below and raised my arms. My fire crystal glowed a deep orange as I felt the flames race through my veins and into my hands. The people below dropped their makeshift weapons, frozen in fear at my creation. A ball of flames the size of the Ritker Desert sand mounds churned above me. Sweat formed on my brow at the effort. This was larger than anything I'd ever made before, and it would destroy more than I ever had before.

"Spirits!" the nearest archer screamed.

Those closest to me scurried from my creation. I could see the rioters who had any fear for their life scramble away, but some still stood, heads held high. Idiotic. With a grunt and a blinding flash, my creation descended upon the crowd. Screams of agony echoed off the stone walls. Everything in my fireball's path was charred within seconds.

"Well done, little one," Imogen said in my mind.

As the smoke cleared, black grass and scorched bodies were all that was left. Fire could be so beautiful when wielded correctly. That beauty sometimes made me forget just how destructive it could be.

As the last of the stragglers hurried from my wrath, I leapt off the roof of the tower, forming a ring of air around me to soften the fall. Pieces of ash were strewn on the stone courtyard, like a blanket of gray and black snow.

"General," I called.

The general I'd spoken to at the start of the riot jogged up to me, his eyes straying to the ashy mess at our feet. His eyes watered and he coughed as his steps kicked smoky particles up into the air.

"Yes, Your Majesty."

"Find a squad to dispose of the bodies."

He bowed. "Right away, Your Majesty."

"Come little one, we have much to prepare."

Chapter 17

Nikos

Oliver's second request appeared to be the very thing that would kill me if this sorcerer didn't show up soon. I had paced the palace garden for at least an hour, and the only thing I'd gained was a layer of sweat making my white shirt stick to my skin. Oliver claimed Ahn spent much of his alone time in the garden, but I'd yet to see more than a few gardeners that had scurried away the moment I rounded the corner.

During the Council meeting I'd eavesdropped on, Ahn had said he would approach me with information about my father and Imogen. He'd claimed they'd done something to me, something that was horrid enough to sway me to their side. What side that was, I'd yet to determine.

I couldn't stay out here until the sun went down, but Oliver would report me if I went back inside without talking to the sorcerer. The sickly odor of rotting peaches wafted into my nose as I wandered into the grove of peach trees. Fallen fruits littered the ground, baking in the heat. A stone bench lay under the largest tree, which barely offered any shade. Finally a place to sit. As I finally took my weight off my sweaty feet, I could feel the heat of the stone through my pants.

This had to be another one of Oliver's tricks. No one in their right mind would voluntarily be in the garden in this heat, not even a sorcerer. And I was wasting precious time I could be using to plan an escape on the way to Croaga. I'd overheard Ilise and Imogen talking about traveling to Croaga to ask for their endorsement to Ilise's rule. But I wouldn't be able to plan anything without finding out more information about the trip. And I couldn't find more information in this spiritsdamned garden.

The humid air pressed down on my shoulders. I struggled to take in oxygen and, despite the heat, a chill traveled down my spine.

Someone was here.

I tensed my muscles and activated my crystal. The green light outshone the blaring sun as I scanned the grove. *Who is there?*

"Show yourself," I demanded to the trees.

"Hello there, young Vikander," a melodic voice said.

I whipped around to find the golden-eyed sorcerer staring at me.

I jumped back, tripping over the uneven stones.

"Are you enjoying the garden? I have yet to see you out here," he said.

He walked off and I assumed he wanted me to follow. I didn't want to spend more time with this sorcerer than I had to, so I decided to address my mission head-on.

"I know you have something to tell me," I said.

Ahn stopped at the edge of the grove. He stared off into the distance, as if the empty sky were more interesting than the conversation he should've been having with me. If my father and Imogen had done something to me, it very well could mean they'd done something to Daeva. She was all I had left.

"Have you come to enjoy the rain shower?" he said. I stared up. There was a singular cloud. What was this sorcerer talking about?

"The sky is clear."

He shook his head, strands of black hair falling into his face.

"It *appears* clear. But that does not mean it will not rain."

What in four hells? I didn't have time for riddles; Daeva didn't have time for riddles. The sorcerer started to walk away and I grabbed the shoulders of his black robes. I leaned in close to him, so that his golden eyes filled most of my vision.

"Look sorcerer, I know you want to tell me what the hells my father and Imogen have done to me, so go ahead and spill it, or I'll tell Her Majesty what you and the other Council sorcerers are planning," I said.

His face remained steady, save for the smallest glint of fear in his sparkling eyes.

"What would that be, young Vikander?" he asked innocently. "I can assure you, the Council is not planning anything, let alone something worthy of Her Majesty's attention."

The corner of his mouth tipped up in the smallest of smirks. He was lying. He knew I could tell he was lying. The Council had said they wanted me on their side for whatever it was they were planning, and yet Ahn was intent on denying the fact he needed me. Antagonizing me and speaking in riddles was hardly the method to sway someone to your cause. Unless...Ahn had his own set of motives.

"What do you want from me, sorcerer?" I asked, pushing him away. He stumbled but kept the fake smile on his face.

"All I want is for you to understand," he said. His voice had the quality of a children's school teacher's, as if he were telling me a fun tale.

"Understand?" I said. I let out a singular, curt laugh. "If you want me to understand, then tell me what in four hells I'm supposed to understand." My skin tingled with fury. My face was surely matching in color to the peaches littering the ground in the grove behind me. He thought he had the upper hand here, he thought he was the one in charge. Yet, he was the one right under Imogen's thumb because of his soul crystal, and he was the one who could only ever live long term on a secluded mountain. How dare he act as if I was the one who needed him? I would save me and Daeva with or without the alleged information he had.

He frowned, letting out a soft sigh.

"Ponder what I have told you about the sky. Only then will you understand," the sorcerer said before disappearing into the peach grove once more.

Chapter 18

Yorena

Two guards led us through the majestic castle. White stone columns wrapped in ivy lined the open walkway, letting in the salty sea air. Perfectly rectangular shrubs acted as a half-wall, the only buffer between us and the sandy beach. Soft waves crashed in the distance and sunlight glinted off the blue water. I could see why the King and Prince Consort had decided to make the castle open to the elements. Everyone's mouth was open wide in pure awe at such beauty.

The guards pushed open towering doors etched with two silver trees.

"What are those drawings?" I asked the guard.

"The new royal crest," he responded. "Our monarchs changed it to pay homage to the Buquo Jungle."

The Buquo Jungle was as important to Croagi as the Spirits were to Ereans. While we believed our elemental abilities were direct gifts from the Spirits, Croagi history said the jungle was the true source of our gifts. They believed the Spirits had imbued their powers in different fruits that grew in the jungle, and the first Imperium were the ones who had eaten the fruit. Part of my early lessons had been about the different histories the kingdoms had for the origin of elemental magic. Mostly to avoid the notion that the Erean version of the Imperium origin story was the only correct one.

Last time I had written to Alyx, he hadn't mentioned changing the crest. Actually, I couldn't remember the last time I'd written to Alyx. I'd been too busy preparing to be Queen. We were due a catch-up. And knowing Alyx, I was walking straight into something barely short of an interrogation.

We were led into the main foyer of the castle. While there were proper walls here, most of them were taken up by enormous windows. It almost felt like we were right on the beach.

"Spirits, it's bright in here. I think I feel a migraine coming on," Kieron said.

I fought back a chuckle.

"Don't be rude," Val chided from behind us.

We walked up a gleaming wooden staircase, the treads of which were covered in a finely woven jungle-print carpet. Once we reached the top, we were greeted by the bright gap-toothed smile of Prince Consort Alyx.

"Thank you gentlemen," he told the guards who had escorted us up. "I will take the lead from here. And would you mind telling the kitchens to supply these good people's rooms with some snacks? They must be famished."

The guards bowed and walked back down the stairs. Our group all bowed to the Prince Consort.

"Oh there's no need for formalities," he said. "Come. My husband is waiting for us in the study."

We walked to the end of the bright hallway, lined with the regal portraits of the past Croaga monarchs, and Alyx led us into a room. Two of the four walls were made entirely of windows, and a third was completely open to the balcony we'd seen him on earlier.

King Titus sat at the desk chair.

"Make yourselves at home," he said with a warm smile.

His cornrowed head was bare of a crown, and in this lighting, I could see the blue flecks in his brown eyes, matching in shade to the sapphire crystal around his neck. Kass, Cain, Val, Rori, and Mathias stood uncomfortably in the corner, as far from the monarchs as they could.

We stared at each other, everyone waiting for the other group to start the conversation. I could imagine there wouldn't be many happy sentiments from the Union members toward monarchs in general. But they had nothing to fear; Titus and Alyx were two of the best people I knew.

It'd been years since I'd last written to Alyx, I realized. As I had gotten older, my "parents" had wanted me to get more involved with palace matters, and I had been glad to, but it also meant I had less time for pen pals, even royal ones. If anything, I'd learned more about being a good leader from Alyx than I had from the King and Queen of my own kingdom.

Kieron nudged my shoulder, a silent request. *Talk.* It seemed he too could feel the building tension in the room. I waved the others forward; I couldn't be the only one talking. Rori didn't attempt to hide their look of displeasure as everyone in our group stepped forward, boots squeaking on spotless white marble. Titus thrummed his fingers on the acacia desk, waiting.

"Titus, Alyx," I said, taking the time to meet both of their dark gazes. "We've come to request your help."

The two monarchs looked at each other, sharing an amused smirk.

"What?" I asked.

"We were placing bets on how long it would take you to come to us," Alyx said. "I won."

Kieron raised an eyebrow at the monarchs.

"Ty over here thought it would take two months, but I knew you were smarter than that," Alyx said with a smile.

So while we were running for our lives, the monarchs were betting on how long it would take me to get here. Somehow, I wasn't surprised. And somehow, it made me feel a little bit better. They were still my friends. But I couldn't dwell on the warm and fuzzy feeling. We had come here for a reason.

Val cleared his throat, gathering everyone's attention.

"If I may, Your Majesties, we are operating on a tight time frame and I think we should get right to business," he said.

"Of course," Titus said, but I could still see the subtle spark of amusement in his eyes. "Yorena, would you care to explain why you and your friends traveled all this way?"

"Friends is pushing it," Rori muttered.

"I'm assuming you two know about what happened in Erea?" I asked, ignoring Rori.

Alyx sat on the arm of the ivory upholstered desk chair as Titus wrapped an arm around his hips. I briefly imagined what it would be like to love that easily, to have the person you care about most always within arm's reach.

"All we know is that your parents were killed. Our condolences. And some girl apparently took over the throne? It boggles the mind," Titus said.

A very loose description of what actually happened, but at least I didn't have to explain everything. I quickly recounted the events of the last several weeks to the monarchs, taking care to protect Ilise as much as I could. None of this was her fault, and I didn't need to make her look guilty of treason.

"So the takeaway here is that, Erea is a mess, and the entire kingdom is out for your heads," Alyx said. It sounded only slightly more hopeless when he summed it up like that.

"Basically," I murmured. "And we request Croaga's help to take back our kingdom whether it be through soldiers or resources."

Titus tugged on the sleeve of his husband's blue robes. Alyx leaned down.

"Should we tell them?" Titus whispered.

"Tell us what, Your Majesties?" Val asked. "Did something happen in Erea that we don't know about?"

News usually traveled quickly between villages between air messages and word from traders. But to another kingdom? We should've heard if something bad had occurred.

"*Queen* Ilise is due to arrive in Rimed within a few days," Titus said.

Ilise was coming here? What could she gain from traveling this far? Why would she leave the kingdom Imogen had only recently forced her to take over?

"Why?" Kass said, striding up to the monarchs' desk. The monarchs shrugged.

My tongue rested uncomfortably in my mouth, dry. I should have been wondering whether the monarchs of Croaga were in fact as firmly on my side as I had originally hoped, but instead, all I could think was that Ilise would be here in a few days. I would see her again in a few days. My heart sped up at the thought for the exact opposite reason it should. Ilise wasn't the one to blame. It wasn't her fault Imogen had forced her to become a monster wearing the face so many of us here cared about. If she saw me, I would be captured. And if she saw any of the others, she would have them killed. All logical reasons I should be terrified at the thought of her coming here. But I needed to see her, I craved it.

"We'll make sure to give you rooms on separate sides of the castle," Alyx said. "And we will bring your request for our help in your mission before the council."

I curtsied. "Thank you, Your Majesties," I said. I looked back to Kieron and Val, pure relief on the brothers' faces. I wished I could feel the same relief. All I could think about was seeing Ilise again. Thinking of the purple cracks through her beautiful eyes was like a punch to the chest. Too many people had hurt her in the past, myself included. I couldn't do anything about what had happened before, but the person responsible for hurting her this time would be within my reach. Imogen wouldn't evade my grasp again.

Two guards opened the doors to the study, their iron-tipped spears gleaming in the sunlight.

"My guards will escort you all to your guest rooms," Titus said. "But Yorena, please stay for a moment."

Kieron shot me a questioning look. I gave him a subtle shake of my head. He filed out the door with the others.

Val was last to leave.

"We'll all be in my room once you're dismissed," he said as he left.

I nodded. The door closed with a soft click, and I was left alone with the monarchs. They stared at me, expectantly. I tried to think of what they wanted from me. Alyx had a tendency to... pry. He always had an inherent need to know the whole story, as if the world would end if he didn't know every small detail. It'd been like this since I first started writing to him. Even through letters, he could tell when I wasn't saying something either because I felt too embarrassed, or I felt like he wouldn't care. But he cared, almost too much. It was sweet, but overbearing at times.

One time I'd been writing to him about how much I wanted to sit in on one of the council meetings, but my "parents" still refused me. I didn't tell him I'd ended up sneaking in anyway, and instead told him I was sad about being left alone in my room. I could still remember the exact letter he wrote back: *That was an unconvincing lie, now tell me what you really did.*

"You know what I'm going to ask you?" Alyx asked.

Of course I knew what he was going to ask. But I could barely say the truth to myself, let alone him and Titus.

"Do I have to answer that question?"

Alyx shot me a look, the meaning clear. *Really?*

I sighed. "So what do you think I'm lying about this time?"

Alyx stood from his husband's chair, swinging an arm around me as he walked me toward the glass wall. The waves had calmed down so they just barely frothed the water with each crash. Pelicans and seagulls cawed as they darted through the sky.

"I wouldn't say you're lying per se," Alyx began, "But I think you're leaving out some details, specifically about this Ilise girl."

I stiffened.

"It appears I'm correct," he said.

"I suggest you tell him what he wants to know, or else we'll be here all day," Titus said. "I would know," he said with an amused smirk.

But they didn't know Ilise, they didn't know her heart. If I told them everything, they might see *her* as the enemy. She hadn't had a choice in this, she didn't deserve to be punished for Imogen's plans. I clamped my lips shut, unwilling to say anything.

"Yorena," Alyx said, softer. "You can tell us."

I took a deep breath.

"It wasn't her fault," I said finally.

"I'm failing to see how a palace takeover can be done unintentionally," Alyx remarked.

"It was like Imogen—she's a powerful sorceress in our kingdom—took control of her soul or something so Ilise would do her dirty work for her." I looked back at the monarchs, their dark skin blanched. "Is something wrong?"

"Oslu Isezsre," Titus said absently.

What?

"I apologize, my Croagi is quite rusty," I said.

Was this a Croagi name for sorcerers? Yes, sorcerers could be terrifying, but I'd never seen anyone that afraid of simply hearing about one. And they hadn't had this reaction when I told them Imogen was a sorceress in the first place.

"Oslu Isezre, Soul Seizers," Alyx said, taking a dazed step back. "I thought they were mere children's stories, a myth."

If only they were.

"You might have heard them be called Imdn Lmetsre, Mind Melters," Titus said as he rose from the chair.

I felt like I'd heard the name once before, but it must have been years ago. Erea called them all sorcerers, no matter how powerful they were. But Croaga had the right idea to give beings like Imogen a different name.

"Well, it sounds like Imogen is one of those, and I'm willing to bet she will be in your castle in a few days," I said. "She rarely leaves Ilise's side."

Alyx gulped and Titus grabbed his hand, giving it a reassuring squeeze.

"Now that we've gotten that unfortunate piece of news out of the way," Titus said, trying to veer the conversation for Alyx's sake, "Tell us about why she took over this girl, Ilise, specifically."

"She wanted her because Ilise has control over both air and fire. She's more powerful than most, but is still less powerful than Imogen, so she was controllable."

It sickened me to think of Ilise that way, a mere weapon in Imogen's war. From the brief time I'd seen her after her transformation, I could tell the power I'd seen her wield was only a small fraction of what she could do. She was already strong on her own, stronger than anyone I knew, but now she would be nearly unstoppable.

"And now Imogen has a double crystal puppet at her fingertips," I said.

My fist clenched. Imogen would pay for this, and it would be by my hand.

"You seem quite fond of this Ilise," Alyx said.

"She's my friend."

Alyx gave his husband a knowing look.

"What?"

"I think she's more than a friend," he said.

My face heated.

"You love her, don't you?"

I wouldn't go as far as saying I loved her. Cared about, sure, loved...

I just wanted to make her the happiest person in the kingdom, and that started with ensuring the people who had hurt her most could never do so again. Especially the man in charge of the group who'd put those scars on her arms, the ones she rarely showed to anyone. And sure, my heart sped up thinking of being able to hold her again, being able to be on the receiving end of one of her rare smiles. I felt sick every time I thought about the type of person Imogen was forcing her to be. And if I closed my eyes, I could easily see the golden flecks that had appeared in her eyes when she'd first used fire, the sharp but subtle curve of her jaw, the plump bow of her lips.

I cleared my throat and forced my traitorous heart to slow down.

"This does not seem like the *appropriate* conversation to be having considering our circumstances," I said.

Alyx gave me a knowing look.

"Fair, you're dismissed. Your rooms are on the first floor, turn left once you reach the bottom of the steps."

I could tell Titus was hiding a little smile behind his hand, but this was no laughing matter. I left the room and hurried through the bright halls. They would be making plans for Ilise's arrival by now, and I didn't want to miss any of the preparations. I turned left at the bottom of the large staircase and entered another corridor. This was the first hall in this castle that didn't have windows on almost all sides. Soft torchlight lit the ivory-colored corridor, more vines wrapping around the regularly spaced white stone columns.

Was I really that transparent? Alyx and Titus had been able to see how I felt about Ilise within a few minutes of seeing me. It was like my heart was being laid bare. But I would endure whatever conversation those two could come up with if it increased our chances of receiving aid.

The faint sound of voices carried from the end of the hall. I followed them. I reached the farthest forest green door and opened a crack to see the others all sitting on the rug in the center of the room. I was about to walk in when Rori's words stopped me in my tracks.

"She's holding us back, we should just leave her," they grunted.

Are they talking about me? I pressed my ear to the door as close as I dared.

"She managed to get us into Croaga, you should give her at least some credit," Kieron said.

"But she's part of the reason why we even had to come here in the first place," Rori shot back.

It wasn't like I'd *allowed* Imogen to use Ilise to take over Erea. I tried to help stop her. I tried to save her, but I failed.

"It's Imogen's fault we're stuck here, Yorena is not to blame," Chafik said.

At least I had some people on my side. I knew Rori was not a fan, but I didn't think their hate ran deep enough for them to want me gone.

"You guys have to admit, she was barely able to take care of that guard when the squad attacked us," Kass said.

Kass too?

"See, Kass agrees with me," Rori said. "She even got Orla killed!"

My heart stopped. My tongue sat like a dry, heavy lump in the back of my mouth. Orla had helped me get out of the fire. I was immune to fire. She should've been the one to go first. She should've been the first to taste the fresh cool air after breathing in all that horrible black smoke. Orla's death was my fault. Her blood would forever be on my hands. I hadn't helped her, just like I hadn't helped Ilise when she needed me. She'd begged for me to see how corrupt Erea was becoming the night Aerilyn was killed, and I'd dismissed her. I'd refused to believe her and she'd run away. But there was still a kingdom full of innocent people that I *could* help.

I steeled myself, wearing the face of an unfazed Princess, a face I hadn't used in a while, now. The door opened with a loud creak and my companions all froze as I came into view.

"I think most would agree with me when I say that deciding someone else's fate while they were being held up by the monarchs is quite rude," I said.

Mathias hid a grin behind his hand.

"And unless one of you was raised to be the ruler of Erea, like I was, I think it's best you don't leave me behind."

Rori stepped up to me, close enough that they had to tilt their head up to look me in the eye.

"I think most would agree with me when I say you shouldn't be acting so smug. After all, you've only made our lives worse from the moment we met you."

I gritted my teeth. I was human; humans made mistakes. Just because I was brought up as a princess didn't mean I wasn't going to make mistakes. I'd had to learn that the hard way. I had no way of fixing the monumental mistakes I've made, but that didn't warrant their pure disgust toward me.

"I've only been trying to help all of you," I pleaded.

The few people I dared to look at as I spoke seemed unconvinced.

"This is what you call help? I'm almost terrified to imagine what you would be like as Queen." Tears sprang to Rori's eyes as they spoke. I tried to think of something to say, anything. Or maybe just give them a hug. But I could tell that was the last thing they wanted. The others stepped forward warily, not sure if Rori was a few seconds from breaking down, or from attacking me. The words I had yet to speak lodged in my throat. How could I say anything to make up for all the damage I'd caused?

"I tried," I said.

Like blowing out a torch, all the heartbreak that was in Rori's eyes moments before vanished, replaced by a fiery anger I was all too familiar with.

"You tried? Is that all you have to say for yourself?"

I opened my mouth but nothing came out. It was all I could say for my-self—those two measly words.

"Maybe we all need a second to calm down, and we'll revisit this conversation later," Chafik suggested.

Rori turned on him, causing him to scurry backward with a single look, one that held the promise of violence.

"I will *not* be told when to calm down," they said in a low voice.

Rori whirled back around to me.

"And you."

I squinted at the light of their crystal as they dragged me forward with a ring of air. I struggled to loosen my arms, but they only tightened the stream more with every struggle. Kieron rushed forward to stop Rori, but they blew him against the wall with another gust of wind. The air was slowly pushed out of my lungs. Tiny spots danced in my vision.

As I desperately looked around for an ally, I saw Chafik take a transfixed Mathias by the arm to the same side of the room as where Kieron stood. Kass and Val slowly made their way toward Rori, arms up.

"Rori, let her go," Val said soothingly.

"I'm tired of having to get along with a spoiled brat," Rori spat. "She is part of the same family that's been screwing us over for years."

"I was a child," I choked out. "Any harm the past King and Queen caused you was not by any fault of mine."

I was not them. I was here, in a foreign kingdom because I was wanted in my own, working with a group of people who would rather see me meet the same fate as my "parents" than work with me, because I wanted to be better. Each new attack Rori delivered made the growing pit in my stomach deepen. I could taste their hate on my tongue. I could feel the old doubts vibrating in my chest—that I was no better than the past monarchs and I would never be a decent Queen. It suffocated me, threatening to drown me.

I could not succumb to it now.

They dragged me across the smooth marble until I was only a foot in front of them. Their hazel eyes bore into mine.

"Do you have anything to say for yourself?"

"It would be easier to speak if you weren't trying to squeeze me to death," I managed to choke out.

A muscle in their jaw twitched before they released me. I slumped onto the floor, sucking in lungfuls of air.

"Speak."

I stumbled as I pushed myself off the ground. The room still spun, but I was able to keep my balance.

"You may not like me, in fact, you may hate me, and I don't really care. But we are all working toward a common goal. You think I don't feel bad about every way I have messed up in the last week alone? It's all I can think about. I can't sleep without seeing Orla's last moments, seeing the ways I could've saved her...the ways I could've taken her place. And every day I re-live Ilise being turned into the last thing she wants to be."

I paused, holding back the tears that ached to fall. I wouldn't win this through pity.

"You need me whether you want to accept it or not. None of you have been training to be Queen your whole life. But me? It's my only purpose, the only thing I know I can do. I know it doesn't look like it to you, but Erea is one of the things I care most about. And I hate what's become of it just as much as you do.

"I know nothing I have experienced comes close to what you have had to go through," I said to Rori.

I looked around the room.

"What any of you have had to go through. But just know I'm trying to understand, and that I want nothing more than to transform Erea into the greatest version of itself I know it can be. The version all of you have been trying to turn it into."

The room was silent save for the whisperings of wind outside the window. I stretched my hand to Rori.

"Can we try to work together?"

Rori stared at my hand, considering. They said nothing as they stepped forward, face set. They didn't shake my hand, but instead whispered, "Fine."

"Now that we've moved past the homicidal rage portion of our evening," Chafik began, "Why don't we start looking through the books we found."

Mathias groaned. "Only you would be able to follow something so exciting with something so incredibly dull," he said.

Chapter 19

Ilise

THE CARRIAGE RATTLED ACROSS bumpy cobblestones as the gentle plains of Newnina gradually gave way to the swaying grasslands of Faveru. After the first hour, Oliver dozed off in the seat across from mine. And after the second hour, Nikos followed. Imogen stared out the window, the same smile plastered on her wrinkled face. It was foreign to see her smiling so much. I must have been doing a good job.

Maybe to her.

My only real company was the incessant voice in my head. It kept trying to convince me to order the driver to turn around and reverse all of my recent policies. I had to hand it to them, whichever one of my enemies had sent this voice certainly was persistent.

Turn around.

I would not turn around. I was growing closer to the payoff for all my pain—my reward for enduring all who had hurt me, and those who had yet to. I took the golden circlet off my head and fiddled with the delicate gold vines. I hardly felt like a Queen at this point. Half my kingdom wanted me off the throne, two of our neighboring kingdoms refused to engage with me, and I had to be stuck in a cramped carriage for days just to get recognized as Queen by the Croagi monarchs. How come I had to work and fight for my crown when the ones before me could hardly be called qualified and were *still* welcomed with open arms?

If I remembered correctly, my false father had originally been from Croaga. I even remembered a few words in Old Croagi, though I was sure they didn't speak that anymore. Except for that one phrase. The phrase I'd told to Yorena in my poisoned delirium.

Miel rof em ym sra. Ilth et yaw rof I aev olt mesfl ot oy. Ot oyru adkrenss, ebuatilu ni et yaw lla civisuo hisg era. Oyru adr ised of et sra, ym sra.

Smile for me, my star. Light the way for I have lost myself to you. To your darkness, beautiful in the way all vicious things are. Your dark side of the star, my star.

I shouldn't think about her. I would find her in due time. There were only so many places she could hide from me. I would find her in Croaga, even if I had to tear the whole kingdom apart to do it.

And I wouldn't hesitate to.

Once the sun dipped below the horizon, we stopped for a quick break. Stars dotted the cloudless sky when I hopped out of the carriage, my legs sore from sitting down for so long. I had elected to wear my old mission suit. The smooth leather was plastered to my skin from the warm carriage. There was no telling what to expect on this journey.

I was glad for it as the cold wind slapped my face, a biting chill rolling through the night. I rubbed my gloved hands together as the sun stole away, along with the last of the warmth. The rest of my company stepped out of the carriage.

"Nikos, grow some wood for me to burn," I ordered. I hadn't spent the majority of my life as a powerless nobody, only to spend the beginning of my reign freezing.

Green light was the only thing illuminating the ground around us as a small tree sprouted from the ground. The thick trunk would last most of the night, but we wouldn't be here for long. I lit the tree on fire, its warmth seeping into my bones. He sat on the ground, staring into the crackling flames. I would never understand that boy, but at least he was obeying me for once.

"How much farther are we from Rimed?" Oliver asked.

"If we make haste, less than a day," Imogen said.

She appeared beside me as if she'd solidified out of thin air, making me jump. I hated when she did that.

"Walk with me," she said. She stalked off toward the carriage and I had no choice but to follow after her fluttering robes. She blew open the door, and we stepped up into the velvet interior, I sat across from her.

"What do you want?" I asked. I was sick of being in the carriage, after all the travel we had done.

Imogen crossed her legs and leaned into the soft seat back, a serene calm on her face I'd never seen before.

"We need to discuss possible distractions waiting for you at the castle."

Distractions? Nothing would distract me from ensuring the monarchs recognize me as Queen. It was all I needed to fully take control of Erea and morph it into the greatest kingdom it could possibly be.

"There's a high chance Yorena is at the castle, and you cannot allow her to distract you," she said.

"She won't distract me, but that doesn't mean I won't make her come back with us."

Imogen sighed. "We are not traveling to Croaga so you can get your Princess back. She should not be on your mind once we arrive."

But it was the perfect time to have her on my mind. Right now, Yorena was out of her element. After living a life sheltered in the palace, she wouldn't last very long on her own, and the Union rebels she ran off with would soon grow restless having to take care of her. Capturing her in Croaga would be ideal.

"And why would she make herself known to you?" Imogen retorted. "If the monarchs allowed her into the castle, they would have told her about your impending arrival."

But Yorena still cared about me, I knew she did. And I'd learned that she never knew when to quit. If she knew I was due to arrive, she would seek me out, no matter how idiotic that plan may be.

"You don't know her like I do," I responded.

Imogen shrugged. "Fine. Let yourself be distracted by a pretty face, see how far that will get you as Queen."

Quiet anger blossomed in my chest. Yorena was more than just a pretty face, and she wouldn't be reduced to such.

"Careful how you refer to her," I said in a low voice.

In the blink of an eye, Imogen wrapped a ring of air around my neck and squeezed, hard. I could finally see her full face in the white light of the crystal. I struggled to fight her with my own crystal; she was stronger. Black spots blotted out sections of the carriage. I resorted to clawing at my neck and to no avail.

"You forget your place, little one," Imogen mused.

Chapter 20

Nikos

"Y OU REALLY OUGHT TO hide your displeasure better," Oliver remarked.

Grass scratched at my skin and the fire Ilise had made did almost nothing to combat the biting chill in the air. It was only September. It shouldn't be this cold already.

"And *you* really ought to not blindly follow the lead of two madwomen."

They let out a short laugh.

I shouldn't be here. I should be in New Teber, making sure they didn't hurt Daeva. There was no telling what they might put her through in my absence, and I wouldn't be able to do anything to stop them. Ilise had nothing to gain by bringing me. She likely wanted to separate me from Daeva as a punishment of some sort, but who knew what went on in that girl's head.

I'd planned on Ilise taking Daeva with us to have something to hold over my head. Then we could have slipped away on the way to the Rimed castle, or we could have run from the castle and made a new life for ourselves near the jungle. It would have also gotten me out of Oliver's third request. They hadn't decided what that would be yet. Though the longer they made me wait, the worse the scenarios my mind conjured.

"Well, the 'madwomen' are on the winning side," they said.

Highly debatable. Assuming Yorena used my small act of help to her advantage, she would make a formidable opponent. I'd underestimated her during our time as competitors, and I would not make that mistake again.

They would all regret what they've put me through. Imogen, Oliver, Ilise, my father, all of them. Half of them were hardly people who should be causing me all these issues. Oliver was a follower. They were like a tiny bug, attracted to the brightest light they could find at any given time. How someone could be content to live a life like that, I would never grasp. As far as I knew, they weren't even forced into this. No, helping The Progression was their whole life.

Sad.

Ilise and Imogen returned from the carriage. Part of me was curious as to what they had discussed, but the more sensible part of me knew it would be of no help to me. Ilise sat far from the flames, a spooked expression on her face. Imogen paced around the fire. That was something I'd noticed about the old sorceress, she was always pacing. Always watching over us like a hawk would its prey.

It was in little ways like that I was constantly reminded of my place. I wasn't in Nitedand anymore, so I didn't have an army of supporters behind me. I was something to be controlled, put on a leash, out of fear I would foil any plans my opponents may have. Still, I couldn't allow myself to fall into a pit of self-pity. Daeva needed me at my best to stay safe. I was doing this for her, and only her. I would wait, quietly. Then I would strike. I just had to observe, and wait for the perfect opportunity to get us out of here, and far from Erea. Far from my father, the Union, and The Progression. I would find somewhere we could live out the rest of our lives without ever having to hear about either of those spiritsdamned organizations again.

Grass rustled, and then there was Ilise, standing before us, looking down at us with her unsettling cracked irises nearly glowing.

"Oliver, Nikos, once we're inside the castle, I need you two to look for Yorena and the Union rebels she ran off with."

Ugh. If Yorena had even an ounce of common sense, she would have left the castle already. Assuming that was where she even was. I hadn't attempted to keep track of her movements, and I prayed to the Spirits that she was far from the castle. Yorena, or more so the need to find her, was likely the only part of Ilise's humanity that was left. If she was captured, Daeva and I needed to be as far away from what Ilise would become after getting Yorena back.

"We leave in two hours," Ilise said.

The driver of our carriage, an old, graying Water Imperium man who could hardly walk without shaking, tapped Ilise on the shoulder. She whirled on him. *Big mistake.*

"Your Majesty, if it would not be too much of an inconvenience, could we leave later? I would just like some more time to rest."

His pale skin blanched and I would swear on my life the man physically withered from Ilise's stare.

"If I wanted your opinion I would have asked, old man," she sneered.

The man shook as he bowed to her.

"My apologies, Your Majesty," he said. "I meant no offense."

He stumbled back to the carriage and fell asleep the moment he was settled into the front seat. Ilise didn't have to scream at an innocent old man for requesting a delay, hells, the request had been on the tip of my tongue, too. I stood and brushed the cold dirt from my black pants.

"I will rest in the carriage," I said.

Ilise waved me away and sat, staring into the fire again. *What is this girl's problem?*

I awoke with a start as the carriage jerked from the dirt road onto a cobblestone street. Ocean waves crashed against the jagged rocks on the coast as the bright castle came into view, orange light blinding my eyes. I returned my attention back to the carriage and found Ilise already staring at me.

"Remember your assignment," was all she said before turning her attention to the window.

Spirits help me.

Chapter 21

Yorena

I worked through the night, staying awake on nothing but pure adrenaline, combing through the single book we had managed to take from the Archives. Tiredness remained on the edges of my vision, and occasionally I could feel myself beginning to nod off. But I couldn't sleep. Wouldn't sleep. Not until I found something to help Ilise and Erea. Orange light shone through the cracks in the curtains, washing the room in its soft light. Everyone's soft snores were the only sound, aside from the careful flipping of the delicate pages.

Page after page, section after section, and not one piece of useful information aside from the one chapter about sorcerers' powers. There had to be more in here besides that one chapter I'd already read through at least a dozen times. Tired grumbling filled the room as the others began to wake up. Maybe they could help me decipher the passage. It may have been in the language of our time, but it was phrased in such a way that it was as if the author was *trying* to confuse me.

We'd all come to an uneasy truce after Rori's outburst yesterday, but we were far from being able to call each other friends. Chafik stretched from where he rested on the chaise lounge, rubbing his sleepy eyes.

"Chafik," I whispered to not disturb the others.

His eyes locked on me and he ambled to my spot on the floor.

"Can you help me decipher what this says?"

"Is it in a foreign language?" he asked in a rough voice.

I handed him the heavy tome and showed him the passage.

"No, but it's phrased really weirdly."

Slowly, the rest of our group migrated to me and Chafik. Kieron's chin dug into my shoulder as he looked at the book.

"Did you find something?" he said, yawning.

I shook my head. "Not unless this spirtsdamned passage turns out to be helpful."

"If it turns out to be helpful you can wake me up again," Mathias said from the chaise before falling back asleep.

"Why don't you read it out loud so we can all try," Val said.

I took back the book and cleared my parched throat before starting, sleep threatening to take me.

"A soul is not one object, a soul is everything and nothing in our world. Sorcerers take this to heart. And through that knowledge, they can mold the soul how they see fit. Nearly limitless are the possibilities, not through every breadth, but still through the limits of their own minds. Only through the power of the five crystals can they accomplish this feat, allowing them to wield the Soul Spirit's Sword."

"What in four hells does that mean?" Rori grumbled.

A tiny headache attacked the base of my skull, the dull throbbing almost like a weaker heartbeat. I would rest soon, we just needed to figure out what this meant.

"Soul Spirit's Sword?" Kieron repeated.

"I don't think that's the information we need, but it could be in reference to the Soul Spirit's will," Cain said.

What did this have to do with the limitations of sorcerers' powers? There had to be something that would be a hindrance to sorcerers. Not even they could be more powerful than the laws of nature.

"The book said *nearly* limitless," Kass began, "so there is a limit to their powers."

"Read the whole sentence again," Val said.

Chafik took the book from my hands.

"Nearly limitless are the possibilities, not through every breadth, but still through the limits of their own minds," he said.

It made even less sense the second time.

"Could it mean the only limit they have is if they psych themselves out or something?" I offered.

"I'm pretty sure that's a limit for every Imperium, Princess," Rori said.

And here I was thinking I would escape that annoying nickname.

"I doubt Imogen has the capacity to be psyched out," they said.

They were right. Imogen had too much confidence to be psyched out. She was endlessly more powerful and skilled than we were; and she knew it. She danced the thin line between confidence and cockiness, and yet she never allowed it to slip into arrogance. Our job would be a lot easier if she would.

The part of the sentence that made it most difficult to understand was the middle portion: "not through every breadth".

If the author had been talking about a sorcerer's breathing, wouldn't they have written "breath"? "Breadth" was typically used when we were talking about how wide something was. What did width have to do with sorcerers' abilities?

"Does breadth have any other definitions beside width?" I asked.

Chafik chewed on his lower lip, thinking. "Not that I know of," he said.

Cain snapped his fingers, a look of revelation on his face.

"In older writings, they primarily used the word to describe distance," he said. "'Nearly limitless are the possibilities, not through every breadth.' The book is saying the almost limitless possibilities do not apply when it comes to distance."

Of course. Their power must diminish the farther the distance between them and the soul they're controlling. Ilise had said Imogen could sense her whan she was close, so we just needed to get Ilise outside the range of Imogen's weird sixth sense.

"But didn't Imogen contact Ilise before she even got to the palace?" Val asked.

"She did, but the palace wasn't that far from where we were," Cain said. "It probably needs to be a much greater distance than a days' walk away."

But how would we get Ilise that far away from Imogen? After all the trouble Imogen went through to get Ilise, she wouldn't let us just take her. Ilise would fight us on it because what Imogen wants, she wants for a reason. And right now, that reason was to bring ruin to the kingdom and kill us in the process.

"Is there somewhere we could even take her at this point?" Kass said. "It was hard enough to get just us over the border."

"Couldn't you guys overpower her?" Kieron said. Everyone stared directly at him and I pushed his chin off my shoulder. "She can't be *that* powerful."

Val rubbed his forehead as if his brother's statement was mind-numbingly stupid.

"She has control over two crystals, half of us have none," Val said.

At that, Kieron clamped his lips shut.

"Can't you just knock her out with a rock or something," Mathias suggested from the chaise. Chafik shook his head at him. Technically, it would work, but not for very long. Also, a very angry Ilise would be the next thing on our list of problems once she awoke. There had to be something else, something that would give us an edge over Ilise's crystals.

"You wake up to join the discussion and *that's* the first thing you say?" Chafik said. Mathias shrugged and shifted so his back was to us once more.

A knock sounded at the door.

"Come in," Val said.

King Titus walked into the room. It was peculiar how he and Alyx never had a guard escort them through the castle. Even before everything fell apart, there had been no less than two guards surrounding my "parents".

"Good morning, friends," Titus said. "Ilise has arrived, and has been put in the rooms on the top floor." *Ilise is here.* Ilise was just a couple floors above me, after running from her for so long.

It was as if Kieron could read my thoughts, because he said, "Don't even think about it, Yorena." I wasn't going to go looking for her, no matter how much part of me screamed for me to. She was under Imogen's control, and there was no telling what she would do once she finally captured me.

"I'm not crazy," I said. Kieron shot me a knowing look. "Ok, I'm not *that* crazy."

"Accusations of insanity aside," Titus said, "We have called an emergency council meeting today, and you all should have your answer by the day's end."

Thank the Spirits. The sooner we got support from Croaga, the sooner we could take back Erea. And I could take back Ilise.

"Thank you, Your Majesty," Val said.

"You're welcome. And please, call me Titus."

Without another word, Titus left the room.

Mathias finally rose from the chaise and joined us on the floor.

"What's the plan for today?" he asked.

"The plan is to stay out of Ilise and Imogen's sight until we figure out how to get her away from Imogen," Val said. We were in for a boring day. We'd already figured out the only information the book offered, and there was no telling where Ilise and Imogen would be. It wasn't like they were the ones confined to their rooms.

Mathias spread out on the floor, using his arm as a pillow.

"Wake me when something interesting happens," he said.

The others spread out across the room, finding something to pass the time. Val and Kass sat huddled together, speaking in hushed tones. Rori took over the plush bed and Cain hovered over them, while Rori tried to unsuccessfully tune out the pair droning on about sorcerers. And Chafik was poring over the rest of the archive book. I knew he knew there was nothing else that could be of use to us, and I was sure he was reading for pure enjoyment.

Kieron bumped my shoulder. "So what do you wanna do while we wait?" All I knew was, I couldn't sit here and do nothing all day. I could go into the garden, but Ilise also liked gardens. Well maybe Imogen-controlled Ilise didn't, but we couldn't take the chance.

"Follow me," a voice whispered. My head whipped toward the door.

"Did you hear that?"

Kieron looked around the mostly quiet room, confused. "Hear what?" That was the same voice I'd heard near the temple ruins. It had told me it would reveal itself soon. Maybe this was that time.

"Remember those whispers we heard that night in the forest that led us to an old temple?"

"The whispers that had me tempted to tie you to a tree before you got yourself killed? Yes, I remember."

"Unneeded comments aside, I think the voice was coming from inside the temple."

He nodded his head slowly. "I thought you said you weren't crazy," he said.

I slapped his shoulder. "I just heard the voice again. And it told me to follow it."

Kieron groaned. "Are you taking me on another wild goose chase?"

I smiled, pulling him and myself up from the floor.

"We'll see."

"Follow me."

We left the room and I led Kieron in the direction of the voice. I wondered if this was what it'd been like for Ilise when she first heard Imogen's voice. I knew it couldn't be Imogen, since I first heard it when we were farther than what should be the limits of her power. And this voice had only started when I was close to the temple. The voice was darker than Imogen's, yet it was inviting, warm—the antithesis of everything Imogen was.

"This way."

The voice was growing louder—I must've been getting closer. The voice led us through the bright halls of the castle. Windows gave way to pale stone; the yellow glow of the sun gave way to the orange light of candle chandeliers. We reached the end of the hall and halted when we were met with stairs.

"Don't stop. Follow me for the answers you seek."

I started to walk, but Kieron stopped me with a strong arm.

"Titus told us to avoid the upper floors," he said.

But something told me this voice wasn't leading us to Ilise. Maybe there was another place of information we didn't know about in the castle. Maybe even a place Titus and Alyx didn't know about. No one had known about the music room in the Erean palace until I'd discovered it. Maybe the Croagi castle had something similar, something that would help us.

I pushed Kieron's arm to the side and bounded up the marble steps. He grumbled in complaint behind me, but followed anyway. At the top of the stairs, we were met with three diverging hallways. I leaned toward each one to see where the voice was the loudest.

"To the left," the voice said.

I took Kieron by the wrist and pulled him into the left corridor.

"This is a bad idea," he said.

"Yet, you came," I shot back. He clamped his mouth shut after that.

"Your answers are in the room at the end of the hall."

I hurried to the last door, but paused when I noticed it was already ajar. Frustrated grunts emanated from the crack between door and frame. I put a finger to my lips and Kieron nodded in understanding.

It had been so long since I'd last seen her, but I knew instantly who was inside when my eyes landed on a familiar shaven head. Kieron inhaled sharply behind me, but I ignored him. I watched the figure train from the small crack in the door. She tossed aside giant blocks of wood like they weighed nothing more than a feather, the blocks crumbling into tiny pieces upon impact with the wall. She even floated herself above the ground with a ring of air. Everything she did was so effortless.

It was terrifying.

This was the strength Imogen had under her control—the ferocity. Ilise had already been a ruthless opponent after training with the Union for years, but this was something different, something bloodthirsty. I knew I should be scared. I should want to get as far away from her as possible. But I couldn't stop watching.

I didn't know how long I stood there watching her. I missed her so much. If I closed my eyes, I could still remember the last time I'd seen her before Imogen took her from me. She was intent on pushing me away, almost acting like she hated me, but had just been scared. Scared of losing me, or scared of the possibility Imogen would take over my throne, I still didn't know.

"We need to get out of here, *now*," Kieron whispered, gripping my arm. I glanced back at him. His neck was tense, his gray eyes wide.

I couldn't leave yet. The voice had led me here for a reason, I just needed to figure out why. With nothing left to smash, Ilise's fire crystal glowed deep orange. She stared down at her gloved hands. *What is she doing?* Slowly, she peeled off the leather gloves. She continued to stare at them longingly as they dropped to the ground.

A timid rope of fire snaked out from her hands, pooling in a flaming pile at her feet. Her hands shook the longer she held it, until it dispersed with a small puff of smoke. Eyes open wide in panic, she rubbed her hands on her clothes, as if they were still on fire. I'd thought that with the discovery of her powers, she wouldn't be as afraid of fire. Ilise dropped to the ground, frantically putting her gloves back on. Her body shook. She was terrified. Deathly scared.

Without the gloves, she couldn't hold it together..This was why the voice had led me here. I knew how to defeat Ilise.

CHAPTER 22

ILISE

I WAS WEAK. THE gloves were a crutch. I couldn't keep them on forever, and there would be a time when I would have to use my powers without them. But if I had broken down attempting to create a simple a spiritsdamned whip, how could I expect to fight without them? As I got dressed, I was close to ripping my red silk dress, stuffing my arms into the sleeves I'd had my dressmaker configure so there was no chance fire would touch my skin.

I should have been rid of all weaknesses by now. I'd rid myself of the ties I'd had with the traitorous Union, of the "connection" with the false family I'd grown up with, and I'd finally stopped living my life without powers, without any strength.

Imogen wanted me to get rid of the gloves. I knew I had to get rid of the gloves. But the fear was still there. I was *immune* to fire, yet the idea of it touching my bare skin terrified me. Depending on how well Erea would react to the Croagi monarchs recognizing me as Queen, I may have to scare them into my control. And how could I do that if all it took was a small flame for me to retreat?

"You aren't weak."

The imposter was still there.

"Leave me alone," I said.

The room melted away and I was once again pulled into my soul. *Now, I was surrounded by blackness, a blackness that was becoming familiar to me, as familiar to me as the training room of my palace. The colorful aspects of my soul immediately swarmed me and I shooed them away. I didn't want warmth right now.*

"I thought I said to leave me alone," I said.

The imposter materialized before me—an almost exact replica of how I used to look. This time, she wore the yellow servant dress that used to be my uniform.

"When have you known me to leave you alone?" she said with a sad smile. "Especially when you speak to yourself so poorly."

"You are in no position to cast judgment," I sneered.

She shrugged.

I didn't need figments of my imagination to tell me I was weak. Everything that came out of her mouth was a lie, and that was the biggest of them all.

"Send me back to reality."

The imposter clicked her tongue, circling me.

"Not until you stop calling yourself weak."

But I was. This fear of being touched by fire, even my fire, would only hinder me. It was the most powerful and most feared element, but it would be useless if I was the one most afraid of it. I looked down at my hands and was startled to see brown skin. Where had my gloves gone? I stared down at my calloused palm, marred with notches from years of training.

"What did you do to my gloves?" I shouted.

The imposter flashed a full-toothed smile.

"Just because you have a fear does not make you weak. It's what makes you human."

I wasn't trying to be human. I was going to be better than that. Being human was to be weak, and to be weak was to be the same as any other monarch Erea had had over the last millennium. I would be better than them. I wouldn't let my humanity stop me from making the necessary decisions.

"I was forced to live as a normal human for nineteen years," I said, "I will be powerless no longer."

The imposter halted and sighed. These gloves were the last thing in my way, yet I couldn't destroy them. I'd put the Primis back in their place, I'd quashed their little rebellion outside of my palace, and I was about to have my place as Queen accepted by one of our most powerful neighbors. But I was bested by my need for stupid gloves.

"Would this be a good time to ask you to stop listening to Imogen?" the imposter asked.

I narrowed my eyes on her.

She pursed her lips. "Not a good time, then. Soon, though."

A burst of light blinded me, and my guest room rematerialized before me. I lay on the marble floor, shaking. Despite myself, the imposter's words rang in my head. *You aren't weak.* I raised my gloved hands, the smooth leather taunting me. I would get these off. Eventually. They would burn, along with every other obstacle I'd demolished.

A knock sounded at my door. I scrambled from the ground and smoothed out the wrinkles on my dress.

"Enter," I said.

King Titus and Prince Consort Alyx walked in.

"Your Majesties," I said, dipping into a small curtsy. The couple waved their hands.

"There's no need for bowing," King Titus said. "And please, just call us by our names."

I nodded. They were quite peculiar. What kind of monarchs would want people to call them by their names? Wouldn't it diminish the effect of their power? Bowing was the most fundamental way to show respect.

"Because they had their crown given to them, little one," Imogen said through our bond. *"They don't have to remind the people who their leaders are."*

I hid my grimace with a sweet smile. They didn't have to fight for their crown, yet the people respected them more. Or at least enough that bowing had become redundant. I wanted that. And I would have it, once these two endorsed me. These monarchs were even more well-liked than I'd expected. This was perfect.

"To what do I owe this visit?" I asked.

The monarchs' eyes latched onto the crystals around my neck, and I smirked. It was so easy to tell when people identified me as something out of the ordinary—something dangerous.

"A ball will be thrown in your honor tonight," Alyx said. "It's our welcome gift to you."

A ball? I loathed balls. Talking to nobles who were without a doubt gossiping right under your nose, having to act like I was truly interested in whatever another guest was saying, all the speeches about hope and coming together. Blech. Though I supposed rejecting a ball thrown in my favor wasn't the proper way to get formally recognized as Queen.

"Thank you, Your Majesties. It would be my honor."

Chapter 23

Yorena

"**D**O YOU HAVE A death wish?" Rori asked.

I'd told everyone my idea of how to get Ilise away from Imogen, and it was not going well. Ilise couldn't use fire without her gloves, so all we had to do was take the gloves, and then we'd only have to deal with one element from her. A strong one, but only one nonetheless.

Titus and Alyx watched silently from the corner. I'd invited them to see what they thought, but they'd yet to say anything.

"It won't end in death if we execute it correctly," I said.

Kieron hid his face in his hands.

"I knew letting you watch her train was a bad idea," he mumbled.

I shot him a look. "I don't see any of you suggesting ideas," I said, making sure to meet each of their eyes. "Taking a pair of gloves shouldn't be too hard."

"Considering she managed to get an entire kingdom under her control in a matter of weeks, I would say she won't let us take her gloves," Rori said.

"She had Imogen to help her, and Imogen can't possibly be near Ilise at all times."

"When would we even do it?" Cain asked.

Titus and Alyx finally moved from their corner and joined us in the center of the room.

"We're throwing a ball in Ilise's honor tonight," Alyx said, crossing his arms over his black and green checkered jacket.

A ball? Balls were full of distractions; the perfect time for us to steal her gloves. And the overall chaos of a ball would help cover us while we took her from the ballroom.

Kieron shook his head at me. "I can see you thinking, you have your bad idea face on," he said.

Kass covered her mouth—to cover a smile, no doubt.

"The ball will cover us," I said. "Don't you guys agree?"

Val, Kass, and Cain all grimaced.

"*If* we were to go with your plan," Val began, "We would need to plan exactly how to take the gloves. We can't go into this blindly."

I knew I shouldn't be getting excited, but that did nothing to diminish the flames of hope sparking in my chest. They actually wanted to use an idea of mine.

"I actually think we can help," Alyx said.

We all turned to the Prince Consort.

"The council denied sending aid to your kingdom, I'm afraid," he said solemnly. "They 'don't want to endanger our soldiers in a silly war'."

What? Then how were we supposed to take back our kingdom? Ilise and Imogen had The Progression, the royal army, and an entire kingdom of resources at their fingertips. All we had were a few Imperium, an ex-guard, a couple ex-servants, and a fake princess. We were doomed.

The air quotes Alyx had used told me he didn't agree with the council's decision, but there wasn't anything he could do about it. Unlike Erea, Croaga used a council to make decisions. On one hand, it made things fair, but on the other hand, it never worked in your favor when you needed it to.

"If your council said no, then how can you help us?" Cain asked.

Alyx cracked his knuckles repeatedly, and Titus took his hand to calm him. *What is he nervous about?*

"I can't help you fight, but I can help you get the gloves," he said.

We all looked at him, confused.

"Love, she looked like she would kill us as readily as she would a fly when we talked to her. I don't think she'll appreciate you taking her gloves," Titus said.

That sounded like Ilise. She was like that even before Imogen had changed her. Alyx leaned into Titus' ear to whisper something, and Titus' dark skin blanched.

"Absolutely not," he said.

The others looked at me for answers, and I shrugged.

"I know someone who can help you," Alyx said.

Titus turned to him, a warning etched in his eyes.

"I'd sooner throw myself into the Fire Spirit's hell than let her out again," he fumed.

Her? Who could make Titus of all people blanch with fear? He hadn't been nearly as afraid when he'd talked about Imogen, and who could be worse than her?

"Let who out?" Rori asked.

"Follow me," Alyx responded.

We all trailed after him, out of the room. We were led down to the lowest levels of the castle. Bright windows gave way to dark stone, and eventually a narrow hallway lit only by torchlights. Damp air swirled around us, and I assumed we were in the dungeons. Were we getting help from a criminal? Alyx nodded to the single guard stationed in front of an iron door and we were led into another hallway, the Earth Imperium guard trailing close behind. He stopped us in front of a wall of stone. *Is this the door?* There wasn't a single seam, a single crack to mark this as an entrance to a cell.

I wondered who could be locked inside. Maybe it was a serial killer they'd barely caught, or the leader of a gang. Or it could be a sorcerer of a similar caliber to Imogen that they'd somehow managed to lock up.

"Let us in," Alyx said.

The guard's green crystal glowed and the outline of a door appeared in the wall, sliding to the side. He held a spear at the ready for whoever resided inside. My mind was blown when we entered a room that looked much like the guest rooms, minus any windows. The white stone floor was covered in fur rugs, and chandeliers blazed around the room. A plush canopy bed with notches carved into the posts sat in the corner with a small figure laying on top.

"Isidora," Alyx said.

The girl turned to face him with an annoyed look on her face. Her ebony skin glowed in the candlelight, her eyes black as night. The silver strands streaked through her thick black braid were like shards of moonlight. She almost looked familiar, with her rounded face and blue-flecked eyes. Titus was visibility tensed, his arms tight at his sides and his face set. Though it didn't escape my notice how he stood slightly in front of Alyx, taking a protective position in front of his husband.

"Everyone, meet my niece," Alyx said.

He has a niece?

Isidora flashed a sinister smile. "To what do I owe a visit from my dear old uncle?"

She stood from the bed to look us in the eye. She was quite short, barely reaching my shoulder if she were closer to me. *What is such a small girl doing in here?* She wore a white tunic and beige trousers; not what women in Croaga typically wore.

"We need your help," Alyx said.

Isidora raised her eyebrows. "*My* help? Why would you need the help of a lowly criminal you can't even bring yourself to visit every once in a while?"

"Why are you in here?" I asked.

Part of me wished it was for a lot of small crimes rather than something big like murder. Erea didn't have a lot of options left, and I doubted someone like that would be our savior.

Her dark gaze landed on me and a chill ran down my spine.

"Alyx over here locked me up for a few *measly* crimes."

Titus exploded before Alyx could respond.

"Measly?" he fumed. "You killed twenty people and robbed half of Rimed within a two month period!"

The girl shrugged.

Great. Alyx thought our best chance at taking Ilise away from Imogen was a murderer. I just *had* to think she was a murderer.

"Ok, I like her," Rori said.

"I thought the pinky was punishment enough, *uncle*."

Titus bristled, but showed no other reaction to her tone.

Isidora wiggled her right hand, revealing that the top of her pinky had been cut off, leaving only a short nub. She didn't look that threatening, but the same could have been said for Ilise. Isidora had a thickset build, probably with more muscle than Chafik and Mathias combined. And her compact form *would* allow her to slip away at a moment's notice when stealing. And if the notches on the bed were any indication, she was stronger than she appeared. I recognized the shapes they made.

They were from her kicks.

"Like your uncle said," Val began, "We need your help."

Isidora put a finger to her lips.

"You don't need my help. You need me to use my skills to get what you want before you cast me to the lions."

Dramatic.

"But Erea will fall if you don't," I blurted.

The corner of her mouth tipped up in a smile.

"Oh? I was wondering where you lot were from." She sat back on her bed, finger thrumming the dented post. "Do tell me more."

I gave her a quick rundown of what had happened with Imogen and Ilise. Her facial expression didn't change beyond mild disinterest throughout the story. I then told her about our plan to steal Ilise's gloves at the ball, and that had gained some of her attention.

"And what does *any* of that have to do with me?" she asked when I finished.

"My friends here would appreciate it if you used your special 'skills' to take the gloves," Alyx said.

Isidora weighed the idea in her head before frowning again. I didn't think this girl smiled often outside of annoying her uncles.

"What's in it for me? From what I can tell," she said, rising from the bed, "you all want me to go on a suicide mission based on how you described Ilise, just so the rest of you lot can go on *another* suicide mission to get your kingdom back. I would like to keep my life, however drab it is." She said that last sentence with a pointed glare at the monarchs. How could I convince her? I hardly wanted to do this, but my kingdom was on the line. She didn't owe anything to Erea, but there must be something that would sway her.

"I have an idea," Kass said.

She whispered something to the two monarchs and Titus' fists clenched.

"When I infiltrated The Progression, they did this all the time to get information out of Union members they captured. More often than not, it worked," she said.

Alyx sighed and walked up to me, leaning close to my ear.

"Your friend suggested we offer to release her if she helps. But we can't allow her in Croaga," he whispered. "Would you be willing to take her back to Erea?"

I looked back to Isidora. We *were* asking a lot, sending her straight to a powerful Ilise, though if what Titus said was true she would be another problem for me to deal with. But, a full-powered Ilise under Imogen's control was harder to deal with than a criminal.

I nodded.

"Isidora," I said. "If you help us, your uncles will allow you to be released, and you'll come back to Erea with us."

Her dark eyes brightened. She let out a harsh laugh.

"How naive of you to think they would ever let me go," she said.

"They said they would," I said.

She couldn't be *that* bad. Between the eight of us, we would be able to control her until we got back to Erea. Then we would decide how to deal with her.

"Interesting." She clapped her hands together. "I suppose I'll help you. What do I have to do?"

Alyx ran out the door after a very stressed Titus.

"I'll stay behind to plan how to take the gloves with her," Val said. "The rest of you should go back and see if any of the servants can find clothes for us to wear to the ball."

Kass, Chafik, Mathias, Cain, and Kieron filed out the door, but Rori stormed up to Isidora.

"If you even *think* about betraying us, you'll have me to deal with. Got it?" they said.

Isidora looked up into their eyes, unflinching.

"I'm not scared of you, freckles."

Rori narrowed their eyes at her before turning to leave. So we had an ancient sorceress, a mind-controlled Imperium with power over two elements, and a Croagi criminal who could decide to leave at any second.

What could possibly go wrong?

Chapter 24

Yorena

CROAGI BALLS WERE SO peculiar. Nobles and commoners danced together in a circle of patterned fabric in the center of the room, and the few servants milling about the room joined in the fun the moment their trays of food were empty. Spears of lamb and overflowing bowls of peanut soup lay across tables on the perimeter of the room, the delicacies disappearing faster than the servants could replace them. Torches surrounded the marble room, matching the setting sun beneath the sea. If this were any other time, I would take the time to join in the party. But I had a mission.

I rubbed my palms on the plum cotton of my dress. Servants had found old formal clothes people had left behind over the years and thankfully they hadn't required any alterations. Three daggers pressed into my skin with every step. All of us were spread out across the room, waiting for Ilise's arrival. After Val had told Isidora the plan, she only added to my growing list of doubts. I wouldn't be surprised if she bolted the moment her uncles let her out of her "cell". But I hoped she would pull through for us. I hoped, I hoped, I hoped.

I was hoping for a lot of things. I hoped Imogen wouldn't spot any of us once she arrived with Ilise. I hoped none of the guests here would get hurt if we were to clash. I hoped Isidora would be able to get Ilise's gloves without getting hurt. I hoped our plan to distance Ilise from Imogen would free her, but Isidora then had said, "Your sorceress lady wouldn't have allowed you to know about the distance thing unless she wanted you to know." I was choosing to ignore that comment of hers.

But at least we actually had a plan for once. I would hide and keep track of Isidora once Ilise arrived, and Chafik would go with her so she wouldn't stick out being alone. Then, once Isidora stole the gloves, we would blow out all the torches to limit Imogen's vision while we knocked out Ilise. And assuming Imogen didn't find us, we would all hurry to the back part of the castle and load up into an already prepared cart so we could travel to the Niongi port in the north and sail back into Erea.

Simple. Sort of.

Drum beats echoed through the marble room, and the space fell silent. All that could be heard then were the crashing waves outside. Titus strode into the room with Ilise on his arm. The room fell away, leaving nothing but me and her. I was mostly hidden behind a pillar, but I could still see her clearly. Her crimson dress hugged her body, leaving nothing to my imagination about what it would feel like to run my hands along the silk at her waist. A large slit revealed at least one dagger under her dress, sharpened to a point. Tulle was wrapped around her arms, littered with pieces of gold to match her glittering crown. My crown.

I forced my eyes off her. I couldn't get distracted. No matter how stunning she looked, radiant as ever. Out of the corner of my eye, Kieron and Val crept closer to the front of the room while Kass, Rori, and Cain moved to block the other entrances. There wasn't much we could do about the open wall, but there were already a few Croagi guards stationed there. Mathias was on the move, tray of drinks in hand. Titus and Alyx had given him a uniform to blend in with the other servants, and distract Imogen while Isidora went for Ilise.

It was my turn.

With shaking hands, I joined the rest of the crowd. I needed to be close to Ilise once her gloves were gone since I had control over her one weakness—fire. I pushed through a crowd of women in large, colorful dresses, children running through small gaps, and the never ending waves of servants handing out flutes of champagnes and oxtail soup. I was halfway to Ilise when I froze in my tracks.

Oliver and Nikos were here.

They strolled into the crowd, eyes scanning every face. I squeezed in with a group of girls that looked to be about my age. They paid me no mind, not even a hitch in their chatter. Alyx had said he told the guests to ignore us, pretend we were regular guests of balls. Given how different we looked from the Croagi with our lighter skin tones, it wasn't hard for them to pick us out. But it also made hiding from Ilise and her entourage a challenge.

"Can you get me closer to them," I whispered to the group of girls.

They nodded and slowly made their way forward.

Animal skin drums and bamboo flutes echoed off the walls and the crowd grew louder, dancing with a new ferocity. A spark of pain spread across my back from bending over for this long, but I was much too tall to stand normally. Oliver pressed further into the crowd behind me. *Finally.* Nikos hopefully wouldn't be a problem; he was the one who had let us out. Imogen was nowhere to be found, but we wouldn't get another chance.

"Thank you," I whispered to the girls as I squeezed myself out of their tight circle.

Isidora and Chafik were mere paces from Ilise, who was deep in conversation with one of the Croagi nobles. I scanned the room for the others and gave them a nod. Kieron and Val gave me a thumbs up and I gestured for Mathias to move closer to the others at the entrances. Once Isidora was a few feet from Ilise, I extinguished all the torches in the room. The room was plunged into darkness, save for the weak light from the nearly set sun.

Go time.

The few guests that weren't in on the plan screamed into the darkness, making a run for the blocked entrances. I swam through the thick crowd to Ilise and Isidora, guided by the light of Ilise's air crystal. I would get her back. I prayed to the Spirits that Chafik wasn't trampled by the mob, but I had to focus. I finally reached Ilise, her back to me, and attempted to pull her arms behind her back.

Quicker than I ever thought possible, she wrenched her arms from my gentle grip, and swung me around so I was in front of her.

"I had a feeling you were here," she said. I looked down at her bare, calloused hands. It only took her a second to notice the gloves were gone. Rage sparked in her cracked eyes. "What did you do?" she seethed.

Breaking my own heart, I slammed my knee into her stomach, kicking the air from her lungs.

"I did what was necessary." I jerked her arms so they were behind her back and leaned down to whisper in her ear. "You're going to come with us, and nothing you do will stop us."

She shot a sinister smirk before hoisting me over her head and slamming me on my back. Pain shot up my spine like lightning. Ilise stood over me, hand on her hips.

"Actually, it's *you* who will be coming with *me.*"

I leapt up and tried to sweep her legs out from under her but she tackled me. We tumbled to the ground with a loud grunt. She pressed all her weight on me, pinning me to the ground.

"Ilise let's be reasonable. I don't want to hurt you," I said.

She laughed, the same entitled laugh Imogen had. Her fire crystal glowed, flames wrapping the tulle sleeves of her dress.

"Once I get rid of the others, you won't be taking me anywh—"

She cut off mid-sentence, eyes wide upon seeing the flames consuming her dress. She rolled off me, hands shaking, and let out a blood-curdling scream.

"Where is it! Who took my air crystal!" she hollered.

And there it was, a singular crystal swinging from her neck. It seemed Isidora hadn't let us down. Now I just had to get Ilise to the exit so the others could help me subdue her. I made a break for the nearest door, Ilise charging after me.

"Out of the way!" I screamed to the guests in my trajectory.

They jumped back upon seeing Ilise, creating a path for me to get through. Kass, Rori, and Cain already had their weapons out once I reached them at the exit. The rest of the guests were being led out by Val and Kieron so they could leave room for us to prevent any...collateral damage. I skidded to a halt, turning to face an enraged Ilise.

"Come on, Ilise. Be reasonable," I said.

She stopped, panting. "I am."

She pounced. I threw up my arms but she sprinted past me. She charged Kass and Rori with the spirit and grace of a warrior. Even without crystals, her skills were unmatched.

"Incoming!" Rori shouted as they ducked under one of Ilise's lethal swipes.

I sprung forward while Ilise prepared to throw a dagger at Kass and grabbed her wrists.

"They're your family, you can't possibly want to hurt them," I said.

She yanked herself from my grip and planted her boot in my stomach. The air rushed from my lungs and I staggered back.

"These people aren't my fami—"

Val tackled her to the ground from behind, using his body weight to pin her down. She squirmed under him, but was still unable to move.

"You're gonna regret this, you'll all regret th—"

I slammed one of her dropped daggers onto her head, knocking her out cold.

I hoped I didn't hit her too hard, the last thing I wanted was to be the one hurting her.

"Do you think I hit her too hard?"

Kieron spared no time in scooping her up as if she weighed nothing.

"She's been hit harder than that before," Val said. "She'll be fine, but we need to get out of here before Imogen comes after us."

With Val leading the charge, we all sprinted out of the ballroom, toward where Chafik, Isidora, and Mathias were waiting for us in the back. Titus had told us they would assign the guards to escort the guests to a separate room to continue the ball, leaving the white stone halls empty.

Too empty. Where was Imogen? I was certain she knew we were here by now, but no one had come after us. Not even Oliver or Nikos. We took a left at the end of the wall and were met with the warm blanket of the moist sea air. The sun had set below the waves, stars beginning to dot the purple sky. Chafik and Mathias waved to us from two large covered wagons. At least one of the wooden wheels on each wagon looked close to weathering away, and the cloth roofs could have been white before, though now they were a dingy brown. But they were stable and that was what mattered.

"Where's Isidora?" Chafik asked.

I scanned the grassy area around us, searching for a familiar head of silver-streaked hair. She had escaped the castle, right? She should've gotten out well before we did. And wasn't she an Imperium too? If I remembered correctly, her eyes had blue flecks—a Water Imperium. And Alyx had said he would give her a crystal for tonight. Maybe she did leave after all. All she'd wanted was freedom, and I guess freedom in Erea hadn't sounded as enticing to her.

"Let's load up before Imogen finds us," Rori said.

They took Ilise from Kieron and stepped toward the wagon when a voice broke through the darkness.

"I wouldn't do that if I were you," a familiar sinister voice said.

We whirled around and saw Imogen standing in her plum robes with Oliver at her side, a writhing Isidora in their grasp.

"I believe you have something I want," she said.

All five of her crystals glowed. She didn't say anything else, but her crystals said everything.

"Hand her over, and your little friend won't get hurt," Imogen said coolly, as if she weren't holding the life of Isidora in her hands.

Isidora had ceased her struggling, her face an eerie calm. Was she not terrified? My hand rested on the hilt of a dagger sheathed at my thigh. I knew it wouldn't do much against five crystals, but it was something. Kieron returned to my side, having secured Ilise in the wagon.

We couldn't give Ilise back. We had gone through too much to get here. Too much was riding on her help. But we also couldn't let Imogen hurt Isidora. I may not fully trust the girl, but all she wanted was freedom, and I intended to give that to her.

"You're not getting Ilise back," I said.

The others all had at least one hand on a weapon, with Chafik and Mathias off to the side. Ok, how could we defeat one of the most powerful sorceresses in the land? Before I could think of the safest option, Rori let out a roar, charging Imogen.

"Rori no!" Kass shouted.

Rori swung their shortsword in a broad arc and Imogen lazily swerved out of the way. *Spirits help us.* Imogen knocked them to the side with a strong gust of wind, forcing them to the ground with a heavy thud. Kass rushed over to half carry, half drag Rori back to our side.

"You have one last chance before the girl pays for it," Imogen said.

I shot a panicked look at Val, hoping he would have any idea what to do. He had a hopeless look in his gray eyes.

Isidora let out a slow giggle, the sound slowly spiraling into something made of nightmares.

"Why do you laugh girl, knowing you are soon to meet your demise?"

Isidora's face spread in a grin. A blue light emitted from under her green cotton gown and she... turned into water? Where Oliver once had Isidora trapped was now water in the shape of Isidora's small form before it splashed to the ground. Oliver looked as dumbfounded as the rest of us, even Imogen.

The water that was once Isidora flowed to where Chafik stood before rematerializing into Isidora. *How in four hells did she do that? Though that explains why she had a solid wall instead of a door.*

"Come close to capture, and you learn a few tricks," she said.

Taking advantage of our distraction, Imogen shook the ground beneath us. I grabbed onto Kieron for balance, causing both of us to topple to the ground. Kass planted her feet, fighting for control over the ground. Sweat beaded her brow, and her muscles shook under the sleeves of her black dress.

Oliver lunged toward Kieron and me on the floor. On unsteady ground, we broke apart. Oliver stumbled but quickly regained their footing.

"Val!" Kieron screamed.

I whipped my head to Val, about to be on the receiving end of one of Imogen's gusts. Kieron rushed toward his brother and Oliver pounced on me. Sharp rocks and gravel dug into the exposed skin on my back, acting like a hundred needles from the continued quaking of the ground.

Oliver landed a kick to my side before running toward the wagon. I needed something to stop them, and my mind immediately went back to the whip of flames I had seen Ilise create. I imagined flames snaking from my hand as an extension of myself. I didn't realize my eyes were closed until I opened them to a flaming whip in my hand. Rolling onto my knees, I lashed out at Oliver's ankles just as they were about to board the wagon. They fell face first into the dirt, screaming from the intense heat.

I pulled them back toward me. They wouldn't take Ilise from me again, nobody would. They attempted to free themselves by dousing the flames in water, but my spark would not be extinguished.

"Don't even think about it, *Oliver,*" I sneered.

They opened their mouth to respond but I nailed a kick across their jaw and their eyes fluttered closed. I should've felt remorse for the line of blood dripping down their face, but I couldn't find it in myself to feel any.

I focused back on what was going on around me. It was quiet, too quiet. I looked back to our wagon, making sure everyone was accounted for. Everyone was there, in varying shapes, also looking confused from the quiet. Chafik and Isidora stood off to the side, almost completely hidden in the night, but a familiar mess of brown curls and sarcastic comments was missing. Where was Mathias?

"Has anyone seen Mathias?" I said.

Kieron was about to answer when he winced and pointed behind me.

"Found him," he said in a strained voice.

Mathias writhed in Nikos' iron grip, held in place by an arm around his chest.

"Sorry," Nikos mouthed.

Sorry? He was holding my friend and had the gall to say sorry? Chafik started toward his friend but Isidora grabbed him and pulled him back toward the cart.

"Are you dense?" she chided. "You're gonna get yourself killed."

"Both of you get in the cart," Val ordered. He looked to Rori, Kass, and Cain. "You three as well," he said as he strode next to me and his brother.

"Give him back, Nikos!" I yelled.

Imogen stood next to him, a satisfied smirk clear on her face. She put a finger on her chin as if she were actually considering it before shaking her head.

"How about I keep your freckled friend and I give you exactly five minutes to get out of my sight before I come after you," she said.

My hands curled into fists and my jaw clenched so hard I wouldn't be surprised if my teeth cracked.

"Just let the boy go before we take him from you," Kieron said.

Imogen sighed. "Nikos," she said.

Without another word, Nikos' crystal glowed, the ground shook. A thick, gnarly tree root sprouted from the dirt, slowly snaking its way up Mathias' body. He ceased his struggling, eyes glued to the plant now fully wrapped around his legs.

"If you try to take him, you lose him. Simple," Imogen said.

Nikos averted his eyes to the ground. Was he ashamed? Did he disagree with what Imogen was making him do? If he was, then why wasn't he doing *something*, anything?

"Guys, I think you should go," Mathias said in a thin voice. I took a step forward and froze when Nikos made the tree move up to his torso.

"We can't just leave you with them," I cried.

Mathias had never even wanted to be with us in the first place, this was no way to repay him. He'd helped me in my first attempt to defeat Imogen and now he was stuck in this mess. I couldn't leave him with her. And he was my friend, and I liked to think he thought of me as his.

"Val? Kieron?"

The two brothers shrugged.

"You heard your friend," Imogen said. "You have four minutes left to leave before I rescind my kindness."

She was allowing us to take Ilise? What could Imogen possibly need Mathias for. There had to be a trick, or some type of trap. Imogen had waited years to have Ilise in her grasp and now she was letting her go? Impossible. I couldn't just leave Mathias here. But I couldn't risk Ilise falling back into Imogen's hands.

Fight. Flee. Fight. Flee. Which was right?

"I promise we will take *good* care of him."

A single tear slid down Mathias' face as he mouthed, *"Go."*

The tree branch was now up to his neck. All it would take was one move from Nikos and he would be dead. I couldn't save him. Just like I couldn't save Ilise, and I couldn't save Orla. I slowly nodded to him and turned toward our wagons. The two brothers followed after me in a heavy silence and we boarded with the rest of our group, now another person smaller. I chose the wagon with Chafik, Isidora, and Ilise.

"Where's Mathias?" Chafik asked, dual-colored eyes darting around the small space.

All I could do was shake my head.

"But he was righ—"

I shook my head again, cutting him off. He clasped his hands over his mouth and turned away from me, his eyes glistening with the start of tears.

I took a shuddering breath and settled down next to a still knocked out Ilise and rested her head in my lap.

"Please work. Please work. Please work."

Chapter 25

Nikos

"They're gone," I said to Imogen.

I didn't want to keep holding Yorena's friend hostage, the poor guy was shaking in the branches on the tree I had created. Imogen waved her hand and I dropped my hold on the roots, causing them to wither off of the boy's shoulders. Before he could run away, I grabbed his arm and tried to ignore the way his breaths came in pants, the way he feared for his life because of me. It wasn't working.

"What do I do with him?" I asked.

Imogen clicked her tongue and took him from me.

"Just get Oliver back to their room, I will put the boy somewhere," she ordered.

Ugh. Oliver disgusted me. They'd been knocked out by a puny dagger. It was quite pathetic. How was this the person who'd been blackmailing me for days? I walked over to them and lifted them into my arms. A small line of blood trickled down their face, but they looked otherwise fine. When I turned around again, Imogen was already gone with Yorena's friend. I wondered where she took him, but unfortunately there was nothing else I could do about it now.

I walked back inside the castle and quickly set Oliver down on their bed on the top floor. I couldn't believe the monarchs were still letting us stay here. Their ball was ruined, Progression members—me—were in their palace, and they had lost the Queen of Erea to a rebel group. They may be the "good guys" here, but it still had to be embarrassing. Even I would have thrown us out by now, and concerning myself with something that didn't concern me was the last thing I enjoyed.

Which was a large reason why I was confused about the servant boy. What would Imogen want with him anyway? She let go of a double element-controlling girl in exchange for a powerless boy who couldn't contribute more to a conversation than a few ill-timed jokes? I'd noticed him around the palace a few times, and he was forever joking about serious matters. Life wasn't something you could aimlessly go through without a care. I hardly thought Imogen truly had a use for him. But what did I care? As long as Daeva stayed safe, I couldn't care less who Imogen wanted for her inane plans.

I walked to my room, intent on forgetting about the events of the last couple hours, when a familiar head of curls and freckled face came into my field of vision. *"I will put the boy somewhere,"* she'd said. Of the countless rooms in this castle, she had decided that my room was the best place to put him? Mathias lounged on my bed as if he owned the place, dirt-caked shoes and all.

"What are you doing here?" I demanded.

He stretched out and released a loud yawn.

"Sorceress lady told me to stay here and give you this note, and I don't have a death wish, so I couldn't refuse," he said. Well, at least he had *some* sense. "What does she want with me anyway?"

"I don't know. But it would be in your best interest to not annoy me," I said. "I hardly want to spend my time babysitting a child."

I walked up to him and snatched the note. A strong part of me wanted to find Imogen and demand she find a better place for him, but I didn't want to sign Daeva's death warrant.

Do not let him escape. I brought Daeva, so you should have much motivation to follow my orders.

-Imogen

She brought Daeva? How had I not seen her the entire journey? I would have escaped ages ago had I known she was here. Dammit.

"I'm not a child, I'm twenty," the boy grumbled.

"So an overgrown child then."

Mathias crossed his arms and huffed. "I rest my case."

I needed to find Daeva. I looked back at the man, boy, child—the person sitting on my bed.

"Don't do anything stupid while I'm gone," I said.

I didn't have the time nor energy to clean up any messes of his. And after losing Ilise, I doubted Imogen was in a forgiving mood.

"Ooo, someone's a grumpy boy," he teased.

For the love of the Spirits. I ignored him and kicked open the door. I couldn't believe Imogen had put me on babysitting duty. Who cared if, according to him, he was technically not a child? He acted like one and had the cleanliness of one. If I had to be stuck with him after we left tomorrow, I just might end up killing him. I despised myself for every life I had to take for Imogen and my sorry excuse for a father's plans, but for that boy, I would make an exception.

I knew Imogen wouldn't tell me where she'd put Daeva, so I went to Oliver's room. They were probably awake by now. I pushed open the door and found them wiping the blood off their face at the vanity.

"Where's Daeva?" I said.

They pretended they didn't hear me, focused intently on making sure every speck of blood and dirt was clean from their face.

"I won't ask again," I said, taking a few steps toward them.

"I wasn't aware I was taking orders from you," they said.

They had a lot of confidence for someone who did all of Imogen's dirty work, willingly, I might add. I'd been stuck with this annoying, shifty, dishonorable person for two years now. My father had placed his people in Ominka's court to eventually take control from the Duke and Duchess, and Oliver had been oh too happy to help with that endeavor. They'd impressed my father so much after they got one of his spies promoted to be the assistant of the Duke, that he assigned them to work with Imogen and make sure I stayed in line. Long story short, it gave their ego an unneeded boost. And I thought they got a sick sense of joy from bossing me around because of that spiritsdamned blackmail.

"Just tell me where she is so I don't have to talk to you anymore."

They swiveled around in their chair, a finger on their chin.

"Give me one reason why I should. You lost Ilise, and you're under my control until I decide on my last request," they said.

Said the person who got knocked out by a small dagger and a half-trained girl. But they had one more weakness. I didn't use it too often, felt too childish, but I would be seeing Daeva before we left. I started it as a small tremor, just enough to rattle the mirror they were so intent on looking into. Then, I increased the quake so they rattled in their chair, hands already clutching their stomach.

"Tell me where she is," I said.

They shook their head.

Fine then. I aimed both of my open hands to the ground and released one of the strongest earthquakes I could. After years of practice, I'd mastered the ability to confine my quakes to a small area, and in this case, Oliver's room. Potted plants toppled over, vases shattering into a mess of root and dirt. Cracks formed on the posts of the bed canopy, and they crouched on the floor, hand over their mouth.

"Fine, fine, I'll tell you. Just stop before I vomit!" I ceased the quake. "She's in the room next to Ilise's," they said.

I left the room without another word. Of course Imogen had put her next to that unstable freak. The thought of Daeva being anywhere near Ilise made me want to rip those crystals off Imogen's neck and show *her* what it was like to be embedded in a tree as she so often liked to threaten.

I briskly walked down the hall to where Ilise's room had been. Surprisingly, the door was unlocked when I tested it, and a familiar head of black hair poked up from the bed.

"Darling?" I said.

She smiled her wide gap-toothed smile. If I could watch her smile all day, I would. Simply for the way it grounded me, reminding me that everything I suffered would be worth it.

"Are you okay? Imogen hasn't done anything to hurt you, right?"

She jumped up from the bed, throwing herself into my arms, and I wrapped my arms around her, inhaling her lavender and citrus scent.

"I'm okay," she said. "She hasn't talked to me since I got put in here."

Good. I didn't think I'd done anything to deserve Imogen's wrath, but I could never be too careful.

"What are we doing here anyway?"

Nothing she should know about. I always avoided telling Daeva exactly what I had to do to keep her safe. Though I was sure she appreciated me keeping her alive, I doubted she would agree with my methods.

"Don't worry yourself over it. You are safe, so everything I've done is worth it," I said.

Who cared if my dreams were plagued with the face of all that have suffered because of me? Daeva made a sound of slight annoyance but said nothing as she sighed into my chest. She might hate me if she knew everything I had done for her, but even that couldn't make me regret anything.

We'd been planning to get married back in Nitedand, until my father had forced me to work with Imogen. One day, we would be able to go back home and have our wedding, and I would do *nothing* to risk it.

"We could try to escape," she said after a while. "Then you wouldn't have to follow Imogen's orders anymore."

I pressed a soft kiss to her head.

"I wish we could, darling."

Spirits knew how much I wished we could.

"I can see how this is weighing on you," she said, looking up at me with those big, deep hazel eyes of hers.

That look shot straight to my heart. I wished I could grant her wish, but I couldn't risk it.

"Let's just go. Please." Her voice broke on the last word and I was surprised that didn't make me cave right then.

"I'm sorry, darling. We can't."

Daeva broke off from the hug, clearly upset with me. I hated upsetting her. Keeping her safe and happy was the only thing that kept me from lashing out against Imogen or Oliver. And now, Ilise. I brushed a piece of lint from her silky hair.

"We're leaving for Erea in the morning, and I'm sure you won't have to be here much longer." I kissed her cheek once more and walked out of the room before she convinced me to run away.

I was walking back to my room and in front of my door was none other than the Prince Consort. He spotted me and flashed me a smile.

"Nikos, do you have a moment?" He said that as if he wasn't blocking the door to my room.

"Of course, Your Majesty," I said, surprising myself by keeping the annoyance out of my tone.

"Yorena seems to trust you. And if you decide to prove her right, she's planning to enter Erea from Linhex." He walked away from my door and I stared after him, dumbfounded. "Do with that information what you will," he said before rounding the corner.

Linhex? That wasn't far from my father's manor in Kentfallsworth. If they were heading there, they must have a death wish. I wasn't going to tell Imogen, but I certainly wasn't going to help them. Too much of a risk. I opened the door and got instantly reminded of my most recent problem.

"You should really keep some snacks in here," Mathias said.

Maybe I would kill that annoying servant, just maybe.

CHAPTER 26

ILISE

I WAS LAYING ON a hard surface, it was shaking, and my back was hurting from the position I'd been in. While most of my body lay on the ground, my head was cushioned by something soft, warm, and rose-scented. There was a soft pressure on my head. No, it disappeared. And then it was back. Someone was stroking my head?

I couldn't open my eyes yet. My head pounded too much. What had happened? My hearing was still muffled, and I could only grasp that there was someone talking, or maybe multiple people talking. The last thing I remembered was walking into the Croagi castle's ballroom, and they'd been about to recognize me as Queen of Erea. The rest was a blur.

Where was Imogen? I could usually feel her presence, almost like a sixth sense. But the incessant pressure of her soul that had been in the back of my head had once been was gone. It was like I could finally breathe normally, have my thoughts to myself for once. Ever since I had let her in, no matter how far I seemed to be from her in the Erean palace, the presence had never gone away. How come it was gone now?

A familiar and unwelcome ache began in my chest, each beat of my heart like an intense labor. What did Imogen want now?

I finally opened my eyes, my head pain gone, my energy returned. I was still on my back, with colorful shadows—my soul aspects—acting as a pillow and blanket. They were warm. Usually Imogen made them act like bricks of concrete. But Imogen wasn't here. Who had pulled me in here then?

I rose from the "ground" and started walking. There weren't any true directions in a soul, but walking felt more productive than sitting in a pile of shadows.

"Nice to see you again," a feminine voice said. I whipped around to find the mysterious entity wearing my face. "Glad to see you somewhat back to normal."

"Was I not normal before?" I said.

The entity flashed a sad smile, crossing the distance between us so that we were only a foot apart. Spirits, we looked identical. They had my same round eyes that were so dark a brown they appeared black, and they had the same rich dark brown skin as me, and full lips. The only difference was that their hair was in the full afro mine had once been styled in.

"You were being controlled by Imogen, you were hardly yourself," the entity said.

The memories all hit me at once. I was Queen now, and I had become worse than the previous monarchs. The monarchs. I'd killed them in cold blood. I'd become worse than anyone in The Progression could've been. I'd destroyed the lives of Primis people, whom I'd sworn to protect from the tyranny of The Progression.

What had I done?

The entity placed a hand on my cheek, wiping away a tear I hadn't realized I'd released.

"It's okay, Ilise. You're going to fix this," they said. "Nothing that happened was your fault."

It sure felt like it was. The kingdom probably hated me now, Imogen would be looking for me, and I was the reason everything was in shambles. This was the exact thing I'd been trying to prevent.

"I can hear your thoughts, just so you know," the entity said. "You can't fix anything if you're intent on blaming yourself."

"What are you?" I said.

The entity opened their mouth but another figure appeared right next to us. We froze. This one looked like me, too. Why did all of these entities have to look like me? I didn't want to be inside my own head right now, let alone have to look at myself.

"We are both you," the second entity said. The only difference between me and this entity was that they wore the golden crown I never wanted. "Except the other one is an imposter."

The first entity frowned. "Actually, you're the imposter."

The second one crossed their arms, taking a step closer to me, close enough for me to see the jagged purple cracks streaking through the silver and gold flecks in their eyes—my eyes. I tripped over my own feet trying to scramble away from them.

"I am what you have become. I am the better version of that one over there," the second entity said, nodding to the first.

I'd become the very thing I devoted my life to destroying. That crown was nothing more than poison, its venom seeping its way into a newly transformed me as soon as I put it on. I'd killed. I'd captured. I'd hurt.

Spirits. I'd even threatened Nikos' lover. Sure, Nikos was a pain in the ass most of the time, but Daeva had never done anything wrong. She was a human being, and an innocent one at that. The fact that I would've hurt her to keep Nikos in line was disgusting.

"Ilise is nothing like you," the first entity said, stepping between me and the second. "You're nothing more than the monster Imogen turned her into. And she will never be that way again."

A large part of me didn't believe that. Imogen had said she'd changed me into something else from the moment I was born. All my so-called memories were lies. I'd never been something other than what Imogen wanted me to be. How could I not be a monster? I have never been my own person, and I never will be. Even the spiritsdamned Council had been afraid of me, despite all of them being more powerful than I could ever truly be on my own. I was awful.

More memories from the night before slowly started piecing together in my head as the two entities argued. Yorena had been working with the Union. How could they still want to save me after all I'd done? Even if I could help them, Imogen would come looking for me and she'd have no quarrels with killing them to get me. And the moment Imogen got back to me, I wouldn't have any problem with it either. I was more trouble than what I was worth. None of them had even tried to hurt me to get me to come with them, they still cared. My throat felt thick, and my eyes were blurry with tears. I didn't deserve this. I didn't deserve them.

A strong hand rested on my shoulder and flinched away. "There there, everything will be okay once you stop listening to this imposter," the second entity said.

The first one let out a sigh of exasperation. "You're the imposter, not I. You're only using her for your own twisted ends," they sneered.

The second one smirked. "It's not considered using her if she wants the same things."

"I will never want the same things. Ever," I choked out.

Thinking of how my mind worked, how I'd wanted to revert Erea to the ideals of Letita, made my stomach twist. Until a few weeks ago, I'd thought I was Primis, and it'd taken so little time for me to see them, my own people, as inferior.

"I think it's time for you to go," the first entity said as they stepped back.

They raised their arms, their limbs shaking as their hands... glowed? The second one screamed from the light, parts of their body, my body, dissolving into a purple mist.

"You can't run from me, Ilise. I will always find you," they said before the rest of them dissolved.

The first entity gathered the mist into a miniature ball, squeezing it between their hands until it finally disappeared with a small puff of smoke. What in four hells just happened?

"They can't bother you anymore," they said with a smile.

I stared at them with wide eyes.

"What are you?"

They placed a soft hand on my cheek, wiping away the last of my tears. "I'll tell you when I see you again, but now it's time for you to wake up."

Without another word, my soul around me exploded in a flash of white light, and I was thrown back into the normal world.

I shot up, immediately regretting that decision as all the blood rushed to my head. Yorena let out a surprised yelp before breaking out in that dimpled smile I'd missed so much.

"Ilise! You're finally awake," she said as she tried to pull me in for a hug.

I swerved from her grasp, my back colliding with the wall of what I assumed to be a wagon. Chafik and a girl I didn't recognize stared at me.

"What's wrong?" Yorena said.

The hurt look on her face only made the guilt mounting in my stomach grow. I didn't deserve her hugs, or any affection from her. I'd destroyed her kingdom, I'd killed her parents, and I'd sent her on the run. None of that warranted a welcome back hug.

I hugged my knees to my chest, trying to get as far from the other riders as I could in the small space.

"I'm a monster," I whispered. More tears welled up and I didn't try to stop them from falling. "You shouldn't have brought me with you."

Yorena scooted closer to me and I tried to press myself further into the wall.

"None of what you did was your fault," she said as she wiped away some tears.

"I risked getting killed over a pair of gloves for someone who didn't even want to be rescued?" the unfamiliar girl said.

Chafik lightly elbowed her before shaking his head.

"You should drop me off wherever we are and return to the kingdom without me," I said.

Yorena grabbed my chin and lifted my head so I was looking her in the eyes. I'd been avoiding her eyes this whole time. I'd forgotten how much the gold flecks in her eyes made her irises glow, and the deep brown of them made it feel like she was staring into the depths of my forever tainted soul. Like I could never hide myself from her.

"You will not blame yourself for this. And wherever you go, I will go."

I would convince her to leave me eventually, but it was clear she wasn't budging any time soon. She tried to wrap her arms around me again but I moved to the other corner of the wagon. She sighed and didn't try to approach me again.

Was all I could ever do was hurt people? Was that all I was meant for? I couldn't even keep Yorena away from me without feeling like I was holding a knife to her heart.

Chafik flashed me a sad smile and didn't try to talk to me. Good. Maybe he knew it was a bad idea for me to be here. I hid my face in my hands and closed my eyes as the gentle rumble of the wagon lulled me back into a dreamless sleep.

Chapter 27

Yorena

THE RATTLING OF THE wagon was accompanied with Ilise's soft snores, her long body curled up into a ball in the corner. It hardly looked comfortable, but she seemed intent on staying as far from us as possible, or maybe just from me. I knew it was impossible for her to not feel guilty for everything Imogen had made her do, but it broke my heart to hear her call herself a monster. She couldn't have done anything to stop herself even if she'd wanted to.

Orange light streamed through the fabric roof of the wagon, and strong winds kept attempting to run the wagons off the road. We'd been riding for two days straight, trying to get ahead of whatever Imogen might send after us. We were almost at the Niongi port, from where we would sail into the kingdom through Nitedand. Linhex was mostly empty, a small port of a town, so there was less of a chance of anyone spotting us. We weren't sure what Imogen was telling the kingdom about Ilise, so we needed to avoid her being seen until we knew for sure.

The wagon ground to halt.

"Finally," Isidora said, stretching out on the floor. Ilise still didn't stir. "I was moments from getting out and walking myself."

She practically jumped out of the rip in the fabric we used as a makeshift door, Chafik following close behind with a trunk of clothes for us to change into. I couldn't wait until we were on the ship and I could get out of this dress. I shuffled over to the corner Ilise had banished herself to and lightly shook her awake. She awoke with a start and immediately shied away from my touch. I quickly moved my hand away.

"We're here," was all I said.

There were so many words I'd imagined saying when I saw her next, but they were all stuck in my throat. And if she felt like she had anything to say to me, she didn't show it. I wished I could hold her until she truly believed none of this was her fault, and that we could make up for lost time. But most of all, I wanted to tell her how I felt, even if I'd yet to find the right words. I walked out of the wagon without another word.

I shielded my eyes against the setting sun, light glinting off the crashing waves of the Picchi Sea. Alyx had said Titus had reserved a ship for us to take back to Erea, and only one ship was at the small dock. It was dilapidated. Most of the exports that arrived from Croaga came into Port Hapow from West Dstos or Rimed, so I guess Niongi didn't have need for an over-extravagant port. Algae covered the faded wood planks of the dock, some pieces missing, probably having fallen into the sea. And rotting seaweed curled around the support posts, slowly washing away with each lap of the waves.

The ship itself was unassuming. It was about the size of any other small trading ship, appearing to have three decks at most. A yellowing sail flapped in the wind, the tall mast rocking with it. The faded outline of a crest marred the side of the ship. Alyx and Titus had likely had someone remove the Croagi crest to eliminate any extra questioning from any guards who might be at the dock. Blank ships like this arrived in ports all the time, usually carrying less precious trade items. No one would question it unless they were *looking* for trouble. The rest of the group walked up behind me, also eyeing the ship.

"Was this the best he could do?" Isidora asked.

For Spirit's sake. "The less extravagant the ship, the less attention we draw," I said. I turned to the short girl and her dark eyes looked up at me with something I interpreted as annoyance. She shrugged and started toward the ship with Chafik in tow.

Val walked up beside me, still dressed in his torn fabrics.

"We need to figure out where we're going once we get back," he said. "Where's Ilise? She hopefully has some ideas, after all the trouble she put us through."

I looked back toward the wagon. Ilise still hadn't come out yet, and I didn't want to upset her more by forcing her out. She'd already been forced to do too much, and I wanted to give her a break. I wanted to give her a choice.

"She's not feeling well," I lied. It was technically true, I supposed.

Rori simply smiled sadly. We all knew that what Ilise had gone through was hellish, and she had every right to be upset right now. I would ask her to come out after she's had some time alone. Until then, we needed to plan out next steps.

"I think we should hide out in Slandslina Forest while we think of a detailed plan for how to take back the kingdom," I said.

Almost nobody lived in the thick forest. The venomous animals, the unbearable humidity, and the lack of space for infrastructure made the prospect of living there nearly impossible. But it wouldn't be too hard to set up a camp for a couple days while we rested and came up with a plan.

And maybe I would be able to find that temple again. The voice I'd been hearing had been quiet lately, but maybe going back to the temple would give me some answers. The voice had been helpful by showing me where Ilise was, giving me the idea to take her gloves. And maybe I could make sense of the weird advice they had given me. *Claim your crystal for it will serve you well.* I needed answers, and we needed time. I didn't see much of a downside to this plan.

"That's a waste of time," Rori said, crossing their arms. "By the time we dock in Erea, we'll have a plan. Stopping in the forest will only waste more time that we don't have."

"But Imogen always seems to know what we're going to do next, and if we take the extra time, we can account for that," I said.

Kieron put a hand on my shoulder.

"I'm sorry, but Rori is right," he said. "Taking the long way would exhaust the energy we need to defeat Imogen for good."

I shot him a stern look at his betrayal.

"Don't say I didn't try to help," he said with a shrug.

"Taking a little extra time won't be the end of the world," I said.

Rori let out a harsh laugh. "That's exactly what it means, Princess. We aren't endangering the kingdom just because you want to hide."

I clamped my mouth shut because I was sure the next thing out of my mouth would end in a fight. I didn't want to hide, I just wanted us not to go into this blindly. No one else would be getting hurt because I'd failed to think of possible ways our plans could go wrong. We'd already lost Orla, we'd had to leave Mathias, and Imogen was probably trailing after us by now to take someone else's soul.

"We'll know our plan of action by the time we dock in Linhex," Val said. "The boat ride will provide plenty of time for us to come to a consensus." Of course Val was choosing to take neither side. *Just as helpful as his brother.*

"Are you guys coming or not? I'd rather not spend more time than I have to in this dump," Isidora yelled from the ship.

I couldn't decide who annoyed me more, Isidora, or Rori. The only one of us Isidora seemed to tolerate was Chafik, and the rest of us, she treated with overall indifference. But even a *look* from Rori in my direction bled blatant hatred.

"I'm coming. I'm allergic to the smell of *cowardice*," Rori said before stalking off toward the ship.

Kieron leaned into my ear. "If I 'accidentally' knocked them overboard, would that be such a bad thing?" he whispered.

I attempted to ignore him for not taking my side. Though a small smile appeared against my will.

"No throwing people overboard, Kieron," Val said.

"How did you even hear me?"

"You're not subtle," he said plainly.

"Also, I told him," Kass said. Val opened his mouth in betrayal and Kass smirked. It would have been a sweet moment if my heart hadn't dropped at the sound of pounding horse hooves behind us.

"Do you guys hear that?" I said.

The three others frowned, squinting in the direction we had come from. Dust flew into the air as three black figures sped toward us. I couldn't see a crest on their clothes, but their sheer speed and the metal swords glinting in the light told me all I needed to know.

Imogen had sent for us.

"Guards!" I yelled.

Val and Kass whipped out the daggers they'd hidden under their clothes and Kieron unsheathed the shortsword at his hip. Small footsteps sounded behind me as Rori joined the group, a dagger in each hand.

How had Imogen even gotten this many guards over the border? Foreign visitors were only allowed a maximum of three guards each. And these had to have been following us the whole time to have caught up already.

"Can't hide now, Princess," Rori said as they gripped a curved dagger.

A smoky smell filled my nose. I turned to see that the wagon we had ridden in began to burn, the dirty fabric cover turning black as the flames licked its surface. Ilise stood there as the roof turned to ash, her fire crystal glowing as bright as the sun. Her face was set with grim determination, the gold in her eyes swirling.

"Where are they?" she said in a low voice.

"Nice to have you back, kid," Kass said with a smile. "We got three of them coming up behind you."

The guards were close enough now that I could see something gold glittering on their chests. The Erean crest. I felt energy rush through me as I activated my own crystal, spheres of fire already gathering in my hands. They would not be hurting, or taking, anyone else. Not as long as I could do something about it.

Ilise hopped down from the wagon, a cloud of dirt flying into the air as she landed.

Val stepped in front of us. His face was set, ready for battle.

"Ilise, Yorena, and I will lead the offensive. The rest of you stay here and make sure they don't get to the ship in case they get through us," Val ordered.

Kass, Rori, and Kieron nodded as Val waved me forward. He stopped in front of Ilise, staring at her with pure concern in his gray eyes.

"Are you sure you're up for this?" he asked.

She nodded. Val sighed but waved for us to go forward. The guards slowed their horses to a stop, one of them already jumping down from the saddle.

"We go as soon as he starts running," Val said. But before any of us could move, Ilise put out an arm in front of us.

"Allow me," she said, not turning to look back. I noticed she must have found her gloves on the floor somewhere in the wagon, and she rubbed them nervously on her ruined dress as if she could wipe off sweat. The flames started from her hands, winding up her arms like a growing vine, glowing brighter with each second. I had no clue what she was planning to do, so I grabbed Val by the sleeve and backed up from Ilise's inferno. The flames had now engulfed her entire body. She glowed like a sun on earth, and I shielded my eyes with my hand.

The first guard charged toward her at full speed, sword raised. I sprinted toward her.

"Ilise!" I yelled.

When the guard was only a few feet in front of her, she released the fire. The guard was instantly charred into something that looked less than human. His blackened, twisted corpse fell to the ground and Ilise merely stepped over him to survey the rest of her damage.

A blast of light and heat shot toward the other two guards. They met the same quick demise as their friend. I ran after Ilise, grimacing as I sped past the dead guards. I grabbed her arm and yanked her into a hug. I'd thought that guard was going to kill her, and to think she was that close to dying had terrified me.

"Are you okay? Did he hurt you?"

She shook her head and looked back to the other two guards. Since they hadn't been as close, you could still tell they'd been human. Though their skin was darkened from the inferno, and blood covered the charred skin. Ilise walked up to the dead guards, kneeling next to them in the dirt. She lightly touched the burned cheek of the first guard with a shaking hand, immediately yanking it away. She stood up and brushed past me toward the ship.

"Ilise, wait," I said.

She halted. "We have a ship to catch. Let's go."

CHAPTER 28

ILISE

T HE DECK UNDERNEATH ME rocked against the waves, only aggravating the queasiness in my stomach. *Why did I burn them?* I knew the guards wouldn't have killed me; Imogen valued me too much. I'd killed them. I'd killed them in the worst, most painful way possible. Something was wrong with me. The damage Imogen had done was stuck with me.

My hand went to my neck on impulse, searching for the golden pendant that had been my only link to my family for so long. But it was gone. Just another piece of myself Imogen had stolen. She'd convinced me they shouldn't matter to me, that they were something to be forgotten. Not even the memory of what I was fighting for could save me now.

Yorena hadn't sounded disgusted by my actions, but I could see it in her eyes. She was afraid of me, they all were. None of them had come to see me ever since the ship had left the dock. The room I'd chosen belowdecks was at the back of the ship, with low ceilings and nothing more than an oil lamp for light. I didn't know how long we'd been at sea, but it had to have been at least a day and a half. A small bed was tucked into the wall, with a threadbare blanket tossed across the compressed mattress.

I would have complained if I didn't think it was more than I deserved. I was a killer. Images of the guards' charred faces flashed repeatedly in my mind. I'd spent years of my life preventing The Progression from doing that exact thing to Primis people. Hells, it was the exact thing they'd done to my village. After what I'd done to them, those guards had barely looked human. They looked how I felt—monstrous, twisted. The guilt had a chokehold on my throat and constricted my chest. Again, nausea gripped me and I took a deep, shaking breath to keep it at bay.

I hugged my knees to my chest, clamping my eyes shut to prevent the tears from falling. Crying was for people who didn't purposely kill three people without batting an eye, who didn't allow themselves to topple the little stability the kingdom had left. My old friends should've left me in Croaga. At least then they wouldn't be on the run from Imogen, they wouldn't be arguing over what to do next. And I knew they were arguing, because I could hear their muffled voices above me. There was no easy solution to the situation I had gotten them all into.

Two short knocks sounded at the door.

"Go away," I said. There were a few seconds of silence before the person knocked again. "I said go away."

The lock on the door slowly twisted open and a short girl stepped into the room. Streaks of gray lined her long brown braid, and the dimness of the room made her large eyes look like black pits with light blue flecks swimming in them.

"Did you just pick my lock?" I said.

The girl tucked a rusted pin into her braid and closed the door.

"You act like it's hard," she said. Without another word she slid down the wall to sit beside me. "Your little Princess friend's been waiting outside for hours. I thought I might meet the person she would go through all this trouble for. I'm Isidora, by the way." She held out her hand and lowered it when I didn't take it.

Why was she here? And why was Yorena waiting outside? Maybe she was on guard duty. After my *demonstration,* I wouldn't be shocked if none of them trusted me anymore. I wouldn't trust me—I didn't trust me.

"I'm not in the mood for this," I said, trying to move away from the girl. There was something odd, different, about her energy.

"You don't want to know why I'm here?"

No, I didn't. 'Cause then that would lead to us possibly becoming friends, or allies. Considering she was able to go wherever she wanted on this ship, Yorena and the Union must trust her. And if we became friends, that would be one more person I would be disappointing. The less people I had depending on me, the better.

"I'm telling you anyway. I'd rather not waste my time," she said. "My uncle is the Prince Consort of Croaga and he had me locked up in the castle for almost two years."

Her own uncle had her locked up for that long? She didn't appear to be much older than I was. She must have been no older than sixteen when she'd been locked up.

"He locked me up because I robbed all of Dyrnie from when I was thirteen until I was sixteen. My family didn't have much before Alyx married Titus, so I had to do what I needed to do to make ends meet." She paused to look me deep in the eyes. "I hear your situation wasn't much different than mine."

I mean, I hadn't robbed my village since we were all struggling, but I wouldn't have been surprised if it had come to that. Isidora snapped in my face and I jumped back.

"Don't look so disgusted, you've done worse," she said.

The nausea was back. Was she here to make me feel better, or to insult me?

"But don't worry, I've done worse, too," she continued. "After a couple years of petty thievery, a young man approached me and hired me to be an assassin. He said that if I did it, my family would be taken care of. I killed twenty people before my uncle found out and had me locked up. By then, he'd gotten married and was helping support the family, but I couldn't exactly stop being an assassin easily. At least not without either faking my own death or fleeing the kingdom."

Spirits, this girl has been through the hells.

"My uncle captured me when a fruit vendor caught me using his well water to clean off one of my knives. And when I tried to run, he chopped off the tip of my pinky, the punishment for getting caught stealing in my town."

Why was she telling me all of this? I'd thought my childhood had been awful, hers had been at least three times worse.

"I can see the pity on your face, and that isn't why I'm telling you this. I'm trying to tell you that, despite all that I've done, you don't see me blaming myself for it. I was a kid. And my life was less than ideal, and while some of it is my fault, I'm not blaming myself for all of it."

I said nothing, staring at her.

"Come on," said the girl. "Put on your big-girl trousers and stop moping. I'm tired of listening to your friends come up with half-baked plans that will surely end in our deaths. I want to be rid of you all as soon as possible, and that can't happen unless you tell them how to defeat your sorceress friend."

"I bet the others just *love* having you around," I remarked.

Isidora shot up from the floor and clapped her hands together. "Oh my Spirits. She can speak."

I scoffed. I hated to admit it, but her tale had made me feel better.

"Looks like my job here is done, remember what we talked about." Isidora was halfway out the door when she added, "And if you tell anyone what I told you, I will kill you, joyfully." The door closed with a slam. I didn't doubt that threat.

"She's right, you know," a voice said.

What the hells? My head whipped toward the tiny window to see the entity I had up until then only seen in the depths of my own soul perched casually on the windowsill. There it was, the entity that looked like the old me, the person I could never be again. They looked mostly solid, though they were blurred at the edges, almost like a ghost. *They are on the windowsill.* That shouldn't be possible.

I backed up against the door.

"How are you here?" I asked.

My hand strayed to the dagger at my hip.

The entity frowned. "Put the dagger down. I'm not here to hurt you."

I threw the dagger in their direction anyway, and it went straight through them, landing in the wall behind them with a loud thud. I was going crazy. That had to be it. This entity was nothing more than a figment of my imagination. Beings from dreams couldn't simply appear in front of me. Unless they were a monster sent by the Spirits, sent to punish me for my crimes.

"Oh for Spirits sake, I'm not a monster. Stop being dramatic." I still hated how they read my mind.

"It's not mind reading, I'm reading the emotions in your soul. Your fear is making me anxious, and I would appreciate it if you would stop." They jumped down from the window sill and crossed the small space between us, sitting cross-legged in front of me.

"What do you want?" I said, pressing into the door as hard as I could. And now I was talking to them. Yup, I'd gone insane. My heart pounded in my ears. My breaths quickened, as if the entity was stealing all the air in the room. Maybe if I closed my eyes, they would go away. They were just in my imagination, right? I shut my eyes, tightly.

"I'm still here," they said. "I had to pull some strings for you to see me without sleeping so we could avoid the imposter. Sit down so we can talk before I run out of energy."

Pull some strings? Run out of energy? What in four hells are they talking about? I opened my eyes. They were still sitting there, as if their presence was a completely normal occurrence.

"I wanted to see how you were doing. I knew you would beat yourself up over what you did to those soldiers." Did everyone on this ship pity me now? Even the imaginary monsters?

"Isidora already gave me what she deemed a cheer up speech, so you can leave now," I said.

I didn't want to feel better. I deserved every ounce of guilt that felt like rocks piling onto my chest, no matter how many people told me there was no reason for it. Maybe if I held onto this guilt, I would never do any damage again.

"I'm not here to give you a cheer up speech, I already know that won't work on you," they said. "I'm here to tell you that you should be helping your friends create the plan for when you get back home."

Home. Was Erea truly my home anymore? For five years, I'd let a hatred for half the people in the kingdom be the only thing keeping me going. My family was long gone, my best friend was dead, and now anyone from the kingdom would probably chase me away at first glance. There was nothing left I could go home to. There was no one left I could go home to. Any home and family I would ever have would always be taken from me, and I would never be able to do anything about it.

The entity placed a hand on my knee. I couldn't quite feel the pressure of their hand; it was more of the idea of a hand being there.

"You do have a home. It's with your friends."

The entity disappeared without another word, fading into nothing but a shadow before vanishing entirely. I turned toward my closed door. Could I really help them all? The entity seemed almost desperate for me to help, but I couldn't. Every decision I'd made in the last couple weeks only made everything worse. I was in no shape to save a kingdom.

Feet shuffled on the other side of my door, followed by a single knock.

"Please," Yorena whispered, her voice cracking, "we need you back, I need you back."

I didn't make a sound. Eventually, her footsteps grew quieter, before thumping loudly up the stairs. A piece of my heart fractured to hear her broken voice, and it urged me to go after her. But would I truly be what she needed, or would I only bring her more pain? Would I be the one to take away what little she had left?

"You do have a home, it's with your friends."

Imaginary or not, the entity was right. I needed to help them take the kingdom back. I had to at least try. I didn't want to lose them, too.

Chapter 29

Yorena

Overlapping voices echoed down the narrow hall as I walked back up to the main deck. We'd been sailing for a day and half already and we still hadn't decided what to do once we arrived in Linhex. The Union had a lot of plans we could use, but all of them were too risky. We weren't going to lose any more people, not if I could help it.

Once Isidora had left Ilise's room, I'd heard Ilise have another conversation. Since I'd been in front of the door the whole time, I knew there couldn't be anyone else in the room with her. She had been through more than anyone else would in a lifetime, so I didn't feel it was my place to ask just who she was talking to. But it was still peculiar. Worrisome, in fact.

Seagulls squawked overhead and I shielded my eyes against the beaming sun as I reached the deck. The light glinted off the blue water. The sea was sparkling. If only my first time being on the water wasn't when we were running for our lives and trying to save the kingdom. Kass noticed me from where she sat with the rest of the group, hunched over a map of Erea on the floor. She gestured to me and I approached her.

"Any luck?" Kass asked.

"I told you she didn't have the guts to force her way in like I did," Isidora said, leaving her spot on the edge to join us. A satisfied smirk was spread across her face. It made the nerves across my skin tingle with fire.

The clearing of a throat forced my attention away from the very strong temptation I had to throw Isidora overboard.

"Well, Princess," Rori said. "While you were sitting in front of a door, we came up with a few options for what to do when we get back."

"I think you mean, you screamed at each other until your voices got tired and decided to present all of the options for the sake of your sanity," Isidora said.

"You talk a lot for someone who has yet to offer up any ideas," Kieron groaned. He was slumped against the wall with his head in his hands. He looked exactly how I felt, but there would be time to let myself feel the defeat once we got somewhere safe on dry land.

"I don't care what we do, I just want my freedom once we get back," Isidora said. "Come get me when you guys actually make a decision."

At that, she walked back to the underbelly of the ship, no doubt coming up with her own plan in case things went south in Erea.

"So what were the ideas you guys came up with?" I asked.

I hated having them take the lead. My family had played a large part in allowing Imogen to take power the way she had. I'd hoped that after all the lessons, all the shadowing, and all the knowledge I'd gained of court politics, I would have at least come up with even a half plan.

Nothing. I could think of nothing. I needed a weakness of Imogen's to exploit, but it was like the sorceress was flawless. She had the power, she had The Progression to act as her personal army, and she had all the resources of a Queen. What was the crack in the armor?

Val rubbed the back of his neck. "I thought we could attack the palace head on," he said. "They wouldn't expect us to go there directly."

Rori scoffed. "Imogen would follow that exact line of reasoning and have a whole battalion waiting for us once we get there."

As much as it pained me, they were right. Imogen would think of all the obvious solutions we could go with, and attacking directly would be taking the easy way out. I mean, it wouldn't be *easy* per se, but it would be the first option we would go with.

"We'd be killed in an instant if we did that," I said finally. Kieron raised his eyebrows, clearly surprised I was willing to agree with Rori. "What are our other options?"

"My idea was to go into Nitedand and take down The Progression from the inside so Imogen won't have her second army anymore," Rori said.

Kass frowned. "Nitedand is hell, our chances of surviving there are just as low as us surviving the palace."

I'd never been to Nitedand before, but from what I'd heard as of late, it was the last place we would want to be. And all of our faces would be known by Progression members by now. We wouldn't make it two steps without getting recognized.

"But you're from Nitedand, wouldn't we have some chance of making it there?" Cain asked Kass.

I hadn't known Kass was from Nitedand. That must explain her pale skin and the slight accent I couldn't place.

"And you were able to infiltrate The Progression not too long ago," Cain added.

She infiltrated The Progression and made it out alive?

"Yeah, and all I saw was a place that looked nothing like my home, filled with people that would kill us in an instant," Kass said in a flat tone.

My stomach curled with guilt. My kingdom had stopped trying to do anything for Nitedand the moment they closed their borders. I couldn't imagine going back to the place you used to call home and finding it changed for the worst. I had my hand halfway raised to give her shoulder a reassuring pat, but lowered it at the last second. Receiving reassurance from the fake Princess of the kingdom that had failed you might not be the best way to make someone feel better.

"She's right," I said, pointedly ignoring Rori's glare. "And the border has been closed for over a month. Nothing could get us in there."

Rori scoffed. "I don't see you coming up with any ideas. Why don't you try helping instead of shooting down everything."

"So now you want my help? I thought you didn't even want me to be here?" I shot back.

"Well, I have a feeling it wouldn't be appreciated if I threw you overboard so I'm stuck with you," they said. "And that should mean we have another person to help plan, but you have yet to do anything of the sort."

"Can you guys not start fighting again please?" Chafik said. I hadn't even noticed him where he sat perched against the door to the captain quarters.

"Then tell your Princess friend to stop being difficult," Rori snapped.

Chafik took a deep breath before standing up.

"Look, I know you're all probably scared, even if you don't care to admit it. I'm scared. I don't have nearly as much training or experience as the rest of you, so if things go south, I'm done for. Yet you don't see me arguing with everyone on the ship because I know none of us have a chance of making it out alive if we waste this time arguing."

It was so silent I could have sworn even the birds stopped chirping.

"I knew I always liked you," Kieron said. Chafik was right. Even if Rori wasn't in the mood for it, one of us had to be the bigger person. "Now let's have a civilized, calm conversation. And if you don't, I can get Isidora who I highly doubt will appreciate being disturbed."

Kass snorted. "I don't think she appreciates being on this ship in general."

After Chafik's comment, we continued our discussion about what to do, but to no avail. Every idea we could come up with ended in us dying in multiple ways before we even got close to the palace. A heavy feeling settled in my gut. We were only eight people, hardly enough to take on a sorceress who had more power than any other, while being on the run from basically half the kingdom.

It was almost time for the sun to set and we were no better off from when we started. I needed to get over myself and talk to the one person that might be able to help us find a way to defeat Imogen.

"I'm going to get Ilise to help us," I said.

Rori raised a skeptical eyebrow. They opened their mouth to say something but Chafik shot them a warning glare that was scarier than anything Rori had ever shot toward me. I was glad I wasn't on the receiving end of that look.

"She always was one of our most helpful strategists," Kass said as she stared out the waves. "But she's also the most stubborn. Good luck."

I nodded and walked belowdecks, lighting the glass-covered oil lamps lining the walls as I went. I reached the door to Ilise's room and my hand hovered in place. I knew the answer to our problem was just on the other side of the door, but I couldn't force my fist to knock. Ilise could barely look me in the eye the entire way to the coast, as if even the thought of looking at me brought her pain. But the kingdom couldn't be in danger because of my overly-confusing feelings. Pushing them as far deep as I could, I finally knocked on the door.

"Ilise?"

No answer.

I knocked again, harder this time.

"Ilise, we need your help," I said.

I heard shuffling on the other side of the door, and I could've sworn she had moved so she was just on the other side of the door.

"I can't help you," she said. "I only bring ruin to anyone I try to help, and I don't want to be the reason any of you get hurt anymore."

My heart broke. I hated that she believed that. All the pain Ereans had suffered was because Imogen had used her as nothing more than a puppet, someone to receive all the consequences of what she had planned for the kingdom. I needed to show her she was the only person who could save the kingdom, the only person who could stop anyone else from getting hurt. But first I needed to get her attention.

"I thought you were stronger than that," I said.

The door handle clicked and I stepped back as Ilise finally opened the door. The look on her face told me she didn't appreciate my response, but it was what I needed to say to get her to open the door.

"Excuse me?" she said.

I pushed myself into the small room before she could shut me out again and perched myself on the rickety bed. Ilise sighed and shut the door, leaning against the farthest wall possible from me.

"What are you doing?" she asked.

"I'm not moving until you fully understand the words I'm about to say." Ilise frowned but didn't object. *Okay Yorena, you can do this.*

"We miss you, Ilise. No matter how much you try to distance yourself from us, the hole you left still hurts."

Her face softened, ever so slightly.

"It hurts to know you still blame yourself for everything that's gone wrong. It hurts that we can't do anything to help you. It hurts knowing I couldn't do enough to protect you from Imogen in the first place, and it hurts knowing I still can't protect you from the effects of her now."

Ilise's expression matched the way I felt, like my heart was bleeding out in front of me. My throat was thick with the start of tears, but I had to get through this. For her.

"I'm not going to let you go, and I'm not going to let you sit here and carry all of this guilt."

Ilise opened her mouth to speak, but I continued before she could say anything.

"I know you feel awful about what Imogen made you do, but it isn't your fault. You can't sit here and blame yourself when you probably have the knowledge we need to get ourselves out of this mess and make up for all the pain she's caused."

I rose from the bed and crossed the small distance between us. I was close enough that she had to look up at me, and I could see the silver and gold flecks dancing in her dark eyes, finally free from the violet cracks Imogen had placed in them.

"Come back to us, please," I begged, my voice cracking.

A single tear slid down Ilise's face and I cupped her soft cheek, wiping it away.

"I'll try," she said, almost in a whisper.

My face broke out into a large smile. *I did it.*

"I missed that smile."

My stomach fluttered and the air between us felt charged with lightning. She pulled away before I could respond and opened the door for us. I grabbed her hand, taking it as a small victory when she didn't pull away, and led her to the main deck.

Val halted mid-sentence when six sets of eyes landed on me and Ilise. Kieron didn't even try to hide his shock, his mouth agape.

"Look who I found," I said.

She wiggled her hand out of my grasp and I tried to pretend it didn't sting.

"Ilise," Rori said with a smile.

They stood up to come and embrace her but before Rori could get to her, she said, "I'm just here to help you plan what to do when we get back to land." Rori frowned but didn't object.

"It's good to see you out of your room, kid," Kass said.

Ilise was being distant on purpose. Clearly my speech hadn't worked as well as I thought it had, but the fact that she was here meant there was still a chance we could convince her to release the guilt.

Ilise took a deep breath and moved to the center of the group.

"Imogen will always outsmart us, the only way to make a jab at her is to go for her superiority. She only has power over people through bully tactics and threats. We just have to take away the things she is using to threaten people."

We all shared a look of confusion. "And what would that be?" Val asked.

"We need to get rid of The Progression before we can do anything else. It's time to cut the head off the beast."

Chapter 30

Nikos

On one shoulder, I had a snoring prisoner who appeared to have never grown out of the sleep-drooling phase, and on the other shoulder I had Oliver's head, their hair taking up all of my room to breathe. Five days of playing babysitter for an overgrown child, five days of no information from Imogen, five days of fighting the urge to break Daeva out and make a run for it. And what did I get for a reward? This. And now, even worse, we had to go visit my father in Kentfallsworth for Spirits knows what.

We'd left the castle the day after Yorena and her allies had fled the castle, and now we were in the carriage on the way to my father's manor. I couldn't see why we couldn't meet at the palace. I hated the manor. It was basically the home base of The Progression—the last place I wanted to be. At least Imogen had sent Daeva back to the palace with the soldiers. I didn't want her anywhere near that place.

The carriage rattled as it crossed over thick tree roots roping across the road. My father was a recluse. So of course, he had to make sure the way to the manor was a difficult one. If we didn't know where we were going, it would look like we were randomly traveling through the woods.

We rode over an especially large tree root and the carriage jumped. Mathias jerked his head up, accidentally bumping his head against the ceiling of the carriage.

"Ouch! What was that?" he said, rubbing his head.

"We just went over a tree root, calm down. And since you're awake, I would appreciate it if you would stop using me as a pillow," I said.

He frowned, but moved to the seat on the opposite side. "And I would appreciate it if you said please every once in a while."

I scoffed. I didn't even know why Mathias was here. Imogen had yet to tell me what to do with him. The only difference between him and me was that I could at least go wherever I wanted in the small area Imogen allowed me to go.

"I wasn't aware I was supposed to be nice to prisoners," I said.

"Maybe you're jealous I don't get treated that differently from you."

"I don't get jealous," I said.

"Sure," Mathias taunted.

I ignored him for the rest of the ride, which was slightly more bearable without him talking. Streams of orange light beamed through the window as we neared the manor. A jolt of danger spiked through me upon seeing the towering white columns, and the chiseled mural of the four Spirits. It'd been years since I'd last been here, and my body was still fearful of the damn place. All because of that one fateful day.

Daeva and I had been on a walk through the main village. It'd been such a nice day, the first warm day of the season, and everyone was outside, smiling at each other as they passed. But while everyone was soaking up the sun we hadn't seen in so long, my attention stayed glued to Daeva.

We were set to marry in a few weeks, and I would finally get to spend the rest of my life with her. She'd smiled at a child who'd run straight into her legs. The mother had started her frantic apologies when she'd recognized me, but Daeva had let them go with a smile. My heart clenched, and I knew I would do anything to keep that smile on her face.

"Are you ready to go home, darling?" I'd asked. She'd looked up at the sky. The sun had just started to set, and pink and orange streaked through the sky.

"The sun hasn't set yet, can't we stay a little longer?"

I'd wanted to take her back to the small house we had on the edge of the town to give her a gift I had prepared for her. Living together before marriage was quite uncommon in Nitedand, but it was safer for us to do so. We had to constantly be on alert for my father, and that forced us to live somewhat separated from everyone here, so I'd made it my mission to make sure Daeva was the happiest person here. She popped out her bottom lip in a pout and I knew there would be no denying her.

I planted a light kiss on the top of her head, tucking her closer to my side. "As you wish. But I have a surprise for you at home," I said.

She beamed at me, and in that moment I knew that no matter how hard it was, keeping her away from my father was worth it if I could see her smile like that for the rest of my life.

"Where do you want to g—" My sentence was cut off as a thick boot kicked me in the middle of my back. I tumbled to the ground, sucking in lungfuls of air.

"Nikos!" Daeva screamed.

I shot up from the ground and charged the man who'd dared to kick me. Everyone in the square had run screaming from the scene, but all I could focus on was the way the man had Daeva in his grip. No one hurt Daeva and lived—no one. The flood of strength from my crystal only did more to fan the flames of my anger.

Thick roots had sprouted from the ground and shot toward the man. Had I still been paying attention to my surroundings, I would have noticed a familiar man come up behind me.

"Don't even think about it, son," my father had warned. I froze. "I think it's time we had a talk."

I was thrown from the memory with a jolt as the carriage crossed over the last root before the dirt road smoothed out into cobblestone. Oliver had finally removed their head from my shoulder and was now looking wistfully out the window. The manor grew closer with each second, its looming structure almost taunting me. And the fact that Oliver looked upon it with such reverence, such awe, made my gut clench with disgust.

"Are you done staring at me?" Mathias said.

"What?" *Was I staring at him the whole time?*

His face broke out in a grin. "If you find me so attractive, you can just say so."

I scoffed. "As if I would find the likes of you attractive," I deadpanned.

The carriage parked in front of the manor, and Oliver crawled over me to get out first. Imogen waited on the entrance steps of the structure, her arms crossed. Imogen had decided to ride ahead of us, and the expression on her face told me she didn't enjoy having to wait for us.

"Let's go before you make the sorceress angry," I said.

I jumped down from the carriage and stared up at the manor. Putting my memories aside, it was a nice place to live. The back structure of the building had an entirely glass roof, allowing the light to shine on what I knew was the library. Was the light good for the books? No. But it was the only part of the manor that showed life—energy.

Out of all the places in the manor, it was the one place I had fond memories of. Sequestering myself away to avoid the flood of Progression members who would come in and out of the house, spending the whole day trying to read as many books as I could before the sun went down, and making my own little garden in the leftover space to take care of and improve my abilities.

The rest of the house was little more than a glorified block. It was meant to impress with the friezes of the four Spirits, gold columns wrapped in vines, and a shining marble floor throughout the house. But I knew it had no soul.

The three of us exited the carriage and followed Imogen into the manor. My boots echoed noisily off the walls, as if to drive home just how hollow of a home it had been.

We passed through a series of golden archways before arriving in the main meeting room. It wasn't as ornately decorated as the rest of the house, with nothing more than a few plush, white, pristine couches, and a wooden table in the middle. I glared at the man already seated at the head. My father. My jailer. Daeva's captor. Part of the reason the kingdom was falling apart. He was a lot of things, and a father was at the bottom of the list.

"Hello, son," he said, his voice devoid of any emotion a father would normally greet his son with.

I stared at him blankly.

"Now, is that the proper way to greet your father?"

"Hello, Father," I said, swallowing my pride. It was like there was a line of electricity between us. The tension in the room was thick enough to cut with a knife. He stared at me. I stared at him. It'd been a year since we'd seen each other in person, and it seemed the time had done nothing to ease the animosity between u s.

"Let us begin," Imogen said.

I sat at the end of the table, as far from the two of them as I could. Oliver sat to the left of my father, their face bearing a look of admiration. I fought the urge to vomit all over the table. Anyone who looked at my father with reverence was a lunatic. But I supposed that was an accurate adjective for Oliver. Mathias sat next to me. It appeared he had at least a little sense to not sit near the people who were against his very existence. Personally, if I were a Primis in his shoes, I wouldn't even be in the same room as us, let alone sharing a table.

"Since Yorena and her *allies* have taken Ilise back, we will have to operate without her from here forward," Imogen said. *Good*. Ilise was the most powerful person in the kingdom who wasn't a sorcerer. At least as far as we knew. People with control over more than one element had never been able to hide it easily. So if we hadn't heard about anyone else by now, there most likely weren't any others alive. What was left of the Union needed all the power they could get.

"A fake princess and a few Union members was all it took to overpower you?" my father seethed. "That girl was supposed to be our best weapon for taking the kingdom, and keeping it."

But at least now she was the person who would kill my father without a second thought. I wouldn't stop her.

"Letting her go will only help us in the near future. Right now it's time to begin phase two of our plan," she said.

My father's mouth quickly turned from a sneer to a grin. *Phase two*?

"What's phase two?" Oliver asked.

"I'm so glad you asked, my friend. We're going to start relocating all the Primis people out of all those nice homes in their villages into more *suitable* places. Only Imperium deserve the best homes," he said.

But that would leave them without jobs, without the places they'd been living in for who knows how long. First, Imogen had made Ilise seize all Primis-owned businesses, and now this? How much more were they planning to take? I didn't say of this out loud of course, and my face betrayed nothing—showing nothing more than mild disinterest.

I'd learned how to do that a long time ago. With a father like mine, keeping all of your thoughts off your face was a required skill. Or else I wouldn't have been able to avoid him for so long while I was planning to marry Daeva. My father had still captured her before the wedding happened, but I'd only gotten that close to getting married and escaping with her *because* my father couldn't discern anything from me.

Another thing I'd learned was to leave when you knew your mask was close to slipping. I pushed my chair away from the table, the legs scraping across the marble with a loud scrape.

"This does not appear to concern me, I'll be upstairs," I said. My father grunted in response and took it as a sign that he didn't care.

I walked out of the room and was halfway up the winding staircase when I heard the clack of quick feet behind me.

"Mind if I join you?" Mathias said.

Can the Spirits not grant me one moment of peace?

Chapter 31

Nikos

"**Y**ES, I DO MIND if you join me," I said. I continued up the staircase, pretending not to hear Mathias' footsteps behind me. "What's the point of asking if you're going to follow me anyway?"

We stopped at the top of the stairs. "Imogen told me to follow you because she was annoyed by my presence." *For once I agree with the sorceress on something.* "And it doesn't sound like you have much of a choice in the matter so..." *For Spirits' sake.*

"Fine. Just don't be annoying," I grumbled. There weren't many places in this house I particularly enjoyed, and the back of the house was off limits unless I wanted to walk back through the main meeting room. With nowhere else to go, I headed toward the room I'd spent the other half of my time in as a child.

My old room was tucked into the back corner of the hallway, as if it had been put there as an afterthought. I twisted the gilded doorknob, the door opening with a loud creak. It had to have been at least three years since I'd last stepped into this room.

Mathias stepped through the doorway after me, letting out a low whistle. "Is there any part of this place that *isn't* as fancy as a palace?"

I ignored his question, but the answer to that would be no. My father cared very much about how other people perceived him, and what better way to make yourself appear better than you were than with an upscale house?

My poster bed had been pushed into the corner, along with my dresser and old desk. My old chairs and chaise had been draped over with a giant cloth, making it appear as if this was the room of someone deceased. *Fitting.* Mathias flopped onto the bed and a large dust cloud was released from the sheets, eliciting a series of coughs from him.

He rose from the bed, waving away the dust particles still swirling around his head.

"Man, if my parents had a house like this I don't think I would ever leave," he said.

Why don't you try living with a sadistic man for a father.

"Why are you so casual about being held captive?" I asked. "Have you no fear for your life?" Where was the fear he'd shown when Imogen had first taken hold of him at the castle? He was acting as if this were a fun vacation.

Mathias strolled around, soaking in every minute detail of the room. The opulent white columns on the wall, and the balcony overlooking a man-made pond on the manicured grounds, hardly felt like the room for a child. Everything in here had always seemed too cold, like even breathing on anything would ruin the beauty of it.

"You aren't half as scary as that sorceress, and she's the one that told you to watch over me so I doubt you're allowed to kill me. And it's rather entertaining how easy it is to annoy you," Mathias said.

I scowled.

"If you keep scowling like that, your face will get stuck that way."

"That's a children's tale."

Mathias clicked his tongue. "Then don't come crying to me when your face doesn't let you smile anymore," he said, grinning. The idea of sewing his lips shut in that moment brought me more joy than I'd ever felt in a long time. Would Imogen really be that upset if I did? My lips twitched into an upward curve.

"See, it isn't so hard," Mathias said.

Oh, if only he knew what was making me smile. The only thing that kept me from following through was the knowledge that whatever annoyances he came up with would be ten times better than sitting at that table downstairs. I may not have been the poster child for being a good citizen, but even I had the decency to not take over a kingdom just to return things to the horrible way they were a millennium ago.

Mathias and I stared at each other for a few moments, neither of us knowing what to do to fill the silence. I could tell it made him uncomfortable. I leaned against the closed door, silently laughing at the way he seemed to squirm under my gaze. That was the difference between me and my father. I might be slightly twisted, but at least I could keep it to myself. At least enough that Mathias wasn't running screaming out of the room. My father was the type of man who made getting away from him more important than taking care of your child. But could I really blame my mother? No.

"So...what was it like to grow up here?" Mathias asked, no doubt past his threshold for standing in silence.

I shrugged. "Fine," I said.

He frowned. "Just fine?" I shook my head and he moved on to toying with the cloth draped over my old sitting area. "I might not have grown up in a mansion, but I could still think of a few more words to describe my childhood than 'fine'," he said, humor staining his voice.

"There was this one time when I—" Mathias' sentence was cut off as he tripped over a box poking out from under the cloth, barely saving his face from hitting the floor. Piles of letters poured onto the floor. "What are all of these?"

I crossed the room, crouching to consolidate the messy pile. "Just some old letters and notes," I said.

When I was younger, barely even a teenager, my father used to leave me notes and letters everyday since he couldn't even be bothered to talk to his only son. Some of them were a to-do list, some were lists of people he needed me to find—no doubt because they were hiding from him—and some were him outlining the latest thing I'd done to displease him. Reading over the faded, cramped, loopy, nearly unreadable handwriting brought a scowl to my face.

Scooping the papers into my hands, I stuffed them back into the box, back to a place where they could never remind me of my old life again. One note fluttered out of my grip, floating to the ground. Mathias grabbed it before I could, squinting to read the probably illegible scrawl.

I snatched it back from him, crushing the paper in my fist. "Did anyone ever tell you not to read someone else's personal letters?"

He shrugged. "It looked older than the rest so I was curious," he said, putting his hands up. *Older?* I uncrumpled the note and smoothed it out against my leg. He was right, the ink on this paper was at least twice as faded as the others. Strange.

"Hmm," I said. Reading my father's handwriting normally was a challenge, with this letter, it was a nearly impossible feat. Deciphering even one sentence was beyond my abilities, but I could make a few words. Daeva, time, love, hold. Why would my father have been talking to someone about Daeva? She wasn't from any of the noble-born families, so my father had chosen to mostly ignore her existence. At least until he had decided to use her to keep me in line.

"I told you," Mathias said. The date was nearly faded as well, but it was just dark enough for me to see. It was from five years ago. That was around the first time I'd met Daeva. I wouldn't have mentioned her at that point, so why was she in this letter? It must have gotten mixed in when my father had packed up my room. And being stuffed unceremoniously into the box must have smudged the old ink.

"Earth to Nikos," Mathias said, waving a hand in my face.

I opened my mouth, ready to demand that he leave, but then I got an idea. "How would you like to do me a favor?" Maybe instead of torturing myself with his irksome personality, I could use it to my advantage. If my father had been meddling in Daeva's life, I needed to know about it. I wasn't normally one to worry about the collateral damage of my father's antics, but Daeva was off limits. She was the one person I would always protect. The only place I could find answers about this letter was in my father's study. And if he walked in while I was searching his correspondence, there was no telling what he would do.

Mathias' face spread in a wide grin. "What kind of favor?" What would I have him do? In a perfect world, I'd have him drag out their meeting by distracting the trio downstairs, but Imogen would either kill him or throw him in a dungeon. That wouldn't help me. I needed a lookout. Depending how deep in the study I had to search, I needed a decent amount of time to erase any evidence of me being there, and Mathias could give me a warning signal.

"You will be my lookout," I said.

He raised an eyebrow. "A lookout for who?" he asked.

"Just make a loud noise when you see my father coming up the stairs."

"Okay," Mathias said, crossing the room to perch himself on the edge of the bed. "What do I get out of it?"

What could I give him? There wasn't much I could do for him in the way of his freedom. Even after Imogen let him go—possibly—he would still only be a servant, so bribing him with more money wouldn't be enticing either. Wait. I was overthinking this. This man was hardly an adult, more childish than half the teenagers in The Progression. I didn't need much to repay him.

"I'll give you extra dessert when we get back to the palace."

"Deal."

With Mathias stationed at the top of the stairs, I teased open the door to my father's study, just on the other end of the hallway. Stacks upon stacks of boxes surrounded the room, making it seem smaller, like the walls were threatening to cave in. Light streamed in through the giant window on the far wall, illuminating the dark space. A light layer of dust coated the mahogany desk. Father must not have been here in a while. Good. That meant there was even less of a chance that he would walk in on me.

Not wasting any more time, I crossed the room to the wall of boxes. My father was meticulous. He organized everything so neatly, even a half-literate toddler could manage to find whatever they were looking for. First, the papers were organized by year, then by the province they came from, by which town they were from—alphabetized, I might add—and finally by the last name of the sender. It didn't take me long to find the section from Nitedand, five years ago.

There wasn't much before the files moved on to Ominka. I moved the heavy box over to the desk, removing all the files from Nitedand at the time that interested me. My eyes caught on another file from Havenwood—Daeva's hometown. I removed the file and returned the box to its correct place in the pile, taking extra care to make sure it looked exactly as it did before. If my father were to notice something amiss, he would instantly blame me. He never could seem to blame himself for anything.

A hoarse scream echoed down the hall. I froze. It sounded like Mathias, and that meant...

Clacking footsteps sounded from the hall. *My father.* I hurried to skim through the slightly crumpled notes in the Havenwood file. I was about to ignore the note until my eyes caught on Daeva's name. The footsteps were right outside the door when I stuffed the discarded notes back into the file, and just as I was about to tuck the letter into my pocket, the thin parchment ripped in half. *Dammit.* One long foot stepped into the door.

I had no time. I stuffed the half of the letter I was able to get into my pocket and tossed the rest of it behind the box it'd come from. I would have to come back later to put it back correctly before he noticed.

"Nikos," my father grumbled. "What do you think you are doing?" I flailed my arms around the desk, searching, praying I would find something.

"I was just looking for a...uh, fountain pen," I lied rather poorly. My fingers grasped the smooth surface of a fountain pen. "The one I was using ran out of ink."

My father narrowed his eyes at me, but didn't outright accuse me of lying. "Get out," he ordered. I didn't acknowledge him as I rushed out of the room, the letter in my pocket almost burning a hole in my trousers. The moment I entered my room, I ripped the letter from my pocket and began to decipher the faded ink.

She will be arriving within the coming days. The school has already accepted my letter to allow her to attend. We expect our payment to be given upon arrival, we would hate for this to get out of hand. And trust us, she will...

She will what? Who was this "she"? Was this letter about Daeva? How could I have been so careless? I had risked my father's wrath just to get only half the information I needed.

Dammit.

Chapter 32

Yorena

WE SAILED FOR ANOTHER day before we saw land. The dreary landscape of Nitedand hunched like a menacing beast in the distance, my sense of foreboding growing as we inched ever closer. It was almost always raining in the province, making much of the land more of a swamp than the grasslands found throughout Erea.

Brooding clouds hovered over Linhex, the small port city of Nitedand. Almost nothing was shipped here, so it was the best place for us to dock. And it was closer to the next destination that Ilise had decided on. Her plan would eliminate one of the biggest obstacles we had between us and taking back Erea—The Progression.

Kieron stomped up the steps to the deck, his arms overflowing with all the rope he could find. "Do you think this'll be enough?" he asked. The thick ropes dropped with a loud thud.

"I think it'll be plenty," I chuckled.

I felt Ilise's presence as if through a sixth-sense as she climbed the edge of the ship.

"Looks like we'll dock within the hour. All of you need to be ready before then," she said. She spared neither of us a glance as she walked back to wherever she had decided to hide herself from us. After she'd told us her plan, none of us could find her. Not in her room, not on the deck, not in the brig.

"Hello to you too," Kieron muttered as she walked off. "Remember what I said about those ghosts in the Archives?"

I nodded.

"I think she got possessed by one, 'cause she just keeps appearing and reappearing."

I let out an empty laugh. However dumb Kieron's ghost stories were, I didn't think he was too far off. Helping us plan out our arrival had seemed to revitalize Ilise, if only slightly. She had even smiled once. But I imagined she almost felt like a ghost, floating around here without quite knowing her place. I would have to try harder to get her to forgive herself. Even just a little to lift the burden she insisted on carrying.

Footsteps sounded behind me, and I turned to find the rest of our makeshift team.

"Are we ready to get started?" Val asked.

Me and Kieron nodded.

Val picked up one of the ropes. "So, who wants to go first?"

Note to self: in case I ever had to bind my wrists with rope again, always keep a layer of fabric between the rope and my skin. The coarse bindings chafed, and I was shocked I hadn't started bleeding yet. Dark clouds floated overhead, the promise of a storm evident in the quick flashes of lighting illuminating the gloomy sky.

My head was hung low, trying to play the part of the defeated prisoner. Though I would have been looking down anyway to prevent myself from tripping over the loose planks on the dock, made worse by the mud squishing beneath my feet. Kieron's heavy footsteps behind me were one of the only other sounds besides the crashing waves.

Ilise marched at the front of our dreary procession. Even without a crown on her head, she carried herself like a true Queen. Our feet met with the softened ground as we walked off the dock, gaining the attention of the two posted guards. Since this port was rarely used, there was hardly a need for an entire squad.

One of the guards, who had a head of blonde locks, held up her hand, signaling us to stop. "State your business," she said. I lifted my head up slightly, watching the proceedings through a shroud of hair.

"I demand entrance into the city and carts for my prisoners," Ilise said, her voice firm. The guards looked at her, and then trailed their eyes down our line.

"Name?" he said.

"Ilise Obrien." When they didn't acknowledge her she said, "Your Queen." The two guards looked at each other before unsheathing the broadswords at their hips. *Hells.*

"Who do you think you are, raising a sword against your Queen," Ilise seethed.

The white crystals at the guards' throats glowed a brilliant white as twin smiles spread across their faces.

"According to the Council of Sorcerers, you betrayed the crown."

My heart dropped into my stomach. How could Imogen have gotten word to Erea this quickly? I shot a panicked glance back toward Kieron, and saw that the expression on his face mirrored mine.

Kieron jerked his head toward the ropes binding our hands, a nearly imperceptible nod. Taking care to keep the glow of my crystal down, I started burning through his bindings. It felt as if the guards could hear the subtle sizzling of the rope fibers, smell the smoke mingling with the damp mud.

"We're under orders to arrest you on sight," the blonde guard said.

"Let's untie the others," Kieron whispered as I finally burned through the thick ropes. I hunched over to hide the glow of my crystal as I quickly burned through my ropes, as well.

"All unoccupied soldiers report to the Linhex port, the traitor Queen has returned," the other guard said, their summoning being carried to the town by the wind. The two guards rushed Ilise, and she blocked them with the staff she'd strapped to her back. Ilise pushed them farther from the dock, taking their fight farther into the mud.

"Hurry up you two," Rori said from the back of the line. My hands were still half-numb from being wrapped in the rope. I fumbled to untie Val, Cain, and

Chafik, attempting to burn through at least some of their ropes. Isidora splashed into a puddle of water before I could get to her, rematerializing in front of me.

"Take Chafik somewhere safe," I said, starting toward Ilise.

Isidora groaned. "Can't I do something fun?" she said.

"Isidora, please," Chafik said. She sighed, but led him some distance up the coast.

Rori and Kass rushed toward the two guards, speeding past me faster than Pamuese cheetahs, so fast I could only see the blur of their crystals and Rori's fiery hair. Val grabbed my arm from behind before I could get too far away, and leaned in close to my ear.

"Follow Kass and Rori, the rest of us will stay back for the other guards they summoned," he said. I gave a quick nod before running after the pair, my boots slipping across the damp ground.

I hated Nitedand.

Ilise stood over one of the guards who was already immobile in the mud, the skin of his face charred and bloody. *Oh, Ilise.*

"Are you gonna actually fight, or just slow us down?" Rori grunted when they spotted me, their sword in a standstill with the other guard's.

Instead of answering, I sloppily, unceremoniously, chucked one of my daggers at the guard they were fighting. The blade embedded itself into his bicep. *I was going for the leg, but I guess that's fine too.* The guard dropped his sword, letting out a scream of agony as he gripped the dagger, attempting to pull it out. Kass ran past me, leaping into the air to deliver a spinning kick to the guard's face. The guard slumped to the ground, unconscious.

"This wasn't supposed to happen," Ilise muttered, joining us.

It wasn't. If the plan had gone as it was meant to, we would have already been loaded up into carts and on our way to Kentfallsworth. If we wanted to eliminate The Progression, we had to get rid of the leader. Wayne Vikander. My stomach twisted at the thought of having to take someone's life. Sure, Wayne Vikander was a horrible, sadistic man, but capturing him would just make our little group a homing beacon. I loathed to think we would have to kill someone. But if it was what would keep Erea safe by crippling Imogen's expansive soldiers, then it would be worth it.

Kass brushed some of the dried dirt off her leather suit, coming up beside me with Rori.

"We need to get carts so we don't have to walk the whole way to Vikander's manor," Rori said.

"We also need to dispatch the guards that are surely coming our way," I added.

Ilise clicked her tongue, running a finger along the sharp edge of one of the blades strapped to her thigh.

"Isidora and Chafik can get the carts. Shouldn't be too dangerous. You and Rori go toward the town and try to slow down the troops while the rest of us get ready for them to come," she said finally.

"Why do I have to go with her?" Rori asked, not bothering to hide their displeasure.

"We need the stronger fighters back here, and Yorena needs someone with good fighting skills so she doesn't get *killed*," Ilise said.

"Fine," Rori said with a curt nod. They stalked off in the direction of town, forcing me to trail after them.

"Thanks for waiting," I remarked. They shot me a deadly glance. "It would be in our best interest for you to stop hating me for a few minutes while we hold back the guards."

They scoffed. "I was able to play nice for Ilise's sake, but she's not here right now."

I grabbed Rori's shoulder, forcing them to stop and look at me. "Look, the only way we're going to take back Erea is if we can all work together. And it's a lot harder than it needs to be right now when you're so insistent on being against me."

Depending on how much protection Wayne Vikander had at his manor, this could be a suicide mission. He'd managed to escape capture and what had to be a countless number of assassination attempts already. We wouldn't scare him. But if we failed to kill him, The Progression would continue to be used as Imogen's cannon fodder. Arguing at every turn would only hinder us.

"You'll only hold us back. You can barely fight, your strategizing skills leave much to be desired despite the fancy education I'm sure you've received, and you shoot down any ideas we have because you don't want to dirty your little Princess hands," they seethed.

"I can do more than you think."

We were both pulled out of our argument by the faint sound of pounding hooves. We turned our heads to see about a dozen guards racing toward us on horseback. Less than I'd expected, but still a lot. Rori nodded toward the incoming stampede.

"You say you can do more than I think? Prove it."

I wasn't completely confident, but I was up for the challenge. I would prove myself to Rori once and for all, I hoped. I may not have been allowed to help the Commander with military strategy—considering there wasn't much use for it until now—but I did know more than a few things about strategy games. I just had to look at the guards like players on a chess board.

One of the quickest ways to win a game of chess was to outsmart your opponent, make them fall for whatever trap you'd laid. We couldn't overpower these guards. But we needed to get them far away from us while we started toward Kentfallsworth. But really, we didn't need to overpower them, just nudge them in the direction of a trap. Rori had power over air, and I had power over fire. Surely that was enough for a little nudge. I turned back to Rori.

"I have an idea."

"If this works, are you ready to admit you were wrong?" I said. The rest of the group and I were hidden in the few trees scattered around the port, ready in case things went south.

"Not a chance," Rori said. They waded in the water up to their knees.

"I'm sure that will change very soon."

Mud flew into the air as the black steeds pounded toward the coast, so close I could clearly see the swords in the riders' hands, the subtle shine of the Erean crest on their uniforms.

I activated my crystal, summoning more fire than I had ever summoned at once. I could almost feel heat coming from the crystal as well, as it blinded me with its orange glow. A wall of fire appeared behind the guards.

"Get to the water!" the leading guard shouted, clearly not understanding where the fire had come from, but eager to get away from it. Rori ducked underneath the dock, readying for their attack. My arms shook as I moved the fire wall strategically, so that the guards would be forced to retreat to the area where Rori was hidden. My pulse pounded in my ears, overpowering the sound of the galloping horses, and the sound of the screaming guards. I felt myself falter, my knees starting to give out.

"You've got this," Kieron said, moving to stand behind me in case I fell. He placed his hands at my waist, keeping me upright. I clenched my teeth together. The guards were just to the waterline. I finally released the wall upon seeing the first splash of water, collapsing into a panting heap on the ground.

"You did it!" Kieron cheered.

I propped myself up on my elbows to witness the last part of my plan. With enough water around, an air crystal could be used the same way as a water crystal. Rori generated a massive gust of wind, their crystal lighting up the bleak landscape. The wave swept up the guards, carrying them far out to sea.

The guards' screams were drowned out by the enormous wave, which was nearly the height of the palace I had grown up in. Now, I could see the heads of the soldiers out in the water. Not so far out that they wouldn't be able to swim back—I didn't want to cause more loss of life, but enough that it would take them quite a while to get back to shore.

"Have anything to say?" I shouted to a soaking wet Rori as they stepped out of the muddy water.

The smallest smile graced their face, and I suddenly realized they weren't as menacing as I'd thought.

"You were right. This time."

CHAPTER 33

ILISE

L UCKILY, THE ONLY GUARDS in the entirety of Linhex had been the ones Yorena and Rori had thrown out to sea. The town was desolate, the only signs of civilization being the few dilapidated houses dotting the marsh. And if anyone had witnessed what we'd done to those guards, I doubted they would report us. Even the nosy old woman every village seemed to have was absent, or minding her own business for once. But the town was far behind us now. We'd mobilized as soon as Isidora and Chafik had returned with carts to get ahead of the guards swimming to shore.

I'd thought nothing would be worse than slogging through the thick mud of Linhex, but where we were now was much worse. We were in the woods. I had traveled through forest multiple times in my life, but this was more than just a forest. The trees blocked the faint amount of sunlight that was able to break through the clouds, and it felt as if the crooked branches were reaching out for us, trying to ensnare us in their grasp. We were still a few hours from Wayne's manor, after riding without a break for almost two days, taking shifts at the reins. As far as I could tell, Val drove the other cart, which was behind mine. There was a light blue tinge to the scant sky I could see, which meant the sun was probably rising again.

I was at the reins now, and a lightly snoring Yorena was curled up beside me after I'd convinced her to get some sleep. She needed it. Her display of power was unlike anything I'd seen from her before—in fact, seen from anyone before. I had to fight the urge to brush aside the strand of hair that had fallen into her face, floating into the air with her every breath.

It was in quiet times like these that I was truly able to commit her face to memory. The soft curve of her jawline, her light brown skin—impossibly smooth, the glow she always seemed to have even in sleep, even in this bleak province, her heart shaped mouth. But at the same time, looking at her sparked too many emotions in me. Anger, fear, shame, and something I'd rather not name.

She and the others could have gotten hurt because my plan to get us through the guards had worked for all of twenty seconds. We wouldn't have had to throw a whole squad out to sea if I'd been able to see that Imogen would never let me go *and* let me keep my authority. That would have given me power over her, and she couldn't allow that. I now understood that her goal was nothing short of a total kingdom takeover.

And what had I done to help with the resulting fallout? I had killed a guard, and then sat behind a tree while Yorena and Rori saved us. This shouldn't have to be their fight. So why did I have to sit there, completely useless?

A few hours passed, until we suddenly broke out of the forest with a large bump, which doubtless woke the sleeping passengers of the carts with a start. The clouds were beginning to disperse, chasing away the earlier chill.

"Are we there yet?" Yorena asked, rubbing the sleep from her eyes.

"Yup," I said, forcing myself to tear my eyes off of her. The facade of imposing manor revealed itself as we trudged up a lush green hill, which served as a stark contrast to the muddy forest we'd just left. I guessed a perk of being an Earth Imperium family meant you could pretend you weren't living in this dump of a province. No offense to Kass, but it was awful.

We pulled up to the front of the house. I made sure the horse was secured to one of the front columns and started walking up the steps, barely noticing whether the others were with me. I felt nothing. I was on the doorstep of the man who had made my life a living hell, finally on the brink of being able to ensure that he wouldn't be able to hurt anyone ever again, and I felt nothing. There was no joy, no excitement, no relief, only what felt like a heavy curtain draped over my heart.

Yorena's footsteps were so silent that I hadn't even heard her come up next to me. She grabbed my hand, lacing our fingers together. I didn't pull away; I squeezed her hand hard.

"Are you ready?" she asked.

I nodded. "We'll shout if anyone attacks," I said to the others. Val gave a subtle nod, and I kicked open the door. The house was quiet—too quiet. Thin streams of light illuminated the dark space, dust particles dancing in the beams. I sniffed the air. Something smelled, a familiar odor.

Yorena coughed. "What is that smell?" she said, pinching her nose between her finger and thumb.

I simply held my breath and walked up the stairs. "Maybe we'll find out," I said. Our footsteps echoed on the marble. "Where could Wayne be?" I asked.

Yorena looked up and down the long corridor. "Let's follow the smell and see if that'll give us a clue as to where he went," she said, wrinkling her nose.

My stomach roiled at the smell—something resembling rotting fruit, or garbage that had been sitting out in the heat. We walked to the edge of the hall, and the stench only got stronger. A door at the end of the hall was ajar.

"Is it coming from here?" Yorena asked.

I shrugged. I pushed open the door and Yorena let out a shrill, horrified scream that echoed through the house. Heavy footsteps pounded up the stairs and the rest of our group burst into the room, swords brandished.

"What? Who?" Kieron yelled before recoiling at the scene. "What in four hells is that?"

In the middle of the room, there were boxes, which had been knocked over, papers spilling out of them, many appearing to have been burned. There was also a desk in the room, and it was broken, smashed right down the middle. The remnants of tree roots snaked through the cracks throughout the marble floor, one lone decaying branch still jutting up. And in the center of the floor was Wayne Vikander, or rather, what was left of him.

The body was charred. One of his arms was bent at an awkward angle, and his face was frozen in a silent scream. Blowflies had already started buzzing around the decaying body. No wonder it had smelled so familiar. I knew that smell better than anything. That smell was my childhood—what had sent me on this path to revenge for so long.

The smell of burning death.

Yorena grabbed onto my arm and I let her. I could at least offer her that small comfort, or maybe she was comforting me, too.

"Is that what I think it is?" she said, eyes wide.

"I think I'm going to be sick," Kieron said.

Staring at the body, I didn't feel disgust, or pity. No, I felt…annoyed. My whole life, I'd wanted nothing more than to be the one to put an end to Wayne's reign of terror, and someone had beat me to the punch. Though it did feel fitting that this horrible man had died the same way he had condemned so many others to death.

"There goes our plan to weaken Imogen," I said finally. "Back to the drawing board."

"Maybe let's talk about this in a room that doesn't smell like death," Rori said.

And at that, Kieron vomited into the corner.

Oh hells.

Chapter 34

Nikos

MY FATHER WAS DEAD. Most people in my situation would cry, feel angry, feel like life had dealt them an unfair hand. I, on the other hand, felt nothing but relief. The silence in the carriage had been heavy, thick, since we'd departed from the manor.

We'd been loading up the carriages when Imogen told us she'd killed my father. Her justification had been something about him not wanting to follow her orders. As much as I hated having to bow down to the orders of that sorceress and Oliver, at least it spared me from the same fate as my father. It was only fitting that the old man's instinct for self-preservation, and the stubbornness that had allowed him to be one of the most powerful people in the kingdom, were the reasons for his demise.

I was thrown into one of my most vivid memories—the day I'd lost all hope for my father.

I'd been sitting in a dark room. My arms were tied at my side. And my father stood above me. It had almost felt like he'd been the one to tie me up. Usually, when a parent's twelve-year-old was captured in the middle of town square, they would do everything in their power to get them home. What had my father done? Chided me.

"What did I tell you about going out alone?" my father had yelled, spittle flying from his mouth and into my face, humiliating me in front of the guards he always tasked with shadowing me if I ever left the house. I had grown tired of being followed around all day. But I was twelve years old, and I had decided I could take care of myself.

I may have thought my father's rules were annoying, but I wasn't completely stupid. I'd simply gone to look at the fish in the town square fountain, and these men, brutish mercenaries, it seemed, had grabbed me. They'd tightly bound me with rough ropes, and had unceremoniously dragged me back to the manor to request a ransom, only for my father to berate me in front of them.

I remembered how the ropes around my chest had squeezed me so hard that it was a battle to speak. I'd taken that as an excuse to not answer my father's question. I couldn't even stand to look at his face, knowing I would see his favorite expression, which was a mix of anger, disappointment, and annoyance all rolled into one. He'd stepped closer to me and the two men behind me shifted closer, one of them resting a heavy hand on my shoulder. Maybe the man had started to feel sorry for me. My father didn't even bother looking at the men, as if the very idea of giving up anything in exchange for my safe return was laughable, something not even worth addressing. That familiar glint glowed in my father's e ye.

"I asked you a question, child." I could still feel the drops of spit that had flown into my face, which the ropes made it impossible for me to wipe away.

"I thought I wasn't in any danger," I'd said quietly. The only thing worse than disobeying his orders, had been talking back to him. I'd only done it once before, and he'd locked me in the library behind our house for two days. I still remembered being so thirsty I couldn't even produce tears anymore.

"Pitiful excuses," my father had said. "I can hardly believe you're any child of mine." I'd lowered my head to avoid the pure resentment in his eyes.

"Just hand over control to the southern section of Nitedand and we'll give you your son back," the largest man had said. "I'm sure you can spare it."

My father had rubbed his chin, as if he was considering it. I was his only son, I'd thought, there was no way he wouldn't hand over some forest land to get me back. Without me, there'd be no one to inherit his power, I'd reasoned.

I'd thought wrong.

I'd been hopeful, expectant. And then, my heart dropped into my stomach and a wave of fear and shock washed over me when my father, with a straight face, had simply said, "No."

"Really?" one of the men had said. "I thought for sure..."

The other man had slapped the back of his head. "He's just bluffing, idiot."

"He's not," I'd said, my voice pinched.

"Correct," my father had hissed. "Goodbye, gentlemen." At that, my father had walked out the door, taking with him my only hope of escape. The metal door had closed with a slam, the final note to my sentence.

I was his only son, and he'd abandoned me to people I was sure would have killed me had I not had some competence with my crystal. I still remembered the shock on the men's faces when I had dispatched them with vines wound around their necks, my first kills. I hadn't needed him then, and I sure as hells didn't need him now. I was glad he was dead. It was one less burden on my shoulders.

"Are you okay?" Mathias asked. The slightly-less-of-an-annoyance thwacked me on the head, knocking me out of the memory.

"I'm fine," I said. He didn't look convinced, but I didn't owe him an explanation.

"Is it because of your father?" The look of concern on his face was such a stark contrast to the indifference I felt about the whole ordeal.

"He may have been my father, but he sure didn't act like one," I said. I wasn't sure why I'd told Mathias that. I braced myself for the usual look of pity that I earned wherever I told anyone about my father, but it never came. Mathias just stared. I didn't like it.

"What?" I said. "No looks of pity, no sympathy hugs, no 'I'm sorry'? Because if you're going to do any of that I would suggest doing it sooner rather than later."

Mathias let out a short laugh. "Why would I do any of that? My father was an ass too, not as much as yours, but still."

I hadn't expected that. Mathias came across as the type of person that had grown up in a perfect little family. With loving parents, at least one or two older siblings, and maybe even a pet dog. His coloring and mannerisms made me think he was from Lasaintbo, and most families there either fished, or worked on farms together. The people there were disgustingly happy.

"You look shocked," he said after a moment.

"I am. You look like your childhood couldn't have been anything but perfect."

He laughed again, though this one was free of any humor.

"My father owned the largest fishing company back home, basically Lasaintbo's version of your father." He paused. "The amount of times some *unorthodox* traders threatened me to get a cheaper offer from him is impossible to count."

I stared at him.

"What?" he said.

"I never thought other people went through that."

For the short amount of time I'd been able to interact with the other children in my town, all any of them could talk about was how great their parents were. It was always about the newest toy they'd received, or about the trip they were about to take to either another province, or even to one of the neighboring kingdoms. It was tiring.

"We're more alike than you think. Well, besides the fact that my father wasn't the one to create an organization to kill people," he said.

I let out a short laugh. "Fair." Perhaps Mathias wouldn't be so much of a nuisance to me, now that I knew we had this in common. He could be someone I could talk to other than Oliver, who I'd been avoiding since I'd finished my second request from them. Maybe Mathias could even provide some insight on the one thing I wished I could ask him.

"What do you know about trading deals?" I asked him.

"Plenty." If I couldn't figure out what the piece of the letter I had found meant, maybe he could. I pulled the scrap of the letter out of my pocket.

"What do you think of this?" I said, holding it out to him.

He scanned the letter, his face slowly falling into a deep frown.

"I'm guessing this was a deal your father had made independent of his trading empire. I don't know who the 'she' is they were talking about, but she must be someone important to your father."

He handed it back to me. "Is this why you needed me to be a lookout?"

I nodded. "I found something in my old boxes, and I need to figure out what it was about."

This involved Daeva. There was no other "she" from Havenwood my father would have been discussing. I needed to understand. And if Daeva was in danger, *nothing* could stop me from doing whatever it would take to keep her safe.

Chapter 35

Yorena

I HAD THOUGHT THAT barely sleeping in a cramped cart would be the worst part of my day, but now, after taking in sights and smells I would never be able to block out, I was sitting in the dining room of a dead man, trying to determine why Wayne had been killed. There I sat, in a smaller, ivory colored version of the formal dining room in the palace I had grown up in.

At this point, we were just waiting, slowly giving in to our fatigue, the adrenaline that had powered us through the day wearing off. Kieron's soft snores began to fill the room from where he was basically using his brother as a pillow. At least the pair seemed to have put aside the tension that had plagued them before.

Val tapped his fingers impatiently. "If Rori and Ilise aren't back in the next minute we'll have to start without them," he said.

Rori had gone to retrieve Ilise who was burning away the remnants of Wayne that had made the house smell like a morgue.

Isidora yawned. "Could you not have said that five minutes ago?" Chafik elbowed her and a look passed between them. I couldn't tell exactly what he was trying to silently tell her, but it was enough for her to attempt to hide the annoyance on her face. Attempt.

"Found her," Rori said as they strode into the room, a stone-faced Ilise in tow.

"We were about to send out a search party for you two," Isidora remarked.

Rori glared at her and took a seat beside Kass.

"Is it too late to abandon her in the nearest swamp?" they said, nodding at the retired assassin.

"I'd like to see you try," Isidora said, her mouth twisting into a sinister smile.

Val shook off his sleeping brother.

"We've made it this far without killing each other, let's not mess it up now," he said, shooting a pointed look at Rori and Isidora. "Before we do anything else, we need to figure out why Imogen would kill Wayne, now, in this manner."

Ilise scoffed as she sat down beside me—the only vacant seat.

"She obviously didn't have a use for him anymore so she got rid of him. Imogen only keeps people alive if it benefits her," she said.

"But Wayne controls, well, controlled The Progression," I said. "Wouldn't killing the leader put them in disarray and weaken a large portion of her army?"

Kass shook her head. "Not if she took control of them herself," she said.

"But aren't they scattered throughout the kingdom?" Cain asked. "She might be able to communicate over vast distances, but I doubt even she could stretch her power over the entire continent."

And, there was nothing to suggest Progression members would even follow Imogen. Wayne had been in control for so long, most of his subjects would still be loyal to his vision, not hers. Depending on where they were stationed, most of the members might not even find out their leader was dead for a while. The Progression might be built on the idea that Primis people were inferior, but the mistrust of sorcerers had been around much longer than that belief.

"She did manage to get a palace full of people loyal to the Schaefers to bend to her will," Kieron said, looking slightly more awake now.

"The palace was contained, and on a smaller scale," Rori said. "A group as large as The Progression couldn't possibly change their loyalties so quickly."

"They could if their lives depended on it," Ilise said.

"But she can't threaten the entire Progression, can she?" Chafik said.

Val considered the idea. "I wouldn't put it past her."

But that would take more than just her power to carry her message with the wind. That would take the entirety of the palace army, and they were probably too busy looking for us. Based on Imogen's treatment of Wayne, I knew for a fact she didn't like leaving any loose ends.

Wait, that might be it. "Ilise, was the entire guard back at the palace while you were in power?"

Ilise's whole body stiffened at the mention of her short time as Queen.

"No, a large portion of them were looking for all of you, being dispatched to villages and towns to move all of the Primis people, and the few that were left had been sent on a mission to find the last of the Union members. There might not be more than ten percent of the army left at the palace."

Now, Ilise got a look on her face. She looked considerably more cheerful than moments before.

"Oh no, she made her idea face," Kieron groaned.

Kass raised an eyebrow. "The what face?"

"Every time she gets that face, the next thing that comes out of her mouth is something that will either end amazingly, or with me aging five years," Kieron said.

"If most of the army is separated, then it will take some time for Imogen to spread her area of power over the entire Progression since they're so far apart," I said, understanding what Ilise had realized.

"And?" Rori said,

"That gives us an opening to get to the palace and take her down while she's the least protected. And between taking over as Queen, completely changing the social structure of Erea, coordinating the army to spread word about her taking over The Progression, *and* looking for us, she'll be at her most distracted. She might start making mistakes or overlooking the security of the palace."

The people at the table stared at me. "That... makes sense," Val said. "But that means we need to leave *today* if we want to get there before her armies are whole again."

"We could be out of here in the next hour, at most," Kass said.

Val looked around the table. "Are we all in agreement? We'll have to plan exactly how to get into the palace along the way."

"Yes," we all said in unison.

He clapped his hands together. "Then be ready to go in one hour. Dismissed."

"Yorena, Chafik, Isidora, can I talk to all of you?" Ilise said.

"Make it quick," Isidora said as she moved to a seat closer to us, Chafik staying next to her. Out of all the people for Isidora to tolerate, I never would have guessed she would choose Chafik. "What do you want?"

Ilise took a deep breath. "I don't want you three to be with us by the time we get to New Teber. This is basically a suicide mission and I don't want any of you to get hurt because of it."

She had to be kidding.

"We aren't going to leave just because you ask us to," Chafik said in a voice firmer than I'd ever heard from the boy. "Imogen and The Progression hurt my family too, and there's no chance I'm going to stand aside when I can help all of you take her down."

"*Someone* has to keep this one alive," Isidora said with a small smile. *An actual smile? Without sarcasm, without an insult attached to it?* "And you people are a *mess,* you need all the help you can get." Ah, there was the insult. She stood, Chafik following her. "Now if you'll excuse us, we need to get ready." At that they left the room, leaving only me.

"Why do you still insist on trying to talk me out of helping you?" I said.

Ilise frowned. "Because this isn't your fight. This is my mess to clean up."

I grabbed her hand, gripping it hard enough so she couldn't pull it away. Every time Ilise blamed herself for the mess we were in, there was nothing I wanted more than for Imogen to never have forced her into being a puppet queen. I wished she could see how none of this could have been prevented.

"I care about you just as much as the others, why can't I help you too?"

She shook her head. "They've been training for this for years. You've barely had a few months." She took my other hand in hers, her eyes pleading. "Let me get your home back without putting you in danger, please."

"It's your home too."

"I have no home." *Your home is with us, with me,* I wanted to say.

"Of course you have a—"

"I have no home," she said again. "The ones I had were destroyed the moment I first heard about the spiritsdamned Progression, and were lost forever the second I joined the Union. Every home I've ever had has been stolen from me. And now, the only thing that's left to take, is everyone in this house. And there's no way in four hells I'm letting Imogen take you all from me."

"But we have a chance to prevent that. You don't have to protect me anymore."

Ilise shook away my hands, pushing up from the table. "Why do you even want to help me so badly? I hunted you, and I'm the reason Erea is in shambles."

"How many times do I have to tell you that isn't true?" I said, also standing from my seat.

"I hurt you. I hurt the kingdom. I don't want you to suffer anymore because of me."

I stepped closer, close enough now that she had to look up to meet my eyes. "And I want nothing more than to keep *you* safe. I failed once, I won't fail again."

I could see tears in her eyes, just like I could feel some in my own.

"How can you possibly still think that?" she said in a thick voice.

I took her face in both of my hands, leaning in so that our noses were touching, so that we shared the same breath.

"Because I'm in love with you, and I never let go of the people I love."

I gasped as Ilise pushed me away as if I were poison, backing up until her back hit the wall.

"Don't say that," she said, her eyes wide. "Don't link yourself to me. It's a death sentence."

She ran out of the room, taking with her the swell of hope I'd let build up in my chest. Had Imogen truly taken her from me? I knew she felt the same about me as I did about her, she had to. I would uncover the same girl who'd risked everything for those she loved, the same one that had opened her heart to me in the first place.

Chapter 36

Ilise

After over twelve hours of traveling, I had come to one conclusion: I despised forests. Actually, I had come to *two* conclusions: Yorena loved me. She'd tried to kiss me. Yet, I still couldn't say I loved her back. It wasn't like I didn't feel the same, I would burn down this whole kingdom if it meant I could finally keep her safe, if it meant I could keep her smiling wide enough for her dimples to make an appearance.

But maybe if I didn't say it back, I could keep away the cloud of death that seemed to touch all the people I loved. It'd stolen my family, my village, Aerilyn, and the base. I wasn't going to let it steal her from me too, not as long as I was alive. Admitting my feelings would only bind her to me and make her even more of a target.

We'd only just reached the forest after pushing the horses as fast as we dared through the swamplands, the sun slowly rising above the horizon. Rotting fruit and rain-soaked shrubbery were a welcome change in smell. Though I barely noticed that—most of my mind was focused on the sleeping head in my lap. Yorena had opted to sleep for the first stretch of our journey so she could help keep watch later. Her hair was so very soft. It was what I imagined clouds to feel like. And even after weeks of travel, I could still pick out the slightest rosy scent emanating from her.

Yorena had helped to come up with the first part of our plan. The only place we could guess Imogen wouldn't frequent in the palace was the Archives. The only books down there were historical accounts and biographies. And frankly, nobody went down there. I wouldn't be surprised if the keeper down there hadn't seen someone go down there in over a decade. And luckily, there was an Earth Imperium entrance hidden at the back of the palace that we could use to enter. Imogen would sense me the moment I got remotely close to the palace, so that meant we would have to act quickly and decisively.

The plan was for everyone to hide in the Archives while I scouted for the places with the weakest concentration of guards. Then, I would summon Imogen to wherever that was using the bond we still shared, and we would ambush her. But there was a major problem with this plan. And that was, how would I be able to resist falling under Imogen's control again? I couldn't delude myself into pretending that speed and adrenaline would protect me. I looked at the other three sleeping passengers in my wagon. Isidora and Chafik had fallen asleep the moment we started moving, Kieron, not too long after them. I may not have known Kieron and Isidora well, but I knew I didn't want them to get hurt if Imogen turned me into a weapon *again*.

Under her control, my moral compass wouldn't exist anymore. And as much as I knew I didn't want to hurt anyone else, I didn't think I had the strength to resist her. There was no way to say I wouldn't put us at an even greater disadvantage because of how easy it had been for Imogen to take over my soul the first time. If anything, it would be easier for her the next time we faced off.

"Hey kid," Kass called from where she held the reins. "We're in a pretty thick part of the forest, you should get some sleep while there's the least chance of trouble."

"You don't know that. Imogen could've sent someone to ambush us," I said.

The forest might be thick to us, but she could've sent some Faveru soldiers who were accustomed to it. The sun was only just beginning to rise, and it was still dark enough for soldiers to take us by surprise. Ever since we'd escaped the soldiers at the dock, it's been quiet, too quiet. There hadn't been a single guard left at the manor, not even a housekeeper.

"I'll wake you if anyone attacks. Get some sleep."

Despite the rattling from all the tree roots and shrubs, I quickly fell asleep. Days of running on adrenaline and pure willpower were finally catching up with me.

Suddenly, it was dark. I shot up from the ground, my eyes scanning the dark for any sign of the two entities I had come to expect in these dreams.

"Hello Ilise." I whipped around.

The entity wasn't wearing my face this time. No, this time they were barely a human, more of the idea of a person. They were nothing more than a black silhouette, small pinpricks of light outlining their figure.

"I thought us to be past the point of me having to appear more human."

"So what are you, exactly?" I asked. The figure settled on the ground, gesturing for me to join them. I sat next to them, leaving ample room between us. They still gave me the same feeling as being around a sorcerer, like the air felt the need to compress around them. But they wore no crystals, no sign of having any power at all other than being able to talk to me in my soul. But who else could do that other than sorcerers?

"I'm something older than the world itself, something that you have a piece of inside of you." Older than the world itself? But the only thing older than the world was…

"You're a Spirit?" The light highlighting Their silhouette seemed to brighten.

"Yes."

I gasped. I was talking to a Spirit, an actual Spirit in the flesh…or whatever they were made of. I quickly rose to my knees, dropping into a bow.

"I think we are beyond you having to bow to me. Sit, child."

I returned to my seat on the ground, trying my best not to stare. No one alive had seen a Spirit. We'd thought Them to be lost to us forever. After Imogen became the first sorceress, the other Spirits had disappeared after the Soul Spirit.

"Aren't you going to ask which Spirit I am?"

"Well, only one of you had any abilities that could allow you to talk to me like this. So I'm going to assume you're the Soul Spirit."

"Correct."

"Aren't the other Spirits chasing after you? Are they going to find you here?" Legend said the other four Spirits had been trying to capture and punish the Soul

Spirit after imbuing a child with their power. I hadn't believed it. But I also hadn't believed it was possible to speak to a Spirit, so incurring the wrath of the other four didn't seem too improbable. I wasn't keen on having four more Spirits coming into my head to capture the Soul Spirit, I'd like my mind to remain somewhat intact.

A twinkling sound not unlike a laugh escaped the Spirit. "Do you humans still believe that silly myth that the other Spirits disappeared to find me?"

I nodded.

"That is merely a lie we let you all believe because we were tired of being asked for help when we received almost nothing in return." Oh. "Do not take offense, but we simply wished to return to where we arrived from." I opened my mouth to ask a question but the Spirit cut me off by saying, "No I am not going to tell you where we came from, we have other topics to discuss." I promptly shut my mouth,

"If you want to defeat Imogen, you will need to be able to withstand her control," They said. But there was no way to stop a sorcerer from controlling your soul, not unless you could also control souls. I might've been gifted with the power of two elements, but it still wasn't enough.

"Imogen's influence over me is too strong," I said. The smallest wisp of purple materialized in the air. I couldn't even escape her stupid imprint for one second. "She's been controlling me since I was born."

What I assumed to be the Spirit's head shook. "Let me tell you a little more about Imogen," was all They said. They raised what looked like a hand, shooting out stars from their fingertips. I liked this version of storytelling much better than Imogen's.

"I met Imogen when she was only a child, one that had only just learned how to speak in full sentences." The stars formed into the crude shape of a little girl, skipping through a small village. "And as you already know, she witnessed how my siblings helped other villagers solve their problems, and she wanted a more peaceful solution."

The stars morphed into the little girl kneeling before a figure that looked identical to the Spirit before me. "She asked me to grant her the power over souls so that she may influence the two villages to cease their fighting."

Starlight from the Spirit's figure flowed into the little girl. "I granted her wish, for how could a little girl cause any trouble?" The Spirit showed a scene of the little girl throwing her influence over the villages, making the tiny pitchforks and torches disappear.

"Now onto the part that is not written in your histories." The scene disappeared, and the Spirit focused Their "gaze" on me. "When one of us Spirits imbues someone with our gifts, we have the ability to see exactly what that person uses them for. And since I had no one else to watch over, I spent my days watching over the girl. And I started to notice something... odd."

I tilted my head.

"It was as if her soul was being tainted by the gifts I gave her. In hindsight, I may have given her too much for her small size. She began to change people just for the fun of it, or so they played games with her. I thought nothing of it at first, thinking it to be something human children liked doing.

"I started to notice a real problem once she reached about thirteen years of age. She forced both the villages she lived near to turn the area into her own small kingdom. And being that she was an orphan, she did not have any elders to discourage her from doing so."

They stopped. "You know the rest. Do you know why I told you this story?"

I shook my head. So Imogen had been power-hungry her whole life. I'd thought her nature had been a result of the kingdoms' treatment of sorcerers and her being cast from society. Turns out she'd been a problem from the moment she had gained powers. Some people were simply born wicked.

"I told you because it shows why so many people are easily influenced by soul magic. Those who do not already have a strong will of their own, a strong sense of self, if you will, tend to be vulnerable. I'm talking about people like children, and people who ignore the fact that they have the ability to resist its control." I felt a strong pressure on my shoulders. "You are not one of those people. You can resist Imogen if only you remember who you are."

I scoffed. I shouldn't really scoff at a Spirit, but They were acting like it was the easiest thing in the world to resist a sorcerer. Yorena had already tried to get me to remember who I was when I'd first fallen under Imogen's control, and that ended up with me chasing her out of the palace and going on a half-crazy manhunt for her and for the rest of the Union. Simply "believing I could" was not what I needed to defeat Imogen.

"You do not believe me?" They asked.

"No. If it was as simple as that, we wouldn't be in this situation in the first place."

"Because you have not been yourself in years," They said. Excuse me? I'd been myself when my family had been murdered and I'd been thrown aside, I'd been myself when I decided to join the Union, and I'd been myself when I agreed to be a palace spy for so long knowing I could have gotten killed so I could help take down The Progression.

"That was not you making all of those decisions, that was your thirst for revenge." Oh for Spirit's sake.

"Disagree with me all you want, but to resist Imogen, you need to become the same person you were before The Progression put all that hate in your heart," They said with a tap to my chest.

"Imogen changed me from the moment I was born. That hate always has, and always will be a part of me."

They tsked. "If you find another way to resist sorcerers, then you can use that way. But until then, I will leave you with that piece of information. I did not help Yorena get you back to semi-normal just for you to not try." They stood, brushing off invisible specks of dirt off of Theirself.

"Also, you might want to wake up. I sense danger."

Chapter 37

Yorena

THE FLOOR UNDERNEATH ME jerked, throwing me to the other side of the wagon. My head cracked against the wood, spots dancing in my vision. Black smoke filled the inside of the wagon, the cloth roof bursting into flames. My vision cleared, and I was able to tell the wagon must have been knocked on its side. *Who's out there?*

"Everybody out!" Ilise shouted as she punched a hole in the roof. The four of us crawled out of the opening while Isidora put out the fire before it could reach the wagon's base. Kass stumbled out of the brush, a large cut gracing her cheek from the fall.

The wagon in front of us was also ablaze, and Isidora sprinted to put the fire out. Val's group staggered across the tree roots to us. At least their wagon hadn't been knocked over, and everyone looked relatively unharmed.

"Is everyone ok?" Val asked.

"What happened?" Cain asked.

"Someone's here," Ilise said, slowly scanning the dark forest.

"Did you see anyone?" Rori asked.

"No. But I know someone's here."

We all stood still, trying to make as little noise as possible. The vegetation swayed gently in the slow breeze, nothing showing evidence of anyone moving in the brush. The only thing I could hear was the soft chirping of crickets, and the occasional forest creature skittering across the ground. How could Ilise be so certain that someone was here?

"Um, I don't see anyone," Kieron said. Ilise's shoulders dropped as she looked around one last time.

"I could have sworn," she said.

"Hello" a chilling voice said.

I gulped and slowly brought my gaze to the tops of the trees. A lone figure sat perched on a branch, the wind flowing through their black cloak. Quicker than my eyes could track, Kass sprouted a thick vine, wrapping it tightly around the intruder. She brought them down. *Odd. They aren't putting up a fight.* I activated my crystal before the figure reached the ground. This could end badly.

Kass' vines gripped the figure harder as Val walked up to them, not attempting to hide that his hand rested on his dagger.

"Are you the one who wrecked our wagons?" he asked.

The would-be attacker giggled. *Giggled?*

"You all are quite entertaining when you are upset," they said. "I thought it would be harder to get all of you where you need to be."

"Excuse me?" Val said, releasing the dagger from its sheath. He used the end of the blade to tip back the cloak's hood. The person he revealed looked to be about middle-aged, with long ashy blonde hair streaked with silver. The moonlight reflected off their pale skin. But it was their eyes that had me taking a step back. Their eyes were bright pink, the color of a freshly bloomed dahlia.

A sorcerer.

Four crystals glowed under their cloak as they burst out of Kass' vine, knocking all of us back. My back hit the nearest tree, forcing the air out of my lungs. I crouched on the ground, trying to compose myself. The sorcerer forced back the vegetation around them with a shockwave of air. Ilise and Rori's crystals were aglow, their faces contorted as they tried to block the sorcerer's wind.

The sorcerer laughed. "You think you can overpower me with two measly crystals," they mused. "Let the fun begin."

The fun? My eyes widened as they activated their soul crystal, generating a deep purple glow. All the wildlife around us seemed to sense the danger and ceased any noise they were making. The forest was quiet, still, deadly promise laced into the dark glow.

"Everyone get back!" Val yelled as he sprinted deeper into the brush. Our group dispersed in all different directions. The limited light made most of the forest floor invisible, making me catch my foot on a thick root. I landed hard on my knee, sharp pain shooting up my leg. Heavy footsteps pounded behind me as I rushed to free my foot.

"Yorena, watch out!" Kieron yelled. He stomped on the root, smashing it in half and allowing me to jump up. "There's a small cave a little ways back we can hide in," he said.

He grabbed my hand, and was mid-step when I knew something was wrong. Kieron halted. And I realized he was now keeping a tight grip on my hand, preventing me from running from the sorcerer.

"Kieron, we have to go," I said, trying and failing to free my hand. I didn't want to use my crystal, I might hurt him. "Kieron?"

His hands flew to my throat, and he slammed me against the nearest tree. I dug my nails into his arms, making him squeeze my throat even harder.

"You must be eradicated," he seethed. White spots danced in my vision as my lungs fought for air and panic flooded my system. I kneed him in the groin and he released his grip enough for me to rip myself out of his hands. I sprinted through the forest, leaping over roots and logs as I went.

"What is wrong with you?" I screamed. Kieron dashed after me, his long legs allowing him to slowly catch up to me. "Help!"

When no one answered, I risked a glance back and followed the orange light in the distance. *Ilise.* I grabbed onto a sapling, using it to slingshot myself back toward the rest of the group. Kieron face-planted into another tree, quickly dashing after me.

"What in four hells is wrong with you!" I yelled. I dodged tree after tree, branch after branch to make it back to Ilise. "I'm not the one you're supposed to be fighting."

Kieron's heavy footfalls grew in volume with every second.

"I will complete my mission," he said.

I finally made it back to the wagons when Ilise's air crystal glowed as if she had stolen a piece of the sun. Howling winds swept up Kass, Rori, and Kieron, confining them to a tight circle. Rori tried to suppress the wind, but Ilise only squeezed them together tighter, so much so that I was surprised they could still breathe.

I hurried over to Ilise. "Are you okay?"

She nodded, beads of sweat forming on her brow from the energy strain. Cain, Val, Isidora, and Chafik joined us again.

"What's wrong with them?" Chafik asked.

"The sorcerer took them over. Rori's eyes had streaks of pink in them, just like the sorcerer's," Cain said.

Hells.

"Correct, my little victims," the sorcerer mused from the trees.

"Victims?" Chafik said, his voice squeaking.

"Imogen sent me. I could easily dispatch you myself, but this method is so much more fun, don't you think?" they said.

Isidora scoffed. "Or maybe you're just scared we'll beat you. Otherwise you wouldn't be hiding in the trees like a *coward*," she said.

I whirled on her. "Are you trying to antagonize them?" I said in a low voice.

She leaned in. "Don't you think it would be much faster to take out one sorcerer instead of two Imperium and Kieron, who's a highly trained ex-guard?"

That was...true.

The sorcerer's eyes turned to thin slits and they leapt down from the tree. They landed with a great puff of dust a few feet from us.

"So be it," they said with a smile. A scalding beam of flames shot out from their hand and we all ducked to the ground. I rolled farther away before jumping back onto my feet. Isidora charged the sorcerer, forming a ball of water over their head.

"Keep them away from Ilise. We can't let the others out until we know they won't be under their control anymore," Cain hissed. I unsheathed one of the thin daggers at my hip, heating it enough for the metal to glow.

"Kill them," Ilise said through gritted teeth. She was kneeling on the ground now, her breaths coming in hard pants. "It's the quickest way to release their control." For once, I didn't disagree with killing someone.

The sorcerer knocked Isidora back with a gust of wind. She hit a far away tree with a loud thud, slumping to the ground. I flung my dagger at the sorcerer. They dodged it easily, the dagger embedding itself in a tree.

"Is that all you can do?" the sorcerer cackled. Val unsheathed another dagger from its hold, so he now had one in each hand. Cain brandished a shortsword, the sharp point toward the sorcerer.

Val gave us a subtle nod.

"Chafik, go get Isidora," he said. At that, the three of us charged the sorcerer. I allowed my flames to become an extension of myself, a thick whip of fire forming in my hands.

I cracked the flaming whip against the side of the sorcerer's face. They crumpled. Val planted a heavy kick to their middle as Cain plunged his sword into the center of their chest. They fell to one knee, staring down at the sword in their chest.

"Finally," they said, coughing up a spatter of blood. Nothing much flowed from the wound, and I realized that the only thing keeping the sorcerer alive was the sword itself, which was keeping most of the blood inside. "Now that they're under my control, your friends over there will die with me. Have fun trying to stop them." At that, they ripped the sword from their chest, unleashing a river of gore, and slumped to the ground.

Die with them? I looked back to the trio trapped in Ilise's wind.

"Ilise! Let them go!" I screamed. Her winds died down and the three of them stared at one another, as if bewildered. I ran to Kieron, trying to rip the sword from his hands. Cain and Val tried to hold back Rori and Kass, but Rori blew the two of them away with a gust of wind. They were shot deep into the woods, much too deep to make it back in time.

Kieron elbowed me in the stomach, knocking me off of him.

"Ilise! Stop them! It was a trick!"

Ilise ran over to Rori, tackling them to the ground.

"Come back! Please," she begged.

I shot back up to Kieron. "This isn't you," I pleaded. Hot tears streamed down my face as Kass grew vines around the two of them. They snaked up their bodies, wrapping around their necks. I desperately tried to burn away the vines, but it was as if Kass grew them faster than I could burn them. I had to get her crystal. I darted to Kass, my arm outstretched to yank it off of her.

She twisted her hand and the vines closed around her and Kieron's necks with a loud crack. The pair slumped to the ground, taking my heart with them.

"No!" I screamed loud enough for the whole forest to hear.

No. It was a tragedy for Kass to be gone. But Kieron. My friend. He couldn't be gone. I placed a shaking hand on Kieron's too-still chest.

"Wake up," I pleaded. If only this were the typical tricks he used to play on me, pretending to be asleep when he didn't want to go along with my antics. But he wasn't playing. It was as if the world was crashing down around me, my heart collapsing with it. I screamed again, my throat going raw, sobbing into Kieron's chest. He was gone. Imogen had stolen his life from him, taken him from his brother, from his family, from his friends, from me.

How could two people with so much life in them be reduced to nothing but limp bodies so quickly? Why? What had any of us done to deserve this?

Ilise struggled to flip a still-fighting Rori so they were on their back. "I'm not letting you go," she choked.

Rori's crystal glowed as they leaned into Ilise's ear. I couldn't hear what they said, but it was something that made Ilise's eye light up with hope.

"Ilise, they're going to—". I didn't get to finish my sentence before Rori's neck broke with a loud crack as they squeezed a tight ring of air around themselves.

Ilise let out a horrifying scream and I felt my heart breaking all over again.

We had failed.

Chapter 38

Ilise

THEY'RE DEAD. WE WERE all together just a few minutes ago, full of hope that we would prevail at last. They weren't supposed to die. No one else was supposed to die. Was there nowhere I could go where death wouldn't follow me? Was this what Imogen wanted?

Choked sobs cut through the heavy silence. Tears burned in my eyes, but I could still see Yorena, Cain, and Val hovering over the broken bodies of Kieron and Kass. Rori had briefly come back to us. Their eyes had returned to their normal hazel, they had spoken to me. They'd been able to break free from the sorcerer's control, it was actually possible. And yet they were *still* taken from me. How could someone who'd been strong enough to break the hold still lose?

Imogen was still alive, and she was still focused on hurting Erea, Oliver was still alive even though they were *choosing* to help the evil sorceress. That stupid Commander who had kicked dirt in my face after Aerilyn's murder was probably still alive. When all the evil people managed to quite happily live out their lives, why couldn't the people close to me stay alive? What had just happened was even worse than returning to my village, only to find it burned, all those years ago. Not because I loved these people more than I'd loved my family, even though they had definitely become family to me, but it was more the fact that I was an adult now, not a powerless child. I should have been able to save them. I could've knocked them out until we could get far away from the sorcerer. Then maybe they would all still be alive, maybe our group wouldn't have dwindled down to only six heartbroken people whose likelihood of succeeding was close to nothing.

"What happened?" Isidora asked. She leaned on Chafik for support as they limped back to our somber group.

Yorena just shook her head, her eyes blurry behind thick tears. She and Val huddled over Kieron's form. I didn't think I'd ever seen Val so...defeated. He hugged Kieron to him, as if he could squeeze the life back into his brother. I crawled over to where Cain was crouched over Kass.

I ripped away the vine Kass had wrapped around her throat. She'd been the first person from the Union I'd ever met. She was the one who had taken a chance on me when I thought my whole world had ended. She'd given me a purpose, she'd given me something to live for, she'd given me a way to ensure my village and family got the justice they deserved. My tears kept falling, and I didn't know when they would ever stop. I closed Kass' still-open eyes.

"We need to bury them," Yorena said.

"We don't have time. We have to get to the palace as quickly as possible," Isidora said.

Val rose, his eyes promising violence. "We are giving them a proper burial," he said. "If you don't want to watch, then get the wagon ready."

Isidora scoffed and walked back to our overturned wagons.

Chafik slowly looked up. "I'll help," he said in a small voice.

Val nodded and we all got to work. We carefully unwrapped the vines from Kass and Kieron and moved Rori next to them. As I lifted Rori into my arms, they felt lighter, almost like the loss of their life had gotten rid of something within them. Something that had weighed them down to Earth, that had tethered them.

"The roots are too thick to dig, we need to cremate them," Yorena said. I looked to Val, expecting him to object, but he nodded. Yorena looked at me, her eyes rimmed in red, her face puffy from crying. I formed a ring of air around all of us to prevent the fire from spreading through the forest. Our hair whipped around us, but the howl of the wind was muffled to me.

"May I say the words of farewell?" Chafik asked.

"Sure," Val said, staring down at his brother and wiping his bloodshot eyes.

"I didn't know many of you well just a few weeks ago, but we've grown closer over the course of this mission. I like to think we are like family now. Our departed friends did everything they could to save us. These last moments, they weren't themselves. I don't know if there is a life after death, but I think our friends here will be in a good, peaceful place." He wiped away the start of tears. "May you all be guided away from this world, and lead the Spirits home to you."

He stepped back as Yorena's crystal glowed. Her flames seemed to delicately flow over their bodies. *Bodies. Not people, bodies.* The harsh smell of burning flesh filled our wind barrier. The bodies disintegrated into flakes of ash. The last of the flames burned away and I released my control on the wind barrier. I gently blew their ashes into the air, so that they could be scattered across the forest, and maybe even waft to further shores. They didn't deserve to be stuck in the place of their deaths.

"Are you guys ready or do I have to go to the palace on my own?" Isidora yelled. What a psycho. I found myself worrying that she would betray us once we got there, that it was worth putting up with her.

We'd all been stuck in the same wagon for three days. No talking, no planning, just pure silence. Only two of the horses hadn't gotten far when trying to escape the sorcerer, and Isidora had opted to be in charge of guiding them, claiming we were "bringing down the mood". The only stops we made were at creeks and grassy patches to water and feed the steeds. I spent most of my time thinking of anything *except* what had happened in the forest. It became much easier when all we could see were the golden Newnina fields.

It was nearing the end of October, and the nights were gradually getting cooler. Yorena still lay with her head in my lap. She hadn't spoken much either this entire ride. Most nights, I was the only one awake, and I could hear her quiet sobs that seemed to plague her sleep. I stroked the soft curls of her head, grateful she was at least sleeping. Val had spent the entire time huddled in the far corner of the wagon. I knew firsthand what it was like to lose your younger sibling. And it was worse for him, he'd been right in front of Kieron before he'd died.

Chafik opened the wagon cover from the front. Bright light entered the space, too bright without the thick cover of the forest. "This is as far as we can go with the wagon, we're about a mile from the palace," he said.

Val nodded.

"I'll scout the area out for any guards," Cain mumbled. He jumped down from the wagon to get closer to the palace.

I gently shook Yorena awake. "It's time to go," I said. She mumbled something unintelligible and walked out of the wagon, Val following close behind.

The glistening waters of the Leekrina River flowed serenely next to the tan stone towers. We'd stopped the wagon atop a small hill overlooking the palace. I couldn't see the obvious black uniforms surrounding the palace, but that didn't mean they weren't there.

Imogen would surely know if I was here—soon, if she didn't already. What if I wasn't strong enough to resist Imogen's control? I couldn't hurt this kingdom again, I couldn't hurt my friends again, I couldn't hurt Yorena again. The person I'd been under Imogen's control was the last thing I wanted to become ever again. Was I strong enough to keep her out? Rori had been able to free themself from the control of that sorcerer, but only for a moment. I would have to be strong enough to keep myself free of Imogen in the long term. No more of my friends' lives would be lost in vain, I wouldn't allow it.

I pushed the last of the doubts to the deep recesses of my mind and took a deep breath, steeling myself. *Less worry, more action.* I finally stepped out of the wagon just as Cain was running back to us.

"There are about two dozen guards patrolling the outskirts of the palace at one hundred foot intervals in the front, and about two hundred intervals around back.

"There should be an old servant's entrance around the back we can use," Yorena said. Those had to be the first words she'd said in days. "It's likely covered by overgrown plants by now, which should work in our favor."

"It shouldn't be too hard to find the tunnel that leads to the Royal Archives," Yorena said. "The only person that's ever down there is Ms. Nettie, and she probably doesn't know any of us are wanted for treason. She's usually much too worried about the few moths that manage to find their way down there, possibly eating the books."

Isidora turned to her, one eyebrow raised. "Probably?"

"Well, she might know, but she wouldn't turn us in. I hope. "

It wasn't a great plan, but it was all we had. We all followed Cain to find the break in the guards' ranks. We reached a large tree, waiting, watching. When it seemed like the time was right, and the guards were patrolling furthest from us, I waved for everyone to start running. We reached the door, tearing the vegetation aside, ducking as low as possible to stay hidden, and I quickly pried it open. A chill rushed out from the tunnels, raising goosebumps on my arm.

"Yorena, do you know the way from here?" Val asked.

She nodded and we all filed in after her. The door closed with a loud slam, plunging us into darkness until Yorena lit a thick branch she had found on the ground. The tunnels seemed to go on forever, every section identical to the one we'd passed meters back. I honestly couldn't figure out how Yorena was able to discern one turn from another. Yorena led us to a less-than-safe looking ladder, and we all climbed down. The ladder creaked with every bit of pressure I put on the rungs, but we all managed to get down without it breaking. We were in front of a door.

"Here we are," Yorena said, snuffing out the torch. She opened the ancient-looking door and my nose was instantly hit with the smell of dust and old paper.

"Ms. Nettie?" Yorena called.

"Is that you, Yorena dear?" the old woman said. "I haven't seen you in months!" She hobbled to us from behind a towering bookcase. There was hardly any room in here to move without having one's shoulders brush against another shelf. Scrolls littered the ground in heaping piles, and some books lay in large stacks. "Where in the Spirits' name have you been? And who are all of these people?"

Yorena's countenance instantly shifted into that of a Princess. A charming smile spread across her face, though it was the fakest smile I'd ever seen her wear. Weariness and grief still dulled her eyes, though Ms. Nettie made no mention of it.

"I've been a *little* preoccupied as of late. These are my friends, and we need to hide out here for a little. Can you promise not to tell anyone we're here, especially Imogen?" Yorena pleaded.

The old woman shrugged. "As long as you don't damage any of my books." At that, she walked off to Spirits knows where.

We dropped our bags to the ground and settled around one of the rickety tables in the corner.

"So, what now?" Isidora asked.

"We get rid of Imogen," Val said.

"Obviously," Cain said.

"Is Ilise going to scout the right area for our trap?" Chafik asked.

Yorena's lips tipped in a smile—a real one, perhaps the first real one in a while. I fought not to stare at the dimples I had missed so much.

"No need for scouting. I know just who to ask."

Chapter 39

Nikos

"**I**F YOU PACE ANY longer, you'll wear a hole in the floor," Mathias said. The floor be damned. If this letter was about Daeva I needed to figure out exactly what kind of deal my father had been planning. He wouldn't hinge a deal on a simple village girl, would he? There was no reason for him to be talking about Daeva five years ago.

"I'm thinking," I said. Had I been too obvious with my feelings toward Daeva? My father had shown me almost no attention after my mother had fled. At least, when my mother had been around, there were two of us to split my father's unwanted attentions, and that'd only been because she'd forced him to interact with me. Why would he have started paying attention to my life out of nowhere?

Mathias sighed. "Is this about that weird letter?"

I gave him a curt nod. "There has to be something we missed, the letter doesn't make sense for the time it was sent."

"Why?" he asked, propping his feet up on the mattress I'd found for him. I was less annoyed with him putting his feet on the bed now that it wasn't mine. Should I tell him about Daeva? He didn't show many signs of trying to escape. He constantly had his guard down. There were times I'd left him alone and he still didn't try to escape, and he more or less obeyed any orders I gave him—excluding the times I'd told him to leave me alone.

"Do you swear to not repeat anything I say? Because I will kill you for it, and there's nowhere you can hide."

He raised his hands in surrender. "You don't have to threaten me, it's not like there's anyone I can tell," he said, gesturing around the empty room.

"Do you swear?" I asserted.

He nodded.

I sat on the edge of his makeshift bed, taking a steeling breath. "Have you ever wondered why I take orders from Imogen?" I asked.

Mathias shook his head. "I can tell you despise her, but people work with people they despise all the time. I assumed there was something you were getting out of it, but it wasn't my place to ask you about it," he said.

I stared at Mathias, taken aback.

He acted like a child, he carried himself like a child—in a way where he was simultaneously taking up as much room in the world as possible while still consciously aware of the fact that it was not his space to take. *Just like I'd been.*

"You don't have to look so shocked," he said after a short while. "But now that you're ready to explain it to me, go ahead."

"The only reason I'm working with Imogen is because my father blackmailed me into it, and now she has full control over the blackmail."

He raised an eyebrow. "What could your father possibly hold against you? From what I've gathered, he doesn't know enough about you to find something to blackmail you with."

A callous assessment, but Mathias wasn't wrong. While my father wouldn't have been able to remember when my birthday was, I'd known him better than I could ever know myself. His motives, his drives, his goal, his desires, his needs. I knew all of them. And it still hadn't been enough to keep Daeva away from him.

"Are you going to tell me what this blackmail is and what it has to do with the letter, or do I need to just go ask someone else? Like, say...Oliver?"

I glared at him. "Imogen is holding captive the woman I love." I leaned closer to him, enough so that he had to tilt his head to look me in the eye. "And should you mention her in Oliver's presence, what Imogen did to my father will seem like a pleasant mercy compared to what I'll do to you."

I've been told my cold stare was a weapon. If there was one thing I was grateful to inherit from my father, it was those bright Vikander eyes. I'd made men twice as strong as me cower with just one look, and all of Kentfallsworth had known to keep their distance upon seeing my eyes flash green. And yet Mathias, this powerless man, was barely holding in a laugh.

"Is something funny?" I said through gritted teeth.

He fell back on the mattress, allowing the laugh he'd been holding back to rack his body. The gruff sound echoed off the walls. This carefree chortling was the opposite of what I'd been expecting. I'd been wrong when I'd decided he understood more than I'd given him credit for. He was an idiot, after all.

Mathias' laughs finally slowed and he wiped tears from his eyes. "You couldn't pay me to *willingly* talk to Oliver. They creeped me out even before we found out who you guys worked for. And you seriously think I would endanger someone you love like that? I had to watch the girl I loved get a sword thrown into her chest and her body get turned into ashes. You think I'd inflict that pain on someone else?"

He gave my shoulder a firm pat. Once, twice. He had a grin on his face. *What is this?*

"You need to learn to allow yourself to look at things in another light," he said. "Letting certain things off your shoulders *really* makes for a better state of mind."

At that, he lay back down on his mattress, stretching out once again. "Or, you know, talking to someone helps too."

I'd never had someone to talk to. My mother had left me with a father who wanted almost nothing to do with me until I was old enough to help him with The Progression. Being in the family I was, the entire town regarded me as if I was poisonous. And I'd always avoided unloading anything onto Daeva so that at least with her, I could pretend I wasn't Nikos Vikander—son of Progression leader Wayne Vikander.

Someone to talk to, such a wild concept.

"So what does this blackmail have to do with the letter?" Mathias asked. I'd almost forgotten the original purpose of this conversation. He shifted so there was space for me next to him on the mattress. He patted the area, and reluctantly, I shuffled closer. The lack of a headboard forced me to slouch slightly to keep myself upright.

"As far as I know, at the time the letter was sent, my father had no knowledge that Daeva existed."

He tilted his head, perplexed. "Are you sure he didn't know, and that he wasn't just hiding the fact until he had a use for the information?"

I'd considered that option, but my father had been trying to find a way to control me for years after the date of the letter. He wouldn't have wasted all of that time to find a different solution when he already had something, or someone to use against me.

"That's not his style," I said.

Mathias rubbed his chin. "Is this Daeva here?" he asked.

I nodded.

"Why don't you just ask her about it? Maybe she knows something you don't."

She might. But no, I reasoned. She'd only just moved to Kentfallsworth a year before we met, *and* she'd lived on the opposite side of the town—the slums in the swamps. My father had never dared to go near the swamps, so she couldn't have known him at all, let alone for him to mention her in a letter.

"My father would have despised the idea of me being with someone like her, why would he have known her years before he ever mentioned her?"

He shrugged. "Still seems like a good idea to ask."

"Darling?" I called, brushing the last of the cobwebs I had collected in the passage between my room and Daeva's off my vest. The tunnels were dark and confusing, but Imogen had two guards stationed outside Daeva's room at all times; they would have reported me the moment I tried to enter her room.

"I'm in the main bedroom," Daeva called. She hadn't been given servants to help her with the cooking and cleaning, leaving four of the five bedrooms in the apartment vacant. I walked into the largest room and my heart dropped into my stomach.

Daeva was packing.

"Why are you packing? You know we can't leave until we're certain Imogen won't follow." But rather than responding, she continued meticulously folding her clothes into a leather suitcase. *Where did she get a suitcase?* "If you leave on your own she'll still send someone after you."

She looked up at me with those hazel eyes of hers, ones I could stare into forever.

"I doubt it. Now that your father is gone, my services are no longer needed." *Services?*

"What are you talking about?" I asked, caressing the soft skin of her cheek. Green light flared, and my eyes caught on the crystal that had returned to her neck. She'd had her crystal taken ages ago. Without it, there was no chance she could escape from my father.

She peeled my hand off her face with an expression that was not unlike disgust.

"Did you really think someone was willing to love you?"

What?

This wasn't Daeva. Daeva loved me. Daeva and I were about to be married until my father decided to wreck any chance of that fantasy coming true. This must have been the work of Imogen, there was no other reason why Daeva's personality and feelings toward me would change so drastically in such little time.

"Are you truly this dense? I was a *ploy*. Your father hired me to get you to fall in love with me so he could have something to control you with."

She will be arriving within the coming days. The school has already accepted my letter to allow her to attend. We expect our payment to be given upon arrival.

I backed away from the one person in this kingdom I'd thought loved me. It had all been a cruel trick. "How could you?" I said, failing to keep the pain out of my voice.

She shrugged, and smiled. "Anything to get out of the swamplands. And it was so easy to trick you. All I had to do was show you the smallest amount of attention and feign an attraction toward you. It was like watching a moth fly into a candle flame."

She placed both her hands on my shoulders—a gesture that would have comforted me at any other time, but now it was like she was stabbing me, like she was sucking the smallest amount of life I had left out of me.

"Oh Nikos, you're so funny," she taunted. "You're nothing like your father." She leaned in close, her breath warming the shell of my ear. "I love you. Of course I'll marry you." The words sounded like the Daeva I knew. They sounded like the words that had kept me bound to her, kept my actions bound to her life. But they were a mockery. They were a lie. A cruel, dirty lie.

I backed away from her. Some part of me wanted to believe this was all one of Imogen's tricks, that maybe she had taken control of Daeva to get to me. But her eyes were the same color they'd always been, the same soothing hazel. How could I have been so stupid, so gullible? Of course no one would love me. My whole village cringed at the sight of me, my father had never bothered to care about me while he was alive, even my own mother had fled our home without me. Only the Spirits knew where she went. Maybe she'd gone and found a man better than my father—started a new family. Maybe she truly loved her new children and had completely forgotten about me.

Daeva waved her hand with a cruel smile. "Goodbye, Nikos," she said.

I stormed out of the room and back into the tunnels. Somehow, I was able to find my room on the first try, and I slammed the hidden door closed.

"So... I'm guessing that conversation didn't go well," Mathias said from where he sat perched in an old armchair. I glared at him and he raised his hands. "No need to take it out on me, I'm just here to talk if you want."

Talk? The one thing I had left to look forward to turned out to be a lie and this man wanted to *talk*?

"You want to talk?" I said. "Then why don't I just go on and on about how Daeva was hired by my father to trick me into falling in love so he would have a way to control me. Why don't I tell you about how this proves that no one has ever cared about me, not one person has been around me by choice despite my upbringing and despite my father."

Mathias opened his mouth to speak but I cut him off. The words wouldn't stop, I knew they wouldn't until I'd gotten every last thought out.

"Or about how this means every person I've hurt, every bad deed, every bit of dirty work I ever did for The Progression was for *nothing*. The only solace I had was in protecting Daeva. That if I listened to this order to recruit for The Progression my father wouldn't think about using her against me, if I listened to a crazy sorceress and her equally insane right-hand, Daeva would be let go, that if I followed 'Queen' Ilise's orders and tortured her former Union members for information, she would stop hurting Daeva. But no, it was all a lie. And now I have no excuse, no justification for *anything* I did."

I didn't feel the warm tears on my face until I'd stopped talking. Mathias just stared. Then he stood, and wrapped his arms around me. And for the first time in years, I let go, I released all the masks I'd been forced to wear over the years.

And I cried.

Chapter 40

Ilise

"**A**bsolutely not," I said.

The whole table groaned. Yorena seemed to think the best course of action was to ask Nikos for help. Had he helped her escape? Yes. Did he choose not to engage during our first battle with Imogen and Oliver all that time ago? Yes. But he was also the one who was actively working for The Progression during the entirety of Heircestrial, he was the one who held back Mathias during the rescue mission for me, from what I remembered he didn't try to go against me when I'd ordered him to torture the few Union members that were left, *and* he was the son of the leader and founder of The Progression, for Spirits' sakes. Asking for his help would be as bad as asking Oliver for help.

"Who else would know the best time to take out Imogen?" she asked, slamming her hands down on the creaking table.

"I don't know," I said. "But he switches sides too easily. What's stopping him from betraying us like Oliver did to you?"

She took a deep breath. "Nikos is the only one that we know for sure is against Imogen, so he's the only one in the palace that we could possibly trust to help us."

"Val? Cain?" I said. Val rubbed the growing stubble on his chin, and got that hardened, determined look he had when he was truly considering something risky.

"It's not like we have many other options, Ilise," he said after a long while. "Imogen needs to go."

"Are you really willing to trust the person who might be the de facto most powerful person in The Progression now that Wayne is gone?" I said.

He stared at me with cold, hardened eyes. "We lost *three* people. One of them was my *baby brother*. I don't care if we have to ask the damned Fire Spirit for help, Imogen cannot hurt more people."

"We're all that's left of the Union, do you truly think we're gonna be able to do this without any inside knowledge?" Cain asked. "I hope you realize she'll sense your presence before we can do anything."

"We have no choice," I said, not bothering to mask the frustration in my voice. The more time we spent stuck down here, arguing, the less time we would have to catch Imogen by surprise.

Yorena rubbed her eyes. "Ilise, can I talk to you in private, please?" She said it with a bite of authority that one could only gain from life in a palace.

"Fine."

Yorena led me to the opposite corner of the Archives. This section was slightly less disheveled than where we'd decided to set up. Place cards bearing dates lined the slightly bowed shelves, some holding twice as many books as they were supposed to. Yorena leaned against the peeling wall, arms crossed over her chest. She had a pinched facial expression, like she was trying to read something from far away.

"Why are you so against asking Nikos for help?" she asked.

"It's too risky. Imogen holds the life of his lover in her hands, and enjoys threatening him with her to gain his obedience." Even I had used her against him at least a few times when I'd been under Imogen's control.

"And approaching her yourself isn't risky?"

"Only for me, and then the rest of you can escape if things go south."

She took a step closer.

"We aren't going to let you become a martyr. The only way we'll be able to beat her is if we all come after her at once, and we need inside information if we want to do that, and make it out alive."

"Or we could prevent having to risk all of us and let her think I came alone."

Yorena raised an eyebrow. "Surely you don't think Imogen's that dumb to think we wouldn't come with you?"

I clamped my mouth shut. I realized the truth, now. That it was so obvious my friends wouldn't leave me that even Imogen could see it, even if I had been in denial. But still, I was running out of ideas, and I couldn't let any of them near Imogen. Not over my dead body.

"We lost *three* people because they got taken over by a sorcerer, I'm not letting that happen again," I said. "Kass, Rori, Kieron, gone in seconds because Imogen wanted us all dead. Because she no longer has a use for me. The one thing we'd been able to count on is that she didn't want me dead, but now, we didn't even have that. Why endanger six lives when we can let me handle the danger I put us all in in the first place?"

Yorena stared at me. I'd sooner stick my bare hand in fire than see any of them hurt, I'd sooner throw myself into a bonfire without my crystal than see her hurt more because of Imogen. Before I could pull away, she wrapped me in a tight hug, resting her chin atop my head. I relaxed into the hug. It felt nice. She felt nice. I could feel her heartbeat speed up, the sound thudding against my ear. I wondered if she could feel mine.

"One person being put in danger knowingly, without backup, is not acceptable. At least with all six of us there, her energy isn't focused on one person, on you. We care about you too much to let you go in alone." She brought her lips to my ear. "I care about you too much."

The slight hitch in her voice formed a tiny crack in my heart. I didn't want to worry her, I just wanted to keep her safe—I wanted to keep everyone safe. I wiggled out of her grip, wiping any reaction to her words from my face. Keeping her distanced would keep her safe until we defeated Imogen. It had to.

"I'll agree to your plan, but only if I can talk to Nikos on my own first."

Reluctantly, the others agreed to let me find Nikos myself—much to Yorena's dismay. I had planned to knock out a guard and stuff them in a closet somewhere, but Ms. Nettie was kind enough to tell me where spare guard uniforms were stored in the basement. The closest one to my size must've been an older version because the royal crest was on the shoulder rather than the chest, but hopefully, no one would be looking that closely. And if they did, my original plan would work just fine.

I followed the subtle tug I felt whenever Imogen was around straight to the throne room. Well, not straight there. Most would probably still recognize my face. The uniform only helped me if someone was looking at me from behind. So, I took the most indirect way there. The only sound in these corridors was from my thick boots ringing against the tile, and my gloved finger tapping against the blade of my dagger. I'd also taken a few more daggers from the training room, along with the same broadsword all guards carried.

I took the servant stairs to the second level, and eased open the back balcony entrance to the throne room. *Where are the guards?* This was too easy. I should have encountered at least a dozen guards by now. Imogen wouldn't have dispatched them all to ensure the kingdom was following her directives. Not with us still at large, and most likely plotting her overthrow. She wasn't dumb. The door creaked. I froze, listening for the pounding sound of guards' boots. Nothing. I slipped through the small crack in the door and crouched below a half-wall.

The room was full of excited chatter. It was loud, buzzing, like I had stepped into a swarm of mosquitoes in the middle of a swamp. I risked a glance over the wall.

The room was packed.

Most of the people there were in patchwork clothes with wooden weapons tied to their hips. Some possessed real weapons, ones that gleamed in the candle light. *Are these all Progression members?* She must be using them as part of her army.

There had to be nearly a thousand of them in here, if not more. This many people fueled by pure hatred would be twice as formidable as a soldier acting on orders.

The main door swung open, and I ducked down so that I could just barely see what was going on. Imogen strode in, along with the Council of Sorcerers, and finally, guards trailing behind. All the chatter ceased, the eyes of the entire room following her. The guards posted themselves around the room, encircling the Progression members. *What is going on?* I needed to find Nikos, but Imogen might be revealing her plan. But this was a strange situation- why were there so many guards here when Imogen was amongst her supporters?

"Honored guests," she sang.

I shivered. Even now her voice sent chills down my spine.

"As many of you have heard, Wayne Vikander has departed this world and has named me your leader." Quiet mumbles spread over the throne room. "And I have a very important announcement to make." Silence.

"All of you have done a tremendous job aiding my mission to return this kingdom to the best version of itself." The room erupted in applause, some releasing loud cheers. Disgusting. How much brain-washing did one group of people have to go through to truly believe that Letita's idea of this kingdom was the best? That Primis deserved to be treated no better than animals strictly because they weren't born with elemental abilities? Then again, I had been brainwashed, like them

"I need everyone's help for one last task. We need to gain the kingdom's trust." *Its trust?* I risked revealing myself to look closely at Imogen. How could I have missed it? The only reason I hadn't been caught yet was because her power was already strained. Her crystal glowed an ever so subtle purple, one that could easily be missed if you weren't looking hard enough. *Who is she controlling?*

"And the only way to do that is to rid the kingdom of you all."

What?

The guards encircling the room stepped forward, creating an unbreakable wall enclosing the Progression members. They screamed. They fought. They tried to knock the guards to the ground, but they wouldn't budge. *Is she killing the entire Progression? Her army?*

Imogen raised her hand and all the guards looked at her. They must've been who she was controlling. Keeping this many people under her thumb must be distracting her from sensing me.

"You are all about to die, but you will die knowing it was a worthy and noble sacrifice for the good of Erea. Guards, now."

I couldn't tear my eyes away from the scene. Fire Imperium guards incinerated throngs of people, reducing them to mere ash. Earth Imperium guards sprouted thick vines, snaking them around dozens of members at a time before squeezing them to death. The last sounds that came from them were gargled screams of agony. Water Imperium guards summoned great spheres of water, drowning their victims with stone-faced expressions. It was brutal. Horrific. And much as I wanted to, I couldn't look away. I was surprised Oliver wasn't here to join in on the fun.

Air Imperium guards kept the whole killing spree wrapped in a tight circle. The few members that somehow wiggled out of the guards' grasp were thrown at the wall with winds the strength of a tornado, killing them on impact. The wind howled, as a thousand screams reverberated off the walls. Bile rose in my throat. I knew Imogen was demented, but this was on another level. I had to get out of here before this ended, and she discovered me here. With all the chaos, I didn't even need to be that careful about opening the door.

I shut the door behind me, stopping to take a deep breath. What had I just witnessed? Had I wanted The Progression gone since I was a child? Yes. But not like that. That was... No human should be able to do that to someone. My heart pounded in my ears, and the sickness in my stomach felt like it was here to stay. I needed to find Nikos and get back to the others. They needed to know about this as soon as possible.

If I was Nikos, where would I be? It couldn't hurt to start with his room. Oliver almost never spent time around Nikos voluntarily, so hopefully I wouldn't have to run into them. I took the stairs to the next floor and ran to the guest rooms. Again, an empty hallway. That couldn't have been all of palace security in there, where were the rest of the guards?

I reached Nikos' room and paused before I blew open the door. Without my longer hair, I didn't have any pins to pick the lock, as I used to do. Voices trickled out from behind the door.

"I'm not honoring your stupid request, Oliver," a voice that sounded like Nikos said. "I don't care anymore. Go tell Imogen whatever your little twisted heart desires, but I'm done being your lackey."

Request? How in the world was Oliver the one controlling Nikos?

"Nikos," a voice that sounded like Oliver said, "put down the vine."

A crash sounded from inside the room and I blew open the door. Oliver lay still on the floor, their lithe form wrapped a vine Nikos had launched from a broken pot. At least that was one thing off my plate.

Mathias shot up from where he sat on a mattress. *Mathias?*

"Ilise?" Mathias said.

"Mathias! Thank the Spirits you're still alive."

"He didn't make it easy to keep him that way," Nikos remarked. My eyes narrowed to slits.

"The fact that you thought about killing him is enough for me to not value your life right now. But Yorena requests your help."

"Yorena?" he said.

I activated my crystal and wrapped Nikos in a tight ring of air before he could run away, bringing him closer to me. "You're coming with me, and if you make the move to escape, don't think I have any reason to spare you."

CHAPTER 41

NIKOS

I FOUND MYSELF IN a dusty underground space with an ex-Queen, a false Princess, two ex-palace servants, a girl who couldn't possibly be taller than the middle of my chest—who was apparently one of the most dangerous criminals in Croaga, and two Union members who looked like they would like to skin me alive. Ilise still had me wrapped in air, but had loosened it after Yorena had noticed my skin had started to turn red.

"Fun group you managed to align yourself with here, Yorena," I said.

She let out a short laugh. "Fun. Right. Now, we need your help," she said.

I scoffed. "*My* help? I thought I told you multiple times that I do not intend to associate myself with your little rebellion." I did not aspire to spend my time cleaning up the mess my father had made. Unlike this lot, I actually valued my life. I was relieved I didn't have Oliver's requests hanging over my head anymore, either. He would likely be waking up by now, and I hoped that vine had left a mark. I would have done worse had Ilise not barged into the room.

"You're the only one with any insider knowledge. We want to find a way to kill Imogen, it's the only way we'll be able to take the kingdom back," Yorena said.

The Croagi girl with silver-streaked hair—Isidora I think was her name—shot Yorena a look that could wilt entire crop fields.

"Oh yeah, go ahead and tell him our whole plan. It's not like that's the last thing you should ever do when asking the enemy for help."

Chafik lightly elbowed her.

"What better way to convince him to work with us than inform him we want to kill our mutual enemy?" she said.

"Your sorceress friend just killed off all of The Progression and we need to know why," Ilise said.

She did what? The whole room stared at Ilise, looks of pure disbelief on their faces. I forced my expression to remain calm—indifferent. It wasn't like I cared much for any of them. They were all pawns. But The Progression had at least a thousand members, how could she have possibly killed all of them? And in the throne room? She may have called a meeting to lure them all there, but even my father had never tried to speak to *all* of them at once.

"She killed them off?" Cain mumbled.

"When did this happen?" I asked.

Ilise blinked, as if she were stuck in her own head. So she was still doing that. She even did that while she was Queen, it was always slightly unnerving.

"Right before I found you. She said it was for the good of the kingdom."

Good of the kingdom, huh. The Progression *was* one of the biggest problems in this kingdom, but it had never crossed my mind that she would kill all of them.

"Why would she kill off her own personal army?" Yorena asked.

Ilise leaned down to me, the promise of violence in her eyes. "That's what I want to know," she whispered. Ilise tightened the ring of air again so that I could just barely breathe.

"Fine," I wheezed out. "I don't know why she would murder them, but the opportunity to kill Imogen isn't enough of a reason for me to help you. If you fail, which you very probably will, then she'll have a reason to come after me too." As long as Imogen didn't see me as a threat to her control, I should be safe. Unless Oliver actually decided to report me.

"You could get back at Imogen for the Daeva thing," Mathias said. My vision turned red. That lying girl was what had kept me working with these idiots for so long. I was cruel. But I wasn't cruel enough to trick someone into thinking you were in love with them for years. I'd killed, I'd swallowed my pride, I'd tortured, and all for *nothing*.

"Daeva? Your lover?" Yorena asked.

Mathias winced. "More like a fake lover," he said. "Wayne and Imogen hired her to keep him in line."

Everyone's faces softened, even Isidora's, ever so slightly.

"Spirits, that's rough," Cain said.

"Don't you want to get back at Imogen?" Isidora asked. "She might be dead by the end of this, but don't you want to see her face as she sees all the work she put into this takeover end up being pointless?"

"Would helping you require me to be in the palace after today?" I asked.

We wanted the same things, but I was not going to put my life on the line, especially for someone who'd threatened my life at least three times in the last twenty minutes.

"No," Yorena said.

I pressed my mouth into a thin line. "I'll give you information, but only if you swear I'll never have to interact with you lot ever again" I said.

"You are in no position to be making a deal," Ilise sneered.

"I'm the only one who can provide you with information. I think I am," I said. "Though I suppose you can go in blind, and risk falling under Imogen's control. *Again.*"

The group traded a look with each other before huddling far away enough that I couldn't hear.

"Don't even think about moving," Ilise whispered in my ear.

For the love of the Spirits, could they let me go before Imogen gained the bright idea to get rid of me. She had to know Daeva had left already. There was nothing motivating me to obey her anymore. Ilise still had me wrapped in this ring of air, the room was cluttered with yellowing tomes and scattered piles of papers, bookcases took up most of the floor space, and they were in the way of the only exit. Maybe I could force a vine under the air and break it. I should have at least a couple seconds to get as far from them as possible and up the stairs. I could knock over a few bookcases for good measure if need be, better to use them to my advantage rather see them as mere obstacles.

"You don't need to sit there plotting," Mathias said. *When did he break from the group?*

"I am not plotting," I said. He shot me a knowing look. "Well maybe I am. But I wouldn't have to if your little friends did not insist on dragging me into your rebellion. Multiple times I might add."

Mathias sat on the ground beside me, releasing a puff of dust. "We're not *dragging* you in, we're *asking* you to join our rebellion."

I tested the ring of air, still strong. "Do you often tie people up when you ask them for a favor?"

"Only ones that have threatened to kill us multiple times," he said with a smile.

"I was playing a part, and you insisted on getting on my nerves so it wasn't my fault."

He laughed. "And you wonder why Ilise restrained you." The group returned, their faces betraying nothing.

"So are you all going to be doing yourselves a favor, or am I going to be stuck down here forever?" I said.

Yorena stepped forward, fiddling with the handle of a dagger at her hip. Could this girl at least *attempt* to hide her nervousness, lesser people than I would use that to their advantage here.

"We agree to your terms. Once you tell us anything that could help us, we will let you go, and never speak to you again," she said. *Finally*

"Could I possibly add in a clause for you to untie me?" Yorena looked at Ilise with a pleading look in her eyes. Ilise huffed but finally released me. Air flowed into my lungs, and my chest pulsed slightly from being half-crushed by the wind for so long. *Could have been worse.*

"You can start by telling us why Imogen killed off her Progression army in the throne room," Ilise demanded.

"Army? Hardly any of them could have been a decent soldier. Most of them came from rich Imperium families who saw successful Primis people as a threat to their wealth. I'd wager on most of them having spent the majority of their lives in their large manors, maybe occasionally stepping outside to take an afternoon stroll. She wouldn't have used them in an army." Well, any sane person wouldn't use them in an army, and Imogen could hardly be called sane.

"But they still did her dirty work all over the kingdom," Val said. "Why would she get rid of that asset?"

"Right before she killed them, she said this final action would gain the kingdom's trust," Ilise said. Of course. The kingdom would never accept her as Queen after all she'd done, not unless she did something for them. By getting rid of The Progression, the people would see her as the hero rather than the oppressor. The kingdom was so close to collapse, they would take anyone who helped them as the monarch. Even if she *was* the reason it was a mess in the first place.

"The people will love her," Yorena said, staring blankly. "If she tells the people The Progression is gone before we can, then we won't just be fighting against her, the whole kingdom will be against us."

"Then we should get rid of her first, easy," Isidora put simply. *Easy?*

I started backing toward the exit. "It appears it's time for me to take my leave," I said. If I didn't leave now, they might try to recruit me for their assassination attempt. I wanted to be far away from Erea when that happened; they would certainly fail. How could six barely adults defeat a sorceress that was over a millennium old?

"You're not going to help us?" Chafik asked.

"We had a deal. I told you what I knew, so I'm free to go."

"He's right. We can't force him to stay," Yorena said. "Thank you for your help, Nikos."

I nodded. "You're welcome." I started toward the exit, and paused. I looked back to Mathias one more time. Although I hated to admit it, he had become the closest thing to a true friend I'd ever had, even if that wasn't saying much. He understood me, he didn't judge me based on my father's actions, and without him, Daeva's departure would have been an even worse surprise. He gave me a short nod, saying goodbye. Maybe I would see him again. If there was anything that would convince me to come back here, it would be him.

"Wait," Ilise called. "Is there anywhere we can catch her by surprise to kill her?"

"If I was Imogen, I would tell the people I killed The Progression during a large event. She'll be distracted with the festivities to prepare for your attack."

I turned around.

"A large event?" Cain asked.

"A parade perhaps. Something to celebrate her victory over The Progression with the people." At that, I walked out of the Archives, leaving my old life behind. It felt freeing, like a great was finally being lifted off my shoulders. No Progression, no Imogen, no father, no Daeva.

Finally, gone.

Chapter 42

Yorena

NIKOS WAS WRONG ABOUT one thing—Imogen didn't call for a parade. No, she called for a festival. Somehow this was worse. Festivals involved too many people, too many risks, too many lives at stake. Food stands had been set up, vendors advertising fresh donuts, grilled lamb kebabs, and steaming bowls of spinach stew. Fire and Water Imperium performers created figures out of their respective elements, entertaining children. There was even an Earth Imperium growing flowers at a child's request.

It could have been any other festival, like how it was after all the Spirit balls—until I looked closer. Soldiers were stationed at every food stand, and the royal guards pushed people into the festival with a sword at their backs. The smiles on people's faces were strained. No one was here by choice. The laughs that would usually accompany an event of this caliber were absent, replaced by quiet conversation to avoid upsetting the guards. The only joy came from the children too young to understand why they were here.

The sun beamed down on city center, far gentler than it did during the summer. A chilling breeze tickled my skin, as if mimicking the way my blood chilled thinking about this last mission.

One last mission.

This was our *final* chance to take Imogen down. The next few minutes would either allow the kingdom to rebuild itself into something even better than before, or sentence Erea to its death. Not once did I think I would be saving my kingdom dressed in rough trousers and a gray tunic at least two sizes too big, only a single dagger because I couldn't conceal all of my weapons in this outfit, and the curls of my hair combed into a frizzy mess to prevent anyone from recognizing me.

I picked my way through the crowd, approaching the spot where I'd stashed my weapons. Soldiers streamed back from the residential area of the city, marching through the street in a river of black and gold. The crowd parted for them, parents forcing their children behind them.

"Is everyone ready?" Ilise's air message said.

I wasn't used to hearing air messages via wind, and her voice made the hairs on my neck stand up. She was somewhere farther back than me. Imogen would sense her more quickly than we wanted her to if we'd let Ilise up front. The others were scattered throughout the crowd, ready to guide the crowd to safety once all hells broke loose. Chafik was even able to convince Isidora to be on crowd control duty. I would never understand why he was the only one she half-listened to.

Trumpets blared and the crowd's attention turned to the towering palace gates. The doors opened and Imogen marched out, a squad of soldiers flanking her. *No throne. She must be attempting to appear approachable.* She wore a gold-speckled black robe, the fabric glittering in the bright sun. Her gray coils bounced with every step, a bright smile on her face. The expression looked unnatural on her.

A silence fell over the square, the only sound being the breathing of the man behind me. I quickly realized I was nowhere near where I needed to be. The plan was to wait until Imogen started talking—when she would be the most distracted. I should have gotten closer to the edge of the crowd, near a palace wall. Instead, I was enclosed on all sides by people, and moving now would draw attention to me. Not to mention that coming for her through the packed crowd would cause too many injuries.

"Greetings citizens of Erea," Imogen said, her voice carried over the crowd by the white glow of her crystal.

We needed to move in, *now.* But Ilise still hadn't found me yet, and we'd planned to attack her together. Three crystals were better than one, or two in Ilise's case.

"I have come to deliver the news you have all been waiting for," she said. *Where is Ilise?*

I couldn't wait for her any longer. I started forcing my way to the front of the crowd, piquing the attention of the soldiers lining the entire perimeter. Hells. They were blocking access to the alley with the rest of my weapons, and the way their eyes followed me told me I wouldn't be granted access. It didn't matter. I had to keep going. At least their inaction meant my disguise was working.

"I'm here," Ilise said into my ear.

I jumped. "Spirits, you scared me," I whispered. "How are you so quiet?"

"Practice," she said. "Now let's go before she delivers her news." Ilise and I squeezed our way through the crowd. It was slow, tedious work. I felt like a child again, running wild through the ballroom whenever there was a party and I'd managed to escape my tutors. Only this time, I was taller than most of the people, so running under their legs wasn't an option.

We reached the front of the crowd, just a few rows of people lay between us and Imogen.

"As many of you know, our precious kingdom has been infested with Progression extremists," Imogen said. *As if you weren't the one who had enabled them.*

"Is there something else bothering you," I asked in a soft voice. Ilise's usual determined gaze was blank, distracted, as if her mind were somewhere else.

She shook her head. "We need to focus. We have to get her before she reveals they're gone."

"I love this kingdom with my full heart, and I will do *anything* to keep it safe. Especially after the reign of terror of Queen Ilise," Imogen continued. Murmurs of agreement spread through the crowd.

"She's too busy raking your name through the mud, we have time," I said.

Ilise sighed, tapping her fingers on the handle of her dagger. "Fine. I'm only nervous. This *has* to go right," she said. "Imogen cannot hurt anyone else."

I weaved our hands together, grateful she wasn't pulling away. "She won't. Because we're going to stop her."

She snorted, the sound was adorable. I hadn't heard it in a while, and it brought a smile to my face.

"Quite optimistic thinking."

I shrugged. "When the odds are stacked against you, the only thing you can do is think optimistically. You should try it sometime."

"Maybe after we get rid of Imogen, I might consider it," Ilise said, the corner of her mouth tilting up into a grin.

"Now without any further exposition, I will deliver my news," Imogen said.

Ilise's face set, mimicking a statue. It was time, we would finally get our kingdom back.

"The future of this kingdom looks bright, but we must rid ourselves of one more thing."

Imogen turned in our direction, and I wanted to collapse in on myself. *She knows.* I gripped Ilise's hand, I was probably cutting off her blood flow but she still wasn't letting go.

"Everyone move forward with the plan. But be careful, we've been compromised," Ilise whispered under her breath, her message carried to the others. I could finally pick them out in the crowd, directing people to go home, fighting off the soldiers who tried to stop them.

"Now Ilise, Yorena. I thought you two were much smarter than that," Imogen said, right before Ilise collapsed at my feet.

Chapter 43

Ilise

"**W**ELCOME BACK, LITTLE ONE,**" Imogen mused. Hells, I was back in my soul. I'd gotten used to mostly seeing the Soul Spirit, Imogen returning was like a slap in the face. But at least this time, she hadn't tied me up. "I'm going to give you one last chance. Either stand down and let me get rid of you, or I'll make you wish I did. I'm tired of you running around and trying to undermine me."

I turned toward her voice, squinting at her form in the darkness. Her face was set, betraying no emotion other than potent displeasure. She clasped her hands behind her back, slowly circling me.

I let out an empty laugh, taking a step closer to her.

"You're the reason my family and village are gone, you killed my friends, and you turned me into a soulless monster. What else could you possibly do to me?"

The leather of my gloves whined as I curled my hands into fists. There was nothing else she could do to me. As long as we were inside my soul, the few people I had left couldn't be hurt by her. I'd spent years of my life preparing to take my revenge on The Progression—on Wayne Vikander. But The Progression was only the instrument of my destruction. Imogen was the conductor. It'd always been Imogen.

"I know you want to kill me," she said.

I spread my feet, readying myself to charge her, gripping the dagger at my hip.

"Then I hope you'll make this easier on both of us and stand still." The crystals around my neck glowed, sending a rush of energy through my veins, into my muscles, into my bones. I sprinted toward her, dagger out in front of me. Imogen swerved out *of my way at the last second, throwing up a thick wall of branches. I skidded to a stop, searching for her in the darkness. The glow of her crystals gave her away and I dashed in their direction, wrapping flames around the blade of my dagger.*

"This is entertaining," she said.

I roared, slashing her side with the flaming weapon. She swiped me to the side with a large gust. I landed hard on my back, the air forced out my lungs and my weapon clattering far out of my reach. I staggered back onto my feet, my breaths coming in short, labored gasps. Imogen gripped her side, where I'd managed to get her. She lifted her hand away, her palm now stained with red.

"I'm surprised you're even human enough to bleed," I wheezed. The soul aspects that had yet to make an appearance wrapped around my chest, crushing my lungs. The already dark landscape dimmed, Imogen's form blurring.

She brought a red hand to her face, like the blood was something otherworldly. It must have been centuries since someone had wounded her.

"You actually wounded me," she said in amazement. "Perhaps I will still have use for you."

Before I could unsheathe my last weapon, her air crystal glowed, a ring of air wrapping around my throat. The cold wind burned my skin.

"I left too much of your past self intact last time." Her soul crystal glowed a deep purple. "A complete erasure should ensure you behave."

The purple shadows returned, swarming me and Imogen with ferocity. No, not again, I couldn't fall under her control again.

"The last of you should be gone in a couple minutes." Imogen faded away, the soul aspects surrounding me with her, "See you on the other side, my puppet."

Imogen was gone, but another figure appeared. They looked just like me, or really what I'd looked like when I was Queen. The crown of golden vines shone brighter than anything else in my soul, a black tulle dress flowing around them.

"So, we meet again," they said.

"Not by choice," I said. I stood, finally able to breathe. "I suppose you're who Imogen wants me to be."

The other me stepped closer, a large grin on their face—my face.

"I'm who we were always meant to be," they said.

We were now mere inches apart. It was terrifying to see who I'd been with my own eyes.

"Which one of us do you think had kept your need for revenge alive, which one of us do you think was strong enough to kill the old King and Queen? They killed Aerilyn. I only returned the favor."

"You plunged the kingdom into chaos and became the very person we spent so much of our life trying to destroy."

They shrugged. "You aren't much for this world anyway, it's time the better version of us become the only version." They nodded to my hand, which was beginning to tingle. I raised it, my heart dropping in my stomach. I could see through my fingers, I was fading away. The tingling quickly traveled up the rest of my arm, my sleeve disappearing with it.

"You're even weaker than the little girl you used to be, crying over the family you left. You are the one who abandoned them, and yet you mourned them as if you'd been forced away from home."

My family. All of this had started with them. All of this had been for them. They may not be my biological family, but they'd been mine in all the ways that had mattered. I still remembered the days we'd all spent in the fields for the fall harvest. The sun would beat down on us as if it were right on top of us, but Mama would always make a stew out of one of everything we harvested. Granted it wouldn't always taste the best, but it'd been something we could look forward to.

I'd left to allow them to have a better life. I'd never abandoned them, I only did what I thought was best for them. It didn't make me weak. If I was weak, I'd have stayed home and suffered alongside them, if I was weak, I'd have never joined the Union to ensure no one would have to suffer as I did, if I was weak, I'd have never even gone back to the palace when Imogen had threatened my friends.

"I'm not the weaker version of us, you are," I said, spitting as much venom in my words as I could. "One of us is doing everything in our power to resist being controlled." I unsheathed my other dagger with the arm that had yet to disappear,

threatening to split the leather of my gloves with how tight I gripped the hilt. "I will never be as weak as you because I will never fall under Imogen's control again."

I plunged the dagger into their chest, twisting the blade until I felt the squelch of their heart being torn to shreds. I yanked the blade out and they crumpled to the ground, the golden crown falling to the ground with a loud clang. I leaned in close to them as they released their last labored breaths.

"You will not be who we are anymore."

The tingling sensation returned to my arm, but the arm that had faded returned. The darkness around me lifted as the figure dissolved into nothing. She'd tried to erase me, but I'd resisted her. There was nothing left she had to use against me. It was time for me to get rid of her for good.

The first thing I heard were the screams. The second thing I heard was Yorena's panicked voice begging for me to wake up.

I rose, shakily, taking in the scene. Most of the townspeople had been able to get out of the city center, and many of the soldiers that had been surrounding the area fled. The food stands were in pieces, and I couldn't even see where the others had gone.

"What happened?" Yorena asked. She forced me to look at her, and I softened. I wasn't sure what I'd looked like whenever Imogen pulled me into my soul, but it must have been enough to scare Yorena out of her mind.

"Imogen pulled me into my soul," I said, giving her hand a reassuring squeeze. "But I'm fine, and we need to find her."

Yorena's eyes widened, and before she could say anything, she was ripped into the air. I whipped around to find Imogen encasing her in a ring of air, tightly.

"Let her go," I demanded, taking a step forward.

Imogen's laugh was accompanied by a wet cough. It appears I'd managed to wound her worse than I'd previously thought.

"I will commend you for resisting the crystal. But this one appears to be all you have left, and I don't intend to let you have her." Imogen retrieved something from the inside of her robes. A silver blade glinted in the sunlight. My blade.

"I've lost *everything*," Imogen said, her normally strong composure cracking. "My soldiers have abandoned me, the Council has cast me away out of fear of retaliation against all sorcerers, and the rest of your little friends have run with the rest of the city. It's time you lost everything too."

She raised the dagger in front of Yorena's chest, and my vision turned red. My hands felt hotter than the surface of the sun, the fire crystal at my neck glowed so bright I was almost blind. But I could still see her, I could still see the weapon inches away from ending her life.

"Put. Her. Down." I ordered.

"Then come get her," Imogen taunted.

I sprinted to them, faster than I ever had before. The world around me was a blur, all I could see was Yorena. I gathered as much heat as I could. It was as if my skin was burning off. I became fire, became heat. Imogen would die, and it would be by my hand. I was inches away from her when Imogen plunged the blade into Yorena's chest.

Yorena slumped to the ground and I released the fire I'd gathered toward Imogen with a scream. Her robes turned to ash first, then her skin peeled away, flaking into the air as soon as it was stripped from her. She whittled from my fire, leaving nothing more than crystals and blackened bones to clatter to the ground. My gloves had burned away with her, but I did everything I needed to do.

Imogen was dead.

"Ilise, help," Yorena choked out.

CHAPTER 44

ILISE

"**Y**ORENA," I GASPED, RUSHING to her limp body.

"Help," I choked out, tears spilling down my face. "Yorena needs help," I said, praying the wind was able to carry my message.

The blood from the wound gushed, faster than I could stop it. Why was there so much blood? No one person should have this much blood inside of them. There was too much to lose, too much to keep inside of you, too much to keep your heart pumping. Too much to keep her heart pumping.

It was all over my hands—sticky, so sticky.

Yorena released a shuddering breath; she was still alive. I weaved our fingers together, as if it could tether her to this world, to me.

"Ilise," she whispered. I cradled her in my arms, brushing back the blood-slicked strands of her hair.

"Yorena," I sobbed, holding her closer to my chest. I tried to press down on the wound to stanch the blood, but it only flowed faster, taking her away from me faster. "You're gonna be okay, you're gonna live." If I said the words out loud, they had to come true. I couldn't lose anyone else, I couldn't let Imogen take more people from me. She was dead. Dead people shouldn't be allowed to take.

"Is she gone?" Yorena asked. Her voice was no more than a hoarse whisper. *No. Please, Spirits, don't take her from me.*

"She's gone. She can't hurt us anymore," I said, running my hands on the back of her head.

Footsteps pounded behind me.

"What's wrong?" Val asked as they all skidded to a stop.

My throat was tight, teardrops mixed with the blood on my hands. "Imogen's dead, but she stabbed her, Val. She stabbed her," I choked out.

He kneeled beside us and studied the wound. "The wound is too big, we need to stitch it," he said.

"We don't have time to find a clean needle and thread," Isidora said. She turned to me. "You need to cauterize it."

Cauterize? "My gloves are gone, I can't..."

"It's okay," Yorena said. I cradled her cheek as she flashed me a sad smile, showing her spirtsdamned dimples.

"I can't lose you," I said.

"You won't lose me." She placed our joined hands over her heart. It was beating slowly, much too slow. "I will be with you for as long as you remember that I love you."

The tears wouldn't stop, they flowed as much as the blood from Yorena's chest. She coughed, oozing more blood.

"You're only saying that because you think you're going to die," I said.

She opened her mouth to say something, but her eyes closed, and her head slumped back.

"No," I said. I lightly shook her, but she wouldn't respond. "Don't you dare leave me, Yorena!"

"For Spirits' sakes, close the wound before she bleeds the rest of her life out on the dirt. You're going to let your fear kill her?" Isidora scoffed.

"Isidora!" Chafik said. His face was wet with tears.

"No. She's right."

I laid Yorena down softly; she still didn't stir. I pressed a slow kiss to her forehead, hoping, praying, begging this to work.

"I love you," I whispered. "I'm sorry if I never got the chance to tell you that."

The light from my crystal was blurred in my vision. I gathered as much heat into my hands as I dared. My arms shook, my heart beat erratically in my chest.

The unnatural heat flowed into my hands. I was terrified, panicked, but I tried to hold fast. *I can do this. I will save her.*

I pushed together the two sides of her wound, focusing all of the heat into it. I needed to stop her from losing more blood. The shaking spread to the rest of my body, so much so I was shocked I was still able to hold the skin together. My crystal faltered, my hands were cooling. No, I could do this. I had survived losing my family, I had survived being a puppet, and I had survived Imogen. I could survive this. My power would survive so that she could.

The smell of burning skin assaulted my nostrils as the wound was seared together. *Just a little more.* I fused together the last of the wound and broke my hold on the flames, releasing a shuddering breath.

I did it.

Chapter 45

Yorena

I FELT LIKE I had discovered a whole new level of pain. My chest was on fire, throbbing, pounding harder than my heart. I peeled my eyes open, squinting against the bright sunlight. I was in my old bedroom, with the mountain of pillows scattered about the bed. I tried moving my hand, and it was like I was moving through honey.

"Yorena?" a familiar voice said.

I slowly turned my head. Spots danced through the air in front of me. I needed water.

"Ilise?" Her blurry face came into my field of view and I blindly reached for her hand. She grabbed it, squeezing it hard. I couldn't tell if it was for me or for her, but I didn't care. She was here, she was alive.

I was alive. She'd saved me. Even though I knew it terrified her to use fire without her gloves, she'd saved me.

"You saved me," I said. She knelt beside my bed, taking my face in her rough hands.

"Of course I did. I wasn't about to let my Queen die," she said with a smile.

"And here I was thinking it was because you loved me," I said with a laugh. It hurt my chest to do so but it felt good. We'd won. The kingdom was ours again, and we could finally get it back to normal. No, better than normal, better than it had ever been.

"That too," she said. She leaned in closer, bringing her lips to mine.

I froze for a second, letting out a small squeak of surprise before kissing her back. Her lips were softer than I could have ever imagined. Her hands caressed the curve of my neck, my skin aflame in every place our bodies touched. I had changed my mind, I didn't need water, I just needed her to keep kissing me like this. She threaded her fingers through my hair and tipped my head up, deepening the kiss.

But then I stopped. I leaned back, leaving only a slim space between us.

"Why are you stopping?" Ilise asked.

"Say it. Out loud," I said.

Ilise beamed. I didn't think I'd ever seen her smile so hard.

"I love you. I'm sorry I didn't tell you before. Everyone I've ever loved is taken from me, and I felt like if I admitted that to myself, you would be, too." She took both my hands in hers. "I almost lost you. But now, if telling you I love you every day will keep you by my side, then I'll do it."

I laughed as she peppered my face with kisses.

"Where are the others?" I asked. She was next to me in bed now. The mattress could hold four people, yet Ilise pressed against my side like we were in a cot, and I wasn't going to complain. She gently stroked my head and I rested my head in the crook of her shoulder.

"Val is telling all the palace workers what happened so they're ready for when you recover, Isidora and Chafik are cooking for everyone, and the others are helping anyone who needs it."

"Isidora? Cooking?" I said.

Ilise opened her mouth to respond, but another voice beat her to it.

"I will have you know, I can make a meal out of nothing," Isidora said from the doorway. "Lunch is ready," she said.

Lunch?

"How long have I been out?" I asked.

"A couple days," Ilise said. *A couple days?*

"Yeah, and I think I speak for everyone when I say we're tired of being Queen for you," Isidora said.

"Technically, Ilise is Queen by birthright," I said.

Ilise scoffed. "I don't think I have the best track record."

I squeezed her hand. "Then it's a good thing you have me," I said. "But you'll be Princess consort, won't you?"

"If it's by royal decree, I don't have a choice," Ilise smiled.

"Okay you guys can stop being cute now," Isidora said. "You have a kingdom to rebuild."

ACKNOWLEDGEMENTS

We made it to the end guys. I'm sad to say goodbye to this wonderful group of characters for the time being, but I wouldn't have gotten to know them without my support team. Thank you to my parents for supporting me through this second book. I could never do this without you guys. Next, I want to thank my friend Megan H for being my biggest fan. I love you, and I'm going to miss you so much in college. (And don't worry, you'll always get the insider info :)) Thank you to Karena for helping through yet another book. I'll always be so grateful for you and the hard work you put into making my books into the best possible versions they can be. And thank you to everyone who read the first book and came back to support me. I could not do what I do without all of you wonderful readers. We will be saying goodbye to Erea for a while, but I hope we will all be able to return one day. <3

About the Author

Olivia Ocran is a young adult author attending Howard University for English. She has been an avid reader for the majority of her life and finally started writing books of her own during the quarantine in 2020. She plans to continue writing through college with aspirations of becoming an English teacher. She intends to create a space where people of diverse groups can see themselves in literature. You can find her writing at random coffee shops in the D.C area or wandering around various bookshops. She can also be found at https://oliviaocranauthor.wixsite.com/my-site or through @oliviaocranauthor on Instagram and TikTok.